I0782121

BLOOD & WAR

BELLE WALKER

aethonbooks.com

To Rowan—My sweet boy. I hope you see this and are inspired to reach for the stars and whatever dreams in life you may have. You can achieve anything your heart desires.

I love you to the moon.

Pronunciation Guide

CHARACTERS
Eire: Eye-rah
Arakiel: Arr-a-kiel
Oriel: Oar-e-el
Theliel: Thel-e-el
Reim: R-ee-m

PLACES
Solis: So-lease
Andorra: An-door-ah
Daire: Die-rah

One

DEMITRIA

Ten grueling years since the Ascension, and still, everything was burnt to ash. Demitria's eyes spanned across the barren landscape that surrounded her. Scanning. Scouting ahead for anything out of place. Everywhere she looked was desolate. Lifeless. The charred remains off in the distance the only inclination that life had once been abundant here. Ten years since the world had become a living hell. *Life never got easier.*

She scanned again. Waiting. Always waiting for something to attack, but like this, without anywhere for them to use as cover and hide, it made her job that bit easier. Nothing, not even the creatures from the damned Underworld itself could get past her eyes in the clear conditions. It was a small reprieve, but one she was grateful for nonetheless. The earth beneath her boots was nothing more than dirt and the burnt remains of what life had once been. A constant reminder that everything she had once longed for now lay dead at her feet in a crushing heap.

"It's clear." Demitria's body twisted swiftly around in the supple leather saddle, holding the beast underneath steady as she called back to her companion waiting behind. The loud hum of the motor from his bike increased as he neared. She sat silently as he caught up to her, wind blowing a crisp breeze, catching a lock of dark hair that had escaped the braid she'd quickly trapped it in hours before. Righting herself in the saddle, Demitria scanned once more to be sure. There was nowhere for the creatures to hide, but it never stopped them from coming. Nothing had moved, but she held her breath anyway.

Never let your guard down, no matter how safe you think you are. Do so, and you die.

Jace's words from long ago echoed through her mind. He'd drilled those words into her, time and time again. Never to forget. A constant reminder of just how much things had changed.

"It doesn't look like we were followed." The whir of the motor quieted as he pulled up beside her. Jace rested his feet on the ground to keep the bike steady. "We're clear to move ahead."

With a nod, Demitria nudged the horse beneath her forward. The beast just as alert as she was swiveled his ears back and forth, always listening for anything Demitria's eyes may have missed.

Up ahead, the traders' large building came into view. She searched for anything out of place. When nothing moved, Demitria came to a halt a few feet from the entrance and Jace followed her lead. Freeing her feet from the stirrups, Demitria swung her leg behind her before her feet touched softly to the ground. She tied the worn braided reins in a loose loop around the hitching post in front of the door. Jace was already steadying his bike beside them.

The patchworked building had been constructed from fragments of timber and massive pieces of scrap metal. Anything that could be salvaged from the wreckage of the once prosperous cities that surrounded the area. None of the structures were much to look at, but they provided shelter and that was more than any of them could ask for.

Tall heavy metal doors sat open, beckoning them inside. She knew from years of coming here that the tin roof had been scavenged from some rubble pile miles away, the mismatched sheets torn and gouged in places that let in sunlight on the nicer days, but nearly flooded the place during a heavy rain.

"Let me do the talking today." Jace looked down at her, eyes narrowing. She knew her place.

Stay still and keep your mouth shut.

It was the usual routine whenever she'd had the chance to accompany him on these outings.

"Whatever you say, Jace." The corners of her lips curved up into a wicked grin. It wasn't like she intentionally screwed these things up. Her mouth just tended to get the better of her at times. "I'll do my best."

"I knew I should have brought someone else." Shaking his head, Jace let out a loud sigh as he fiddled with something in his jacket pocket. He hadn't mentioned anything about the item they would use as trade, but it seemed small in comparison to what they were after.

"You and I both know you don't mean that." Her laughter was infectious, and soon his own soft chuckle echoed inside the building, signaling their arrival.

For weeks now, trading days had proved to be chaotic as neighboring communities became frantic for supplies, making hard to acquire items even more scarce. Demitria knew that the other settlements in the area had been running out for some time now, they all were. It would only be a matter of time before there was absolutely nothing left. She never asked how they came into their stock. Didn't want to know for that matter. So long as her people had the supplies they needed, she didn't care.

Demitria quietly fell into step beside Jace, hand subtly resting atop the pommel of a blade she'd concealed beneath the dark fabric of the cloak billowing around her. Jace had no weapons hidden within the confines of his worn jacket, the deep brown of the leather faded in spots from years of wear.

"By the gods, I swear if you pull that thing out again today, Demi..." With a shake of his head, Jace raked a hand through his wheat-blond hair as he let loose another sigh. She didn't say a word, but followed behind as they entered.

The same rules no longer applied, she reminded herself. There was no honor system, no safety in those walls anymore. Bad people took the things they wanted, whenever they wanted. And they didn't care if they had to kill to get it. She wasn't about to let Jace get attacked over supplies. The blade was needed, despite his protests every single time she'd brought it. Jace believed that making a show of weapons set a certain tone about them, but she wasn't so sure that was a bad thing.

Demitria thanked the gods she had never needed to use it here. Yet. She let her hand fall back loosely against her side.

The building was dimly lit with large candles placed precariously along the unpainted walls, the flames flickering as the breeze crept inside from the cracked front doors. At the counter, an oil lamp lit the counter area in a warm glow.

She counted five men with the clerk, each one older than her and Jace by many years. Each one with varying shades of gray peppered throughout their once dark hair. She recognized one of them, Augustus, the leader of Valencia, one of the largest communities around. Demitria found her hand hovering back toward the weapon at her hip, feeling the pommel warm in her hand. There wasn't supposed to be anyone else in the building with the clerk. It was their time to trade.

"How nice of you to finally join us."

The clerk narrowed his gaze, blue eyes fixed on them as they walked further in. Demitria's grip tightened around the weapon as they stopped before the large counter in the center of the room. The man had been kind to them in all their encounters prior. Most times, anyway.

"We're early." Jace's voice was loud, firm as he rested a strong hand on Demitria's wrist.

She released the sword, only slightly, still feeling the edge of the blade at her fingertips. They had arrived earlier than their meeting had entailed, much earlier in fact, to avoid any overlap of time slots should their trades take longer. Jace pulled out the item he'd been toying with from his pocket. Her eyes caught on the intricately carved pocket watch that she'd recognize in a heartbeat. It had been his father's, gifted to Jace on his last birthday, spent all together so many years ago. The engraving of his father's name had been rubbed smooth in spots along the underside, his fingers always grazing across the cool metal as it lived in the pocket of his coat. She'd never seen him without it. Another constant reminder of what once was. Had he really come here to try and trade it today? One of the only pieces of his family he'd had left? She wouldn't let him.

"Quite early, in fact." Jace added.

"I can't promise your resources will be available." The clerk set his hands on the counter before clenching them into tight fists. Eyes roaming over the others before him.

And so, it begins.

She'd heard about other communities paying off a clerk to help with sales. Offering them goods or services to raise prices and greatly upping the revenue for both. It surprised her as this particular clerk had never done so in the past. The traders had their fair share of scum, but this was a new one. Their luck was due to run out at some point though, and today seemed to be that day.

The air left Jace's lips in a rush as he stopped before the men. "We're here for the medical supplies we were promised two weeks ago, nothing more."

"So is everyone else, get in line." To their left, what looked to be the oldest of the men, Augustus, chimed in. The corners of his eyes creased with age, lips set in a tight scowl as he gave them both a once over.

Demitria knew the type. They were the youngest there, and these men would use that to their advantage.

"My people are suffering. This is no place for petty teenagers to get their fix." Augustus said. He carried himself with an air of importance that made Demitria's blade hand twitch.

"Surely you aren't that stupid." Demitria couldn't help as the words quietly slipped from her mouth. They hadn't met often, but enough times that he knew exactly who they were. Knew they had a community to look after. Jace's hard stare stopped her before she could say anything else.

"These are hard times, and the merchandise is in high demand." The man standing within arm's reach directly to her right piped up. "As if it wasn't already."

"I have what you're looking for, but not for the price I know you're willing to pay. Not anymore." The clerk sighed, shaking his head.

Pain medicine, bandages, antibiotics. Demitria watched as the clerk set a small amount on top of the table. It was significantly less than last time, and she knew they'd ordered double—triple the amount to be here today, had stood beside Jace as he'd bartered for it.

"What'll you do?"

"That's not what we agreed upon." Jace's voice rose to meet the clerks. He would stand his ground for his people, unwilling to back down. They needed the supplies, no matter what it cost them.

"The recent attacks have sent everyone into a frenzy. What makes you think you get special treatment, boy?" Augustus snapped, his deep voice harsh.

"What do you mean attacks?" They'd all been suffering from various attacks since the Ascension. That was why they were in this mess in the first place, but it was the first she'd heard about anything new. Their community hadn't seen anything out of the ordinary, and due to their small numbers, they were usually one of the first ones hit during a raid. "What kind of attacks are we talking about?"

"Andorra, Serenity, and Ashton were all hit this week."

The blood in her veins grew cold, turning to ice as her stomach tumbled to the floor. The clerk watched them with a sharp gaze, brow raised as her face paled, knowing Jace's expression must have mirrored her own.

"A whole pack of demons. There's hardly anything left."

The bile rose to the back of her throat. Aside from Valencia, they had been three of the biggest communities. Just... gone.

"Those that survived came here, bought up most of my supplies. They need it more than the lot of you. This is all I got left." The clerk held his arms out toward the product, showcasing that what was on the counter was all he had.

"How much?" through clenched teeth, Jace's voice was quiet. "What do you need?"

"Who says it's yours?" Augustus chirped. "We deserve it just as much as you, if not more."

She clenched the hilt in her hands, fingers aching against the metal. "The influx of attacks isn't something to take lightly. If we're on their path, we need them." Demitria said.

Jace ran a hand through his hair once more. Something she'd often caught him doing in an agitated state. "Our community cannot go without. My people need their supplies just as much as everyone else."

The mention of the demon attacks had pulled her from the current situation, scattering her thoughts. She knew they needed the supplies, but the attacks took precedence. While the attacks had been common, this was too frequent. Too severe. Three communities obliterated in two weeks was terrifying. Horrific.

The men in the room were silent as they exchanged tensed glances. No one wanting to make the first move. Despite it being their time to trade, another community leader, Augustus, had shown up. And while she may not have cared enough to know who the others were, she could only guess they held similar positions. They were no longer playing fair. They now had to play the game their way, bidding for supplies.

She'd accompanied Jace for backup, but after ten minutes, Demitria lost track of the back-and-forth banter between the men around her. It could have easily been longer, but she needed to take a breath, her head spinning as the men argued over one another. She was useless during a trade, her demeanor too hostile to gain any favors.

The outside hadn't changed since they'd gone in, and she made sure to walk just far enough out that she could still keep a watch on Jace, keeping him in her peripheral should anything go wrong. None of them seemed to be carrying any sort of weapon, and Jace was more than capable of taking care of himself, but she worried nonetheless. She inhaled a large breath, the breeze still crisp as it nipped her face despite the sun glaring high in the sky. It was early spring, but the landscape around them said otherwise. It had been years since the world was covered in an array of lush green foliage. She couldn't remember what grass felt like beneath her bare feet. Only the cool dirt beneath her boots remained. Another thing the creatures had taken from her. From them all. Everywhere they went they left death in their wake.

Filling her lungs with one last cool breath, she returned to Jace.

In the dimly lit room Jace was rummaging through his pack before clipping the bag closed. He still hadn't mentioned what he'd be trading for the supplies, and she wondered what it was he'd just given up. The medical supplies still sat on the counter and she didn't know if they'd gotten what they came for. His eyes met hers for a brief moment where she caught the slight nod of his head, the only inclination that they'd succeeded. She didn't let herself smile. If they truly did get the supplies, that meant several communities now went without them. She never wanted to take away from anyone, despite knowing it was going to happen no matter what, knowing they didn't have a choice.

"What do you want for the horse?"

The question caught her off guard, and she stared at Augustus, dumbfounded. Her lips thinned to a straight line. Had she heard him right?

"He'd sure feed a lot of my people."

"He's not for sale." The words left her mouth in a rush as she shoved the hood on her cloak back, chin raised as she stared down the man before her despite their height difference. *Feed his people?* The thought made her sick. She was horrified that someone had even entertained the thought of eating him. Demitria's gaze traveled up and down the older man. Waiting for the fight. Willing it to come. Augustus outweighed her by more than fifty pounds, but with her skill the take down would be easy.

His weathered eyes narrowed into a glare at her reaction before focusing his attention to Jace standing beside her. "Name your price. My people need their food." He demanded, refusing to acknowledge the answer she'd already given him.

Demitria's eyes roved to the clerk standing quietly behind the table. He'd known about the horse. Had seen her with him for years since she and Jace had been trading. He knew exactly what the horse meant to her, but watched anyway, brow raised in a curious look.

"I said he isn't for sale." She growled, her hand tightening so hard around the hilt of the sword her knuckles were white. The smooth metal warmed in her palm as the blood within her veins boiled. A rage built inside of her, ready to explode, when a strong hand upended her by the back of her cloak. In an attempt to regain her balance, her legs buckled at the knees. She fought to stay upright, unwilling to tumble down to the dusty floor. She would have hit Jace had he not caught her off guard.

"Enough, Demitria!" He bellowed. "Go wait outside with Atlas. I'll finish this on my own." His tone harsh, angry.

She could see that fire swirling within his gaze as he stared her down.

It would be a useless battle to try and argue with him, that much she knew. Jace being angry with her was almost unheard of, the fact that he'd so openly looked ready to tear her to pieces was a telltale sign she needed to leave. Now.

"Fine." Her eyes found their way to Augustus one last time, the warning in them clear before she began her retreat outside.

"It's time for the adults to do their business." Augustus quipped. The audible groan from Jace was the last thing she heard before her body turned back of its own accord, shutting out the room around them as she homed in on the man before her.

To hell with being complacent, and fuck letting it go.

Demitria swung. Her fist arched through the air in one rapid, glorious movement and connected with the older man's jaw. Augustus stumbled backward into the counter as he nearly took out the rest of the men behind him when he fell. With glazed eyes, his body ricocheted from the wooden counter to the floor, blood dripping from his nose in a swift current, mixing with the dirt floor beneath him.

She didn't stay to utter threats. Her movement fluid as she left, despite the anger that still roiled within. She had felt some release with the punch, but gods she was so ready to just lose herself to it. To let that rage take hold of her body and let it do with her as it willed.

Outside, Atlas stood patiently, waiting for their return. Dark ears flickered in Demitria's direction, and his low nicker reverberated through her chest. A smile spread across her lips at the sound.

"Hi there, boy." Holding out a hand, the horse nuzzled into her palm, letting out a long sigh of content. "I wasn't gone that long." Chuckling, she couldn't help running her fingers down the soft fur of his muscled, sleek black neck. Atlas inhaled deeply before letting out another sigh as he attempted to nuzzle into her cloak. Each stroke of her hand brought wave after wave of calmness that tangled with her rage. Satiating it for the time being. A side the beast always seemed to bring out in her. They'd been inseparable for years now, owing each other their lives.

In the earlier days of their war forsaken planet, their community had been ravaged by a creature out for blood. An angel, so consumed with rage, had annihilated anything and everything in his path. Tearing through the homes of their community, tossing aside the Guardians like they were nothing more than fallen leaves on the wind. Demitria had been prepared to stand her ground in those moments. Prepared to lay down her life for those that couldn't fight. In the end she'd stood alone, the others too injured to be of any use. But she fought back.

The kill had been something she never enjoyed. The smell of blood, or the sound of flesh being cleaved in two. It made her sick to her stomach. Even after years of bloodshed it never got easier, but the need to protect those she loved was too much. The need to protect *Jace* was what had been her driving force for so many years.

Demitria's hands found the silver scars along Atlas's back. The angel had flown in on a magnificent dark horse with wings that looked as if they'd been carved from obsidian. The creature had been injured in the crossfires of the battle and rendered useless. With his wings broken, the horse had been discarded by its master. Abandoned and left for dead.

Demitria had tried to end his suffering once the battle had been over, but looking into the creature's deep brown eyes, she'd wavered, the blade falling from her hands and clattering to the ground at her feet. After so much killing... to take another life...

Despite the harsh comments from the other residents on housing—caring for one of the creatures, it had taken her months to slowly nurse him back to health. She'd spent excruciatingly long nights changing and washing bandages from scraps of fabric that she'd managed to get her hands on, and applying salves made from yarrow, one of the only plants she'd been readily able to find and that Stella, their community's "healer," had shown her how to make, to ward off the infection that threatened to settle in. His wings had been beyond repair, but he wasn't broken. Others thought differently of the choice she'd made, but none of that had mattered to her. Atlas hadn't left her side since.

Jace rounded the corner, reaching her in three large steps. "Get on the horse and go. Now." He growled, eyes narrowed as his lips held in a thin line. "One job Demitria. One fucking job..."

Demitria met his glare, not wavered by his anger. "Don't start with me, Jace." What had he expected? She knew the punch had probably been a tad overboard, but she was not about to tuck tail and let Atlas go for food. Like hell she'd let that happen.

"You can't go around threatening people with your sword, or punching them whenever you're angry, Demitria. Especially a leader with a community as large as his." He scolded, gripping the bridge of his nose before he quickly secured the pack around him. Jace drove his point across, as if hoping that she'd understand the ramifications of her actions. Demitria knew what she'd done was wrong, she just didn't care. She'd fight for the things she cared about, regardless of the consequences on her or anyone else.

"You know he didn't give a shit about what I had to say. I was communicating my feelings in the only way he seemed to understand." She could feel the corners of her mouth tugging up into a grin. Untying the reins, she tossed them back over the horse's head before easily swinging her foot into the stirrup and mounting.

"Are you mad?" Jace exclaimed. "We'll be lucky if they don't tear down our entire community. You could have started a war!" His hand raked through his hair once more. "You should have at least listened to what he had to say!"

"Excuse me?" Had Jace not seen an issue with the man demanding they sell Atlas? As food, nonetheless! "He is not yours to take from me. He's one of the only things I have left." Gods, she could feel the prick of tears in the corner of her eyes. Crying was something she hadn't planned to do. It most certainly was not the first time Jace had seen her cry, but she sure as hell didn't like when it happened.

Weakness. That was what crying was, and weakness got you killed. After everything they'd been through, she couldn't afford to show it. To feel it. Not again. Pulling the hood over her head she nudged Atlas forward, away from her companion.

"That's not what I meant, and you know that!" His voice carried easily over the whir of the motor as he kicked it started, pushing the throttle down as it jolted forward in a burst of speed. He met the horse's gait easily. "I'm sorry."

"I'm going home." With another soft nudge Atlas exploded beneath her. His powerful legs thundering across the ground as they made their way back to the community. Jace would catch up within minutes, he always did. Atlas was running, but not nearly as fast as she knew he could. They were still too far away from home to not be in pairs. It was too dangerous to be out so far alone, and she wasn't stupid. Mad yes, but that didn't matter out here. Leaving anyone alone would be a death sentence, and Jace was the one person she couldn't bear to ever lose.

Demitria could be many things. Angry. Sarcastic, even brash. But cruel was not one of them. Even in a petty rage.

Two

DEMITRIA

Despite the anger that had settled into the pits of her stomach, their silent streak had not lasted long. She was still upset, but the anger dissipated with each beat of Atlas's hooves, and it wasn't long before she and Jace were both in significantly better moods than hours before. She always struggled with the thought of being mad at him, and knew he felt the same. But deep down, she agreed with his words. She could have started a war.

They rode side by side to the tall metal gates that surrounded their safe haven. Its large walls had been built two years prior and had taken months to complete. Those that had been able spent hours salvaging scraps from around the area and helped construct them. The days had been hard in the months it took to build them with so many bodies beyond their community and not enough Guardians to protect them. She had felt safer when they'd been able to spare two for the trips to the decimated cities beyond, but more often than not, whatever group had been out scavenging would only have one. The gates had been the saving grace their community had needed to survive in that new world of nightmares, and they'd done it together, Standing at nearly fifteen feet tall, the gates were the best barrier between them and the creatures that roamed outside, their first line of defense against the nightmares that came crawling.

Demitria reined the horse in beneath her, slowing his gait to a walk before bringing him to a halt. She turned in the saddle as she waited for Jace to bring his bike up beside her.

"Did we get what we needed?" She asked.

His shoulders lifted in a shrug. "It'll have to do." She already knew that the supplies on that counter wouldn't sustain Solis for nearly as long as they needed.

"Were you at least able to get anything more?" If he hadn't, it was because of her. Because she'd acted like an absolute idiot and nearly started a war between their communities.

"A few things, but nothing as important as that medicine would have been." He said, hand rubbing down his face as the sigh slipped from his lips. "I did get a few things for Stella in the greenhouse, though. So that's a win?"

"Food is always a win. We eat, we get to see another sunrise." Demitria forced a smile.

"Maybe." He chuckled, but it didn't meet his eyes. They could have all the food in the world, but the minute those monsters came crawling, it wouldn't matter how well fed they were. Many demons killed to eat, but even more did so for sport. For the thrill of the hunt. And with fangs and talons, food was the least of their worries at that point.

"Maybe..." Demitria let her voice trail off.

Solis wasn't large, by any means. The smallest in the area in fact. With only twenty-five inhabitants inside, it was easier to look out for one another. Most communities that surrounded them had far larger numbers, containing hundreds of people within their walls. Up until now, those places had never really been hit hard. The sheer power of their Guardians, people who had been trained by any means necessary to wield a weapon and fight, was a deterrent to the onslaught of raids following the Ascension. But the smaller numbers had its perks as well, fewer mouths to feed, fewer people to keep safe and healthy. As a community, they had decided to take the risk if it meant no one had to starve or die.

Demitria glanced around them, scanning the terrain to make sure they hadn't been followed. Nothing moved. They were surrounded by miles of dirt and rock that was seemingly their new normal, with the odd bush dotting the horizon. The only plants that still seemed to grow around these parts were inedible and did nothing more than act as cover for the small creatures that scurried around at night. She'd been lucky to find Yarrow a few times, but it had been nearly a year since she'd last seen the plant. Granted, she hadn't spent much time beyond the gates or wandered far enough out to look. Their area hadn't fared as well as others had. She'd heard stories by travelers who'd stopped in for the night about communities far off in the distance that were filled with greenery and clear water. Technically she hadn't seen it for herself, but the stories always filled her with the one thing she knew she shouldn't feel. Something she'd lost long ago in the early years when that darkness had enveloped the world in its terrifying embrace. *Hope.*

Before the Ascension, her own home had been surrounded by breathtaking forests. She and Jace had lived in a little rural town that bordered hundreds of acres of natural farmland. It had been quaint, but they'd loved it. Swimming in the river and lake every summer, playing throughout the trees, pretending they were in some fantasy land with mysterious beasts. But when the mysterious beasts had actually come, they had wreaked havoc on their town. On the entire world. Gone were the games they had once played. In some ways, they'd all but come to life. They tore nations apart, splitting the world into a million different pieces that she didn't think they could ever recover from. Pieces she tried to pick up time and time again, despite the agony it always caused her.

Hope that she could go back to something resembling her normal life. Hope that she would wake up from this never-ending nightmare to find out it was nothing more than some sick dream her mind had concocted from hearing far too many ghost stories her mother had told her and Jace. That she'd wake up to find her parents, alive, sleeping soundly in their beds. She didn't dare to hope anymore.

Jace had founded the community a little over five years ago, and she hadn't left once. In fact, she'd never done any traveling since the Ascension. Why would she leave when she had a safe place right here? As much as she tried to lock it away though, Demitria found her mind wandering. Longing for the old ways. Missing what it felt like to lay out on the beach and feel the warm sand beneath her feet, or swimming in the glistening pools of the crystalline water of the lakes that surrounded their home that was so far away from where they were now. As soon as the nightmare began, they'd run as far away from the little town they were supposed to grow up in. Away from every happy memory she'd ever experienced and the people she had loved. Demitria missed it all. They all did. More often than not, she found herself questioning if it was all worth it. The fight? The struggle? Sometimes she didn't know anymore.

"What's on your mind?" Stopping in front of the gate, Jace held the bike upright with one hand as he got off, resting his other on her calf as jade-green eyes met hers. "You look troubled." His hand was warm under that touch, but she didn't move away. It was a welcoming feeling in the crisp air. "Is it the demon attacks? We'll be ok, you and I."

"Just thinking." Her shoulders lifted and fell in a shrug. She slid her leg over the horse's neck and jumped down in front of him. Jace didn't take a step back, and they remained close. Feeling the warmth of his breath as it caressed her face, the familiar smell of mint filling her lungs. She tilted her chin up slightly to meet his gaze, his broad physique filling the world around her in their nearness. Somewhere in the distance, she could hear the motor of another bike. She hadn't paid much attention on who was out patrolling, and she paid them no mind.

"About?" Jace pushed, nudging her softly with his shoulder. He could be persistent at times, but it was always for her own good. Demitria knew it was because he didn't want her shutting everything out again. She'd done it years ago after a particularly bad raid when another had fallen on her watch. She'd done her sweep of the perimeter and hadn't found anything within Solis. She'd cleared the building she'd told the young Guardian to station himself beside while they waited for the injured to be moved. How could she have known the demon had crawled inside after she'd left, waiting for its next victim. While it hadn't explicitly been her fault, she'd taken it on and the pain and guilt had festered into something so much worse. Until she wanted to just stop existing. Those days she'd hardly left her rooms. Hardly ate. She had been nothing more than an empty husk, begging for *something* to end the pain that coursed through her. Demitria knew it worried him every day. They'd spent a significant amount of time together, even before the world fell apart and went to literal hell. But that one time had been different, and the both of them knew it. Jace hadn't left her side once, making sure she did enough to keep her breathing. To keep her alive, and she wasn't sure she could ever repay him for what he'd done for her. She wasn't sure if she'd even still be fighting if he hadn't spent those weeks by her side.

"Everything." Lifting the reins over Atlas's head, she stepped away from Jace and brought her hand down hard on the gate. The pair waited in silence for a minute and slowly, the heavy gates began to slide open, hinges groaning as the weight shifted and the entrance widened. They were greeted by the Guardian on duty, his boyish smile bright as he waved them inside.

"Come find me once everything is put away." Jace told her, giving her shoulder a slight squeeze. Her head nodded in answer and they separated. Her job was to bring the other items to the back of the community where Stella, who had been unanimously chosen as the communities' matriarch, lived and worked. She didn't know how Jace had managed to secure the new seeds for the woman to grow, but she wouldn't question his methods, either. She just hoped he hadn't traded his beloved watch to get them, or even more of the medical supplies.

Demitria quietly led Atlas down the cracked cement street, his hooves thudding loudly behind as they slowly made their way to their destination.

She was lucky. Lucky for the friends she had, where she lived, Atlas. During these times, she was truly blessed. Demitria couldn't count the number of people she'd witnessed with nothing. No family, no home. No one they loved. Absolutely nothing. It pained her to no end to see the suffering. The loneliness in the eyes of those around her. She'd never truly been alone. Jace had always been there. From the very beginning, he had always been at her side. She didn't even remember a time when he wasn't there.

"Stella?" Demitria's voice echoed throughout the large greenhouse as she quietly poked her head inside. The building had been constructed partially underground to make it easier for the Guardians to protect the food supply. Atlas nudged her forward, and she led him inside. Mirrors had been installed along the ceiling to reflect the sunlight inside. It took two bodies to turn the panels that opened the roof. In doing so, it not only reflected the sunlight in, but on the days when the weather was poor, it let the rain in so they could save on the already dwindling water reserve. It was an ingenious invention a few of the inhabitants had come up with, and their hard work had more than paid off. They had been able to grow an array of different crops, and no one ever went hungry. They were one of the luckier communities when it came to agriculture. Their small numbers were the biggest factor.

The older woman smiled as she rounded the corner, making her way toward where Demitria and Atlas waited patiently. Demitria assumed that Stella was in her late sixties, and quite often tied the mop of messy gray curls into a loose bun at the nape of her neck while the unruly strands framed her soft face. Her long, green skirt flowed around her as she walked, white button up blouse softly blowing in the small draft that had crept in through the roof.

"Were you able to get some good items today?" The glee in her voice was something Demitria couldn't describe. Stella loved her job. Gardening was something she'd done before the Ascension, and the woman had been thrilled to continue afterward. Especially if it meant doing her part to contribute to the community.

The older woman was reaching for the bags before Demitria had a chance to hand them over. Stella had been the light of the community since she'd arrived. It hadn't ever mattered what was going on around her, she'd always continued to be the rock they all needed. Her positive outlook on life was infectious. Her demeanor, despite everything, had remained true to her ways, never letting any kind of bad news darken her thoughts. It was a trait Demitria wished she possessed, and she envied her for that very reason.

"Great stuff I'm told."

The bag left her hands as the woman tugged it free. Atlas let out a soft nicker as he watched the exchange curiously.

"He always knows." A beautiful smile graced her features as she reached into a hidden pocket in her skirt, producing the item she'd been hiding. "Don't you, old friend." His ears perked forward as she extended her hand to him, the carrot disappearing in mere moments. Atlas nickered at her again and she scratched the middle of his forehead. "You're lucky to have each other."

"I know." She knew it. Had watched as it got harder and harder for people to keep animals as pets. When food supply was so scarce it was tough to keep an animal in good health. If it didn't produce something, it made no sense to keep them around. Now, everything had to have a purpose, whether that be food or protection. Very few people kept animals as pets these days, most having set theirs free in the early years to fend for themselves. It was common to see packs of the now feral animals roaming beyond the walls.

Demitria didn't know how, but Atlas seemed to manage fine without any proper feed. He'd thrived on the weeds that, while inedible to her kind, had proved to be enough to sustain his large frame. She often found herself wondering if it was because he truly was so much more different than the creatures that belonged on their planet. If his heritage, wherever the hell that may be, had him evolving faster. After the initial pushback from the residents, it had been a relief for those close to her when he'd continued to flourish. They'd formed an unbreakable bond during the months she'd spent healing him, and he brought out the best in her.

"You know... not everything in this world is black and white." Blinking, Demitria's eyes found Stella. She'd been so lost in thought that she hadn't noticed the woman had already begun preparing the soil for planting until she spoke. "Good or evil. What does that really mean, anyway? We kill for the sake of what... good?" She rambled, but Demitria stood there, listening to what the woman had to say. "Does that make us any different? Truly?" Stella's hand stilled in the dirt for a moment. "Sometimes... change is good, too. Sometimes you just need to give it a chance."

"I don't know what you mean?" Stella's words had confused her, more than they should have. Standing from the edge of the garden bed, the woman ambled around an old oak table as she sorted the seeds.

"It won't be easy, but you'd do well to give it a chance." She repeated herself. "It's a difficult road, but hope. You need hope." Without saying another word, Stella disappeared into the back of the greenhouse.

Demitria loved Stella, there was no doubting that. But she

wondered at times if the Ascension had muddied her thoughts like it had done to so many others. She imagined it had been harder on the older population when the demons came. They'd all had more to lose, and at least from what little of the world she'd seen up until this point, it was the younger crowd that seemed to have adapted better. With a shrug, they left the greenhouse. Atlas once more happily plodded behind. She'd settle him before finding Jace. Hoisting her lithe body up into the saddle, she let the reins fall free around his neck. She wasn't technically in a hurry, and the rhythm of his walk was one of the few things that seemed to calm her most days, silencing the thoughts that tended to come swarming back, no matter how many walls she'd raised against them.

Three

DEMITRIA

Demitria found herself wandering the community in search of Jace a few hours later. Having tried three separate locations, he hadn't been at either. For the fifth time, she came upon the gate. Smiling once more at Tyler, the same Guardian on watch when they'd returned, she gave another sheepish wave.

"Have you seen Jace?" She finally called to him.

"He was at the Smith's about ten minutes ago, not sure if he'd still be there, though." Ocean-blue eyes watched her, waiting for her to move. "Everything alright? I'd be happy to help with whatever you need." She groaned, having been there *fifteen* minutes prior. The Smith's hadn't been anything fancy, but it did the job. With the Guardians and their need for weapons, they'd needed someone to deal with forging and repairing. Although quaint, the job had always been done well. A hobby, in another life, she'd wager. The Guardian smiled, and she hesitated to return it. Too friendly. More than his usual.

"Everything is fine." Demitria forced herself to chuckle. Jace must have mentioned something about her mood earlier, and Demitria made a mental note to have a word with him about that, too. "Just wanted to talk to him is all." Shoulders raised in a shrug, Demitria gave a curt nod before turning swiftly on her heels, beginning the path to her new destination.

"I'm here if you ever need me!" She cursed under her breath. The boy had always been kind to her since he and his family had come to Solis, but even this was beyond his normal. Unsure on who else Jace had found the time to conveniently chat with, Demitria kept quiet as she ducked left down a short pathway. Refusing to meet the eyes of anyone else around as she continued.

Having worked out in her favor, Jace had been exactly where Tyler had said he'd be. Jace was deep in conversation with their smith, Evan. The man's hair had grayed quickly upon his arrival to Solis, and he had a tendency to keep it cut short to his scalp. Despite his age, the muscling in his forearms was prominent as he demonstrated his newest creation to her friend.

Casually leaning against the doorway, Demitria crossed her arms as she waited for them to finish. Interrupting would earn her a stern scolding from Evan, and that was something she wasn't in the mood for. Fixating on a loose thread at the hem of her dark shirt, she waited. The flames of the forge crackled in the center of the room. The heat leeched several degrees warmer into the street. Her eyes wandered the room. An array of weapons adorned the walls around them. His creations were impressive, she'd give him that. The sword he'd made her two years prior had been the best she'd ever wielded, and having been thrust into a Guardian role from the early stages of Solis, she'd handled a lot. Demitria wasn't sure when, or even how, but the smith had found the time to engrave delicate detailing into the edge of the blade. A mixture of florals and greenery. It was beautiful, and she quite often found herself regretting having to dirty it every single time.

Demitria hadn't been waiting long when the smith noted her presence. With a slight nod, he motioned her over.

"I was just showing Jace my newest." Evan held the blade out toward her, and she eyed it up carefully. Beautiful, but not like the one upon her hip. "Glad to see yours is still serving you well." The smile lit up his harsh features. Having lost his entire family before his very eyes in the beginning, Evan had suffered more than anyone ever should. He hadn't been able to do a damn thing about it and was the only survivor, forced to live on when everything he'd ever cared about had been ripped from his grasp. He'd been bound and forced to watch by the sadistic creatures that ended their lives in a heartbeat. Demitria had only ever heard him talk about his family once when he'd first arrived after spending a night in the tavern, the wound still fresh in his mind. He had a wife and two little boys. Evan claimed that they hadn't suffered. That it was over quickly for them all, and that was more than anyone could ask for. Maybe it was better that way. Better that the children didn't have to grow up in a world where they lived in constant fear. Fear of the next attack. The next raid. Their world was no place for a child, not anymore.

"I take it with me everywhere." Playing with the pommel of the sword, she returned the smile. That very weapon had saved her life more times than she could count.

"She does. I don't think I've ever actually seen her without it. She sleeps with it on her nightstand." From beside the smith, Jace's laughter filled the shop. It was infectious, and the smith was laughing along with him. Demitria hadn't found it particularly funny. After everything they'd been through, she was well within her limits to be paranoid at night. Having the blade within arm's reach was comforting in a way. Helped her sleep at night.

"It is a fine blade. One of my best. How does this one feel?" Evan tossed the newest in her direction, and it landed swiftly in her hands. She waved it around, testing it. Feeling the weight of it in her hands. It was heavier than hers, the blade a good six inches longer. Demitria already knew it would be deadly, but still, she preferred her own.

"I like this one." She told him, "But mine feels more balanced. This one is too heavy for me." She handed the weapon back to him.

"I figured you would say something like that." He shrugged, placing it back down on the counter behind him. "Which is why it wasn't meant for you. This however, was." Hanging on a hook was a plain, brown leather sheath. Only the handle of the blade peeked out the top. Snagging it off the wall, Evan tossed it toward her and she caught it with ease. "I had you in mind when I made it." Another smile spread across his face. Evan loved what he did. It was probably one of the few things that brought him true joy these days.

Unsheathing the weapon, her own lips tugged up into a smile at the sight of it. He'd designed a near identical blade to the sword, down to the intricate detailing, but in the form of a dagger. Where her sword's detailing descended down the outer edge of the blade however, the one on the dagger ran along the middle, reaching to the pointed tip. Demitria turned it over in her fingers, admiring the beautiful work of art in her palms.

"Don't encourage her with weapons." Jace could only groan as he watched their interaction. But he knew her role. Had been the one to put her in the position of Guardian so many years ago, and as such, it was only logical for her to have weapons. "Can't you just be repulsed by the fact that you have to use that?" His brows gathered and a pained expression crossed his face. Demitria knew he regretted it the moment the words had left his lips, but it stung regardless.

She was silent for only a moment. "Did you really just ask me that?" She would like nothing more than to be sickened by the fact that she had to kill something. But she couldn't. Wouldn't feel sorry for those monsters. Not when they'd taken everything from her. "You know exactly why I can't sit back and do nothing."

Jace just stood there, listening as she scolded him

"As our leader, you put yourself in danger every single day. I refuse to let you go out there alone and sit back and not do a thing when I *know* I can make a difference too." Because every damn time he went beyond those walls without her, a piece of her ached. When he met with other community's leaders without her there. She didn't know whether any of them had good intentions or not, but as their leader, Jace took that chance time and time again. So, she did her part. She settled into her role as Guardian years ago and fought for those that couldn't. Protected those that couldn't.

"I know." He sighed, the sound weighing heavy on her. She hated getting mad at him, but sometimes when he said stupid shit like this, it couldn't be helped. "Everything looks great Evan, we'll get out of your way." She turned from Jace, eyes meeting Evan's for a fleeting moment before Jace did the same.

Raising his hand in a quick wave, Jace's free arm wrapped around her shoulders as he led her outside. They walked in silence for a few blocks. They passed by the small homes of the community, all lit up by candlelight ahead of the oncoming night sky. Jace nodded at the residents as they walked, not stopping to talk with anyone. A trait that was very unlike him, but she was grateful for it tonight.

"I'm sorry." He finally broke, stopping in a secluded area. "You don't have to keep going out there. To keep fighting. I don't want you beyond the wall." He sighed, rubbing the back of his neck. "I get why you do it, I do. I just—I hate watching you put yourself in danger to protect these people. I want you safe behind these walls where I know they can't get to you as easily."

"You know I can't do that." She whispered. "You know why." Something in her voice cracked. It was barely audible, but she knew he'd catch it. He always did whenever those ironclad walls wavered as they threatened to break.

"Then you understand why I say the things that I do." His arm slowly dropped from around her shoulders as he moved to face her. His hand gripped tight to the sleeve of the fitted dark shirt she wore as the other tucked a stray hair behind her ear.

"I do." Before either of them could say anything stupid, he embraced her. Arms wrapping around her small frame as he held her body close. Demitria couldn't help but unravel in the warmth of him.

Home.

Jace had been her home through it all. Her family.

"Every time you go out a little piece of me goes with you. Every time I even fathom that you're out there, putting your life at risk when I'm not..." His grip tightened, fingers biting into her skin. Shielding her as if the longer he held on, the less chance he'd have of her going out those gates. She didn't move away.

"You think it's easy for me when you're gone for days?" Her voice quiet, muffled from his chest, she didn't break from him. "Not knowing if you survived the night, or got caught in a raid at another community?" The sigh left her lips and she didn't try to stop it. "I hate it. I hate every second of it, but I do it. Because the thought of losing you to one of those... *things.*" Demitria saw them every time she closed her eyes. Remembered the feeling of the attack as she watched on helplessly.

It was early evening when they came. She remembered the sun's rays barely lighting the sky as it descended behind the mountains, casting the world around them in a magnificent red glow, one of the most beautiful sunsets she'd ever witnessed. It wasn't until everything went dark that her parents knew something was wrong, and by then, it was too late. Her parents had shoved her small body inside a low wood cabinet in the living room. The slates in the doors were just big enough that she could see out. Jace was shoved in after her, the cabinet barely able to contain both of them as they watched silently while the monsters attacked. Darkness seeped into the house like an ominous mist, engulfing everything it touched. Demitria remembered *her* eyes when the creature came upon her mother. Seeking her daughter's as she begged her to stay. To not make a sound. Her blood pooled underneath her mother's body, staining the thick carpet. Eyes dull. Lifeless. Demitria's mother didn't scream once as the monster ate her alive. As it killed her. Demitria knew she'd done it for her. Back then, she hadn't known what they were when they'd first come, only that they were something from her nightmares. Demons, she'd found out shortly after.

"You're going to be ok." Her mother's lips whispered without making a sound. She was in pain, but her mother remained silent to make it easier on her. So she wouldn't have to remember the screams.

When it was finished with her mother, its eyes found hers. Crimson. They were raging pools of death. They haunted her. Taunting her with their power. The demon slowly crawled its way toward the cabinet but stopped short. It was her father that screamed, she remembered that too. The wail that escaped him at the sight of his wife lifeless on the floor still echoed in her ears. It turned into horrific shrieks as the creature tore into him, too. Jace's own father was there with them, right behind her dad. But she closed her eyes then, unable to watch her only remaining parent die at the hands of this creature.

Demitria couldn't save her mother. She couldn't save any of them, and it haunted her every single day. She was right there. Mere feet away as her family took their last breaths as they tried to shield her from the horrors that befell them. Her mother's outstretched hand reached for her daughter one last time, her sleeve forever stained with her blood, her father's blood...

The demon was almost upon them when something caught its

attention, the shadowy figure receding on unnaturally fast legs as it disappeared from the room. Jace had pulled them from the cabinet then. Through the carnage in her home and out the backdoor as they ran away from the screams of terror that echoed through their little town. He'd mentioned only once since that he'd seen his mother's lifeless body in the yard, but he kept running. Dragging her away from the pain that coursed through her.

With a shuddering breath, Demitria blinked the haunting memories away. She didn't deserve Jace. Didn't deserve anyone for that matter. Since the attack, she'd struggled letting anyone in. She couldn't hurt if she didn't love. Love had proved to bring the highest form of pain. Jace had been her one exception. Her rock time and time again. The one soul she could lean on, no matter what happened around them. He was there when she hadn't been able to muster the strength to help. When she couldn't move a muscle and watched it tear both their families away from them. She could have done something. *Should* have done something, anything, to stop the attack from happening. The guilt ate at her every waking moment. Like an infectious wound that refused to heal.

When her shaking body finally stopped, Demitria stepped into Jace. Fingers clenched into the fabric of his shirt as she took a step closer to him. Breathing him in. Needing the comfort until the memory finally stopped repeating itself.

"I can't even begin to comprehend the thought of losing you."

"Maybe I'm selfish," He whispered, nestling his head into her dark hair. She felt his long intake of breath before he continued. "but you're the only one that matters to me here."

"I guess that makes two of us."

Four

DEMITRIA

The room erupted with boisterous laughter that echoed off the walls of the building. The other patrons around the makeshift establishment shot glances toward the back of the room, as if startled by the sudden outburst at the table. Along the walls, a number of oil lamps and candles lit the tavern, high enough along the walls should any foolery happen, they wouldn't be knocked over and cause a fire.

"If you don't do it, I will!" Demitria's hands lay flat, fingers splayed across the wooden table beneath her as she shouted. From the chair beside her Jace laughed, shaking his head as the chuckle left his lips.

"He's terrified, he won't do it." From her left another Guardian spoke up. His unkempt, wavy red hair peeking out from under the hood of his dark cloak.

"I'm not scared." Tyler piped up. Demitria knew he was. Could tell in the way he carried himself. From the way he nervously thrummed his fingers along the table to the way his blue eyes darted back and forth around the group. She knew he didn't want to come across as afraid, especially with the twins, Will and Sam, present. She knew it was a losing battle and felt bad for him.

Almost

"Prove it."

His smile contorted into that of a sneer, and Tyler stood. Not before taking a large swig of the ale in front of him. He wouldn't admit to himself that he was nervous, and she knew the mouthful of liquid courage was a necessary feat.

Snaking her gaze from side to side, Demitria eyed the men around the table. Cory and Jace sat on either side of her while the others sat adjacent around the small table. There were five of them tonight, plus herself. The other three Guardians were on duty, staggering their nights off. One stationed beyond the wall, the other two inside. The night off was greatly welcomed. Especially among the company surrounding her. Most of them, anyway.

"I still say he's going to chicken out." Sam laughed, leaning back in the chair as he crossed his arms behind his head. Nearly identical to his brother, his chestnut-brown hair fell disheveled around his face.

"Give the guy some credit, Sam." The redhead spoke up once more. "At least give him a chance to man up." Never one to truly get into the nonsense that usually followed the twins, this night had been different. Once in a while, Cory would let loose.

"If he backs out, you're taking his place then." Sam shot him a challenging look. Demetria knew Cory would without a doubt. He trusted the group, her especially. Knowing she would be the first to volunteer. Demitria was sure he could see the glint in her eyes.

Tyler stood quietly, as if hoping that by keeping quiet the others would forget. She already knew they wouldn't.

"We need an apple." Demitria grinned, shouting as her mug hit the table after downing the remainder of her drink. Tyler groaned, and she mentally apologized for what she was about to do. "What, would you rather we shoot at your head?"

"No!" He shrieked, voice rising louder than intended, cheeks taking on a pale shade of pink.

"Gods help me." Tyler muttered, positioning his body against the wall, Sam balancing the apple atop his head.

"There are no gods." Demitria said as the dagger left her outstretched hand and the blade struck the old, rotting wood a hair's breadth from Tyler's cheek. A small yelp escaped before he had the chance to muffle it, causing a round of vigorous laughter to explode from around the table. She could see the raw fear in his eyes as he watched her. Too terrified to move. At least he'd trusted her enough to keep still and refrained from flinching. She took a step back, stumbling slightly as she did so. Another round of laughter coursed, and this time, an audible gulp passed through the clenched lips of the Guardian standing in front of her.

"Are you sure you're coherent enough to uh... do this?" Tyler asked, having just watched her guzzle two full mugs of ale only minutes before. Knowing she was never one to back down from a challenge, no one made a move to stop her.

"I'm fine." The giddy laughter escaped as she fumbled the remaining two daggers in her hands, dropping one to the floor as it slipped through her slender fingers. "Oops."

Jace shook his head again at the look on her face. He knew her all too well, especially when she was fully prepared to scare the absolute wits out of Tyler as she played up her drunken state.

"Jace..." Tyler whimpered, flashing the whites of his eyes as Demitria closed one of her eyes, teeth biting into her tongue as she focused on the dagger and lined up her shot. She stumbled once more, and Tyler winced at her movement.

"Ok, now you're just messing with him." Jace finally broke, sitting himself up in the seat, eyes hovering in their direction.

"You ruin all the fun." Demitria groaned. Before Tyler could react, her posture straightened. Both eyes opening as her daggers flew simultaneously from her outstretched fingers. His body frozen in shock, mouth hung ajar as his eyes bulged from his head when the apple tumbled to the floor at his feet. Both of her intricately designed blades stuck side by side in the center. "Told you I was fine." With a wink she sauntered over, plucking the apple up off the floor and her remaining blades from the wall behind the boy before resuming her seat once more. She silently cut into the fruit, taking a piece off the tip of the dagger slowly into her mouth, offering another to Jace sitting beside her as he laughed.

"Show off." Sam grumbled from across the table. The glare had been instinctive. Something she couldn't help. She toyed with the idea of saying something she would more than likely regret in the morning, but with the way Jace had been looking at her, an almost silent plea in his gaze, she wavered. It was a known fact that she and Sam did not get along. His twin brother had been no different. Finally, she let it go with a sigh, hopping to her feet.

"With that, I'm off to bed. You boys enjoy the rest of your night." With a nod at Jace and Cory, Demitria turned to walk away. Leaving before things could escalate was the right move. When it came down to the twins it was only a matter of time before fists or other objects would fly, and she'd hate to be the one to destroy one of the community's only establishments that brought the residents joy.

"I'll walk with you." Jace was on his feet, his hand warm on her back before she could manage a step or protest his departure. She wanted to tell him to enjoy his night off and leave her be, but he hadn't given her a chance.

"I can walk myse—" He'd cut her off with a hiss in her ear, and she knew when to keep her mouth shut. They were silent as they weaved their way around the remaining patrons and tables. Some nodding or congratulating her on the impressive throw. Demitria didn't break until they hit the cool night air. It stung her cheeks, and she was thankful for the drinks she'd had less than an hour before, the liquid tingling her body with a fiery warmth.

"I'm fine, Jace." She huffed, shrugging out of his reach.

"It wasn't you that I was worried about." He chuckled, remaining close but not touching her. She didn't look at him. "I know how you are when you get mad at those two." Jace knew her too well. Demitria would have been the first one to throw a punch. Without a doubt, no questions asked. Years of bad blood lay between the twins and her. From the way Jace seemed to favor her around the community, to their opposing ideals on how patrol should be done, they agreed on almost nothing. Nearly every conversation they'd shared would turn into an argument.

"I'm not actually going to bed." She caved, changing the subject before letting herself get even more irritated at the thought of the twins. "I just wanted to walk. Maybe go up on the roof?"

"I figured." He sighed, already leading her in the direction. It was where she always ended up, even on days when she didn't want to tear into the twins. It gave her a good vantage point above the community.

But it was also calming. Being up high enough, away from the other residents, she was able to just... breathe. "I was ready to leave, anyway. Going to do my rounds."

"Aren't you off duty today?" She questioned as they continued on down the cracked concrete streets that lined the community. They passed a few rundown buildings. Some with boarded up windows with whatever solid material they could find, while others sat open, their doorless archways beckoning inside. Most of the buildings around Solis were used to house supplies they'd scrapped from the rubble of the larger cities that had fallen in the early years of the Ascension. A few of the residents had staggered their living quarters around the small town, but most tended to gather at the far end. Everyone helped one another. It was why they liked to live in such close proximity.

"I'm never off duty." He sighed.

"Not even for one night?" The street was nearly dark aside from the small lanterns that lined the road every ten feet. Flames shielded from the wind by thin panes of glass that surrounded them. They flickered slightly, the design not quite perfect as the chill breeze still found its way inside.

"Do I really need to answer that?"

He didn't. She knew as well as he did that a night off just didn't exist for them, despite how badly they wanted and truly needed it. In the hellish world that was now their home, a day off could mean death for everyone around them.

They quieted once more as they pushed on. Listening to the world around them. Something scurried far off in the distance, and her hand instinctively attached to the hilt of her weapon. Demitria couldn't help the laugh that echoed into the night, knowing full well that the noise had been nothing more than a mouse.

Right, some night off.

Always watching. Listening. Scouring the community for any sign of a threat. An attack. It was never an if they came back. It was a matter of *when*. The war wasn't over. At times, it felt as if it never would truly end, and that thought scared her more than anything. Spending the rest of their lives just struggling. Fighting to stay alive—

She often wondered why they'd even come after their home. Why earth? Why had the angels followed after? As far as she knew, no one had truly figured it out. All the creatures did was slaughter her people and the creatures that had lived here first. Had taken over and lived as if it was their home, and the humans were the invaders. They'd decimated massive cities in mere hours as that terrifying darkness took over. Killing and eating their fill of any being that wasn't like them. And when the angels came? That was when she'd known the world had truly fallen. They waged their own war against each other, and it didn't matter what, or who, got in their way. The angels may not have eaten her kind, but they fought just as hard for the vast lands around them. Fought the demons and humans until there was nearly nothing left.

With a sigh, she slowly lifted her hand from the weapon, dropping it back to her side once more.

"I saw that."

"Shut up, Jace." His laughter exploded, filling the cool night air and she couldn't help but smile at the sound. "You coming with me?" She asked, motioning toward the familiar building close to the front gates of the community. The boarded windows were never a deterrent for her. She'd been the one to put them there.

"Of course." He gestured for her to lead the way. With a smile, she disappeared through a wide doorless entrance, coming into a large, open room nearly empty aside from a few wooden crates spaced throughout. An old steel ladder attached to the far wall led to a hatch in the ceiling. She took a running jump, hands latching onto the rungs as she pulled up with ease and climbed, pushing the door open at the top. Jace followed quickly, emerging into the cool night air behind her.

There was nothing on the roof but a sealed container that she'd spent a painstaking amount of time bringing up more than a year ago. It wasn't big, but it held a few items and managed to protect them from the rain. Taking the tattered blanket from the box, Demitria spread it across the ground, letting her body sprawl along it as she lay down, staring up at the glistening expanse above. Jace sidled in beside her and she welcomed his warmth as the two of them gazed out into a sky of endless stars.

"Do you ever miss it?" She wondered out loud. "When it was just you and I? Before the community. The responsibility." She thought of the days when the only people they needed to keep safe was themselves. For so long it had just been the two of them after their parents had died. Moving from one hellish town to the next, trying their best to avoid the nightmarish creatures that now plagued their world. They'd had far too many close calls along the way where both had nearly lost their lives. She'd lost count how many. But they had been just kids when the world had gone to shit. They didn't know how to survive or who they could trust. It was a miracle in itself they'd made it this far. But they did, and had the many scars to prove it.

Mesmerized and unable to tear herself away, she continued staring up at the glittering sky. It was a rare beauty that she hadn't been able to appreciate for a while with the duties of a Guardian, and she reveled in it. The simplicity of laying out underneath them.

"Sometimes," Jace hugged her body in closer, voice near silent. "But I like the safety of it here. Knowing we have a better chance..." He didn't need to say the words, she'd known exactly what he was getting at. They had a better chance than *they* had. Their parents. Demitria didn't know if this was the life they wanted for them, but at least they were alive. It had to count for something.

"Are you worried? About the attacks?"

"Would you believe me if I said no?"

"No." She didn't want to tell him that she'd had nightmares about it since they first found out. That she'd woken up nearly every night in a pool of sweat, reliving their own nightmare. Waiting. Wondering if that night would be the one they were attacked, and she truly would lose everything.

"If Solis is going to fall, you and I will run. We'll leave all of this behind, and it'll just be the two of us again. Know that I won't let anything happen to you. Wherever you go, I will follow. Always."

"We can't abandon everyone here." They had a duty. To this place. These people. When he'd decided to found this community, they had lost the ability to run. She knew if he did, it would be something he regretted every day for the rest of his life.

"Sometimes the ones we care about come before duty and honor."

Five

DEMITRIA

The bright light of the sun's first rays slowly trickled through the makeshift windows of Demitria's home, caressing her face with its warmth as it stirred her awake. She couldn't remember the last time she'd gotten a full night's sleep and her body protested the early rise. She was aware of every ache in her heavy limbs, but it came with the territory. As a Guardian, the days were long. She didn't patrol beyond the wall often, but there was always work around the community. Someone always needed help in some way, or something always needed fixing.

Being stationed inside the gates was boring but necessary. You were the last line of defense should anything go wrong. But by then it would be too late anyway.

Demitria couldn't help the loud groan as she finally left the warmth of the bed. Sometimes it was the small trivial things that were the hardest. With one last longing look toward the blanket, she dressed in a hurry, pulling the form fitting dark pants up her legs, followed by a similar fitting black shirt. They didn't have uniforms as Guardians, but anything dark was usually worn, especially on patrol at night. Anything to help them blend in. Unseen. It was easier to gain the upper hand if they didn't know you were there. Despite the creatures' impeccable sense of smell, the dark clothing seemed to work in their favor most nights. But the demons were always still waiting. Because they were nothing but darkness and shadows with taloned fingers and razor-sharp teeth, some walked on two legs while others traveled on four. She hated those ones the most. Vicious, rabid things that swarmed like predators, tearing their way through anything in their way as blood and gore dripped from their snarling maws.

The sword weighed heavy on her hip. Always be ready. Always be prepared. Demitria was quick to pull the leather boots on her feet, tying them in one swift motion. Fastening the cloak around her body she made her way toward the gate where she knew Jace would be waiting.

Outside, the air was still. Quiet. She had risen early, but someone would usually be milling about. The stillness of the community around her was an odd sensation, but she shrugged it off. The sun was just beginning to emerge over the mountains, slowly spreading its light through the rest of the community.

Demitria wasn't sure what shocked her more, the crowd at the gate or the fact that its doors hung wide open, beckoning the world in from miles away. Picking up the pace, her legs moved into a run. *Something had happened.* Jace was standing there, raking his hand through his hair. Brown leather jacket discarded to the side. He'd donned a similar outfit to her own, dark fitted shirt hugging his toned figure.

Had she slept in? Should she be angry that he hadn't woken her?

"What's going on?" She asked, coming to a stop beside him.

"Sam set off a flare." Jace's green eyes met her own, and her body turned to ice. The blood in her veins ran cold.

"Why didn't you wake me?" She shouldn't be angry, but she was. The fact that he'd had the time to leave his house and come here without getting her on the way was infuriating. They *always* did morning patrol together. He knew that. "Why was Sam even out there? I thought Braun was on patrol last night?"

"Braun said he couldn't keep going, and Sam offered to go out. You'd already fallen asleep. He just set the flare off moments ago. I was passing the gate when I saw it." Demitria could tell he was worried. Jace tried not to show it as he shifted his weight from one foot to the other, but she knew him too well. The look in his eyes had given him away.

Wide and seemingly looking through everyone around them. The way he spoke.

"Are you going out there?" Positioning herself to stop him, she readied her body. He wasn't the one that should be investigating. It should be her. She was expendable, and as their leader, every single person in their community needed him more than they needed her.

"Will beat me to it." Jace sighed, and she understood his frustration. Knowing full well that the twin had broken a rule to find his brother. The warning wasn't to call for backup. It was to alert the community of an oncoming threat that they needed to prepare for within the walls. It meant something was coming. Demon, angel or otherwise.

"That idiot." Muttering a string of curses under her breath, she peeked out the gate into nothingness. She couldn't see the twins. Couldn't see anything, actually. Just dirt for what seemed like miles and miles. "Where'd they go?"

"I don't know." He answered through clenched teeth. Jace glanced out the open gate then back to the community, repeating the movement several times. She knew Jace warred with himself over the decision to close the gate or not. To keep their own, and whatever else beyond the safety of the wall, out. Did they risk something coming in to wait for them? Losing two Guardians would be a blow that they couldn't really afford, but if they lost the entirety of Solis?

In the distance, a blurred object caught her eye, shifting her attention away from Jace. Murmured voices erupted around them, and they all watched with bated breath as it neared. Growing in size before splitting off into multiple figures. One. Then two. *Three.* Demitria's hand found the pommel of her sword, readying the weapon for whatever was coming. Her boots pivoted in the dirt.

"Don't." Jace scolded, knowing full well that she was prepared to meet whatever was on its way head on with her sword swinging. She wouldn't let it get to them with the gates wide open. They were too vulnerable waiting like that. He should send away the remaining curious residents that hadn't already fled when the figures had appeared. More than anything, Demitria knew she needed the space to do her job, and with the bystanders in her immediate vicinity, they'd only serve to get in her way.

"Wait." He instructed.

Reluctantly, she listened. As the figures got closer, she could see the matching chestnut hair of the twins. They were alive, at least. Hatred for them aside, she should be happy.

Darkness. Whatever it was, nausea rolled through her, itching her skin as if a thousand tiny creatures had burrowed under her flesh. The third figure struggled within the twins' grasp, writhing back and forth within their grip as they dragged the being between them. She narrowed her eyes, taking in the dainty but lethal body of the creature as it fought against their hold. Female in stature, by the looks of it. Long, dark inky hair clung to its face. Female in stature, by the looks of it.

Bound by her wrists, the creature bared a set of razor-sharp teeth at the men holding her captive. But it was the scarlet eyes that gave her away first. She snarled an animalistic sound that sent a wave of shivers up Demitria's spine.

But still, the twins brought her closer and closer to the gate.

"What are they doing?" Jace reached out to her, holding her arm steady, unwilling to let her go out. *He was really going to let them bring that thing in here?* Jace said nothing as she moved to inch closer to the gate, his grip tightening around her. Burning into her in an effort to ground himself.

Though her wrists were bound, the female tried to claw at Sam, but he managed to evade her attack before she made contact. Dark, murky blood dripped down her face in rivulets from a wound somewhere on her head, streaking down across the pale flesh of her skin. Her blood, not theirs. So dark as if it was poison. That's what they all were. Poisoned beings that didn't belong anywhere on their planet.

The twins crossed the gates' threshold before they quickly shut behind them as the last of the onlookers darted away. Demitria hoped they were returning to their homes. Will kicked the female to the ground, her knees buckling as she crumbled underneath herself. Like a rabid animal, she snarled. Biting at them, but didn't make to get away. Eyes filled with rage, she watched each and every one of them as if the demon was burning their images into her mind, never to forget their faces. When she met Demitria's own, she stopped. The snarl disappeared only to be quickly replaced with a sadistic smile. It grew wider and wider as she zeroed in, one long spindly finger pointed toward Demitria, nail sharpened to a deadly point.

"You." The female erupted with laughter. The sound almost maniacal.

"Are you absolutely mad?" Demitria exclaimed, trying to tamper down the anger that was rising within her.

"Why did you bring it here?" Jace moved his hand to her shoulder, squeezing it as if willing her to calm down.

"We wanted her to talk." Sam stepped on the hand she'd placed on the ground, the bones popping under his weight, yet the demon didn't flinch.

"We tried everything." Will added, nodding at her. The demon's bloodied face made sense. They'd beaten her for information, and she hadn't yielded an ounce of it to them.

"You risk the entire community bringing that thing in here!" Demitria's voice rose an octave, despite the restraint she'd tried to keep. She couldn't let the other residents within earshot hear the worry in her voice as the demon just smiled. "Surely you have a better reason than wanting it to talk."

"You know as well as I do that there is *always* more than one. This piece of shit wandered up all alone." Sam narrowed his eyes, looking from the demon on the ground back up to her.

Despite looking human, the creature was far from it. Hadn't ever been close to it. It wasn't an uncommon thing for a demon to take on a different skin. To blend in with humans and infiltrate their communities. But she could have just as well had human ancestry somewhere up the line. Someone having been forced to bear the spawn of the underworld. The thought sickened her.

Demitria waited for Jace to say something, but he remained silent. His hands wound into tight fists at his sides, brows knitted. Thinking. Questioning what to do. Knowing he was battling with a decision that could backfire on them all. No matter what he chose, it would end in bloodshed. Whether the demon's today, or one of their own members down the line. It was only a matter of when. Each time they killed a demon, more came hunting for the humans that slayed them. A vicious cycle turning round and round that never seemed to end.

It had happened more times than she could count. Sometimes only two or three would come. Those were the times they got lucky.

"Who sent you here?" Will's boot connected with the female's back and she buckled underneath the force, her body connecting with the dirt. A new wave of blood dripped from her face, the dark liquid spurting from an array of cuts across her beaten lips. Sam and Will took a step back, waiting to see what the creature would do. She righted herself, finger resuming its position toward Demitria as she laughed again. More hysterical this time. Phantom fingers traced down Demitria's spine, taking hold of her body.

She didn't think before pulling the deadly blade from the sheath at her thigh. Her newest dagger came free as she stepped forward in one swift motion before embedding deep into the female's chest. She could feel the resistance as her blade fought to go deeper, catching between her ribs but Demitria shoved harder. Finally pushing it home. She'd been ready to evade whatever strike the demon unleashed, but it didn't move.

Again, the female laughed. A dark, bloody smile graced her terrifying features. "They'll come for this place." She hissed with a ferociousness Demitria couldn't explain. "Come for you."

Jace was the one to speak next, pushing Demitria's body aside as he stood before the demon. "Speak now and I may let you live." He nearly growled. "Who is coming for her?" The demon didn't answer, but spat out a mixture of saliva and that vile, dark blood on his boots. Demitria could see the anger swirling through those familiar green eyes, yet he managed to hold his composure.

"They'll take everything away from you," The female's eyes found hers once more. "Tear the handsome blond one limb from limb." The demon's eyes drifted up toward him, licking her lips in a way that meant she'd eat him, given the chance. Demitria could feel her body shaking, vibrating as her own eyes saw red. The rage swelled within at the threat uttered toward Jace. Toward all of them. The demon continued anyway.

"*He* will come for you. For you all, and he'll burn this fucking place to the ground." The demon's legs shouldn't have been able to support her with how beat up she was, but the female stood tall on steady legs. "You have no idea what's coming. No idea what you're up against." The female laughed again, bellowing through the yard. Demitria freed the weapon resting at her hip. Her sword tore through the flesh of the demon's throat in one clean motion as if it was nothing more than paper. Tearing through the sinewy muscle and bone with ease. The eerie sound was cut short, replaced with a gurgled choking as she bled out on the ground.

Jace didn't take any chances, lighting a match and tossing it to the female's body. Spread out, the remaining Guardians stood, watching as she burst into flames. Flames that burned different shades of orange and red before turning nearly black. The smell of burning human flesh was never something you got used to. A demon's was even worse.

"Are we not going to talk about what the hell just happened?" Sam bellowed, eyes wide as he turned from Jace to her.

She couldn't find the words to answer. Couldn't even think straight. The demon attacks on the other communities were one thing, but this? She'd targeted them. *Someone* had targeted them.

"We don't know that her threat has merit." Demitria said, looking back at Jace. Jace ran a hand through his hair, not meeting her gaze.

"She knew you." Will stepped in front of her, blocking her path should she try to leave. "Why did she know who you were." Demitria didn't care about whatever he'd had to say. Had already tuned the annoying sound of his voice out the moment he'd spoken his first word.

"No, you answer me. Why the hell did you go out that god damn gate? You know the rules. We don't ever go out after a flare has been shot!" She took a step into him, ready to square off should the need arise. "You could have put so many people in danger—"

"We're not starting a fight between each other, now back off." Jace interjected.

Her eyes remained fixed on Will, her jaw clenched so tight her teeth might break.

"Demitria, I mean it." Jace growled, and she could hear the frustration in his voice.

Demitria snorted, finally moving away from Will.

The demon's body was still burning, and Demitria found herself fixating on the flames that engulfed the creature before them. Charring the clothing it wore as the female's skin bubbled beneath the dark flames. The smell, rancid and vile, filled her senses. She was grateful for the lack of food in her system. Demitria replayed the words the female had said over and over again. The threat she'd knowingly made against Jace as if the female had known what he'd meant to her. What it would do to her should anything befall him. Then she'd threatened Demitria's home. The only place she'd known for half her life, and it drove her mad. Sent her spiraling into her own mind as she contemplated her next course of action. Did they amp up patrols? Station as many Guardians as they could spare? Maybe they needed to properly arm the residents. Begin training every single person that could hold some sort of weapon, starting today. She would never take another night off again. They couldn't afford it.

Demitria racked her brain for a solution. For something to help them. To save them for whatever threat may be coming. She'd tuned out the arguing between Jace and the others as she stared into those dark flames.

She'd be damned if she lost anyone else, vowing to kill anything that got in her way.

DEMITRIA

All hell broke loose.

It had been expected, given the circumstances. After the outright threat from the demon, it was only a matter of time before panic ensued. As Demitria made her way through the streets she could hear the whispers around her. Several residents stood together outside the largest of the two housing complexes in Solis. More than half their people resided inside the rundown building, and she spied several of the families huddled around one another. As she neared, their voices quieted. She could feel each set of eyes on her as she passed. Could hear the wavering in their voices as word of the demon floated through the air. She could still smell the burning flesh of its corpse from this far back, and knew the others did too. They were no stranger to the putrid smell, and it heightened the panic that much more.

"Everything is going to be okay." She tried to reassure them, but they did no more than look at her before disappearing into the building. To talk out of earshot, no doubt.

Demitria let out a heavy sigh, tilting her head back and letting the breath rush from her lungs for a brief moment before resuming her walk to another building midway through Solis.

Jace gathered the Guardians for a meeting to discuss their next course of action, how to move forward with their everyday life. The community was attacked before, but this seemed different. Every single one of them felt it, like a change in the air that gripped them by the throats. Despite wanting to believe that the demon's threats were nothing but empty, Demitria had a nagging feeling in the pit of her stomach that refused to subside, roiling around and around as it grew.

Each of the Guardians filed into the room they'd chosen as head-quarters. Like everything else around them, it wasn't much, and truly only served the purpose of these meetings. On the smaller side, scuffed beige paint lined the walls as cracking white tiles lie beneath their feet. In the center of the room sat a large wooden table for them to sit around, fashioned from the wooden doors of a long-forgotten building that Evan had built for them a few years back. The paint peeled up in spots, exposing the red wood beneath.

Jace stood at the front of the table, one hand clenched tight into a fist as the other held firm on the bridge of his nose. She tried to smile at him as she passed, but he wouldn't meet her gaze. She slipped into the empty seat beside him without a word. Cory slid in beside her, tapping his foot against the leg of the table in a nervous gesture. The twins exchanged a glance before sitting across from them. Braun, Tyler and Pieter seated themselves in the remainder of the seats. Each of their features held in a grim line.

The tension was high, each one of them refusing to be the first to talk. No one knew what came next. Did they take extra precautions? Carry on like normal?

"I know right now everyone is worried." Jace started, meeting the gaze of each of the Guardians around the table. She could hear his own worry as his voice wavered for a moment before pushing it down. He refused to sit down, his hands now flat against the table as he leaned his weight into the surface.

Sam snickered in his seat, and it took every ounce of restraint Demitria possessed to not bark at him to shut the hell up and listen.

"Understatement of the year." Will quipped from beside his brother.

"We are the only defense for the people here. This won't be the first attack we've faced, and we are still standing." Jace narrowed his gaze at the brothers with a pointed look.

"What about Andorra?" Will responded. "They were nearly wiped out and they're twice the size we are, have at least double the Guardians."

As much as she hated to admit it, Will was right. Andorra, Serenity, and Ashton were massive in comparison, and they'd been nearly annihilated. If they were up against whatever it was that had attacked Andorra, they didn't stand a chance.

"We don't even know if the threat is real." Cory piped up in Jace's defense. Always the voice of reason. "Even if it is, we don't know that we would be facing the same threat as the others."

"So we train the others. Anyone that can fight, we train." Demitria said, her eyes fixed on Jace, "Put weapons in their hands, and make them fight. Even if the threat isn't real, we train them anyway as backup."

Jace smiled down at her from where he stood, nodding his head. "I think between all of us, we can figure out a training regimen. Put out a call to all the able bodies—"

"Like hell they would," From across the table, Demitria watched as Sam rolled his eyes, his muscled arms crossed over his chest. That same disinterested look clear as day painted on his face. "We all know not a single one of them will fight. That's what we're for. To bear the brunt of it all. To keep this town going."

"How little faith you have in humanity." Narrowing her eyes, Demitria glared at him. At Will too for good measure. "Faced with annihilation, you'd be surprised what people are capable of." She'd been down that road before. Knew firsthand what it felt like to be front row to your own death sentence. She'd lived it too many times to count, and each time it made her stronger. Fight harder to *survive*.

"Since you're so keen to push aside everything that bitch said, are we going to talk about the fact that she called her out?" Braun had never said much during the meetings, but when he did it was usually an opinion most didn't want to hear. "The demon knew her."

"What are you trying to say, I'm one of them?" Demitria challenged, pivoting so easily from the topic before.

She'd tried to like Braun, truly. But his allegiance had always tended to fall with the twins, which was something she just couldn't get behind.

"Who's to say you aren't?" Sam added, siding with the older man. "They took everything from me, and you dare say I'm one of them?" Demitria poured her focus into the unyielding grip she'd had on the table, knuckles turning white. It was the only thing she could do to not hit the stupid look on his face.

"Demitria is not one of them. This conversation ends now." Jace commanded, his voice echoing throughout the room as his fist thumped down loudly on the table. He was good at that, commanding those around him, getting their attention when it tended to stray from the topic at hand. That was why he did so well as Solis' leader.

"She may not be one of them, but we don't know that she isn't working for them." Sam moved closer to the table, his arms clenched tight over his chest as he glared across the table at her, his mouth still curved up in that saccharine smile she hated so much.

She was seething under it. Her blood near boiling at the accusations he'd tossed out.

"How dare you." She could be mean. Hell, she could be a monster if she so chose. She would use her own two hands to tear that fucking smirk off his face, but she reined her anger in. Sealing it within that iron-clad wall where too many of her emotions went to die.

Across the table, Tyler sat stark still in the wooden chair. Refusing to meet the eyes of anyone in the room as his eyes darted around the small space, looking anywhere but at them. Demitria stole a glance, watching as he fiddled with his fingers. Gently drumming them along the table. He had something on his mind. Something that they sure as shit did not want to hear, she was sure. Waiting for the opportunity to interject. "Whose patrolling?" He whispered. Tyler may have intended to keep his voice quiet, but they'd all heard it as if he'd screamed it.

The room fell silent once more. No one wanted to patrol on a good day. It was dangerous and tiresome as you patrolled the outskirts of the wall alone. Beginning in the early hours of the morning and not ending until the sun rose the next day. Solis wasn't big enough to station more than one Guardian outside, and together, they'd decided it better to have most bodies inside as the last defense. It'd do no good if they lost their numbers beyond the wall, before something even reached the community.

"Thanks for volunteering." Sam said as he and his brother both sported matching looks, their lips turning up in a wicked grin as they stared Tyler down. How easy they must think this works. She felt bad for Tyler. The youngest out of all of them around the table, he trended on the quieter side. It made him an easy target for the twins, when it wasn't her, anyway. Yet somehow, he'd still seemingly fallen into their grasp. Following along with whatever heinous thing they decided to do next.

"I didn't volunteer." Tyler's eyes never left the floor, too uncomfortable to even look at the others after the question he'd posed.

"We're not sending him out there." Demitria drew the line at that. At fifteen, he was only five years younger than she was, and she couldn't send a kid out there, alone, when he seemed afraid of his own shadow since the demon's ultimatum. His parents would never forgive Jace if anything happened to him. She wouldn't forgive herself, either. She owed that family far too much after Callum, the Guardian death on her watch a few years ago. Callum was a relative of Tyler's they'd taken in during the early years of the Ascension after his own parents had died, and he'd quickly volunteered to be a Guardian upon his arrival to Solis. He hadn't been much older than she was when he'd died. She still blamed herself for it every day, and she'd be damned if another member of that family died on her watch.

"Like you have any say in this." Braun shot a warning look in her direction. He leaned back in his chair as it creaked in protest. She could feel the fire behind it, but refused to cower and back down like he wanted. *She bowed for no one.*

"You never even go out there." He hissed, venom dripping from his voice as he made his true feelings known. "They seem to want you anyway. I say Demitria is patrolling."

"Agreed!" Sam and Will shout in unison.

"NO!" Jace's voice reverberated off the walls around them.

She could tell when Jace had hit his breaking point, shouting being the most obvious sign. He'd far surpassed that.

"She is not going out there!" He rounded the table in mere steps, hovering over the twins as he spoke, voice harsh. The favoritism he showed toward her was blatantly obvious, and Demitria knew they resented her for it. That was why Tyler wouldn't look her in the eyes when he'd spoken. She was sure of it.

"What if it makes the difference in us being attacked? Her going out—"

"I said no." Jace didn't give Braun the chance to finish.

"I just don't understand why she never goes on duty beyond the wall when the rest of us do." Will challenged. He was aware of the family history between her and Jace. They all were. It shouldn't have changed anything with her duties, but it had. Despite handing her a weapon and being the one to help her train, Jace had begged her not to commit to the roll of Guardian when he'd founded Solis. He'd wanted her to be able to defend herself, but nothing more. But she wasn't able to sit back and not help. Not again.

"Because I said so! End of story." His voice had escalated to the point of yelling, and she flinched at its intensity. It was hard to get his temper going like they had, but when you did... you needed to steer clear. Jace's reason was pitiful, and laughter burst from the twins at the audacity.

She'd heard enough. "Oh, for crying out loud." Throwing her hands in the air, the chair she'd been sitting on tipped backward and fell with a loud thud along the tile as she stood, turning toward the door in a rush. Fastening the cloak around her neck once more, hood pulled up over her head. "I'll do the damn patrol." Turning the knob, Demitria left. Already tightening the belt at her waist to better position her sword.

Atlas had been silently napping near the greenhouse, but at the sound of her footsteps had quickly roused, trotting over with a soft nicker. "Time to go, boy." He closed his eyes, letting out a loud sigh as she scratched his forehead. It was always a favorite spot for him. "Come on." Patting his neck, he followed her down the short path toward their home. His bridle hung outside on a hook at the blue painted front door, and it took only moments to get him ready as she slipped the leather over his head, feeding the bit into his mouth. When she did patrol, Demitria preferred to leave his saddle behind. It was easier to be conspicuous at night. Hoping he'd blend in, as if nothing more than a horse that had been left wild.

Heaving her body onto his back, they started toward the gate. Atlas already knowing their destination without needing direction.

She'd reached the gate by the time the others came rushing out after her. Whether they'd been too stunned or were fighting amongst themselves she didn't know. Didn't care, really. Jace was sprinting toward the gate after her, his eyes wild with a fear she felt in her chest. Cory walked behind him, his pace brisk as he caught up. None of the others dared to come forward. The twins took one look at her, and without so much as a wave, disappeared down the street toward the back of the community. Tyler gave her a sheepish nod before following behind them. She turned away before she could see Braun or Pieter.

"You aren't going." Jace's hand was firm on the sword hanging by her thigh, refusing to let go. Like that alone would keep her grounded. Like his hand was the only thing she needed to stay. "I'm doing patrol."

"Let go of me." She demanded. Jace had it completely wrong. Like hell she'd let him go out those gates after everything. "You're not going out there, Jace. I am." Demitria knew he wouldn't want to hear what she was about to say, but he needed to hear it. They all did. "You are somebody that we absolutely cannot lose. Look around you." A few of the residents had left the housing complex and stood back from the gate, surely roused by the arguing they'd no doubt heard minutes earlier. Motioning to the others and the community, she continued. "You keep this place going. You give this community something to live for. We're better off losing someone like me, not you." Her gaze on him never wavered. Piercing.

"I can't lose you." He responded, hand slowly leaving the sword and resting on her leg. The other tightened around the bridle, clenching so hard she could see the blood draining from his fingers. "You're all I have left."

"It's one shift. I'll be ok." She rested her own hand atop his, hoping the warmth from it was enough for him to let go. To see the bigger picture.

"You're going to be the death of me." With a sigh, Jace took a step back. Giving her hand a tight squeeze before he was out of arm's reach.

She could see the struggle on his face as the gates slowly opened to let her out.

Nudging Atlas into a smooth walk, Demitria tore her eyes away. They'd just passed through the gates and she knew they'd be closing behind her already. "I'll be ok!" She called back as Atlas broke into a canter.

The thud of the iron clicking into place was loud, but she imagined him alone, still standing there, staring at the spot she'd just left.

She was alone too.

The air around her felt cooler as the horse's pace quickened. The wind whipping her hair behind her. In her haste to leave she'd forgotten to tie it back, but it felt freeing, in a way.

Her hand never left the hilt of the sword. She never did patrol much beyond the wall, but she knew exactly what she was doing. It was a simple job, really. The task was to confront any incoming intruders—angel, demon, or human—and deter them from getting into the community. It was rare for another human to come this way, especially this time of day, but it did happen on occasion. Most had good intentions, but with the recent attacks and low supplies, one could never be so sure. Anything else that showed up was fair game. If she had to kill then so be it, and doing it alone was part of the job.

Her mind couldn't help but roam as they rode on. She didn't know whether she could trust the threats the demon had spoken. If Solis was truly in danger. If Jace was in danger. Demitria couldn't think of a single instance where she'd fucked up badly enough to have a price on her head. Was so sure that she hadn't killed more than the next Guardian at any of the communities still standing. So why her?

Why her?

She'd made a vow to Jace all those years ago, standing in the forest at ten years old as the nightmares around them raged on. They would do anything in their power to keep the other safe, no matter the cost. A promise to be there for each other, even if things went sideways, and nothing was to come between that. And if those monsters threatened his life because of her? She'd damn well become just like them to keep her family safe.

She would train the other residents when she returned the next morning. Would instruct Evan to make any weapons he could for those strong enough to wield one. Would work with them every waking moment of the day if she had to. Because Solis was her home. Those were her people, and they needed to be prepared for whatever came their way.

The sound of Atlas's hooves thudding along the hard, dusty ground was the only thing Demitria could distinctly hear for hours. The sun had fallen low in the sky once more, and the residents inside the wall would begin settling down for the night. The noise coming from the community was nearly non-existent, but she'd traveled far enough out that she could no longer see it, either. She knew if they slowed the sounds of tiny little creatures scurrying away from the thundering beast beneath her would be heard as she interrupted their nightly prowl for food. Rats, mice... whatever the hell was still out there.

The sky darkened, but Demitria had trained her eyes to focus over the years. She knew this landscape like the back of her hand and could easily tell when something was amiss.

Her feelings were the same as everyone else's. No one ever wanted to be on patrol. It was the worst of the duties as a Guardian by far.

Sometimes it scared her. Sometimes it didn't.

Demitria ventured off further away. Further into the darkness. She'd done more laps around the community than she could mentally keep track of. Nothing moved. If there was danger either she or Atlas would be sure to hear it. They pushed forward for hours. Even further into the dark abyss. The moon, high up in the sky, cast an ethereal glow along the ground, illuminating the world. She reined Atlas in, bringing him down to a walk as her eyes adjusted again.

It grew quieter.

Too quiet.

Not even the sounds of the rodents cut through the night. She heard nothing.

Absolutely nothing.

Nothing but the sound of Atlas's hooves and her own breathing. Demitria urged him into a slow canter once more, looking around at their surroundings. Eyes searching for anything out of place.

Her heart nearly stopped when she saw the hooded figure up ahead.

Large and broad shouldered in stature, Demitria could tell the being was male as he sat astride his mount. The fabric of his long, red cloak billowed behind him, a stark contrast against the moon's glow. He seemed to wear little to no armor aside from a thick leather chest piece that she was sure would do little in a true fight, but he looked like a deadly warrior, regardless. It was as if his horse had materialized out of thin air, and suddenly, he was nearly upon them.

The rider closed in fast, his magnificent horse charging across the land. It was as if fire erupted from its hooves with each massive step it took, embers glistening in its wake with every stride. The horse's coat was a sea of fiery red, like a flame dancing in the night.

She was irrevocably fucked.

Ambushed, she realized. The silence that had surrounded them. The creatures that had all but disappeared—She should have known the warning signs. Should have known that he had been baiting her further out. He'd set her up, and she'd fallen right into his trap.

She'd barely had the chance to watch him dismount, it all happened so fast. Her body left the warmth of the horse beneath her as the male was suddenly in front of her, his strong grasp hauling her body off Atlas as his arm wound around her middle, and Demitria found herself soaring through the air before crashing to the ground below. The air in her lungs escaped her in one short exhale, her back hitting the compact dirt hard. She landed nearly ten feet from her horse who'd kept pace a few strides more before finally skidding to a stop.

Couldn't breathe. She couldn't breathe. She lay there for what seemed like minutes, but it had been no more than a heartbeat.

Get up.

Get up. Get up. Get up.

She repeated the mantra over and over in her head until her body cooperated. She stood on shaking legs, taking all but a moment to find her balance, Demitria drew her sword, poising herself for battle as he stalked toward her. She could tell just by the way he moved that he was one of *them*. Not human in nature as he prowled toward her with a predatory stance, full lips curved up into a menacing snarl. He pushed the hood of his cloak off, his hair, as dark as the sky itself, cascaded into soft waves just above his shoulders, the top tied back into a loose knot.

Demitria didn't know what the hell he was, but she knew enough that his presence wasn't good.

Her body ached from the impact, but she shoved it aside. Pain was something she couldn't afford to feel, and she wouldn't let it slow her down. Not right now. With clenched teeth, Demitria bit back the wince.

He swung, and her sword met his as she tried to block the blow. So hard, the clash of metal was almost deafening as it echoed through her ears. He swung at her again and again in an unrelenting rhythm, Demitria had killed demons and angels alike, but he was even stronger than she'd initially thought, and her blade wobbled beneath each one of his swings. Arms aching with the force of each impact. She'd hold her ground for as long as she could. Then? She didn't know what she would do. Demitria dodged another of his strikes as she rolled away across the dusty ground, hand reaching to what should have been a small leather sheath at her hip, and her body nearly froze upon finding it not there.

Fuck.

She'd messed up so badly. In her haste to leave, Demitria had all but forgotten to grab the flare gun from within the Guardians' building, and she had no way to signal Solis of the massive threat that was upon them.

She had to last the remaining few hours until morning. Jace would know something had happened, and the community would be up in arms. An impossible feat, but she had to last. Had to do whatever possible to give Solis their only chance of survival.

He dealt blow after blow and Demitria staggered to keep up. Her body was battered, but she was thankful he hadn't managed to wound her more than a few minor cuts. She could feel him gaining the upper hand, faster than she would like. Her arms began to strain with each of his blows she'd blocked. Her movements grew slower with each heaving breath she took, her heart beating what felt like a million beats a minute. The male hadn't faltered once with each of his swings. His body lithe. Graceful as he sidestepped each time her blade came for him. She'd given up on any sort of offense quickly, her movements slipping into a defensive position. It was the only way she knew to make herself last the longest. She couldn't quit. Hold out. Sword up. Keep going. She refused to go down without a fight.

Demitria cursed. At this *creature* trying to kill her. The nightmarish world and barren landscape they barely survived in. She cursed at the fucking darkness that surrounded her, and at the moon that didn't give off enough light for her to fight like she wanted. And she cursed herself for not pushing Jace to station more Guardians. Because someone had come for her, exactly like the demon said they would.

She didn't know when he moved to her right. Losing track of him was her biggest mistake. Legs buckling as he kicked them out from beneath her, Demitria closed her eyes as she hit the ground hard. She wasn't sure what hurt more, the fall from Atlas or this.

His body bore down on top of her as he pinned her to the ground, and she blinked up at him several times from the sudden weight on her hips. She could feel his breath, warm against her face as it slithered across her exposed neck. His smell, woodsy and almost sweet, felt suffocating with each strained breath. In one hand his sword held firm against her chest, the other clenched a dagger pressed against the pale flesh of her throat. She could feel the cool metal as it bit into her skin. Not hard enough to break through, but the blade hurt against her nonetheless. Full lips pulled back into a feral snarl as he leaned in closer, azure eyes narrowed into a piercing glare.

Her death was coming. She wasn't one to pray, but gods she hoped it was quick. She didn't want it to hurt. She knew better, though. Knew that the pain would be excruciating, and he'd drag it out. That's what people like him did. Demons. Angels. Whatever the hell he was, because she was absolutely certain he could not be anything close to human.

An array of different, useless thoughts swarmed through her head as he pressed the dagger into her skin. Could feel the sting as the blade drew that first bead of blood from her throat. She'd done everything she could, and it still wasn't enough. Had done everything in her power to gain the upper hand, but it was futile. He'd gotten through her so fast she'd barely had a chance to defend herself, let alone the community. There would be no saving Solis. Not this time.

The community would be an easy target, completely unaware of the incoming attack nearly at its gate. The female had been right, it seemed.

The wretched demon that had threatened her home and those she loved had been telling the truth, and it killed her that they hadn't put a plan into place before she'd gone out. That she'd spurred herself into action too quickly before getting any more information from the demon, and instead, had turned into a fight about where her loyalties lie. Now she fell defending those that questioned her, and the beast of a male would be unleashed on Solis. Demitria just hoped that with their numbers they'd be able to fend him off.

Her last thoughts shifted to Jace as she winced, readying herself for the pain of the blade that would soon cut across her throat, or the sword that would plunge into her chest. She hoped he'd be able to recover from this. To find the will to move on. There'd been so many things they'd never gotten to experience. So many memories they hadn't gotten to share. Too many things left unsaid.

"Just get it over with." Eyes narrowing into a stern glare, Demitria stared her attacker dead in the eyes.

Seven

KELLAN

"What are you?" His blade held firm at her throat.

She lay there, as still as if she'd given up already.

Pathetic.

"Shouldn't you know that already?" Her words were laced with venom, eyes narrowed like a viper ready to strike. He'd expected more of a fight from someone with the reputation she had. For him to be dispatched, he'd expected *more*.

"Don't make me ask you again." His elbow pressed tighter into her throat and she winced as the weight of him nearly crushed her windpipe, cutting off the air she needed to breathe.

Good.

"Your little bitch henchmen seemed to know exactly who I was." Beneath him she struggled again, but he'd put a stop to it quickly, pressing down even further. The council had been so keen to have her eliminated, yet how quickly the female had fallen.

"Henchmen?"

Her face paled, brows knit as confusion took over her face. "I don't work with anyone." Aside from his siblings, but that was a given. He had no followers. Didn't need them.

"Shit." The girl shifted once more, face laced with panic as her eyes darted into the darkness. "Shit." She repeated, her lean body struggling beneath him.

Demitria Collins was their target. The only reason he and his siblings were sent to the god forsaken world. The fact that she'd thought he'd have underlings was alarming.

"Do you know who I am?"

"You're no different from the other monsters that attacked my home. Why should I know who you are in particular. I don't give a fuck what your name is."

Her home?

"You're human."

The council had neglected to tell them that little piece of information. *The Horsemen had been dispatched for a fucking human.* Out of everyone that could have easily eliminated her, they'd chosen him. His siblings. He couldn't decide if he should be angry or insulted.

"What else would I be?" Like a caged animal, she growled at him. "Let me go." With wild eyes, she shoved at him in a desperate attempt to free herself. Her hands balling into fists as she hit him across his armored chest. He dropped his dagger and nudged it out of the way when she tried to claw at him like a creature fighting for its life. She was, in a way. Grabbing her small hands in one of his own, he held them above her head. He didn't pity the human.

"Not an option." *Idiot.* "We were sent to restore the balance that you so graciously destroyed." Her body stilled for a moment as another wave of confusion crossed her face before hardening into stone once more. "Do you have any idea the beings you've killed?"

"Monsters. I've killed monsters like you to protect my home." The girl hit him and his laughter erupted, echoing into the night. It only made her madder. He recognized the look on her face. The fire that burned beneath her stare. He'd worn it many times himself, even.

"I'll spare you the trouble of overworking that little human brain of yours." Slowly, he removed his elbow from her throat. She wasn't a threat. Her strength had been nothing compared to his own, and he didn't sense any growing power within the girl. "You have single handedly pissed off the entire High Council of Eden." He couldn't help but smile at how her features faltered, and continued on. "You've killed

Demon Lords and Archangels, and the council seem to think you're here to exterminate both."

"If I could, I would." Demitria snapped. "I'd kill you all in a heartbeat to save my family." Despite being completely incapacitated, the human still had fire. He'd give her that.

"We were sent to restore the balance on Earth, and one side cannot continue without the other. You see where I'm getting at?"

Twenty yards away her horse whinnied loudly as he tried to get closer, dust kicking up at his heels. *Obedient.* His own mount blocked the beast at every turn he'd made. Upon his quick glance, Kellan spied the silver scars lining the sides of the creature. The horse wasn't of this world, that much he knew.

Interesting.

"Get off!" His side burned for a moment as she embedded the dagger, breaking free from his grasp.

She'd stabbed him. The human had actually stabbed him. The blade pulled easily from his side and he stared at it for a moment, watching the crimson liquid bead to the dirt at his feet. He hardly felt the open wound, only the initial stab as it pierced through his skin, and it was nothing more than a nuisance now. He stared at the dagger again. Small, but exquisite. If he hadn't been a Horsemen, the blow would have been deadly.

Demitria ran, sprinting into the darkness. He knew the girl had no idea where she was going as she blindly took off, but he expected her to do anything to get away from him. He gave her a few moments before beginning his pursuit.

He enjoyed the chase.

The woman sprinted toward her horse as she pulled the dark cloak over her head, trying desperately to blend in.

"I can still see you." He taunted, chuckling as her speed increased.

The air changed when he was nearly upon her, chilling, as a spark surged through him. Something was approaching from behind, far faster than he would have liked. He could sense it was something not human. Now he was irritated.

He let the girl go. Watched as she mounted the horse and made to leave, then watched as she turned back toward him and stopped.

"Quite the surprise to see you here, War." The angel's voice held a sinister tone as he touched ground before the Horseman. White wings stretched wide from the males back as strong gusts of wind blew toward him with each powerful beat of the angel's wings. Those familiar golden eyes of the male's kind pinning him with a smile.

Noel.

Now he was both insulted *and* angry.

He was a revered Horseman on Eden. Had done the high councils bidding for a millennia doing their dirty work, yet here he stood. War, Horseman of the fucking Apocalypse, and they sent a god damn Archangel.

They were a different race, the angel and him. The Nephilim had been part human once, but that was long ago. Before his time. Neither human nor angel, their blood now ran pure.

It was rare for the angels and Nephilim to intermingle. While him and his siblings were the warriors of Eden, most of his kind lived along its western coastline in a forested village, Daire. It was the council who sought them out. Created out of malice and forever paying the price for the choices their ancestors made, they didn't get a choice if chosen. The high council saw to that, threatening families if they didn't comply. From a young age they were brought up as fighters, training most of their days.

He was really, truly angry. Noel was here for the girl. Had to be.

Pulling the sword from its sheath, he blocked the path between them. Readying the blade. He and his siblings were the ones dispatched. She'd be his kill, and no one else's. Not even his siblings would be the ones to end her, now. Had marked vowed to be the one to kill her the moment she'd drawn his own blood.

"Noel." His voice was hard, angry, as he spoke, which only made the angel smile. "What do you want?"

"Give me the girl, and there won't be any problems." The Angel moved closer, weapons drawn. "Hand her over, Kellan."

"Why are you here." Kellan asked, his hand at the ready as he gripped the hilt of his sword tighter. Clenching his fingers around it.

"I could ask you the same thing, Horseman."

"You're saying you didn't know we were dispatched?" His brow rose as he eyed the Archangel, not showing an ounce of the uncertainty that threatened to take hold at the male's arrival. As an angel for the council, there was no chance Noel wasn't aware of the reasoning behind The Horsemen's dispatch. If he wanted the girl, it had to have been because he wanted answers just like himself. Wanted to know why the Horsemen were dispatched to kill a human when they could have easily sent someone else. Someone like Noel.

The angel didn't answer his question. "Be a good little dog and give me the girl, War."

Kellan didn't understand her importance. The council was adamant she needed to be eliminated. It was the only order given to him and his siblings. Kill Demitria Collins by all means necessary. She was not to survive if they were to restore the balance. How was a mere human causing such an uproar on Eden? In the Underworld?

The council's lack of information had been unusual. The decision to split them up had been as well. Something didn't add up, and if he let Noel get to her, he would never figure out what she was hiding. She had to be hiding something for everyone to be so up in arms. How else could he explain why they had sent a fucking Angel of Death on top of the famed Horsemen.

"I'm afraid I can't do that."

The Archangel advanced, his blades tying with Kellan's. The gold embellishment of the Angel's twin silver weapons held an unnatural glow as he entwined them with his, their curvature locking his sword in place.

He hated angel blades.

Noel blocked his next swing before feigning left, the top of his curved blade penetrating through the thick leather armor on Kellan's shoulder, cutting into him, searing as it tore through flesh. He hated those fucking blades even more. With a wince, he continued on.

He was going to be so irrevocably fucked by the time they completed this mission. The Horsemen were known as the council's guard dogs. They did the shit the council, or other angels, couldn't bring themselves to do. To put it mildly, he should have been kissing the dirt beneath Noel's feet. But the Horsemen were faster. Stronger. Better suited to the fight that had been instilled in them, and he hated more than anything having to bow to the lowlifes that were the Archangels.

His kind may have been classified as lowborn, but the council had treated him and his siblings kindly enough. But they were the chosen Horsemen. Warriors of Eden that never failed, and upheld all honor.

And now he was trying to kill an Archangel.

With a slight glance behind, he noted the girl still stood, poised atop her horse.

Stupid Human.

Even given the chance to flee, the girl stood there. Whether she was frozen with fear or something else he didn't know. He didn't quite care either, but it would make his job easier if he didn't have to run after her. Either way, Demitria wouldn't get far, that he was sure.

Kellan rolled out of the way of Noel's next strike, his own blade easily tearing through the flesh near the angel's shoulder. Had the male been wearing armor, his sword wouldn't have struck. Cocky bastards, they were. He'd yet to meet an Angel of Death, a select group of Archangels that killed for the council, wear anything but the crisp white robes of their brethren. Their only difference were the weapons they bore.

"War! Give her to me!" Noel shouted, pulling him from his thoughts. The angels blade poised high in the air as if to strike him from above. "I want the girl!"

"You'll have to get through me first." Protecting her had not been part of the assignment. Far from it, yet here he was. Whether that was because of his own morbid curiosity at the council's reasoning behind their dispatch, or his own stupid pride in not wanting someone else to take the kill from him, he couldn't be certain.

"Very well, Horseman." Noel lunged once more, both of them advancing on the other. But Kellan was faster. Always faster. The sword left his hands as he launched it straight forward toward the male. The throw had caught the angel off guard, the look of utter disbelief taking hold as he fell back to the dirt. The blade protruded from his chest, pinning him there from the force of Kellan's strike. Striding toward the fallen angel, the anger radiated through him. A familiar feeling, welling inside like the deep churning sea.

"Whose side are you on, Horseman." He coughed, blood spurting from his mouth as he spoke. Kellan knew he'd punctured the angel's lung. If he left the angel now, he'd heal. Slowly.

"I am here to restore the balance." Kellan didn't blame the angel for wanting to know. In his position, he would have done the same. He would have killed to get those answers. He *was* killing to get them.

Noel wouldn't have come here without being sent by the council. There was no reasoning that Kellan could see behind their choice to dispatch an Angel of Death and the Horsemen. The fact that the council thought Noel could do a better job than him, apparently, made him even angrier. The council knew something that they weren't telling him. Telling all of them.

"I will do what is necessary to restore the balance!" His boot fell heavily on the angel's chest. Gripping his wings in his fury, Kellan tore them clean from the angel's body. He felt the soft feathered wings crush within his grasp as he wrenched muscle and bone from flesh. Noel's scream ripped from his throat, echoing through the night.

He wasn't finished.

Noel lay there, panting in a pool of his own blood. "Pathetic. You Horsemen disgust me. Your entire race disgusts me. A bunch of half breeds is all you'll ever be." He spat. The Horseman answered with force, pushing his sword the remainder of the way through his body. Kellan could feel it pierce down to the earth where it stuck. Noel's body went limp.

Kellan's breathing was heavy as he stared down at the dead angel's body. It took a moment before he pulled the sword free, wiping the gore from the blade across Noel's chest before returning it to its sheath. The council would be pissed. Very few Archangels did this job, and he'd murdered one of them over his own morbid curiosity.

Kellan you fucking idiot.

Eight

DEMITRIA

Shit

She needed to get away from here. If what the angel had called him was any indication on what was to come, she needed to get back. Needed to warn the others.

She needed to get Jace out.

War. The angel had called him War, as in the Horseman. By the brutal carnage he was so easily displaying, Demitria knew her suspicions were correct. They had seemed to know each other, yet he'd still murdered him. He was a horseman of the Apocalypse, and she was in so much trouble.

Watching him tear the wings from the angel without even a second thought had been vile, and Demitria very nearly lost the contents of her stomach at the sound it made, and what she'd bared witness to. If he so easily killed his own kind, what would he do to the community? *To her?*

Atlas stood patient but alert as she heaved her body onto his back. He was tense beneath her. Watching intently as the events unfolded. Had they known each other? Him and the angel? Him and War? She'd only been assuming, but Atlas must have been from Eden. That was where the Horseman had said this High Council was from.

Demitria's mind was racing, and she couldn't make him move. The High Council of Eden. She couldn't think about that. Couldn't dwell on the fact that an entire council of people, *creatures*, wanted her dead. Not humans, monsters. And if she did nothing, they would come after her home. They would tear Solis to the ground, effectively ending the lives of everyone she cared for. Jace would not survive.

Finally, she nudged Atlas, and he ran. Ran from the bloody mess of the angel. Ran from the Horseman who'd tried to take her life. The community couldn't afford for her to be weak or afraid. No matter how badly she wanted to leave everything behind, she'd stay for them. For Jace.

Demitria chanced a glance behind her and saw nothing but the dust cloud Atlas's hooves kicked up. The moment she turned back, the Horseman was standing in her way. She didn't even have time to reach before her body was in the air once again.

"You." He snarled that predatory sound, his hand gripping into the fabric of her clothing as he wrenched her from the horse like she'd weighed nothing.

This time she went down swinging, her hands clenched into fists as they connected with the Horseman over and over again across his chest. His face. He barely seemed to flinch with each blow that landed. She kicked. Screamed even, but he still had her body splayed out in the dirt before she could do anything else. The sheath around her thigh was empty, her sword dug into her back She'd lost the dagger after stabbing him.

"Let me go!" She roared, fighting against his ironclad hold. Still screaming as she clawed at whatever fleshy spot she could. He'd thwarted everything she'd thrown at him, and it still wasn't enough.

"You should be thanking me, human." He seethed, pressing into her harder than before. Immobilizing every limb.

Demitria wasn't sure how much time had passed since the initial ambush, but the world around them had become notably lighter. The Horseman was bigger than she'd initially thought, his hulking frame wide above her and she knew she truly didn't stand a chance of getting away. "It's because of me you're still alive."

"I never asked for your help." She spat, eyes narrowing at the smug look that lit up his face. The wound to his right side, where she'd stabbed him, was stained red in his blood, yet it didn't grow. She could have sworn she'd hit an organ with her blade. He should be bleeding everywhere, yet he held her there with ease as if he hadn't even broken a sweat between his tangle with her and the angel. Demitria had too many questions. About him, and how he was still standing in particular. There were so many things about them that she didn't know or understand, but *why* she was being hunted was at the top of her list.

Why had they even come to Earth in the first place? Why had both of their kinds warred over this planet? She wanted answers.

The Horseman didn't move as he held her to the ground. Staring, as if calculating her next movements. He held his face in an almost stone like expression that accentuated his sharp jawline. As the sky lightened even more, she could finally take in the details of his armor. The rich tones of the plain, dark brown vest buckling in the front of his chest. His shoulder pauldrons had a running horse stamped in the center, the rest studded with what looked like brass rivulets holding it together. A long-sleeved black shirt beneath. It was simple, but intricate at the same time. He wore plain dark pants and a pair of matching leather boots to the rest of his armor. He looked every bit the warrior the angel had said him to be. And if it hadn't been so dark, Demitria was sure she would have truly known *what* he was.

He looked deadly.

"If you're going to kill me, do it now." She'd tried to muster enough malice in her voice as she could. Knowing who he was... what he'd done, it didn't take much.

She hated him. Hated everything like him. The angels, the demons... she didn't want anything to do with them.

"You'd like me to just end it all, wouldn't you. Take the easy way out." The Horseman scoffed. Sneering down at her as if she was nothing but dirt under his boots.

Demitria could feel her glare intensify as he continued.

"That's what you humans are like. Time and time again I get dispatched to this shit hole of a planet to rescue your race from destruction. To be frank, I'm getting sick of it."

There was never anything about the Horseman coming to Earth before. Nothing in the history books or schools. Granted she hadn't had much time in school. Just how long had he been around?

"I was sent here to kill you. To end your life where you stand. But I'm not going to let that happen just yet. Now *I* want answers." He loosened his grip only slightly. "He wasn't supposed to be here."

He meant the now dead angel.

"What's that supposed to mean? What are you doing with me?" Out of habit, her fingers inched toward the sheath at her thigh, but his laughter had caught her off guard. Loud, as it boomed throughout her chest, vibrating at their closeness.

"Looking for this?" The Horseman pulled out a familiar looking dagger from a hidden sheath in his own armor, casually waving it in her face. "I might give it back. Haven't decided yet. Now get up." He laughed again before tucking it back away.

Her body felt like nothing more than a rag doll as he hauled her to her feet. He bound her wrists tight with a leather bind before she could protest. "What are you doing with me." Demitria demanded once more, her voice still harboring that icy edge. She matched the stone-cold expression he'd given her right down to the fiery glare that refused to leave her eyes.

War let out a sigh, as if her very presence annoyed him. It probably did, and she swore she could see it on his face.

"I told you, I want answers. We're going to find my siblings."

"I'm not going anywhere with you. Untie me." The leather bit into her skin as she fought to free her hands. She could feel the leather warm from the friction of her protests. Rubbing against the soft flesh of her wrist, irritating it. If she kept this up, wounds would form. Wounds she couldn't afford to have, especially out here where the risk of infection ran high. He laughed, but didn't do as she demanded.

The Horseman took a step away from her, drawing *her* blade as he did so. She watched as he dragged it across his palm in a horizontal line and beads of crimson blossomed along the cut, welling up to its surface. War clenched his fist, dripping it into the dirt at his feet.

"I summon you, council of five." He growled.

Demitria waited for something to happen. For something to burst free from the ground and come for her, but nothing moved.

"I summon you, council of five." He repeated, voice rising, deepening as the words rumbled through his chest. When still nothing happened, she felt her brow raise. War clenched his fist tighter, squeezing more of the crimson liquid from his palm before shoving it into the dirt. "I invoke you, council of five! Fucking answer me!" He bellowed, and she swore she felt it in the marrow of her bones as the sound reverberated through her chest. When they didn't answer, the Horseman was on his feet.

"Move."

She stood her ground and kept her feet planted. She wouldn't follow just because he'd told her to. Like hell she would. With a harsh hand the Horseman shoved, her knees hitting the dirt.

"My patience wears thin." Another loud sigh escaped through his lips as he took up before her. His hulking frame towering over her. War leaned in close, azure eyes pinning her as full lips curled in a sneer. Her own dagger pressed firm against the pale flesh of her throat.

"I'll give you two choices." He seethed. "Option one, you give up this fucking fight of yours and come with me. Or option two. You continue this little hero charade and I'll force you to watch as I burn down that little place you call home." He pointed toward her home. "One by one as I gut them then tear them apart limb from limb."

Her lifeline.

His lips twisted in an expression of disgust. "If you have any sense of integrity and duty to your people you'd pick the latter."

Demitria couldn't move. Her body rooted to the spot as she stared at the monster in front of her. The murderous weapon that had been sent here to rob her of her life and all those around her. He claimed balance. It felt more like an annihilation than anything.

But Jace.

Stella, Evan, Cory, and the others. Their faces flashed before her eyes. She could almost see the carnage he threatened. See the community as it burned to the ground. Hear their screams. Jace kneeling in the middle of Solis as the Horseman stood over him. Helpless. She was always so fucking helpless.

It took everything in her not to empty the contents of her stomach into the dirt. It was more than enough to make up her mind. She couldn't let that happen. Couldn't let their deaths be on her. She'd do everything in her power to ensure they remained safe.

She glared at him, shoulders tensed. "If I go with you—"

"You are hardly in a position to bargain with me." He smirked. She wanted to slap the stupid look off his face.

"If I go with you," Demitria repeated, louder this time. "My people remain safe. My community goes untouched. Only then will I go willingly." Give her life for theirs. It seemed like a fair trade, her life for over twenty lives.

Jace wouldn't know what had happened to her, and he probably never would. She couldn't bear to think of the hurt that it would cause him. The pain when she wasn't at those gates by the time the sun was up. It nearly broke her, but weakness was something she couldn't do right now. Not when it was the difference between her people surviving or not.

"I will not harm your community." Demitria's features softened for a moment, and the tension in his body slackened slightly.

To her surprise, the Horseman bowed his head. *Honorable.* The gesture was something she didn't think a being like him was capable of. At least not toward her kind, and it caught her off guard.

"Mount up, we leave now." War unbound her wrists, guiding her toward Atlas. Demitria was grateful for his presence. One familiar face she could count on no matter what happened. He nudged into her shoulder, easily cracking through the barrier she'd erected. She mounted with her usual ease, but riding Atlas had a finality patrolling never did.

They didn't speak. The Horseman rode slightly behind her and Atlas, to make sure she didn't run again, she was sure. She wouldn't. Not after the threat he'd made. She knew him capable, the tearing of the angel's wings replaying in her mind

The sky grew light as dawn finally broke. Soon, the world was illuminated in its glow. Everything remained quiet. As if the world knew who was present, and would do anything to go unnoticed, or bow at his feet. Their mounts kicked up a whirlwind of dust as they rode away from the only place she'd felt safe in the last decade. It took nearly all her strength to hold back the tears that had been threatening to fall.

Jace.

She reminded herself over and over again.

She did this for Jace.

Nine

DEMITRIA

Everything was dark. Black. The air inside musty yet cool as the breeze drifted in from the mouth of the cave. Underneath her, the rocks had been worn smooth—by what she wasn't sure. Blinking rapidly, Demitria forced her eyes to adjust to her surroundings. Stalagmites formed in clusters along the ground. She'd tucked her body against a large column midway into the cave the moment they'd entered, wanting to put as much distance between them as possible. *She must have fallen asleep.* Demitria hadn't remembered dozing off, let alone feeling the lull of sleep. But given the events that had led her here, it didn't surprise her. They'd arrived at the cave by nightfall after hours of traveling. It had been dark then, but now? She could barely see her own hand in front of her face.

Further back, she could hear the soft breathing of their mounts. Content. Atlas hadn't seemed worried, despite her own cautions. Her own fears. Maybe he really had known them in a previous life. She'd contemplated asking the Horseman, but knew it would get her nowhere. He didn't seem like the type for idle chat, and if she was being technical, she was his prisoner. He didn't owe her an explanation for a single thing.

Demitria's gaze drifted toward him, seemingly fast asleep at the entrance to the cave. His body bathed in the moonlight as it penetrated inside, as if chasing away the darkness that threatened to escape.

What have I gotten myself into?

She didn't know how to get out of this mess. Still didn't quite understand how she'd fucked up badly enough to have gotten into it in the first place. Humans had been fighting back for *years*. So why her? Why now?

Glancing over at the sleeping figure of the Horseman once more, she sighed. *Great. Just great.* Demitria knew he'd purposely stationed himself at the mouth of the cave, knowing she'd try and get away from him. To escape when he'd least expect it, but even that would be a slim chance. Demitria had no weapons to defend herself with. She could just make out the hilt of her sword on the other side of him, in the center of the entrance. Nothing would work.

Think.

Demitria edged closer. Silently sliding her feet across the smooth rock floor. Her dagger had been haphazardly tossed on his side—closest to her. For a supposed Horseman he was an idiot. What kind of being left a weapon within arm's reach of their prisoner?

Her body inched closer and closer. Ten feet. Five. Two. Demitria held her breath, fingers stretched to their limits as she reached for the dagger before snatching it back and retreating to her spot at the back of the cave in a heartbeat. She hadn't dared a single breath until she was safely tucked back where she'd awoken. Acquiring the blade had been a small win, but a win regardless. She would take whatever she could get right now.

Her eyes never left the blade as she toyed with it in her fingers. Could you even kill a Horsemen? He'd claimed she had done immeasurable damage to the beings of the Underworld and Eden. Archangels and demon lords alike, yet he seemed different. Like he was on a completely different level than the others she'd faced. Could she even do it? Or would she just be wasting her life—not like she currently had much going for her anyway. She had to at least try. On the off chance that she could do it and get away, *she had to try.*

Slipping undetected even further into the cave, she readied Atlas. His bridle had been discarded off to the side when they'd first come in, and she retrieved it quickly. Slipping it over his head, her fingers trembled as she fumbled with the buckles, but managed to do them up without making a sound. The horse huffed as his soft, velvety nose nuzzled into her in greeting. Demitria didn't dare speak, but softly rubbed his favorite spot in the middle of his forehead. For the first time since she'd run into the Horseman, she smiled. Even if she didn't go back to the community, she was grateful to at least still have him.

It seemed like hours before she finally had the courage to leave her perch, but had only been a matter of minutes. Having taken her far longer than she would have liked to talk herself into going through with the idea of killing him. To stab him as he slept. It wasn't honorable, but killing never really was. Did that even really matter with creatures like them? Like him? He'd threatened her family. Almost killed her. Maybe *killing* him was the honorable thing to do.

War's chest rose and fell in rhythmic beats, breathing even. Her body crept closer; dagger held before her. Ready. Waiting for her moment to strike, the hood on her cloak pulled up over her head, shielding her from the moon's luminescent glow. He didn't stir as she advanced, and soon found herself mere inches from him. So close she could feel his breath on her skin. It was warm, an unwelcome feeling as her skin crawled. Demitria held the dagger to his throat, the deadly edge pressing ever so slightly into his skin. She watched as a single bead of crimson bubbled to the surface.

Azure eyes met her own, and her entire body froze at the intensity in his gaze. "You'd be making a grave mistake should you go through with that." The Horseman leaned in closer. Pressing the blade deeper into the sun-kissed flesh beneath her dagger. "Do it." His lips curved, teeth near bared in a feral smile as another bead of crimson trickled along the edge of the cool metal in her hand.

She hadn't realized he'd gripped her wrist in an iron hold before it was too late. Hand squeezing so tight she thought the bones in her wrist would shatter completely. The dagger clattered loudly to the floor, echoing in the near silence of the cave. He didn't let her go. She was held prisoner in his grasp.

His eyes bore holes into her very being, face turned to stone. Unreadable. For someone who had almost been killed he made no inclination of anger. Demitria wasn't sure what startled her more, the sheer power he seemed to possess or the innate calm that washed over him as his eyes never left her. "How did you know?"

"I was awake before you even took the dagger." He continued with that deadly calm. It unnerved her.

She was the stupid one.

The anger surged within her when he didn't let her go. Struggling against him, she was inevitably stuck, as if her hand had been encased in cement. When he finally let her go, she fell backward, landing hard on her back. The air left her lungs in a rush, the wind knocked out of her upon impact. Demitria lay there a few moments before mustering the strength to get to her feet once again and retreating to the spot where she'd been sleeping earlier.

"Not going to take your blade?" He laughed. She was furious as the sound struck a chord in her. Building and building until all she wanted to do was hurl *something* at his head. She hated him.

"Go to hell!" Her shout rumbled through the cave, echoing off the walls. Behind, the mounts startled at the sudden outburst. Their hooves thudded against the rock floor as loose pieces scattered beneath them as they skittered further back into the cave.

"Already been there." Demitria could practically hear the smirk in his voice as he spoke, and she saw nothing but red. "Not much to see." He was baiting her with every word, she realized. Like it was a game, knowing that whatever he'd say would make her angrier and angrier until finally, she'd snap. Biting her tongue, Demitria stopped responding. "Humans... such tempers." He chuckled to himself. When he finally stopped mocking her, her mind wandered for hours. Wondering what was happening at the community. The Horseman had said the demons had nothing to do with him, so had they left Solis alone? What had happened when she hadn't returned that morning? Had they sent someone looking for her? Did Jace go looking? Demitria hoped that in her absence, he had amped up patrol. That he'd seen the need to arm the other residents and teach them to truly fight. Because when a Guardian didn't return, it always meant the worst possible scenario. She hoped Jace wouldn't mourn her for long. That losing the last piece of family he had left wouldn't break him. His last reminder of life before the Ascension. They'd made a promise to each other so many years ago that they'd never leave the other's side. That no matter what happened, they would stick together. She hadn't been given much of an option, but it tore her apart. Just another thing she couldn't do. Another promise she couldn't keep.

Another thing she'd failed at.

Stella's words fluttered through her mind. *Hope,* she'd said. She needed to hope. Where the hell would that get her? Where was the hope in this? An assassination attempt, a kidnapping. How was one truly supposed to hope when all she'd ever known was blood and war.

Demitria's head hit the rock behind her, chest heaving as the sigh left her lips in a quick burst. There was no hope. Not anymore. Not like this.

Any chance of hope had died the moment *he* came into her life.

Ten

KELLAN

The moment dawn broke, Kellan was awake. She'd tried to kill him on multiple accounts. It had been the first time a human had ever attempted to. If she wasn't his target, he'd almost be impressed. The look in her green-gold eyes as she brought the dagger to his throat with such confidence, like a wolf silently stalking through the woods, waiting for that perfect moment to strike. For a human, she was fire. It raised his suspicions further. Had him asking himself more questions than he had answers to. Why was the council so invested in her death? Why this particular human? Why even a human? *Why wouldn't they answer him?* He'd tried summoning them three more times after the girl had fallen asleep, and they hadn't come, refusing every call or maybe ignoring him, there was no way to know for sure.

Despite his direct orders, Kellan fumbled the assignment. She was to be killed on sight. Instead, he'd found himself a prisoner. He needed to find out why the council had found her so... special. Killing her could always come later.

Kellan watched her sleeping for a moment. Her lean body curled around itself as she slept soundly, unaware of his presence above her. The curves of her chest rising and falling with each deep breath. He didn't understand the council's infatuation with her death. Didn't understand the allure of the humans in general. Such fickle, frail creatures they were. But the girl had shown a fire that none of the others in his experience had, and that troubled him more than anything.

With each rhythmic breath, he found himself fascinated with the woman, and unable to look away. Enthralled with the way this fair skinned being seemed to raise so many questions within him. She groaned in her sleep, breaking him from the thoughts swarming in his mind. He shouldn't be so curious. Kill the girl, that's what the council had said.

"Get up." His boot connected with her side. The audible crack loud as she yelped awake. Clutching her ribs, she staggered to her feet. "We're leaving. Mount up." Demitria stumbled toward the horses without a word spoken, face pale as she clutched the side he'd just wounded. The sight of her shying away, skittish, stroked something inside him and he delighted at the thought. Bloodshed was what he did. What he was known for. The Horseman War, revered for his innate ability to maim and kill things. A harbinger of war itself, and he smiled at the thought. She needed to fear him. All her kind did. It made his job a hell of a lot easier that way. Kellan strolled after her, determined to get out of the musty cave and on his way to reuniting with his siblings. He readied his mount quickly, tightening the cinch on his saddle before ushering the girl out the mouth of the cave where they mounted.

His eyes roamed the expanse of the landscape around them. Nothing but dirt and dust far beyond what his eyes could see. He'd been appalled the moment he'd returned to this planet. Kellan hadn't been to Earth for many, many years, and the sight before him was disgusting. There was nothing outside. The world had been tossed into a state of chaos. Dead. Everything around was dead. So different from how he'd remembered it. Even if the war hadn't happened, it was much different than he'd remembered. The cities grew vast, buildings stood taller than even the largest trees in Eden. All that remained now was nothing more than a shell of what it once was. *Maybe that was for the best.* Earth had once reminded him of his home. The lush greens and crystalline waters. That was what he remembered. Before they'd changed it. *Ruined* it with their structures of steel. Just another reason he hated them.

She continued her silence as they rode, never so much as glancing away from the path ahead of her. He didn't care, let her drown in those emotions. He had bigger things to worry about. Reuniting with his siblings was the first task. Because he'd fucked the assignment up royally, failing the one task given to them, he needed the input of the other Horsemen on how to proceed. If it had just been him, killing her, while slightly delayed, would have been forgivable. But an Angel of Death showing up for their same assignment? *Killing* that Archangel? Kellan didn't know if the council would punish him. It wouldn't have been the first time. Not by a long shot. For the bloodlust that plagued him for so many years. But he always got the job done, sometimes just in an unorthodox way, and that was always cause for punishment. He knew they took pleasure in the torment. The High Council was savage and cruel on their best days.

They rode for hours under the warming sun, over an endless sea of dust. The last time Kellan had ridden through here Earth had been beautiful. Alive. He glanced over at the girl. Demitria's face had changed, hardened into a stoic look as they eased their mounts into a slower gait. It caught him off guard when she finally spoke.

"I have something that might be of interest to you." Voice no more than a whisper, she refused to look at him. Kellan heard her anyway.

"I doubt anything you say will be of interest," The laughter couldn't be helped. He took no pity on her. "But enlighten me anyway."

"I need something in return."

"You seem to think you have all the bargaining power here." Pulling his mount to a halt, they both stopped. The girl turned in his direction then, the same narrowed gaze from earlier taking over the dainty features of her face. Waiting, ready to strike. She had proved to be interesting if nothing else. Intriguing—almost—by how easily she'd been able to control her emotions. Because anyone else would have broken down at his feet by now. Within minutes, really.

"I saw the confusion on your face, Horseman. You and I both know there are some things you don't know." He hated that she'd read it on his face. *How perceptive of her.*

"You're so sure I don't already have this information?"

"Considering you had no idea who I was talking about earlier, yes. I'm fairly confident that I have the upper hand." Her full lips curved in a wicked smirk. She had so carefully crafted the deadly look on her face, any sign of fear had ceased to exist. Surprising, for a human.

"What do you want?" Kellan decided to indulge her.

"I want the safety of my people." Demitria's green-gold gaze never left his own. Piercing through him as if doing so would gain his favor.

"We already agreed on that."

"For you, not your siblings. If I tell you this information, you and your siblings do not touch my home. My people remain free and unharmed."

Kellan had absolutely zero plans on coming back to the hell hole once they reunited, but she didn't need to know that. It was an easy decision for him.

"You have my word, again, that your people will remain untouched." With a nod, he urged her to continue.

Demitria nudged her horse foreword once more, Kellan quickly following behind. "The morning you showed up, we had a run in with a demon." She started.

Given the current state of the world, this was not news. There were demons and angels everywhere. Opening his mouth to tell her as much, she cut him off with a raise of her hand.

"She knew who I was."

That was news. It was uncommon for demons to know humans. Their only true aspirations were to feed and follow those in command. Their orders were never anything more than destruction. Demons fed on the flesh of humans. On their souls.

"What do you mean she knew you?" His own eyes narrowed in, searching. Looking for answers in her features.

"She said someone was coming for me. For us." The human girl sighed again, tearing her gaze away from his as she looked across the horizon. Something in her face hardened once more, like she'd slipped into a mask, devoid of her emotions. "Threatening my home. Threatening J—" She stopped mid-sentence as if having said too much. Finally, she continued after another moment of silence. "She threatened everything. Everything that I have left, and said they would burn it to the ground."

"Why did she know you?" Kellan repeated. He hadn't expected her to have the answer. "Who was she?"

"I don't know."

"Where is she?"

"Dead." Demitria met him head on. Serious. Coiled and ready to explode. "I killed her before she could say anything more."

"You idiot." Had the human not realized that could have been his only lead? She had been so swept up in the turmoil of her home, that she'd killed the only creature that could give her the information she'd wanted. That he now wanted.

Fucking useless.

A familiar rage began to bubble. With aching fingers, he gripped the pommel of the saddle. Willing it. Begging it to dissipate before he'd do something he would later regret. Killing the human would end most of his problems, but it wouldn't answer any of the questions that had been brewing. In the years he had served the council there had never been a doubt in his mind about anything. Never a need to question the orders he'd been given, but there had never been a mission like this. Never had they sent a fucking Angel of Death to clean up after them. It had *always* been the other way around.

Kellan had been sent to kill something for the council more times than he could count, but never like this. The Horsemen weren't the ones who failed. They were the ones who always did the job right.

The anger bubbled higher and higher the more he thought about it. Like a dam ready to burst.

"Shall I give you a moment, Horseman?" She pursed her lips, and he could hear the lilt in her voice. Could picture the gleam in her eyes as she stared in his direction. Every word that left her mouth, the angrier he got. Every breath she took. Killing her would have ended so many of his problems. Too many questions, not enough answers.

He dismounted. The charred tree feet away crumbled into nothing as his sword collided with its bark. Like the smoke from a fire, pieces of it drifted up into the air. He mindlessly hacked away at whatever was in front of him. Another tree, a bush, he didn't care. But the anger at the unknown slowly left his body as he continued.

Kellan didn't know how much time had passed when he returned to his mount. The human sat waiting astride the beast beneath her, watching the outburst he'd unleashed on the world around him.

"All that over a demon?" A smirk found its way to her lips and he very nearly lashed out at her. Could picture her head as it lolled to the side, blood dripping from a gaping wound that he'd inflicted. "I should have killed you." He growled, "Could still kill you."

She laughed then, calling his bluff as if she knew he was using her for nothing more than answers now.

"Move out." He barked, pointing ahead. The smug grin never left her face.

By midafternoon, they had been riding for hours, the sun high in the sky as it scorched into their backs. The landscape around them hardly changed the further out they went. Nothing but that same barren terrain for miles. They'd passed through the remains of what he'd assume had been a town before the Ascension, but hardly anything remained. Buildings stripped and foraged for all possible resources while rock and stone lay in rubble heaps. He'd noticed the widening of the girl's eyes as she'd tried not to look surprised, but the sudden change hadn't gone unnoticed.

The days on earth had been hot, nights cold. Different, again, than he'd remembered. The last time he'd stepped foot on this planet the days had been less temperamental. The human remained quiet, but her mood had lightened slightly. At his expense no less, he was sure. His outburst hours earlier had surely caused a lapse in her fear toward him. Despite it, her face was sullen as her eyes grew dark. They had been traveling for nearly two days with little sleep in his quest to reunite with the others. She looked...exhausted.

"You look as if you're about to keel over." He noted aloud. *Let her die. Make my life easier.* Do the job he'd been sent to do. Would killing her make restoring the balance easier? Make it harder? Could one human really turn the tides that much? And why did a petty demon claim to know her?

She barely turned in his direction. Barely even acknowledged he'd spoken before answering.

"I haven't had anything to eat or drink in two days." She snapped, brows furrowed as her jaw tensed, her lips forming in a thin line. As if in answer, his own stomach grumbled at the mention of food and he silently cursed its utter betrayal. No matter how badly Kellan wanted to deny it, the human had a point.

"Why do you have no food?" He found himself saying, knowing he'd already sounded like an idiot the moment the words left his mouth.

"Because I had so much time to pack a bag of supplies before I was so kindly threatened then taken against my will." She glowered, eyes meeting his in challenge as that same fiery gaze returned. One she knew she'd never win, but a challenge nonetheless. He shouldn't have respected her for it, but he did.

She had a point... again.

"We'll stop in a few hours. Find food and somewhere to sleep." The human only nodded before pushing her mount forward once more.

They passed through a large canyon sometime later, the smooth edges of the red rock towering tall above them, higher than even his own eyes could see. Before the planet's ruin, he'd wager some form of water system had once ran through it as evidence of a riverbed wound its way throughout. But in the distance, Kellan could faintly make out the trickle of water tucked somewhere in a shallow cavern. Aside from themselves, it was imperative their mounts got water if they wished to continue. He led them toward the sound, coming to a stop at the wide arched entrance in the canyon.

Dismounting, he held up a hand, listening. Waiting. Searching for anything that was inside. He heard nothing. Couldn't sense anything more than small creatures scurrying about, and he knew it was safe. For now, at least. Inside, the sun bounced off the walls, illuminating the interior of the cavern. Stalactites of varying sizes hung from the roof. The drip of the water off the largest echoed throughout. They let their mounts drink first. Demitria was quick to cup her hands under the steady drip before slowly and carefully bringing it to the dark horse. Kellan watched as he slowly gulped the water in her palms, eyes never leaving those of its master's. She repeated the process three more times before he finished, bringing a soft muzzle to her neck as he nuzzled into the girl. He wondered how she'd acquired such a mount, let alone formed a bond as strong as they had. He had an inclination on what the horse was, due to the heavy silver scarring marring both of the beast's sides, and if his suspicions were correct, they only bonded once, and a human sure as hell wouldn't have had one from a foal.

More questions.

Who the hell was this human? He couldn't stop asking himself the question over and over, echoing through his mind. Balance, he had to keep reminding himself. The council said she'd thrown off the entire balance of his world, not to mention her own. But why? He couldn't answer any of it. Might as well focus on the imminent task.

"We need food." Kellan said, unsaddling his mount after he'd had his own fill of water.

"Shall I materialize it out of thin air?" The ever-knowing smirk returned to her face, lighting up her dainty features. He nearly back-handed it off of her, only stopping himself as he knew it wouldn't change a thing. Kellan had always been known by his siblings to have a temper, but he'd done well at keeping it in check over the last several years. He couldn't tell if it was her defiance, or that fire dancing through her eyes, but she'd managed to continuously have him teetering on that edge...

"Useless human." Her kind were already loathsome. She'd proved to be absolutely infuriating, nearly making him reach his limit. It bothered him that she didn't cower in his presence like so many humans had done before her. He was the predator and she was his prey, yet she acted as if she were his equal. Something he could not let continue. "You need to catch food."

"Me? That's funny, I think you meant to say *we*." She put emphasis on the last word, arms crossing over the curves of her chest as she stared up at him. Her eyes narrowed. Kellan had lost track of how many times today alone she'd repeated that same gesture. "I sure as hell am not risking myself out there to get food. If you want it, you help."

With a huff, he exited the cavern. "Fine. If you don't catch it you don't eat. Simple as that."

She followed behind him.

It took an hour for him to track down the damned beast. An hour of painstakingly stalking through brush with thorns so large they managed to snag his clothing in the gaps between his armor. He'd curse if he hadn't needed to be quiet. Up ahead, the human had advanced faster than him, her movements louder than a thundering horse. He could hear the crunch of her boots with each step she took. Each curse as her own clothing caught and tore.

Gods help him.

If they went hungry it would be because of this stupid human.

When she pounced, knife ready, Kellan felt his own body fly. Like hell she'd get it first. The boar squealed as it wrestled its way out from underneath her, fleeing in a frenzy into the thick brambles.

"Are you stupid?" He hollered, not bothering to look back as he instinctively followed the animal into the brush. His own blade left his hands with enough force to break bones. Embedding itself into the skull of the boar who skidded to a halt as it fell.

"You almost let it get away!" Still yelling, his feet carried him toward her as she sat on the ground panting for air. A crimson stream trickled down her forehead, indicating she'd been injured. The boar had nicked her with a tusk during the short tussle. She'd been lucky she hadn't lost an eye. Or her life. Kellan nearly laughed at the thought.

"I would have had it if you didn't come flying at me." She grumbled, peeling her body out of the dirt, brushing it from her pants. "I played every part in that as you did." Demitria was quick to add.

"Whose blade took it down."

"That's beside the point!" Tossing her hands in the air, she was shouting. If anything else was around she would draw unnecessary attention to them. "That takedown happened because of me! It only got away because you're the idiot who nearly crushed me!"

Anger swelled but he squashed it. At least she'd tried.

"We'll share it." Through gritted teeth, he let a sigh slip through his lips. "Now would you keep your voice down?" Kellan had been equally as guilty of not keeping his own down, but she'd managed to push every single one of his buttons. He blamed it entirely on her.

Before she could make another remark he returned to the boar. Making quick work of the carcass as he cleaned and skinned the animal, a skill he'd learned back home from a very early age—taking with them only what they needed. He could sense the scavengers all around now. The smell of death and blood in the air having drawn them out from wherever they'd been hiding. Their near yelling match hadn't helped much either, but Kellan was confident they'd stay away given his presence. The beings could take what they wouldn't use, and he knew none of what the beast offered would go to waste.

"You're bleeding." He mentioned as they neared the cavern. Demitria touched a finger to her head, pulling it away to confirm.

"So I am." She groaned. Inside, the girl returned to the dripping water. Cupping it in her hands and splashing it to the wound. Her face scrunched into a wince at the contact, but she continued anyway, flushing it out as best she could.

Useless. These creatures were useless. With his own groan, Kellan put the meat down and joined her. Washing the blood off his hands before tearing a small chunk of cloth from his cloak and soaking the fabric and stepping before her.

"Put pressure on it." She didn't protest as he placed the fabric against the wound, staunching the bleeding. "These beasts carry disease. You need to make sure it stays clean."

"What I need are antiseptics." She said, but didn't move away.

"Just stop the bleeding. I'll find you a medicinal plant." He didn't give her the chance to utter another word or stop him before he left the cavern. He'd spotted the fauna while they were out hunting the boar, and knew it wouldn't take him long. He'd be back before she could even think about running away.

When he returned a few minutes later, the girl sat along a low edge, still clutching the fabric to her forehead. Kellan said nothing as he rinsed the plant under the steady drip before making his way toward her.

"Hand me the cloth." He held out his hand and she did as he'd said, placing the bloodied fabric in his outstretched palm. He rinsed that too before returning to her side, laying the fabric on the smooth stone. Swiping a loose rock from the floor, he began grinding the plant into the fabric, mulching it up as best he could, given the materials at hand.

"This has medicinal properties that will help fight off infection."

"Yarrow." She nodded, her body relaxing as she watched him work.

"You know of it?"

The girl nodded again. "Someone back home taught me a few things. We make do with what we've got these days." She gave him a sad smile.

"Where I'm from, you typically chew the plant before putting it on a wound. I'll save you the horror." Demitria made a choking noise, and he could have sworn she'd nearly laughed.

"I appreciate the gesture...I think." She looked away from him as he picked the fabric up from the rock. Kellan said nothing as he dipped his finger into the green mixture, swiping it across her forehead as he packed it into the wound.

He was only keeping her alive to get his answers. She had to live long enough for him to reunite with his siblings, then figure out what the council wanted. After that, he didn't care if she keeled over on the spot.

Eleven

DEMITRIA

Warmth.

Demitria didn't know when the cavern had gotten so warm. The night had grown cold rather quickly, almost to the point of freezing, as if a layer of frost had swept over the cavern, turning her core to ice. She'd curled up as close to the burning embers of the fire as she could last night, watching as the flames danced across the walls. Willing the heat to envelope her in its warm embrace until she'd drifted off into a deep sleep, and it had still barely been enough to keep her from shivering.

Her eyes wouldn't open. Reveling in the heat that now radiated through her. Reminding her of the community back home. The warmth of her bed, curling up with the quilt that Jace had Stella make for her birthday a few years ago. It had been mostly cotton, made up of an array of greens, purples, and blue fabric. He'd spent months slowly gathering the supplies needed for it, acquiring most from the traders, but others he'd gotten from their trips beyond the walls. The trips that she hadn't been able to go on with him. Demitria remembered the crippling anxiety waiting for him to return. That feeling of complete helplessness as she spent each day pacing the streets wondering if he'd come home. She couldn't think about the community any more. Going home wasn't an option now, not with the price on her head. Unless she found some way to get out and figure all this shit out, she wouldn't see them again. Wouldn't see Jace again, and she didn't know what unnerved her more. The realization of never seeing his smile again, or her impending death at the hands of the Horseman.

Stretching the aches from her limbs from several nights of sleeping on a cold, hard surface, Demitria froze. Breath catching in her throat as the solid wall of muscle behind her stirred, ripping her from the sleep induced grogginess. It took a heartbeat for that fogginess to pass before she was pulling the dagger from the sheath around her thigh. The Horseman hadn't taken her blade back last night, but from what she'd gathered, it was nothing more than him being cocky. Knowing he was invincible. That she couldn't touch him. *She'd show him.*

Demitria turned around in haste, rolling her body so she was face to face with the wall of heat.

"Get your filthy hands off me before I end your life right here, right now." Dagger pressed hard to his chest, her every word laced with venom.

The Horseman's laugh reverberated throughout her entire body and she fought every bone that threatened to shiver at its warmth.

"This again? You couldn't kill me if you tried." He grinned. "You humans are so fickle. You should be thanking me for keeping you alive. You were pale and cold as ice when I looked over." Every breath he took seemed to feather over her skin and she cringed at the closeness. "Had I not moved over when I did, I doubt you would have woken from that sleep."

She'd like to think he'd been so generous as to keep her from perishing in the night, but she knew better. Knew he wanted something from her, but that didn't negate the fact that he'd saved her life... again.

"You should have left me to die. Wasn't that why we're here? What's ending my life that bit sooner?"

"So quick to forfeit your life, are we? Contrary to what you might think, I'm not the bloodthirsty monster you've conjured up in your mind. My purpose is balance, and I want to know why the council really wants you dead."

It hadn't taken much for him to give up his real reasoning behind keeping her alive, and the admission surprised her.

"Killing you now won't give me the answers that I seek."

"You are exactly what I think you are and nothing more. War, bringer of destruction." Demitria meant for her words to bite, she could only hope they did. All of them were nothing more than monsters. She didn't care what any of these beings said, it didn't change how she felt.

"Kellan," He said, "My name is Kellan. My siblings and I are the four Horsemen, but not in the sense that you humans think. I bring destruction when it is needed, but keeping the balance is what I live by."

"Ok *Kellan*," She emphasized his name for show. "You are nothing more than those fucking creatures that attacked my home. Remember that."

"A thank you would suffice?"

"I have nothing to thank you for." Sheathing her dagger, Demitria rolled her body away faster than needed before scrambling to her feet and brushing herself off.

"You have everything to thank me for." Azure eyes brightened as he followed suit, getting to his feet far more casually than she had with that unearthly grace of all beings like him. She hated that he was right. That he'd kept her alive when he shouldn't have.

"Thank you." She bit out, hands curling into fists at her side. Some sick, twisted part of her felt as if she owed him something, and she hated that too.

"Was that so hard?" He laughed, turning his back to her as if he didn't view her as a threat before sheathing the weapons that had been tossed haphazardly to the side of the small fire he'd built the night before.

She found herself angry once more.

"You are unbelievable..." Demitria clenched her jaw tight, feeling the pressure ache in her teeth as her features contorted with rage. "We should get going." Not daring to turn even a glance at him, she pulled the cloak tight around her body before wandering to the mounts at the back.

Atlas let out a soft nicker at her approach. A smile stretched across her face. Without being able to return home, he was her rock. Her only ties to Solis. Her arms found their way around his neck as the sigh left her lips.

"What are we going to do, boy?" She said, no more than a whisper, but she knew Kellan had heard. She didn't care. If it made her look weak, so be it. She'd lost her home—again—the day he found her. Watched it get torn away as he picked her off Atlas, pinning her to the ground. She could see it in his eyes. She'd known she wouldn't be returning home right then and there, despite her protests. Her fighting.

Letting loose one last sigh she made quick work on readying Atlas. He stood patiently as she slipped the bridle over his large head, taking the bit with ease. The worn leather buckled easily at his cheek. Craning his neck, he looked at her expectantly, nudging her with the soft velvet of his nose. Demitria couldn't help but stare into his soft, large brown eyes. They were kind. Soulful. She couldn't even begin to think about the destruction he'd most likely seen. The worlds he had been to. His master had been cruel from the moment she'd set eyes upon him. The way the angel discarded him as if his life was worthless. Like he'd been nothing but a tool, despite the loyalty the horse had probably shown him.

It wasn't her that grounded him. She didn't think she'd ever be able to forgive herself if it was. The man who had, did not live to see his next day, an angel having slaughtered him moments later. It was brutal and gruesome when Atlas fell. His cry as he hit the ground, wings torn away as he bled out on the ground beyond Solis, was something Demitria didn't think she'd ever be able to forget. The sound was haunting.

He was the one creature she'd ever cared for. The one being she couldn't bring herself to hate. She wanted to hate everything about the beings and creatures that had taken over her home, yet one look into his wounded eyes had shown her everything. She knew he didn't like the fighting any more than she did. Here, horses were peaceful creatures. Majestic. She could only assume that his kind was similar. The wings had been the biggest difference, his brain a close second. Atlas was one of the smartest creatures she had ever known. Attuned to the world around him. He acted as if he understood the words they'd speak. Sometimes she swore he even knew what she was thinking.

The day something should happen to him would be the day another little piece of her died. Demitria didn't have much left. He and Jace were it. She was already losing Jace. Losing them both would probably kill her.

Twelve

KELLAN

They had been riding for hours once more. Something he had grown used to over the years, but he could tell the human was struggling with it. Long days was what he did, especially when out on an assignment. This particular one had been his worst, in more ways than one, by far. Kellan had never questioned the council in all his years. Had killed for them because they wished it without even a second thought. But something had felt wrong the moment he encountered his charge. Tainted. And since then, everything had just been a never-ending spiral of shit, and the only blood on his hands since arriving was an Angel of Death. Thinking this was his worst assignment to date was the biggest understatement of his life.

His gaze wandered toward the girl as she fussed with her mount, and he couldn't help the curiosity spiking through him. So many questions about her past and why the council had to get involved. Why she seemingly shared a bond with a creature from his home that so few ever experienced. After all this time serving the council, why a human? Would she just be the first of many that they were to eliminate? Death seemed to defeat the very purpose of balance.

They'd left the canyon that had been their refuge for the night only to emerge into what was once a grove of trees. The only colors Kellan could see were charcoal, like a deep and endless sea. Gone were the branches that once teemed with life as they grew, reaching tall toward a blazing sun. They'd been ravaged into nothing more than husks. He was sure if he felt one it would crumble at his touch. A fire had blazed through there. Through the entire planet when the Underworld lay waste to these lands. But this area seemed to have been hit one of the hardest. This had been a vast ecosystem once, abundant with life. Hundreds of species, animal and plant alike, had once called this home. He remembered it from long ago. By the remains of the vast number of trees spread around them, it seemed as though not much had changed since he'd last been here. Like it had been left wild and free from the clutches of their steel buildings. At least the humans had done that right.

His own home—Eden—was a place of natural, wondrous beauty. Those that resided there took pride in their home. They hadn't plowed through the wildlife to build bigger homes and cities. They knew better. Understood the importance of keeping it raw. It was just another reason he hated the human species. Destroying themselves well before they even got there.

Despite the hatred that fought to take hold, he pushed on into the nightmarish trees. The air still reeked of smoke and ash. He could feel it burning his senses, dulling them as if a thick fog had taken hold of his brain. The flames no longer blazed, but it was as if they had only just been put out with how badly it smelled.

The Demons were wretched creatures. The angels too, in fact. If they hadn't been so damn greedy, he wouldn't be here. Neither of them thrived on Earth, and he didn't see the allure. Not to mention... a world infested with humans...

"We—" Kellan had opened his mouth to tell the human that they'd be stopping to give the horses a break when something moved ahead. Fast. Too fast for his liking. Slinking through the shadows as it weaved around them in a taunting manner. He cursed aloud, the smell had done more damage than he'd thought. Hadn't even noticed that the world around him had gone quiet. He'd been hearing creatures scurry for miles, but nothing moved. The only sound had been the beating heart of the human before him, and the drag of hooves in the dirt.

The girl finally stopped, catching on to his hesitation. Her eyes met his, looking to him for an answer. Kellan didn't have one for her.

His eyes darkened as it neared, and his fingers inched toward his blade, itching to grab hold and swing just as the familiar stench finally hit his senses head on.

"Run." He told her, not taking his eyes off the moving shadow that slithered around them.

The human stood frozen in place. He shouldn't have been surprised, but it angered him nonetheless. They never do as they're told. Never listen. Her body stood frozen in fear. In one swift motion Kellan leaped from his mount, his boots touching effortlessly to the ashen ground below. His blade was already drawn, ready for whatever hellish creature was rushing in. The hair stood along the back of his neck. Something from the Underworld, that much he knew. Angels and the Underworld were mortal enemies, and with the traces of angel blood flowing in their veins, heightening their abilities, it was a normal reaction when in the presence of the creatures. It made his job easier time and time again.

The demon was shadow incarnate, with a humanesque body as black as the abyss. Swallowing up the world around it like a void. Crimson eyes tore through him. Searching. All he could see was death. Rage. This creature brought nothing but the end of days. Lived for it. Enjoyed it. Just the thought of it sickened him. Worse than humans, demons were nothing more than scum beneath his boots.

Its clawed hands sharpened to deadly points, a thick substance near oozing from the tips. Poison. If it hit true, he'd be imbued with a deadly toxin that would incapacitate him within minutes. Upon its head sat two horns, curving up toward the sky.

All color was gone from the human's face as she stared at the demon in front of them. She'd gotten as far as dismounting from her horse, but hadn't moved since. If he hadn't wanted answers so badly, he would have tossed her at the demon himself. Be done with it. He'd have to protect her. Again.

She'd just made his day a hell of a lot harder.

Thirteen

DEMITRIA

Guilt.

Fear.

Demitria couldn't lift a limb even if she tried. She'd lost all control. Like her body had ceased to exist. Nothing lived around her except the demon and her. A demon she would recognize anywhere. An array of emotions coursed through her for the millionth time in a sheer moment. Terror. Anger. Regret. Guilt. Always back to guilt.

"I know you."

Its voice rumbled through her. Her entire body shook violently at the sound of it. Taloned fingers pointed at her, so still she felt as if they pierced through her chest. The demon, no more than a few feet away, could reach her within steps.

"I remember the taste of their flesh."

The tears exploded before Demitria could stop them. Streaming from her eyes in a rush, like a dam bursting. She fought for control, but it was a pathetic attempt. A courage she just couldn't bring herself to muster as the lifeless eyes of her mother flashed before her. Her father. She pulled the dagger from its sheath at her thigh, but her feet stayed rooted to the spot.

"I said run, dammit!"

The movement didn't register until it was too late. The Horseman's blade collided with the demon inches from her body as he put himself between them. He grunted, as if having been hurt, but didn't falter, his weapon colliding with its sharpened talons. He swung at the demon, but its lean, lanky body slithered just out of reach each time as if it was nothing more than a game.

"Who sent you?" A familiar growl left the Horseman's lips as he eyed the demon. Kellan gripped his sword with one hand, his other held firmly to his chest to staunch the wound. She could see the blood pooling beneath, dripping to the ashen ground below as it seeped through his fingers in a trickle of dark red.

"You hide this girl, but he knows. He always knows."

The sound of the creature's voice ran a shiver down her spine. Demitria tried to move. To lunge at the monster that tore her life apart with her dagger held steady, but the Horseman stepped into her once more. Blocking her from advancing any further. The screams of her father echoed in her mind, like that last thread pulling apart before the seams came undone. She felt as if the ground was shaking beneath her as everything began to crumble around her. Every wall she'd built up to safeguard that ache deep within her chest.

"He will come for her."

"How do you know her?" War demanded. He swung his sword in its direction, but the creature evaded easily. The Horseman was fast, but the demon was faster.

"There are many things you do not know, Horseman. Things you have not been told." The demon toyed with him, a wide grin brimming with razor, shark-like teeth taunting him. "Join us if you wish to survive."

"Who sent you?" Kellan sounded angry now. Before he just looked determined. His own teeth bared in a snarl as even more blood pooled between his fingers. He swung again, and that rage deepened. Even wounded, he was dangerous. Murderous.

"I will return for her."

The words hit her in her core. She was choking.

Its familiar, crimson eyes met her own. Staring longingly before vanishing into nothing.

Numb. She was completely and utterly numb. The walls she'd painstakingly spent years building up, trying to forget its face came crashing down around her in a matter of seconds. It knew who she was. Ten fucking years later and it still remembered.

She still remembered.

The dagger that was held firm in her grip clattered to the dirt at her feet. Demitria felt sick to her stomach and nearly vomited what little food she'd had left in her system. Her parents... she couldn't help the sob that raked through her chest. She didn't care that she was breaking down in front of the Horseman. The pain was too much. Too raw. Of all the creatures that had walked this earth, why had this particular one come back? Why this demon?

A new wave of tears took over. She couldn't see anymore. Didn't want to. Everything she'd worked toward, everything she had fought for, and she'd come undone with one glance.

"What the hell is going on?"

Demitria couldn't answer him. She wouldn't. She had relived that night so many times since the attack, but seeing the demon that cleaved her heart in two triggered the memory as if it was happening again before her eyes. Her father's screams as it tore him apart. The look on her mother's face as she was eaten alive. The smirk on that monster's fucking face as it sought her out. Her parents' blood bright red, dripping from its mouth as it came to finish her off.

A wound, still so raw, had torn wide open.

"What did it mean?"

No.

"The words that it spoke. Tell me the information, human!"

War was screaming, but she couldn't do it. All she could muster was a shake of her head, that moment replaying again and again.

Blood. There was so much damn blood. Could feel it on her hands. She remembered slipping in it when Jace dragged her out of the cupboard. Coating herself in it as her legs gave out beneath her. No. Not again.

Please not again.

The Horseman collapsed. His body slowly crumbled to the ground, and her senses returned in a rush, like a tether had snapped, freeing her from its clutches.

"Horseman." Demitria crouched over his body, but he didn't respond. "War." She looked him up and down, eyes catching on the rounded hole in the thick leather armor on his chest. The red blood she'd watch seep through his fingers had darkened to an unnatural color that dripped down his front. "Kellan!" Finally, he gazed up at her, azure eyes glazed over. The veins on his body grew dark as they snaked across his skin.

Shit

"Kellan what the hell is going on?" She shook him violently, desperate for him to answer. The veins in his face had darkened to the point of being black, matching the blood oozing from the hole in his chest. Nothing about him looked *normal*.

"...fine." He mumbled through clenched teeth "m' fine"

"Sure doesn't look like it." She scoffed, "Definitely not fine."

"Need...time..." He groaned again, but didn't move from the ground. His limbs heavy at his side as he lay there, near motionless as the blood forming around his wound looked like a pit of inky black.

The panic began to set in as she scanned around them. The charred trees surrounding them for what seemed like miles. The sun, still so high up above, seemed to hide behind a thin haze. The demon could be anywhere. Waiting to attack the moment the Horseman fell. She didn't want to admit it, but without him she was vulnerable. An easy target. Its return had scared her senseless, shaking that unyielding fear free from whatever confines she'd managed to cage away in the last ten years. Facing it alone wasn't something she could do.

The Horseman mumbled again, but it was inaudible. He mumbled once more, repeated himself. "Don't... go anywhere." It took him a moment to get his words out. Longer than she'd liked. Demitria felt her nerves stretch taut. "Don't.... go... home." The thought hadn't even crossed her mind until he'd mentioned it. "Favor...stay away." He uttered again.

Something nagged at the back of her mind. That feeling of a debt owed. Sure, he'd treated her like shit, but he'd also saved her life twice now, even if it hadn't been for her benefit. She couldn't leave him there to die. It should have been her on the ground. The demon had been after her, and he'd taken the hit.

Why did she have to care?

Kellan was out cold. His chest rose and fell as jagged breaths left his lips. The blood that pooled from his wound still ran dark, matching the color of his veins. Grabbing hold beneath his armpits, Demitria pulled. He didn't move. His body was as heavy as he was big. A huff left her mouth before she could stop it. She scanned the surroundings again. They needed to go. The shadows danced around them eerily, playing tricks on her mind. The shaking of her fingers began again, she had to get out. Had to get away before she shut down again.

Demitria whistled for Atlas, knowing his mount would be useless to her. Atlas trotted over quickly, lowering his body beside the Horseman's as if he could read her mind. She didn't deserve him. Grabbing hold of the Horseman once more she pulled. The muscles in her back fought against it. Screaming at her to put him down, but she pushed them harder. Begging them to hold out a little longer.

She shouldn't care.

She hated that she cared about a stupid debt. Fuck the Horseman. Fuck the angels. Fuck the whole gods' damned war.

A scream of frustration exploded as she finally balanced him atop Atlas, who jumped up with the poise and grace she wished she'd just displayed. The Horseman's mount walked over then, snorting in her direction as he pawed the ground before her.

"I'm not going to hurt him." She whispered, extending her hand toward him. The horse shook its head, turning away from her outstretched limb. He didn't trust her.

The feeling is mutual.

Strapped to the saddle was her sword. Demitria had never been so happy to see an object in her life. Before the horse could flee, she lunged for it. Managing to snag the tip of its sheath and pulling it free before the horse took off, kicking up dust as it went. She strapped it around her body once more. Grateful to have it back, that feeling of safety washing over. She wasn't safe, but she at least had a chance to protect herself now.

With his body as secure as she could manage behind her, they rode out. The positioning was awkward at best. Demitria had done her best to prop him, but his body hung eerily close for comfort, arms haphazardly draped around her waist in an effort to keep him from sliding off sideways. He'd stayed upright well enough, which could only mean he had to be semi aware and not fully unconscious like she'd originally thought. The warmth of him radiated through her in a deadly embrace that had her on edge. He was too close.

They rode back toward the canyon that had shielded them the night before. Praying to whatever gods were out there that the cave was still empty. Demitria glanced behind her, watching for a brief moment as his mount followed behind in the distance. She doubted it would enter the cave with her, and hoped the beast would survive on its own.

When the canyon stood tall above them, the sigh of relief rushed through her parted lips. She hadn't seen anything out of the ordinary and took it as a good sign. As they neared the mouth of the cave, she dismounted. Gently settling the Horseman along Atlas's back before leading him the remainder of the way on foot. Hesitating for only a moment before crossing the threshold.

"You should come in." Demitria called out to the horse several feet away. Rearing up on its back legs, the stallion snorted, shaking his head in displeasure. "It'll be safer inside. I promise to give you your space." She beckoned it over, hand outstretched, but it didn't move toward her. "If you change your mind, we'll be waiting." With a sigh she went deeper.

Near the remains of the fire, Atlas curled his legs beneath him as he settled his body on the ground. Demitria slowly pulled the Horseman off and settled him against the smooth side of a stalagmite.

"Kellan, you need to wake up." Gripping him by the shoulders, she shook him. Sweat beaded along his brow. "Wake up." Her eyes travelled the cave as shadows seemed to dance along the wall. Reminding herself they were nothing more than that, she shook him again. At his groan, she stepped back. Inky veins snaked paths down his cheeks. From his eyes. The color of his face pallid. Nothing of the sun-kissed skin remained.

"Kellan." She repeated, but the only thing that moved was the rise and fall of his chest in an irregular pattern.

Every bone in her body told her to leave him. To let him die in this cave where no one would be the wiser. She took a tentative step backward, toward the mouth of the cave before her feet stopped. If she left him, would that make her no better than they were?

"Fuck." She cursed, running a shaking hand down her face in frustration. She was better than this. Despite her hatred for beings like him, *she was better*.

A life for a life.

Letting another heavy sigh pass through her lips, Demitria stepped up to the Horseman. Deft fingers worked the buckles of his armor as she peeled it from his chest and discarded it beside him before painstakingly stripping the shirt from his body, her muscles straining against his dead weight. The fabric clung to the wound, ripping it as another wave of the inky blood oozed from the gaping hole in his chest. Her breath caught. So much worse than she thought it was. Rimmed in black, the same dark veins snaked across his torso, thick as she *watched* the poison coursing through his body. As each vein darkened to that same color as it passed through his bloodstream. A thin sheen of sweat covered his upper body, his skin hot to the touch.

Demitria gently touched a finger to the wound, pulling it away and testing the blood between her fingers. Thick. Wrong.

"Shit."

She didn't know if she could help him. Didn't know if there was anything she could truly do to change his fate. But he'd saved her, nonetheless, and she had to try to save him.

Pulling the hood on her head, she exited the cavern on foot, leaving Atlas with the unconscious Horseman. The only plant she would find would be yarrow. Kellan had found it somewhere seemingly not too far off, and she was confident she'd be able to do the same. Her feet carried her down the winding trail in the canyon. Around a tight bend they hadn't gone through the last time, but she pushed on for another few minutes before the grayish-white flowers came into view. Picking enough sprigs to last the night, she returned to the cave. In her absence,

Kellan's mount had entered and was resting quietly with Atlas along the back wall.

Demitria rinsed the plant in the steady drip of water off the stalactite before finding herself in front of the Horseman, watching the rapid rise and fall of his chest. He'd told her how his own people had used the plant, and she did the same. Taking pieces into her mouth as she chewed the leaves, the sweet yet bitter flavor filled her mouth. She worked it for a few moments before spitting it into her palm and crouching before him, packing it into the wound as best she could. Kellan didn't flinch as she worked.

When she was finished, she took a step back and took him in. The muscled planes of his chest. The body that looked so much like her own people's, and the thin, silver scarring that seemed to mar so much of his skin.

"Shit." Demitria cursed herself, running a hand down her face once more as she pulled herself from the Horseman.

She stared longer than she should have.

By the time the sun rose the next morning, Demitria had changed out the makeshift poultice four times. Each time the green leaves turned the same thick, inky color of his blood.

"Kellan." She spoke, her hand gripped firmly to his broad shoulder as she shook him. The Horseman shuddered, but made no other movement. The darkening veins nearly covered his entire body now, the wound to his chest even more gruesome than before as the sides of his flesh had turned black around it, oozing that thick substance that she could only assume was toxins from the demon. Every part of her wanted to tremble at the thought of it, her hands shaking.

She needed to leave before it came back. Or before Kellan died.

Demitria paced back and forth within the cave as she decided on her course of action, warring with the thought of still leaving him to die. Doing that would make her no better than the rest of the creatures. Cruel. *She wasn't that.* No matter how much she hated them, she couldn't leave him like this to suffer. She contemplated ending his life. Putting him out of his misery wouldn't get her anywhere, either. She wouldn't be able to return to Solis as if nothing happened. The angel...

the demon, had said something was after her. Multiple beings, in fact, and she still didn't know what that meant. If she returned now, without any answers as to what was going on, Demitria was sure Solis would fall.

But if he got whatever answers he was after, maybe she could survive and one day return to her home. To Jace. So, Kellan needed to live.

Demitria only knew one way to do that.

Her boots heavy along the smooth rock floor of the cavern, she marched toward their mounts at the back. Coaxing his horse from the wall with an outstretched hand, it snorted, shaking its head at her approach.

"I need your help." She stated. "Don't make this difficult for me." The red stallion balked out of her reach, hooves thundering along the ground as it darted for the mouth of the cave and disappearing somewhere beyond. "Useless beast." She cursed, kicking a stone in the direction it had run off in.

Atlas nickered at her, and despite the frustration roiling through her, she smiled. Bringing a hand to the center of his forehead and scratching in his favorite spot. He didn't take long to ready, and soon the beast was lowering himself to the ground behind the Horseman. Demitria dressed him quickly, her muscles still screaming in protest at the unforgiving weight as she pulled the dark shirt over his head before buckling the armor and cloak around him once more. Kellan was nearly dead weight in her hands.

"I don't know if you can hear me, and I know I'm going to regret this, but you need help." A sigh passed through her lips. "It's my turn to want answers, now." Linking her arms around his torso, she heaved with everything in her. Muscles straining at the movement as she righted him upon Atlas once more. Much like she had done on the way to the cave, she seated herself in front of him. Holding his arms tight around her waist as Atlas slowly jumped to his feet, and left through the opening into the awaiting sunlight beyond the cavern walls where Kellan's mount stood waiting for them off in the distance, as if it knew she was taking his master. Nodding at the red beast once, it followed behind several strides away.

Demitria knew the Guardians were going to kill her the moment she stepped foot in front of the gates. Or would it be the other way around?

Would the Horseman turn on them the moment he was better and slaughter her people anyway? He'd warned her to stay away from her home, even with the poison coursing through him, and yet... she was doing just that. Had told herself it was because he needed the medical attention. That he'd die without it, but was one life really worth that of potentially the entire community? More than Jace's?

The decision should have been easy. She should have been able to walk away the moment he'd gone down, but she'd faltered. That nagging in the back of her mind her driving force to do better. To be better. And what? She was now bringing an enemy right to their front door.

Killing that angel hadn't meant a thing to her. But the demon? As she stood there terrified, fumbling the weapons that were supposed to save her, he'd taken whatever blow had been meant for her. That poison that was meant for her.

A life for a life.

Atlas slowed, coming to a halt as if understanding the battle warring within. Peering up at the sun's position in the sky, she realized she'd been riding far longer than she'd thought, time having slipped away into nothingness. Like it didn't exist. They'd made good time. Exceptional time, actually. Atlas pushed himself harder than she'd ever felt, the speed faster than she could have ever imagined, and it almost felt as though they were flying across the barren land around them. She didn't know if it was a power of his that she'd yet to discover. The ability to run at a speed unheard of for creatures like him. The stamina to endure the pace. It was one of the many things that made him so different from the usual animals that belonged on their planet.

Demitria made the choice to return home with him, life debt weighing heavy over her head. His kind didn't deserve it, not after everything that they'd done to her own people.

But she couldn't let him die.

If she wanted any chance at a life, the Horseman had to live.

Nudging Atlas forward once more, he broke into a slow canter. Instinctively clamping her arms over his to keep him remaining steady and upright. His head slumped over her shoulder, strands of dark hair falling free from the knot they'd been tied in tickled against her cheek.

The shiver racked her body, like an insect crawling across her skin. Each jagged breath hot against her neck as the hint of that sweet, woodsy smell filled her senses. Another shiver, and she cursed, pushing Atlas harder. Fucking Horseman.

Fucking life debt.

DEMITRIA

The ever-familiar large iron gates came into view and Demitria nearly cried at the sight of them. It was something she never thought she'd see again. Atlas had perked up the closer they approached, his gait lengthening to a smooth canter as her own mood shifted with each step closer. Despite her lifting thoughts, her chest felt heavy at their return.

The Horseman's eyes were open, but unseeing. Glazed over as if trapped in some fevered dream. Making sure he wouldn't fall, she dismounted. To her surprise, he stayed upright. She hadn't heard him say so much as a word or lift a finger in a day, and it was a miracle in itself that he'd stayed seated behind her the entire ride, let alone after she'd dismounted. For how long would be the question. Leaving Atlas standing fifteen feet away, her fist pounded four times, hard, on the gate. Everything remained quiet. More than it should be. She had expected Guardians to meet them the moment they'd appeared on the horizon, but instead, there was nothing but silence. They must have been on high alert. Minutes passed before it finally opened.

Slowly at first, only enough for one single figure to emerge.

His arms wound their way around her body before she could take in the height of him, engulfing her in a tight embrace.

"I thought I'd lost you." Jace's voice wavered, arms wrapped tighter, nearly cutting off her air. She didn't care.

"Harder than that to get rid of me." Her voice was no more than a whisper, but knew he'd heard. The familiar smell of mint taking over her senses, mesmerizing her entire body as neither of them could back away. The leather of his jacket was soft against her cheek. A feeling she hadn't realized she'd missed so badly in the days she'd been gone. She returned his embrace.

He finally released her and took her in, his gaze moving up and down her body. Dark circles rimmed his green eyes, eyelids drooping, heavy with weariness as fatigue strained his features.

"What happened to your head?" Jace's hand grazed against her cheek where his fingers touched softly to the wound on her temple. The incident having completely slipped her mind given the days that followed.

"Run in with a boar. I won." She didn't dare tell him that she wasn't the one who ended it.

Shit.

She'd nearly forgotten about the Horseman atop Atlas. Had been so caught up in seeing Jace again that she'd lost all rational thoughts on why she had returned in the first place.

The scraping of the gate echoed around them as it was pushed wider. Identical faces emerged, and her heart sank. They were not who she wanted to see.

"What the hell do you think you're doing?" Sam was angry, his eyes anchored behind her, and as much as she hated to admit it, rightfully so. She'd brought the enemy home. One look at the Horseman and you just knew he wasn't human. He'd had a supernatural air about him, unconscious or not. If his sheer size alone wasn't a dead giveaway, the running horse embossed into the leather of his armor had been another. Like a beacon, announcing his heritage for the world to see. She supposed that's technically what the Horseman wanted. They were a force of nature, not to be messed with. He at least looked the part.

"He's not a threat." She said, motioning toward the wounded male practically splayed out on Atlas. Demitria took a step back from Jace's warmth. "He's a Horseman, and I know it looks bad, but he saved my life on multiple accounts. We were ambushed, and I'm repaying the debt that I owe him. That wound was supposed to be for me."

"Like hell he's not." Weapon drawn, Will notched an arrow, aimed straight for the Horseman's head. His twin followed suit, but pointed it toward her.

"You'd be making a huge mistake by letting those fly." On the defensive, the growl left her lips as she glared back and forth between the two. "Stand down now. We're coming in whether you like it or not." Demitria made to push past them both when Kellan hit the ground with a loud thud, laying in the dirt at the horse's feet. "Does this really look threatening to you?" Mumbling, she strung along an obscene number of curses toward the twins as she returned to the fallen Horseman. The inky veins along his face seemed to have darkened even more, his chest pounding in an irregular rhythm,

Hesitating, Jace's eyes roamed from her, to the community, and back again as if unsure what to do. She knew bringing him here had been a lot to ask of him. Of them all, but she couldn't think of anywhere else to go. Anyone else to ask. He needed help, and he needed it now. Despite Kellan saying otherwise, he clearly was not ok. Finally, Jace slowly made his way over to them. His eyes met hers. She saw fear. Fear of what this could bring upon them. Confusion. It was the disappointment that hit her hardest. Jace had been there when everything happened. They shared the trauma. Now she'd brought the enemy home.

Kellan's horse didn't follow when they entered, despite her attempts at whistling and coaxing him over. She felt bad leaving him beyond the wall, but nothing could be done to get the mount inside. The gate closed as the fiery red stallion stormed back and forth around the community, pacing as his rider disappeared out of sight.

Demitria had never been so grateful to have the infirmary so close to the gates as she and Jace managed, barely, to get the Horseman to the building where they placed him on a too small bed. His large frame engulfed it, as if it was made for a child. Inside, the walls were sickeningly white, illuminated by the sun's rays and an array of lamps placed around the room. They didn't have electricity anymore, so any procedure had to be done by lamplight.

Shelving sat half empty of supplies. She hated taking it away from her people, especially when they were using it on a Horseman, but she still couldn't shake the fact that she owed him after the demon.

"I refuse to work on him! Get him out." Braun roared, exploding into the room. His eyebrows pulled together, lips curling inward as he snarled. The door hit the wall so hard she thought it might break.

"Then I'll do it myself!" Demitria countered, shoving the sleeves of her shirt up to her elbows. The dark blood oozed onto the floor. Making quick work, she began tearing at the buckles of his armor, tossing it aside to better reach the wound. The veins were even worse there, darker than the night sky as they snaked across his sun-kissed skin. Like the poultice she'd painstakingly put on all night had done nothing. She knew she made the right call in bringing him. "He needs a shot. Something to counteract the poison. Where is it?" She'd searched three shelving units, shoving things out of the way, but evidently, she didn't actually know what she was looking for. Pharmaceuticals was not her area of expertise.

"Leave it to Braun. He knows what he's doing." Jace placed a soft hand on her shoulder, stopping her from searching another shelf for the second time. Reluctantly, she took a step back, letting Braun work. His eyes burned holes into her and Jace as he walked by, begrudgingly working on Kellan. Her eyes never left his hands, watching his every movement. Tracking what he did. She knew she should, but she didn't trust him. Not right now, at least.

Jace slid a chair up beside her. It scraped, loud along the tiled flooring, but she was grateful for the seat and happily let her body fall into it. She loved riding Atlas, but a cushioned chair under her battered body was a sensation she didn't want to leave. Wasn't sure if she actually could, for that matter.

Demitria watched for two hours while Braun worked. The welcoming they had received was proof that she couldn't leave Kellan in the Guardians' hands, especially if his life depended on it. For all she knew they'd purposely kill him, seeing it as a major win for their side. Nobody would treat him unless she was there. She may have known her fair share of first aid, but anything complicated was out of her element. Ask her to stitch a small scrape? Great. Give an injection? Sure. Counteract a poison, debride, and deal with whatever the hell they were dealing with was way over her head. She could admit that without hesitation.

"This was out of line, Jace." Braun sneered, that same look harsh across his features. He walked toward the clean bucket of water on the counter, scrubbing the inky blood from his hands. "Saving one of them? Are you out of your fucking mind?" Grabbing a clean infirmary top from a nearby drawer, he moved toward the Horseman once more, pulling it over his head. The pale blue shirt clung to Kellan's body, the fabric stretched taut over his broad shoulders and chest. Jace's steady hand on her shoulder was the only thing that kept her in the chair. That and the fatigue that had taken hold of her body.

"You know I value your opinion," Jace started, "You are one of our most trusted, Braun." The Guardian opened his mouth to speak, but Jace continued. "I trust in Demitria's judgment that the Horseman means us no harm." The fact that Jace had remained so calm through everything amazed her. She had so many different emotions swirling within she had been ready to explode. "He saved her life, and for that I am eternally grateful."

Braun's face darkened. "Everything is always in some benefit to her. We all know it. You claim we are all equal, but she has always been held on a different stature, as if you worship the fucking ground she walks on. Bringing him here was one strike, Jace. Saving him? That was the biggest mistake you ever made." Braun forcefully shouldered past Jace as he left, slamming the door behind him.

Jace teetered, but kept his balance. He said nothing. Did nothing as the Guardian walked away.

"How dare he." Demitria's eyes stared at the door that slammed shut, hard enough as if Braun had tried to break it. "He can't talk to you like that. I could kill that asshole."

"He has a point." Jace ran a hand through his hair, his frustration evident in the small gesture. "You brought a Horseman here."

"He couldn't even walk!" She turned the anger on her best friend, hating herself for it. "He needed our help."

"Demi..."

"Don't do that, Jace. I owed him."

"He's not Callum. You owe these beings nothing." But she did... despite the order to kill her, the Horseman hadn't. She owed him her life.

Demitria had reached her limit. Couldn't talk to him about it anymore, afraid that if she did, she'd say something that she would regret later. Getting into a fight with him was something she just couldn't do. Their friendship meant too much to her. Pulling the chair closer to the bed, she settled down once more. Staring at the sleeping Horseman. Jace stood there, unmoving. He didn't say a word. Minutes went by before he finally let out a sigh. The soft click of the door was the only indication that he'd left.

The anger at the situation was roiling around inside, like her body was in an endless spin. She was angry with herself for bringing him there. Angry with the others for the hostility toward *her*, when all she'd ever wanted was the best for them. Felt as if she couldn't discern right from wrong. Because she understood their worries. Some part of her knew that bringing him back to Solis was bad, but they hadn't been there when the demon showed up. They hadn't been forced to face the living nightmare that had haunted her for ten fucking years. To have a being that she loathed with every fiber of her being save her from it. If she didn't have any sort of moral code—humanity, would they be so different from the demons that slaughtered them? Demitria refused to regret her decision.

With a sigh, she let her head rest in her hands. What the hell did she get herself into.

Kellan hadn't awoken in three days. Due to a growing concern of his assassination while he slept, Demitria hadn't left the infirmary once. The chair Jace had brought in upon their arrival had become her perch. Watching. Listening. Waiting for someone to come in and make a move. They wouldn't while she was there. It'd be a stupid plan if they did. More than likely a death sentence. By her hands.

She had moved to the side of the bed. Kellan's body lay still, unmoving, except for the steady rise and fall of his chest. The tone of his skin evening as the inky veins had all but disappeared. A drastic change from when he'd collapsed outside the gates.

"How is he?" The door clicked shut and she didn't need to turn around to know it was Jace. No one else had dared to set foot in the room, and she knew he was only doing it for her.

"Still no change." Her voice soft, quiet, but she met him with a smile. Jace handed her a steaming mug of tea, a special blend that Stella routinely made. Growing and drying the herbs herself. The sweet aroma of blackberry and hibiscus filled her nose. Eyes closed, she inhaled the smell, breathing it in deeper as she let it fill her senses. Stella may grow everything herself, but it was still a luxury.

"Why are you so adamant on saving his life?" With his body leaning against the far wall, a good distance away from the Horseman, Jace's eyes didn't leave hers. Searching.

"It's... complicated." She sighed. "He saved my life; I'm repaying the favor." Demitria stared into the mug, watching the billowing steam slowly rise and disappear. "When one gives you life, you repay the favor. It's a debt I owe." Forcing her eyes back up, she met Jace's once more. "You understand that, right?"

"I'm grateful he saved your life. For that, I'm indebted to him." He was upon her in two large steps, pulling her up from the chair. The mug nearly clattered to the floor. She managed to stash it on the side table before it did so. "I just keep wondering why... What happened out there?" His brow wrinkled with worry, his gaze anchored to her own.

"The things I saw out there..." Choking on her words, it took everything in her not to cry. She still felt completely and utterly raw from the encounter. Like a wound that just wouldn't close. "You have no idea, Jace." When his arms wrapped around her small frame, she didn't protest. She never did. His touch had always been calming. Safe. She felt so safe in his arms.

She couldn't bear to tell him about the demon. The one who had single handedly torn their families apart. They both had been through so much, and she wouldn't put him through that again. Not when it remembered her. Because if it remembered her, it would remember him. That was more than enough reason to keep that knowledge away from him. She didn't know what he would truly do if he knew it still roamed these parts. If he knew it was coming after her.

"I don't like having a Horseman here." He sighed, arms tightening. She understood his worry, truly. Hell, she'd felt the same way at first.

Questioning if she had made the right decision in bringing him here, but one look at him on the infirmary bed had steeled her thoughts. She didn't think he would have made it if they hadn't.

"I know." Her words came out in barely a whisper. She'd had nothing more to say at this point. Didn't know what to say for that matter. "Once he walks out of here unharmed, my debt will be paid." She wouldn't tell Jace that she'd be walking out with him. The safety of Solis was imperative on that. And if there was some small chance that she *could* survive this, she'd find her way back to them. She just needed her own answers first. To find out why they wanted her dead, because maybe, she could fix it. Change whatever fate that had been laid out for her.

And just maybe, at the end of it all, she could return *home*. To Jace.

DEMITRIA

The light in the infirmary was dim, and it took everything in her to try and rouse herself awake. Demitria's eyes wouldn't open, the feel of a bed beneath her head, and the blanket Jace had gently wrapped over her shoulders was too enticing. If it wasn't for the strong shove that nearly sent her to the floor, she probably would have given in and let the sleep take hold of her exhausted body.

"Tell me exactly where we are, or so help me God." A deep voice, husky from the lack of use rumbled through her.

He's awake.

Rubbing the sleep from her eyes, she couldn't help the yawn that escaped her. "We're at my community." Blinking rapidly, willing herself to focus and just wake up. Gods she was so comfy...

"You're an absolute idiot." Kellan growled, his full lips curled back in an almost animalistic look as he stared her down, azure eyes narrowed. He tossed the blanket from his body like it had burned him, bare feet touching the cool, cracked tiled floor as he jumped out of the bed. His gaze roamed over the room. Back and forth as if taking it all in. Memorizing it should something happen. His hulking figure taking up entirely too much space in the small room.

"Excuse me?" Demitria exclaimed with just as much animosity.

Well, she sure as hell was awake now. "You were the one who fainted, then fell off my damn horse. And you're calling me an idiot? Where else was I supposed to go?"

"I told you specifically not to come here." Kellan closed his eyes, pulling in a deep breath as he grabbed the bridge of his nose in an attempt to calm himself. When he continued, he spoke in almost a mocking tone. "In case you've forgotten, I am the Horseman War. It will take a hell of a lot more than that to kill me." He shrugged out of the infirmary top that Braun had put him in to reveal a smooth, chiseled chest. Any sign of the wound had vanished without a trace. "Where is my armor?"

"How is that possible?" Her eyes bulged as she abruptly stood before him, placing a hand where the wound had been days before. The gaping wound that had been oozing inky blood just days before had healed into a thin, faint scar. His skin was hot to the touch beneath her fingers, like a burning inferno and it took every ounce of her self-control not to gawk as her cheeks burned. She hated every piece of herself that noticed him like that.

Shit.

"Do you not understand the meaning of immortal?" He exclaimed, a hint of amusement flitting through his voice. She chanced a glance toward him and immediately regretted it, azure eyes fixed solely on her as something danced within his gaze.

Oh god, had he noticed?

"I do not recall humans being *this* stupid…" And just like that, every forbidden thought that had been running through her mind vanished into nothingness, like it had never existed in the first place.

She crossed her arms over her chest. "Despite your insults, you're welcome." With a roll of her eyes, she sauntered over to the cupboard at the back of the room. Gathering the armor in her arms, she quite literally threw it at him, taking great pleasure as it smacked him in the face, reveling in the way it thudded against his body. "I was repaying my life debt, and now it is nearly finished."

He watched her, brow raised. It lasted only moments before that all knowing smirk returned. "Life debt? You do realize I was sent to kill you? Not to mention, I tried to kidnap you…"

She may have felt like a complete idiot for bringing him to her home, but she didn't regret what she'd done. "I do, but you did not have to save my life out there. For that, a debt was owed." Visions of the demon swirled before her. The sickeningly sharp teeth, the glaring crimson eyes. The shudder threatened to break free, and she barely managed to hold it back.

Absently toying with the hem of her shirt, Demitria couldn't meet his eyes. The scrutiny in them as he looked her over in what she could only assume would be disgust. He hated humans as much as she hated his kind. There was no way around that. The feeling was mutual between them.

She found solace in the shadows from the lamps twirling along the white walls. Shadows that soon turned into nightmares. *Shit*. Why did everything have to end in those fucking nightmares. The trauma of it all always poured through, no matter what she did. No matter where she was. She didn't think that was something that would ever go away.

"Demitria Collins... I did not take you for the honorable type." The change in his tone was surprising. Against her better judgment, her eyes found his. The Horseman bowed his head at her, sincere, and her jaw nearly hit the floor. "And despite my ability to heal, I thank you for the effort."

Sixteen

KELLAN

The look of confusion was something he was growing used to with the girl. His thanks had sent her into a stupor. The widening of her eyes, the paling of her face, he recognized it all. His own had probably mirrored hers at the mention of the life debt. Something he had not expected in the least, especially from a human.

She'd proved to be so unlike the others he had encountered throughout his time. He'd found her interesting.

Infuriating, but interesting.

The room around them grew silent as neither dared to say a word. He focused on their surroundings. Listening. Taking count of the bodies that wandered around the building.

Three. With weapons.

The humans hadn't realized that their weapons couldn't hurt him. No regular weapon could. Kellan could count on one hand the number of times he had been severely injured. Twice. While not severe, three times if he counted the run in with Noel. Angel blades were the only thing that could truly hurt him. Anything forged on Eden proved to be deadly for not only his enemies, but his own people as well.

"Are you... Did you really just thank me?" The soft tone of her voice carried throughout the room, breaking Kellan from the trance-like state he'd been in.

"You say that as if it's the most shocking thing in the world." With a slight chuckle, he began to dress in the clothing she'd so carelessly tossed his way, pulling the familiar dark shirt over his head. Tugging at the hole in the fabric on his chest, he sighed.

The human watched with curious eyes, and he could practically see the questions she harbored, but couldn't bring herself to ask. He supposed she didn't really have experience with his kind, none usually did. If she decided to ask them, he might give her the answers. It was still up for debate.

His body ached. Not from the wound itself, but from being immobile in that thing they called a bed. While the poison would have run its course naturally, whatever they had done had sped up the process. He guessed it was better than being left in the middle of nowhere for days on end while his body healed.

"It is shocking. I did not take you for a thankful per—being." She corrected herself quickly.

He watched as she busied herself around the room. Dumping a small pail of water down the sink before making her way once more to the other side of the room. He watched the way her body moved. Confident. Sure of herself. *Unafraid* of him. Swinging open a plain cabinet door, he watched as she turned a dial on the surface of whatever was inside before the girl pulled a familiar object from the interior and tossed it on the bed beside him.

"I wasn't supposed to give you this, but I trust you'll keep your word, then?" Her green-gold eyes flickered to the sword she'd tossed toward him.

Kellan nodded. He would not bring harm to her people. "Again, I'm not this blood thirsty barbarian your kind makes me out to be." There were so many emotions playing on her face. So many things she wanted to say, but held them back. It only made the same questions arise. She seemed to have little knowledge of his kind beyond the Ascension, and yet the council had deemed her such a threat. He didn't understand it. Any of it.

The click of a door pulled him from his thoughts. Somebody had entered the building. His body tensed, hand discretely reaching for the sword on the bed as he tapped into his senses. *Unarmed, non-hostile.* Kellan's hand returned to his side. One set of footsteps, walking toward the room. He had his eyes on the man before he entered through the door.

"You're awake?" He sounded surprised, but smiled anyway. Such curious beings...

"I am." He nodded, his gaze not leaving the man.

The girl beside him didn't say a word, but the air around her changed as the man had entered. Lightened, somehow.

A friend, perhaps?

"I wanted to thank you for saving Demi. She told me what happened."

Kellan raised a brow in surprise. Had she really? He didn't think the man would be thanking him if he'd known what his plans had been. That he had meant to end her life before kidnapping her. Or that they were now on their way to reunite with his siblings. His eyes meet hers. The subtle shake of her head gave him his answer. *Interesting.*

"I don't know what I would have done if she didn't return."

"You're welcome?" It hadn't been by choice. She had been saved purely for his own motives. Answers. He needed answers, and obtaining some of them would prove a hell of a lot harder if she was dead. The demon wanted her alive. A conversation with the girl afterward seemed imminent. He always needed more answers.

"You are welcome to stay a few days to regain your strength, but nothing more." The *boy* was abrupt and to the point. "For the safety of my community, that is all I will permit you. That seems like more than enough time for someone like you to be back on his feet." He was much taller than the girl. Muscled, yet lean. Kellan could tell by the way he moved that he was a fighter for his people. The way he sized him up without even an ounce of fear.

"She will be leaving with me." He stated, stepping in to meet the human before him. The top of his head coming to his own nose.

"The hell she is." Jace squared his shoulders, as if in challenge. Like a predator ready to attack and defend what was his. "That is not an option." The fight would be over before the man could even blink.

"Jace you idiot, stand down." She gripped his arm, pulling him back a step. "I'll explain later, but I am leaving with him."

The way he looked at the girl spoke words he didn't have to, his entire demeanor shifting. *More than friends, perhaps?* With a heavy sigh he nodded at her as he made to leave. Only turning around once to point and utter

"Three days." Before slamming the door behind him as he left.

"You will come with me, either of your own free will or force. That choice will be yours." Kellan pinned her with his stare, driving a clear message. "I promised I would not harm your people. When I instructed you not to come here it was an act of mercy. You staying here is a risk that I'm sure you don't want to take."

"I don't want any harm to come to them." She whispered. The girl had shunned his gaze and kept her focus on her hands as she spoke. "To Jace... I'll do whatever it takes."

"Very well."

He fastened the remaining buckles, securing his armor against his chest. With a slight nod in his direction, Demitria quietly left through the door after the man, leaving Kellan alone with his thoughts.

Seventeen

DEMITRIA

The air around them was something fierce. On any normal day, the community would have been teeming with life as residents milled about their daily tasks. Today it was like a ghost town, and Demitria knew the reason was the Horseman at her side. He walked with an unearthly grace that she wished she possessed. His face was hard, devoid of all emotion as he took everything in. The cracked streets, the buildings boarded down. If she was being honest, Solis wasn't much to look at. But she was proud of her home and what they had built.

Demitria didn't know what Eden was like for him, or how he lived his life there. Seeing the way they lived was probably just another thing he found disgusting about them, but they hadn't always been like this. Earth had been beautiful once. Maybe not like he was used to, but beautiful nonetheless. The Horseman was silent as they walked the street, and she couldn't help but wonder what could be going through his mind. What he was really thinking? This must have been so odd for him, being there, walking like they were... so... *mundane.*

There she was being held hostage by this being for days, and now she'd taken him to her home. Practically giving him the grand tour of it all.

She hated having to do it. Being forced to make that decision.

Yet, he'd been different than she'd expected. Different from their initial encounter. Did he take pity on her? The poor human girl who'd done nothing but protect her family from beings that threatened them, and now had a price put on her head. An entire High Council wanted her dead. She hadn't done anything important enough to warrant it, at least not in her eyes. Had killed no more than the next Guardian in other communities, she was sure. But somewhere, along the way, she must have fucked up badly. She didn't see it like that, though. Because if it came down to it, she would do it all over again and again if it meant the people she loved were safe.

"Traitor."

Ripped from her thoughts, the two people she hated most came around the corner before them. She had really tried to like them once upon a time, but they saw things too differently.

"Demon-loving bitch." Will sneered, both he and his twin glancing from her to the Horseman beside her. Their eyes narrowed, shoulders squared as if in challenge.

The muscle in her temple twitched. Well, that did it.

"Before you go spewing your idiotic mouths I'd get your damn facts straight." Her temper flared, and made no inclination on dying down any time soon as she stepped into their path. "You should be groveling at my feet for the sacrifices I've made. You're safe because of me." Finger pressed firmly into his chest, Demitria shoved Will so hard he toppled to the ground. The color drained from his face and the quick flash of the whites of his eyes was a wondrous feeling that she could have basked in for hours, but Sam was quick to help his brother up. The two uttered a string of insults as they glanced sheepishly at Kellan one last time before slinking back into whatever hole they'd crawled out of.

There were residents on the street now, watching her. Whispering to one another. To them, it probably looked worse than she'd intended.

Gods, maybe they all think the same.

"You've created quite the commotion." His voice drawled in a low whisper, close to her ear. Her entire body shuddered at the closeness as the warm breath ghosted over her ear. It took everything in her to suppress the shiver that threatened to crawl down her spine. "Some of the things they're saying..."

She was doing this for Jace. She was doing this for Jace. She was doing this for Jace.

Demitria repeated the words in her head over and over. She just had to play the game for two more days until they left. Pretend that she wasn't actually being kidnapped and forced to go with him to his siblings. That he wasn't actually trying to kill her. Because if Jace had any idea of what was really going on, it would be an absolute blood bath. One she knew Jace wouldn't walk away from. Neither of them would walk away from it, because she'd fight tooth and nail until she was battered and bloody to protect him. She'd fight until her last breath.

It was no surprise that he and Kellan didn't get along. For more reasons than one. It was the only reason she was showing the Horseman around the community in the first place. Keeping them apart had been her only goal. She couldn't have him killing off the only family she had left and if their only interaction was any indication, neither one of them was ready to back down.

"I couldn't care less about what they're saying about me. You and I both know it isn't true." She stared ahead anyway as she kept walking, her hands clenched into tight fists at her sides. They passed a few buildings, but no one called out a greeting like they usually did. Instead, the whispering continued, or they turned away from her gaze. Refusing to meet her eyes. Even after all she'd done for this community. For the sacrifice she'd made to keep them safe. Putting herself on the front lines during every attack... *It's fine.* They were just nervous about him being amongst them. At least, that's what she told herself, anyway.

They passed a number of empty buildings. Ones they'd been using as storage for extra repair supplies. There was no one working in them today.

The tavern was nearly empty as well. *Odd.* During the day it doubled as the towns' meet- up spot where they served varying brews of Stella's famous tea.

Stella. The older woman was rounding the corner when she stopped at the sight of them. Her face held in a grim line as she watched, head tilted slightly to the side. She wore her usual billowing skirt and blouse, but today the colors had been soft earthy tones of greens and maroons. She'd left her hair down for the first time in months, and it cascaded around her petite face in gentle waves. She stared at Kellan, and he stared right back. Demitria couldn't place the look in her eyes. Something flashed across his face, but when she blinked, it was gone. Fast enough that Demitria thought she imagined it.

Finally, Stella smiled. Bright and boisterous. Infectious, as she found herself reciprocating and smiled back at them. Stella nodded at the Horseman before disappearing into the darkness of the greenhouse.

Demitria was grateful for the woman's reaction. The one soul in the entirety of the community who wasn't condemning her for a split-second choice she'd made while beyond the gates. Stella had always been the kindest soul she'd ever met. One she would miss quite dearly when she was gone. Her knowledge of the world was astronomical, and she was a person Demitria often found herself gravitating toward when she wasn't with Jace. Quite often the woman would teach her about gardening, and she truly did love every moment of their time together.

"Is there anything else you'd like to see?" Demitria turned her body back toward him, pulling her gaze from the greenhouse.

"Anything I'd like to see? I didn't even want to do this to begin with." Kellan scoffed. He spoke as if he had some sort of entitlement because of who he was, but she didn't buy it for a second. Horseman or not, she could care less. "Being stuck with you has been less than appealing."

"Excuse me?"

Don't do it, Demitria. Don't do it.

"In case anyone has never told you before, you're a grand asshole." After going above and beyond for him, she was done. Probably exploding more than she should have, but the events of the day had pushed and pushed her until she had needed that release. All of it could be summed up to the fucking Horseman at her side. "Find your own way back."

Demitria knew he wouldn't have even an ounce of trouble getting back to the infirmary, but she didn't care. The message had been clear enough.

She should have left him to rot in the open.

Eighteen

KELLAN

By nightfall Kellan was still wandering the town alone. Watching the people that dared to poke their heads out from whatever building they'd holed up in as he neared. He could tell these people had suffered at the hands of beings like him. Could see the devastation that lay within the cracks of the town, the weary looks on their faces as they peered at him with wide, frightened eyes. In a way, he found himself feeling...almost sorry for them.

The girl hadn't returned. It wasn't hard to locate her within the community, and she was very clearly avoiding him. He just hadn't made it a priority to find her. She'd had hours to herself, and was sure to have leveled out by then.

Ducking into an empty building, he entered a large room. Wooden crates littered the area, dust settled on top of them in a thick coat. Along the back wall a ladder led to the roof. Upon inspection, a hatch was propped wide open.

So, she'd been hiding here all day.

His movements were swift as he ascended, popping his head out the top. The human sat there with her back to him, transfixed along the horizon beyond their community. Staring. Watching for anything that should come this way.

"There is nothing out there." He said, climbing the rest of the way out.

She didn't turn to meet him. Instead, the girl pulled the hood of her cloak up and over her head as if it was a shield. Little good that would do.

With a sigh he added, "Your community is safe."

"I don't like you being here anymore than they do." She said, "I'm trying to do what's best for them. But out there... I panicked the other day."

Her expression was hard when he took a seat beside her. Against his better judgment.

The air here was cool. Colder than he remembered, but the night sky was just as beautiful. Deep blues faded into black as a million little iridescent stars lit up the sky. The full moon cast a soft glow along the buildings. He'd have to admit, Earth did have its beauties.

"You didn't hesitate when I showed up, which leads me to believe you don't simply just...freeze up. What happened?" Kellan kept his eyes trained on the shimmering sky above them. He didn't expect her to answer. If their roles were reversed, he wouldn't have.

But the human surprised him.

"When the Ascension happened ten years ago my family was attacked." She started. "I was only ten when it happened." The girl closed her eyes as her expression turned grim. Pained. Like she was imagining the words she was about to say. "My mom hid Jace and I in a cupboard when that *thing* came for us. We watched, silent, as it ate her alive. Tore her to pieces in front of our very eyes. Her eyes never left mine the entire time. She didn't scream, just silently cried. She didn't want us to be afraid." A heavy sigh left her lips as she tilted her head up, gazing into the sky above. The moon's glow pale on her skin, illuminating it. "I couldn't utter a sound, or do anything to stop it. And it knew we were there. Our fathers came in as it was stalking toward us. We watched as our only remaining parents were torn to pieces." She gulped, and he knew she'd been holding back tears. He could almost *taste* the salt in them.

Kellan and his siblings were told about the early years of the Ascension when the underworld had originally risen and some of the angels had gone rogue, but this? Hearing her firsthand account wasn't what he'd expected. Sure, he'd done some gruesome things himself, but he had done them because he didn't have a choice while under rule of the council. The attack she'd described was horrifying. Sadistic. Kellan didn't have words to describe what her kind must have faced.

"I remember the look on its face when it killed them. Rage, but something else. Glee. It enjoyed killing our families. Seeing the absolute terror in our eyes as we hid. It smiled—fucking smiled with their blood still dripping from its mouth." Her body trembled. "And then out there, it remembered me from that night, and everything—" Kellan turned to face her as she choked back a sob, her words cut short. He watched the tremble of her fists clenched in her lap. Seeing the demon the other day had shaken her, he could see that now. It was no wonder the girl had been nothing more than a ghost of what he'd glimpsed when they'd fought.

He didn't know what to say at her confession. Emotions... *humanity* were not his strong suit. But the girl had brought him here to save his life, even if she hadn't needed to. Had sacrificed their safety for his own. Honorable. And as the nagging feeling of his own childhood was threatening to break through, Kellan knew he could find some form of common ground with her. The trauma he'd endured similar to her own. It was something he and his siblings had all pushed aside for far too many years as an unspoken rule, never to be mentioned. But this felt right.

"Long ago, before any of this, I lived with my family on Eden." The quickening of his own heartbeat was unexpected. He wasn't used to emotions besides rage, much less sharing. "I watched my mother die, through no fault of her own." He joined the human in gazing up at the stars once more. "Angels and man were not supposed to cohabit together, but some broke the rules. We lived in a small forested village along the coast called Daire, where many of my kind resided. We were Horsemen, and we lived peacefully with our families. Our fathers were around when they could be, but we weren't supposed to be there." He paused for a moment, unsure if he should continue. She still hadn't faced him, but Kellan knew she was listening. "The women—our mothers, were stolen from here... taken to Eden without their consent and hidden away. Some were forced to bear us, while others grew to love their captors. Our fathers. Committing themselves for as long as the males would have them. When the High Council found out about us, we were punished. They made our fathers watch while they slaughtered the wives. That was the only repercussions they faced for interfering with humans. I was no older than you were when they killed her in front of me. Punished for a crime my father had committed."

"Kellan, I—"

"I remember the sound she made when the council slaughtered her," He admitted. "When they drove my father's own blade through her chest. Hearing her scream in agony before they slit her throat from ear to ear and forced us to watch as she bled out on the ground before us." Kellan wouldn't admit to anyone that her screams still haunted him to this day. "They beheaded her. Gave it to my father as consolation, but he wanted nothing to do with her, and forced my siblings and I to discard her body. I held her desecrated head in my hands while my brothers dug a grave, and my sister wept beside her body." That was the first time he'd ever felt blood dripping through his fingers.

"I'm sorry." She whispered.

Kellan stared at her, at a loss for words at the softness on her features that had something within his chest tightening.

"I'm sorry you had to go through that. Losing a parent... someone that you love is never easy. It changes you."

As unusual as it was, Kellan knew she meant it. Knew that as she uttered those words to him, she was talking about herself, too. Going through the things he had incited its own war within, and he could only imagine she'd suffered the same. Kellan felt himself feeling sorry for her. It was a strange feeling for him. One he hadn't felt for years. Eons, even.

"This war... it should have never happened." His eyes refocused into the darkening night sky, and his words came out slow. "But we cannot interfere until requested to do so." Kellan ran a hand down his face.

"Why did it take them so long?" Guilt. The sound of her voice. The pained expression in her eyes. "Why did it take *you* so long?"

He glanced at her. *Green.* Inexplicably green watery eyes flecked with gold met his own, wrenching something within. He felt...guilt that it had taken the council so long to send them. His siblings had been aware of the carnage for many years. Had been informed about it the moment the Ascension happened, but not once had they ever thought to defy orders. To dispatch themselves. Not even when some of the angels had gone rogue, staking their own claims to the nightmarish wasteland that quickly followed the demons. "I don't know." It was all he could say. He didn't have the answers that she was after, yet part of him wished he did. If only to ease his own reeling mind. He hadn't known how bad it truly was here. The savagery these people had seen. And when the council wasn't concerned, he didn't need to be either. He'd never had a reason to question their ways, so why would he have?

But that had changed, hadn't it? He'd done nothing but question their decision since being dispatched. Because nothing they told him made sense. This human girl wasn't a threat to their kind. She wouldn't throw the balance any more than the next human stationed within their communities. So why? Why her? Why this human? Unless...

They were wrong.

Kellan sat up straight, eyes widening. The council was wrong. The thought should have never crossed his mind, but he couldn't break from it. Should have tasted acrid in his mouth, yet it hadn't felt more right. Had they lied to him? To his siblings? Is it why they refused his summons?

"You're not who the council says you are."

Demitria jolted upright at his words, craning her neck toward him. It was her turn to stare.

"You're not a threat. Not like they say you are." A heavy sigh left him, and he continued. "I don't know why they wanted you eliminated. Why we were tasked to go after you alone. I don't understand it." He wouldn't even touch on the fact that, according to the demon, someone else clearly wanted her as well.

His mission was already failing. When he was initially dispatched, it was to eliminate what the council had deemed a threat to the very balance of their worlds. A monster. Instead, what he'd found was a human girl trying to survive. To protect her family the only way she knew how.

He hadn't expected to find any common ground with her, not when he'd had his eyes set on the kill. So why had the council wanted her dead so badly? Why was she such a threat?

What weren't they telling him?

"I'd never even heard of this balance until you showed up."

Kellan watched as she slowly unfurled her fingers as a new wave of emotions took hold of her features. That softness she'd shown him had disappeared, replaced by the fiery look he was growing used to. The hard line of her full lips, the narrowing of her green-gold eyes as she took him in. A familiarity struck him. The anger, the rage, so akin to his own.

"I've only ever wanted to protect my family. I have done nothing to warrant this price on my head."

"I believe you." Kellan hung is head for a brief moment. He didn't know why he knew she was sincere, but he did. So why had they ordered her death? Had it just been an unlucky coincidence? He didn't buy that for a moment... "I told you I am not the bloodthirsty monster your people depict me as, and I stand by those words."

"What do you mean by that?" She raised a brow at him, her body turning to face him head on. Dark hair billowed around her in soft waves, framing the curves of her figure.

"I..." He ran a hand through his hair. What had he meant by that? "I will not kill unnecessarily." Even seated, his frame towered over her own. So small. Frail wasn't a word he'd use for her. He was well aware of the body she'd honed for years to survive in this hell. Could see it in the way her clothing seemed to hug along every toned muscle. He blinked down at her. "I refuse to."

Kellan had never disregarded an order from the council before. He may have completed assignments in unorthodox manners, but never had he defied them.

Nineteen

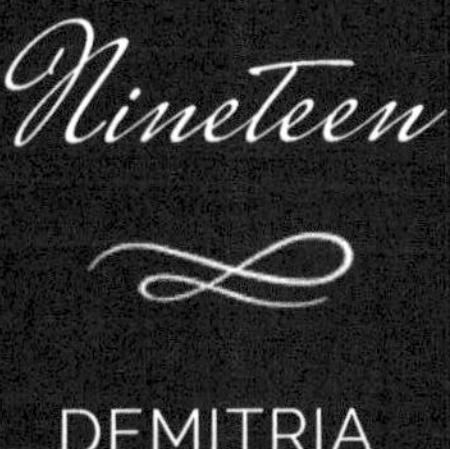

DEMITRIA

Demitria awoke as the sun broke over the horizon. After last night with the Horseman, she'd made up her mind. Their conversation replayed over and over as she dressed for the day. Kellan. It was strange to think of him as anything but War. A bringer of carnage and chaos. Yet last night he'd seemed almost... *human*, somehow. Like they'd connected.

It was odd, really. He didn't understand the order to kill her anymore, and from what she gathered, it seemed as if he wasn't going through with it. Despite that, she still had to leave. Not because she needed to go before his siblings came to finish the job, but because her presence would bring nothing but bloodshed and destruction to the community.

Kellan had been right the other night. The longer she stayed the more danger she brought to her home. She had to leave. She'd do anything to protect them.

She'd contemplated for hours after returning home about what her next steps should be, pacing back and forth until she was sure she'd worn tracks into the old wooden floorboards. Every minute she spent in Solis meant her people were in danger.

She could only think of one solution. In the middle of the night, she would sneak out with Atlas. Leave without Kellan and seek out her own answers.

Demitria had a vague idea of where she needed to go. For years, they'd been keeping an eye on a group of angels a few days ride from the community. From their observations, the beings had never raided any of the communities, and dare she say, they'd been peaceful. She didn't know if they were part of the council or not, but it was her only lead. She would find them, ask them her questions, and hope to whatever gods were out there that she'd get answers.

But hope was always a dangerous thing. She hated to even think it. Feel it. Because there was nothing in this world but dread and terror. It was an illusion of something so far out of reach. Hope for the night-mares to end. For a better world, and those that felt it, believed in it, well...

Hope was the deadliest thing of all.

Shaking her head, Demitria quietly closed the door of her house as she made her way into the early morning air. Small pebbles crunched under her boots with each step she took down the cracked roads of Solis. Toward the large greenhouse in the middle of the community where her first goodbye would be. By morning she was supposed to be leaving with Kellan, but when that time came around, she already planned on being long gone. Last night she'd thought about waiting it out and following the plan he'd set, but Demitria knew she probably wouldn't get her own questions answered. And she had several. Espe-cially after their talk. Leaving early was not only for the safety of her people, but for *her*.

The loud sigh past through her lips as she walked by a few of the empty buildings. Not a single soul was awake at this hour. She pulled the cloak tighter around her body, fighting off that early chill. She'd left her hair loose, flowing around her in soft waves as to not take up even more time. There were too many things she needed to get done, and just not enough time to do them.

"Stella?" Poking her head into the greenhouse, her voice barely above a whisper. The woman was usually an early riser, and Demitria was sure she'd been puttering around for hours already.

"I'm in here!" Stella called. A mop of gray hair popped out from behind a wall, so she entered. Proving her suspicions right, the large wooden table was littered with plants of all different varieties. Herbs, flowers, and an arrangement of seeds. She must have been rearranging and transplanting. "I've been preparing these for you." Stella motioned with an old withered hand toward a pile in the corner and began to expertly wrap them in a dark cloth before handing the bundle over.

"What for?" Demitria asked.

"For your journey." Her eyes met her own in a sad smile. *How did she know?*

"What do you—"

"When you've been around as long as I have you pick up on these things." Stella winked, quick to return back to her work. Pocketing the seeds she'd been given, Demitria watched the woman work for some time.

"I still don't..." Demitria's voice carried off.

"It's best not to question these things." Stella's laughter fluttered through the greenhouse, the sound filling her with a profound sadness at the thought of never hearing it again. "An old woman's mind works in funny ways. Knows many things."

Demitria toyed with the bundle in her pocket. She may not have had a ton of experience with the agricultural side of Solis, the woman had still taught her many things. Stella's knowledge on the subject was vast, and she loved watching the older woman work. She herself had spent many hours with her hands in the dirt, following the woman's instruction. Demitria firmly believed the only reason Solis thrived was because of her.

It wasn't long before Stella shooed her out the door with a knowing look. Right. She had others that she needed to say goodbye to.

With one last lingering wave, Demitria left through the large greenhouse doors, back into the cool morning air. The sun was higher now, still ascending into the bright sky above. She didn't let herself linger in front of the doors. It would be harder if she did.

She found herself slowly walking down the street, watching as the town slowly began to come alive. Residents exiting out of the housing building to her left, nodding in her direction once, but never saying a word. She knew their distance was because of the Horseman, but she shook it off anyway. She had her reasons for bringing him, and even if they couldn't see it, she still didn't regret that choice.

She found Cory sitting outside the tavern, sipping on some of Stella's brew.

"Aren't you a sight for sore eyes this morning." Waving her over, he shot her a charming grin. She took a seat in the cool iron chair, pushing it up to the table. "You seem awfully busy this morning."

"Couldn't sleep." She lied, shrugging her shoulders. Watching as a few residents entered the building.

"Where's that friend of yours?" He nearly laughed, but caught himself as her eyes narrowed. Demitria bit her tongue. They weren't friends. At least... she didn't think they were, anyway.

"Not sure." She shrugged, "Probably sleeping." She highly doubted it, but whatever. Kellan was more than likely planning for the morning somewhere. Whatever he had in mind now she had no idea. She could feel it last night, that change in his beliefs. Demitria knew he was still adamant on reuniting with his siblings, but after that? Regardless, he wouldn't be happy to find her gone tomorrow.

Cory nodded. "I wish you would have stopped in sooner. I'm due for patrol soon." He sighed, downing the rest of the steaming liquid in the mug he cradled in his hands.

"Oh, okay." With a sigh she pushed to her feet. She'd been up for over an hour already, and her list was very nearly complete. A list that had been positively pitiful, she'd realized. And clearly hadn't let nearly enough people in. She wasn't sure if that was a good thing, or just downright depressing.

"See you around?" He called, on his feet and already yards away. Demitria could only nod. She didn't have it in her to truly lie to him. With one last wave, she watched as the redhead disappeared behind a building.

Alone again.

Demitria wandered aimlessly around the community for a while to kill time. Jace usually had meetings in the mornings, and he was the last on her list. She'd been dreading this one the most. It was why she'd saved him for last, knowing his would be the hardest. Leaving Jace behind would very nearly break her.

After another ten minutes of walking she gave up, making her way toward the large building he'd taken residence in.

It had to have been a small office building at one point, but when they'd founded Solis, Jace had knocked down several walls, creating a fairly open floorplan with a few larger than normal rooms she'd spent far too many nights in. His place had fared better than others around the community. The large wooden front door sat unlocked—as usual—and she casually let herself in. Jace wasn't one for decorating, and he only displayed a few trinkets from their childhood. A single photograph of their families on a camping trip hung on the wall.

She stared at it for some time. They were smiling. Genuinely smiling. She couldn't remember the last time they'd been that carefree. They'd hugged each other in close as another camper had snapped the shot. She could see the flames of their fire in the distance. The trees around them were exuberant and *green*. So alive.

Her mother's eyes were happy. Demitria liked seeing them like that. Happy and so full of life. The image of her burned into her mind was from her very last memory. Her mother broken. Bleeding everywhere. Those once hopeful eyes silenced. Dull.

Gods, she couldn't look at this anymore. With a deep breath, Demitria tore herself from the photo, begging the tears to withhold their siege.

She let herself into his bedroom. It was much larger than her own. The ever-familiar scent, another one of Stella's wonderful creations of scented soap, of mint wafting over her. Through her. Closing her eyes, she let her body fall onto the soft mattress. Would she really be able to leave him behind?

She didn't have a choice.

She was leaving for him. To protect him. The High Council wanted her dead, and by the sounds of it, someone else did too. Being in Solis only put him in danger. Leaving was for the best. It had to be.

Before long, the door shoved open, a weathered looking Jace slowly sauntering in. Dark circles were prominent under his eyes much like when she'd returned. Or maybe they had never left? His skin paler than normal, that soft glow from long hours in the sun had all but vanished. He ran a hand through his hair, a sigh passing through his lips before noticing her on the bed. Despite the fatigue plaguing his features, his eyes lit up at the sight of her.

"You're here early." He grinned, collapsing on the bed beside her. His arm draped lazily over her when she scooted in closer.

"I wanted to see you is all." She shrugged.

"Oh?" He elbowed her rib in a playful manner, and she could practically hear the grin in his voice without having to look over.

"Don't let it go to your head, Smith." The laughter came easy with him. It always did. "Stressful meeting today?" She asked, staring up at the painfully white stucco ceiling above them.

"Yeah... Augustus sent a man over early. There's been another raid." Demitria could feel her stomach churning at his words. Her body froze, despite the warmth of him beside her.

Another demon attack. They were getting more and more frequent. She wouldn't ask which community. Just another thing for her to feel guilty about.

"This isn't on you." Jace said, voice matter of fact. She could feel his eyes piercing into her. "I know you think these attacks are your fault after that demon, but it isn't. This war is not your fault." She tried to believe him, but it just got so hard. With the death of their family still so fresh in her mind once more, and her own death looming over her head, she didn't know what to believe anymore. Was she paying a price like Kellan had? She wondered if she was being condemned from something she hadn't even committed yet. Like she'd been set on a course for some mass destruction in the future that truly would tip the balance of their worlds. Was that why so many of these beings seemed to want her dead? Had she done something so bad that she was being punished?

"I know." The words hadn't come easy, but she'd said them anyway. If anything, to put his mind at ease. The less he worried about her the better. "As much as I enjoy your company, I did have a reason to come here."

"Do you ever really need a reason?" He asked.

"No, but I still need to talk to you about something."

"You're leaving, aren't you?" His gaze still hadn't left her, and she didn't dare turn toward him now. "With him, just like he said."

"It's... complicated." She sighed, finding a pattern in the swirls of the ceiling. Anything to keep her from meeting his eyes.

"Then uncomplicate it for me."

"Jace, I—" She refused to tell him about the demon. About what the thing had said to her. How it remembered that day...knowing that if he knew the truth, he'd lock her away someplace he thought was safe. He'd probably try and go after the monster himself, and she couldn't let that happen. Finally, she turned to him. "Do you trust me?" She stared into those familiar green eyes that had been her lifeline time and time again. The sharp features of his face.

"With my life." He answered.

"Then know that I wouldn't leave without a valid reason. I went further than I'd ever gone while I was out there. Saw things... heard things that I can't stomach the words to repeat." She wasn't lying, per say, but withholding some of the information. But all of it was her truths. "When I go with him, it's to keep you safe." Demitria touched her fingers to his cheek, willing him to believe her.

"Then I'll go with you. We'll do whatever it is together." She could hear the panic rising in his voice. "You don't have to do this alone."

"I'm not alone." That was a lie, and she hated the taste of the words in her mouth. Bitter, sharp, like they burned. "I will come back. I promise you." It took every fiber of her being to hold back the sob threatening to break through. Because she didn't know if she'd ever come back. If she'd even survive...

"I can't let you leave."

"Jace, you're my best friend. I'm doing this for you. For us. For everyone in this damn community." She sighed. "I don't like it any more than you do."

"You will come back." He said, voice stern. Like he was speaking it into existence. *Hope.*

If she let the conversation continue, Demitria knew she'd break.

"I could stay here all day." Changing the subject, she let herself curl into his warmth. Jace was quick to hug her body in closer, refusing to let go. He'd been her safety net for so long. She didn't know what to do now that everything was changing.

So, she focused on the little things. Imprinting them in her mind so she would never forget, not that she ever would. She'd remember the way his arms felt as he held her like there wasn't anyone else in the world. She'd remember the warmth of their bodies side by side, and the soft soothing caress of his hand on her arm.

She would remember *them*, because she didn't ever want to let that

Demitria blinked up at the ceiling, willing the room into focus. They'd fallen asleep and had completely wasted the day away. She wouldn't have changed it, though. Being able to spend the day with him was what she had wanted anyway.

With a yawn, she untangled herself from his muscled frame and stared out the window. Someone had already lit the lamps outside, and the sun had begun to set over the horizon as hues of pinks and reds streaked across the sky. She hoped Jace hadn't had much to do today, but was grateful for no interruptions. Almost as if they'd known.

Climbing out of the bed, she stretched on aching legs when Jace stirred. He blinked up once, twice, then settled his gaze on her.

"Apparently we slept the entire day." She laughed, tossing the dark cloak over her shoulders and clasping it at her throat.

"Must have needed the rest." He shrugged, lifting to his elbows and pushing his own body off the bed. Jace ran a hand through his hair, smoothing out the golden strands that had fallen out of place during their slumber. He grabbed the leather jacket he'd discarded on the chair hours earlier and slipped it back on. "I am absolutely starving. Any plans for dinner?"

"I do now." She motioned toward the door and they left in a hurry. The street had been busier than the morning as people milled about. Kellan was nowhere in sight, and she knew that was more than likely the reason why. She wondered what he'd gotten up to all day in her absence. Had he stayed in the infirmary the entire time? Had he come looking for her?

She told herself she didn't care. She'd spent the day with the one person in the world she truly loved, and that was the only thing on her mind. The Horsemen could do what he wanted. She would take her last day. *Her last day free*, because who knew what the hell was in store next. Even Kellan didn't know anymore.

They reached the tavern in record time, stomachs rumbling in a course of growls with the lack of food. Upon seeing Jace, Mitchell, the man that ran it, had them seated in moments as he waved them toward an empty table in the back of the building. It was never busy enough to be waiting long, but it had been the fastest she'd ever gotten to a table. Her stomach thanked him for it.

She let her eyes wander around the room. At the residents seated all around them, laughing as if they hadn't had a care in the world as they ate the meal being served, or sipped on whatever brew Mitchell had chosen to serve. The drink hadn't been high on their list of needs in Solis, but the man had been brewing before the Ascension as a hobby and thought that little bit of normalcy would boost the spirits of the residents. He'd been right, and since then the little tavern he'd created had patrons every day.

He returned a few minutes later with mugs filled to the brim with ale. Demitria hesitated, knowing she'd need her wits when she left tonight. She pondered it for a few moments, staring at the mug in front of her as she contemplated her next steps.

One wouldn't hurt.

Demitria and Jace took a swig in unison, the bitter taste of the cold liquid biting at her taste buds. Mitchell brought out two small plates of food. It wasn't a huge meal, but it was what they had. Root vegetables that Stella had grown in the greenhouse and a thin slice of meat. She didn't know what it was, and she wouldn't ask. They must have caught something last night. She swore to the gods, if he was feeding her a rat...

She didn't eat the meat.

"Are you worried about the attacks?" Her voice hushed, Demitria pushed away the plate. She didn't want anyone else to hear her question. Better to save them from going into a frenzy just yet.

Jace shook his head. "I think it's inevitable that an attack will come." He started, "But knowing that they're becoming more frequent means we can prepare. Have more of us stationed outside. Arm some of those that are inside." He shrugged. For what they'd been through he was oddly nonchalant about it all. It worried her, but she was glad to hear him taking the same necessary steps that she would have.

They thanked the owner and left, resuming the walk they'd started before the meal. Jace led their direction, and he turned left upon leaving the building, down the street toward her small home.

"Will it even make a difference?" She finally asked, now that they were out of earshot from the others.

"I'd like to think it would." With a sigh, he looked up toward the stars. Neither one of them wanted to mention her departure. Her leaving meant one less able body to protect the ones who couldn't fight. But maybe leaving would mean they didn't have to fight at all.

Jace stopped in front of her door, waiting for her to make the next move. Waiting to be invited in. She couldn't. Not this time. He'd spent the night with her numerous times in the house. As her safety net. Her best friend. The only family she had left. Demitria wanted nothing more than to spend her final night alongside him, reminiscing about the old days. About life before the Ascension. But her plan was to slip out in the middle of the night when Solis was fast asleep. She knew the guard rotations at the front gate and would only have minutes to get through unnoticed, and having him here would only complicate things more than they already needed to be.

She also didn't even know how to say goodbye.

"I will be here before sun up. There's no way in hell I'm letting you leave with him before I get to see you."

As if realizing that she wouldn't ask him in, he gave up. Demitria didn't know what to say, so she didn't answer. Jace wrapped his arms around her in a warm embrace, her fingers gripped hard into the fabric of his dark shirt. Unwilling to let him go.

It took every ounce of her self-control not to cry.

"I'll see you in the morning, okay?"

All she could do was nod. He wouldn't. Reluctantly, he released his hold and took a step back into the street. Demitria stared at him for longer than she should before making her way inside. And when she closed the door, her heart cleaved in two.

She watched through a crack in the window as he stood outside for several minutes, his eyes fixed to the door. It didn't make it any easier. She let the tears flow freely, releasing the gates that had barely held them back outside. When he finally walked away, the back of her head met the front door before her body slowly slid to the ground in a heap.

Demitria cried until the world was consumed in darkness. She wasn't going to wait until tomorrow.

Twenty

DEMITRIA

Atlas waited patiently outside as she saddled him in the dark. Nothing moved around them, the cool evening air still, and she was confident that everyone had retired to their homes for the rest of the night.

It was for the best.

They stuck to the dirt paths, making sure to avoid the concrete so the sound of his hooves made no sound. They would only have one shot at this. A few moments were all she had.

They waited in the shadows as the Guardians changed out. One minute, and she counted it down. The second Demitria watched the t'ins' heads disappear around the corner she bolted, Atlas followed behind her on silent steps, as if he knew exactly what was at stake. Heaving with everything in her, she manually maneuvered the large gate, just enough for the both of them to get through. Her arms ached from the force needed, but she shook it off. Mounting swiftly, they shot into the night. Leaving behind the only thing in the world that had kept her grounded for the last ten years.

Demitria was aware of the soft whir of the motor off in the distance. She knew Cory was out patrolling, and between her eyes and the beast beneath her, she was confident of her ability to stay hidden.

Scanning the dark abyss around them, she pushed the mount into a slow canter, holding the edges of the cloak taut around her body until she was certain they were far enough away from Solis.

Several minutes passed, maybe even an hour, before she finally stopped hearing the motor in the distance. Demitria let a shaky breath escape through her parted lips. She wouldn't look back. Couldn't. Fearing that if she did, leaving would be that much harder. Her eyes scanned the landscape again, begging for this journey to be easy. She didn't have the elevated senses of the Horseman, and part of her wished she'd just waited until morning, but she knew her own questions wouldn't be answered if she did. If she could just figure out why they wanted her dead, maybe she could change whatever it was they were so afraid of. Walk a different path than the one she was on.

She didn't want to die. Had fought so damn hard to survive in this fucked up nightmare that she would push to her limits for just one more day. One more year. For her entire life, because twenty years was too soon for her. Her parents had sacrificed themselves so she could *live*, and she'd be damned to have some...some monsters take that away from her.

She pointed Atlas in a similar direction to the one she'd taken with Kellan. The last reports she'd seen placed the angels along the edge of the canyon somewhere. She'd start her search there, looking for any sort of clue on their whereabouts. They'd been spotted from time to time in the ruins of the old city beyond the mountains, and she wondered if they hid out in one of the many abandoned buildings. Her people hadn't entered the cities in years as most had been overrun by demons the moment they fell. She would risk it, though, if it meant getting her answers.

The rhythmic beats of Atlas's hooves pounded in time with her throbbing heart. Each step away from her lifeline brought her closer to answers. She hoped, anyway.

Hope.

Demitria couldn't help but laugh at the audacity of her thoughts. Despite Stella's urging to let herself feel it, to believe it, she just couldn't open herself up for the hurt she knew would follow. So, she locked it away in the darkest corners of her mind, behind that steel-clad wall she'd erected and enforced for so many years.

Atlas flicked his ears back and forth, listening for anything that moved across the barren land that surrounded them. From memory, she knew they wouldn't run into any other community for days yet. There was nothing until after the canyon, beyond the ruins of the city. When they perked forward again Demitria knew the area was still clear. She wouldn't let herself feel relief, it all could change within the blink of an eye.

Her thoughts drifted back toward the community. To Jace. Even to the Horseman that was probably sleeping soundly in the infirmary. Their rooftop conversation had been... enlightening, and she hadn't expected most of the things he'd had to say.

Kellan had been through much the same as her. Losing his mother in a most gruesome way that no one should ever have to experience. Even if he was one of *them*, that didn't matter. At least...not to her anymore.

She wondered about the council. About their involvement in the lives of the beings they'd openly slaughtered. Why hadn't any of them revolted? Why hadn't *he*? Kellan had mentioned his siblings on numerous accounts, and she wondered about them, too. Were they similar in the way they moved? The way they thought? Would they have the same questions about her involvement with the very balance of their worlds? She and the Horseman had come to an understanding on that rooftop. Like an unspoken truce between them, despite every bone in her body protesting against it. She hated to feel it. To...trust someone like him, but there was a nagging in her chest, *roaring* at her to believe it.

Pulling Atlas to a halt, Demitria looked up at the sky. At the moon shining bright overhead and the flickering stars above. Her thoughts drifted to Jace. That feeling of despair and grief welled in her chest with each stuttered breath she took. She let the tears burst free and fall freely down her cheeks as she buried her face in her hands, the sobs wracking through her body.

She would let herself cry. To show that weakness that she hated so much. For nearly twenty years they'd been by each other's sides. Her rock. Her soul. The only family she had left. They were supposed to stay together, no matter what. Had made a promise to one another all those years ago, and she'd seemingly fucked that up too. Demitria hated those creatures. The High Council, and whoever else wanted her dead. So, she made a vow to herself.

She would find the angels in the mountains. She would get the answers to all her questions, and would beg if she had to. Would get to her knees and do anything they asked of her if it meant changing the course of her life.

She would go home.

Twenty-One

KELLAN

Kellan's fist thudded loudly on the old wooden door three times, but there was no answer. Listening for any noise from within, he rapped again with more force. "Open up!" Whispering harshly, he scanned around behind him. The whispers directed at the girl the other day had been harsh and entirely not what he'd expected from them, so he'd tried to keep himself scarce and unseen for her sake. He'd wanted to give her some form of peace on her last day, and had done his best to not disturb anyone else in the community.

He had succeeded for the better part of the day, but only because he didn't try to find the girl. Kellan imagined she'd probably been avoiding him. He didn't blame her. Not after how her own people had treated her for bringing him here. He didn't know what puzzled him more. The animosity toward her, or the fact she'd felt the need to save his life.

A life debt, she'd told him. He couldn't fathom the thought of any human feeling that way toward one of his kind. Most wanted him dead. Human and supernatural being alike. And the lengths she'd gone to had been honorable. *Strange*, but brave. More so than most of the beings he'd met in his millennia. Especially since he'd been in service to the council.

When she didn't answer again, he knocked louder this time, the sound reverberating into the night air as it echoed throughout the empty streets. Kellan cringed at the noise in the early morning air. He could tell by the look on the horizon that the sun was about an hour out from its daily ascent, and had planned on getting an early start to their journey. He wanted to get as far away from this community as he could, but he hadn't wanted to wake any prying eyes in the process.

Kellan was met with silence once again. He waited a heartbeat before pressing his ear to the door. Listening. There was no one inside.

His boot connected with the door. With a loud crack it snapped off the hinges, splintering as it tumbled into the house, crashing to the floor before him. Stepping foot into the house, he took in the surroundings and was met with darkness. His eyes roamed over the room. At the barely furnished interior, despite looking heavily lived in. A rugged blanket was tossed haphazardly upon a worn gray couch, its cushions torn and fraying in several spots. Several candles lined the area, the wax melted and pooling at their base on each surface. The girl was nowhere in sight. He wandered further into the house, swinging open any door he could find in his quick search of the place. The rest of the home looked much the same as the first room. He didn't linger in the bedroom, despite her scent being the strongest there. That familiar light, fresh floral smell. So strong, he could almost picture her laying in the bed in front of him. With a shake of his head, he slammed the door. Not a single weapon had been found during his search, and he froze.

Shit.

Retracing his steps, Kellan exited the building, walking along the side of the house to the covered overhang he spotted. The horse was gone. *Shit, shit, shit!* He had been so aloof all day, dead set on giving *her* time to say goodbye to her people, and she'd gotten away.

Kellan wasn't quiet about the string of profanities that left his mouth, racing to the entrance of the community. Even after their conversation last night, she'd fled. *Fucking humans!*

The iron gates came into view, surrounded by the town's Guardians, weapons drawn.

"You woke up half the town." He couldn't remember the names of the twins. Didn't care to, actually. "You think you can just come here and destroy our homes?" The nearly identical bodies stepped toward him, long daggers held firm in each of their hands as they glared in his direction, the challenge in them clear. He would have laughed at them if he wasn't in such a hurry to get out.

Ignoring them, Kellan's eyes met those of the girl's companion. "She's gone." Jace's features fell, face paling at his news. Kellan almost pitied him. "Open the gates and let me pass."

The man's face hardened, hands clenching into tight fists at his sides. "She wouldn't just up and leave. Not without saying anything to me. We spent the entire day together, and she didn't mention a thing." He muttered, more to himself than those around them.

"Are you humans really that stupid?" Kellan asked, readying his weapons for the trek ahead. He whistled low, knowing his mount would be waiting on the other side. To his right, one of the twins opened his mouth in rebuttal, and Kellan was quick to silence him with a hand. His conversation was with the leader. The girl's... *friend*. "She left to protect *you*." On instinct, his eyes formed into a tight glare, fixated on the human with the hindering connection to the girl.

Jace looked like a fish out of water, opening his mouth and closing it as he tried to find the right words to say. Finally settling, he replied. "What do you mean?"

"She ran to ensure no harm came to your home." Kellan took a step forward toward the Guardians who retreated a foot back at his advance. Jace held his ground, his fingers clutched tight around the sword in his hand. "Let me out."

"What, so you can hunt her down and kill her?" Aside from the girl, he may have been the only human to ever outright challenge him. Most had stared at him as if they'd intended to, but only this one had held his stance, refusing to back down. Kellan knew he cared for her. Probably a lot more than he was letting on.

"I don't plan on killing her!" Kellan's temper was flaring, voice coming out louder than he'd intended as he advanced another step. "Not anymore."

"She knew you were going to kill her, and she still saved you." Kellan watched the realization spread across his face as the man's eyes widened, his mouth hung slightly ajar before schooling his features into something harder. Could see the hatred in Jace's eyes at the thought of it.

"Yes. Now move aside so I can leave." He could get by them all if he'd really wanted to. Even the lot of them couldn't hold him back. But he had given his word that he wouldn't harm them, and throughout his life had always made damn sure to never go back on it. Even if he so desperately wanted to. "Let me out before someone else does the job that I was supposed to."

Jace barked orders without a second thought. The redheaded Guardian scrambled toward the large sturdy gate, motioning toward another to help push it open, and within moments, it was groaning open just enough for Kellan to squeeze through.

"Bring her home." Jace said.

Kellan couldn't do that, and he was sure the man already knew that.

"Just... promise me you'll keep her safe. Please."

His mount stood just outside of the gate, pawing the ground as he neared. He didn't turn back toward Jace as he left.

That was a promise he couldn't make either.

Twenty-Two

DEMITRIA

Four days.

Demitria had been on her own for four days with no idea if she was heading in the right direction. She just rode. She wanted answers no matter what, but was quickly reaching a point that the only thing she cared about was putting distance between her and Solis.

Glancing up at the bright blue skyline above, she guessed it must have been near noon. The sun was high in the afternoon sky as it beat down on her and Atlas. The day had grown hot, muggy, and she could feel as Atlas began to slow beneath her. They'd been pushing so hard with little to no water. She knew he'd need to rest soon if they were to continue the journey to the angels.

"Whoa boy, let's rest for a little while." His hooves dragged along the dirt before slowing to a stop, letting out a huff as he did so. Demitria swung her legs from the stirrups as she dismounted, loosening the girth around his stomach to give him a bit more room to breathe. Gathering the reins in her hands, she led him on foot for some time. Despite the current heat, they'd been rained on the night before. There had to be a source of water somewhere, a puddle from the rain that hadn't evaporated yet. Demitria shook the flask at her hip, letting out a sigh as it rattled. Already half empty. She'd blown through the water faster than she'd liked. They would need to find a spot to refill if they were to continue any further.

They walked for another ten minutes across the barren land with watchful eyes, scanning for anything before spotting the shimmer along the surface of the shallow puddle several feet away. Demitria quickened her pace, Atlas trotting alongside her. Closing the remaining distance, the water was murky with dirt and gods knew what else. Perfect for Atlas, but her flask would have to wait. He gratefully lowered his head and drank, the cool water soothing his overheated body. He stayed head down for minutes, drinking his fill as if he knew they probably wouldn't find more for some time. Once he was done, they resumed their journey. Continuing on foot for the next little while, pace slower than before. The break had been nice for them both, and it felt good to stretch out the aching muscles in her legs.

Alone. She was completely alone.

The thought hit her, weighing heavy on her chest. She had struggled most days back at the community. They may have had more food than most, but you were never properly fed. She couldn't remember the last time she'd truly had a proper meal, and it had grown harder and harder to stay hydrated. Living was hard enough, but they'd always had each other to help weather whatever storm came their way. Now? Demitria didn't know what the hell she had been thinking. Finding food was a near impossible task. She couldn't grow anything. Didn't have the time, as staying in one place long enough to grow something wasn't an option. She could try to hunt like she had with Kellan, but it was clearly obvious she was no good at it. Out there, beyond the wall alone, was a death sentence. She couldn't protect herself from all the creatures that lurked, not at the rate they'd been attacking the other communities. Not that many at once.

She should have left with Kellan.

Demitria ran a hand down her face as she groaned. What had she been thinking, leaving like she had. She wasn't prepared to be out like this. Sure, she'd survived beyond a community before, but never alone. Jace had always been beside her every step of the way. Now? She didn't know the first thing about survival on her own.

Her destination was unknown. Where had she truly planned to go?

They had never been able to find the angels exact location, only the areas they tended to frequent. What if she couldn't even find it? So far, she'd really only managed to get as far away from Solis as she could. She could see the canyon in the distance and could probably make it by nightfall if she pushed, but it would more than likely be later than that. To preserve whatever strength she could, and let Atlas recover from their grueling pace of the last four days.

She should have just gone with the Horseman and reunited with his siblings. They probably would have killed her upon first glimpse. *Maybe that would have been for the best.* Maybe then she wouldn't have had to worry about her home every waking minute of every gods damned day.

Leaving alone had been stupid.

"I'm an idiot." She whispered, head hung in defeat. Atlas nudged her back softly, but it did nothing to lift her souring mood.

Demitria lost track of how long they'd been walking, but her feet drug along more and more with each step. They were completely and utterly exhausted. She knew they would need to sleep at some point. Having been on the move since leaving, never stopping for more than a few hours each time, neither she nor Atlas had gotten much rest. She weighed her options. She would need to risk sleep no matter what, but the timeline was another story. She could wait it out, sleep when it was dark. Or they could find a nice, hidden spot and nap while the sun was still high, and move again after dark. It was an easy choice. Easier than she'd anticipated.

A sea of rocks was some twenty feet off in the distance. They could rest there for the next several hours. The tall outcropping was semi shaded, and it would be nice for both of them to get out of the heat. She left the saddle on Atlas in case they needed to make a quick getaway, but kept it loosened slightly for his comfort. Hoping she would be able to take the two seconds to tighten should it come down to it.

Wiping the sweat from her brow, Demitria's body lowered to the ground. It was hard and uncomfortable beneath her, but her body welcomed the rest. Stretching her legs out in front of her, she glanced at Atlas who was already dozing a few feet away. Unbuckling the sword at her hip, she sat it down beside her. Within minutes, she followed into a much-needed sleep.

The impact to her stomach was unlike anything she'd ever felt. Coughing. Gagging. Gasping for air as Demitria tried to calm her breathing. It was nearly dark outside, and she knew she'd fucked up and slept longer than she'd intended.

Demitria was met with something she'd hoped to never see again, its haunting body hovering over her.

"I told you I'd find you again." Acrid bile rose up the back of her throat as her body threatened to be violently ill as the demon's deep voice rumbled through her. She gagged and finally took a breath, too consumed with fear to do anything more than lay there as her eyes blazed with terror.

"What do you want?" She gasped, the sound of her own voice weak. Pathetic.

The creature smiled, showing a mouth full of those razor teeth. The image of her mother's blood dripping from his mouth flashing before her. Hurried eyes tore across her surroundings, the dark shadows of the large rocks around her, but nothing familiar caught her gaze, Atlas nowhere to be found. She was really, truly alone now. Demitria hoped to whatever gods were out there that he'd gotten away safe.

"Your Horseman is not here to protect you." Those glowing, crimson eyes tore through her. Anchoring her to the spot. It extended a taloned claw toward her, brushing along the smooth pale flesh of her throat, but it didn't break skin. The shiver worked through her body at the thought of those claws. At the poison that had coursed through Kellan's body from them.

She regretted leaving. Regretted thinking she could even do this on her own. Why the hell didn't she just wait for Kellan. *He was right.* Humans were completely and utterly useless. Stupid. Every decision she'd made since meeting him had been absolutely stupid.

"He will be so pleased that I've found you alone."

Somewhere. Somehow, she found the courage to speak again, despite the trembling of her body. "Who?"

"The Dark King." It whispered, flashing another sinister smile.

Had she been standing, her body would have collapsed as another wave of fear rushed through her. She didn't know who the demon spoke of, but the name alone invoked a wave of fear through her. Someone else had put a price on her head. Someone seemingly important.

"He's been looking for you. We had hoped your Horseman would cooperate, but there's still time."

Kellan? Cooperate with what?

"He will join us in due time."

Kellan must have known that she was gone by now. Would he be able to track her? How far had she actually made it? Would his desire to find answers push him enough to look for her in the first place? Demitria knew she couldn't count on the Horseman to rescue her again.

She felt the weight of the weapon at her side. In a moment of blind fear, she ripped it from its sheath and swung. Not caring where and what she hit. His clawed fingers parried her sword easily, knocking it from her hands as if her blow had been nothing more than a feather in the wind. The scream ripped through her as she bore his weight on her chest, pinning her to the cool rock below. The deadly points of his claws danced along her skin in a taunting manor, inciting a new wave of terror. Poisoned. If he broke skin, everything would be over. Knowing full well she wouldn't last nearly as long as Kellan had. Her heart would probably stop beating almost instantly. Demitria didn't struggle, her body giving up before her mind did.

The weight lifted, only to be replaced by a swift kick, the air rushing out once more as he pulled her to her feet. To her right, the sword lay a great distance away. She couldn't risk making a dive for it, and somewhere in the scuffle Demitria knew her dagger had come loose by the weight missing on her thigh. She couldn't fight back. Couldn't do anything, so she walked, obedient, and she could just make out the looming shadows of the canyon in the distance. At least they seemed to be going in a similar direction. She couldn't discern if that was a good thing or not.

"What does he want with me?" Her voice shook, despite the strength she willed into it.

"Your soul, for one." He spoke. "Me? It's the delicacy of human flesh."

She wished she hadn't glanced behind her, catching him licking his lips at the thought of it. Whatever happened, she hoped she wouldn't meet the same end her parents had. Not by this same creature. Their sacrifice would have been for nothing.

"If you're going to kill me, just do it now." Turning on her heel, Demitria faced the creature. The blow caught her shoulder with such force she reeled backward in pain. The blood welling beneath her clothing as the panic set in. Eyes darting to the wound, her fingers prying at the fabric of her shirt, she nearly let out a sigh of relief. She was bleeding, but hadn't been poisoned. He'd hit her so hard, the power behind the blow had broken the skin.

Her arm ached. She could feel the blood dripping down her finger tips, falling to the dirt as he pushed her on. She didn't dare speak another word, knowing that if she did, it would only end in pain.

The silence was awful. It was giving her more time to think than she'd ever wanted, really. About life. The people in it, including the fucking Horseman. Her upcoming death. That was something she didn't want to think about, even though it seemed inevitable at this point. She truly didn't know who this monster spoke of. So many beings that she hadn't experienced, and, keeping track of them nearly made her head spin. The price on her had from the council was worrisome, but a price from this unknown? A Dark King? The thought alone was terrifying, more so after the talk with Kellan back at the community. If he didn't know who—*what* else was in play...she was petrified.

How would her death happen? When would it happen? Demitria didn't know the answer to either, and probably wouldn't until it was too late. Without weapons, she was useless. Against their power, she was useless. As a human... she was just utterly useless. Always so fucking useless.

At some point they veered away from the canyon as the shadows seemed to change. They'd been walking for hours it seemed, and instead of the wide path and those tall canyon walls looming over her, the demon looked to be leading her toward an opening at the base of a mountain, instead. Under the canyon, perhaps? She didn't recall anything of the like when they'd initially been tracking the angels, and wondered how the hell it got there.

"Down this way."

The demon gave her another shove and she stumbled to her knees. Feeling the bite of the uneven rocks beneath her as it tore into her flesh. She wanted to cry, wanted to cry so badly, but she refused to give the damned creature the satisfaction. Curling her hands and taking a deep breath, she willed her body to calm.

"Get up!" Another kick sent her stumbling forward, but she hadn't been ready to get up. Hadn't had a chance to steel her nerves. Just a few moments, that was all she needed to regain her composure. The air emptied from her lungs at the second kick, head colliding with the rock. Demitria lay there, gasping for breath as the creature laughed, grinning as she fought to breathe.

It grabbed at her arms, yanking her up to her feet like she was nothing more than a doll. He shoved again, and they ventured into the cavern. Much like the one her and Kellan had stayed in what seemed like a lifetime ago, when it had really only been a little more than a week. This one was massive in comparison. Demitria wasn't familiar with the area anymore, and she stumbled over her feet at the new terrain. Had they created it somehow? She wondered if they'd been converging down below. It would make sense for the rise in attacks on the surrounding communities. Why so many had fallen?

They continued down the tunnel, and nothing but darkness invaded her vision, as if she'd gone completely blind. Her feet slowed, but the demon held on by the back of her cloak, yanking her around as he guided her down, his talons almost imbedded into the fabric at her neck.

No supplies, no water, no food, no weapons, and held hostage by the creature that had killed her family.

There was no coming back from this. Not this time.

The tunnels were scarily quiet the further they went, the only sound their feet crunching on the loose rock beneath them as the floor dipped in a slight decline. The smell inside the cavern was stagnant. Musty. What she wouldn't give for the crisp night air to fill her lungs as she gazed up at a sea of stars.

The demon pushed further down into the tunnels. They must have been at least a hundred feet below ground, she was sure of it. After what seemed like hours, they came upon a large gap before them, lit up by the glow of flames from beyond the opening. Thick claw marks dug deep gouges into the wall as if the demons had broken through themselves. *How long had they been down here?*

The cavern opened up into another large room, the red-orange blaze of the fire causing a ripple of shadows that danced along the walls. Demitria didn't want to think about how they might truly be alive as they writhed around the outskirts of the room.

"We've found her, my lord." Behind her, the demon spoke. "He will be pleased."

From the shadows, another figure emerged. The being looked disturbingly human, but she knew better. Ever since the war started, things had not been as they seemed.

He wore no helm, but the dark metal of his armor reflected the luminescent glow of the flames, like a raging fire in the night. Large hands held a massive sword that curved into a perfect, lethal point. She knew he wasn't truly human at all.

"Demitria Collins." His voice held a deadly edge, a shiver working its way through her body at the mention of her name. She hated how they knew her when she knew nothing about them. The skin along her neck itched, and she squirmed uncomfortably at the feeling. "We've been looking for you." Something told her that he wasn't the Dark King that she'd been told about, and another shiver coursed through her at the thought. But with the armor and the blade, she knew he must be important. The demon lord's inky eyes watched, roving up and down, giving her a once over, making sure she was truly who they were looking for. His gaze held no color, and it was like looking into deep pools of the abyss. Empty. Black. Void of *anything*.

Using up whatever courage she had left, Demitria's body straightened. "Why does he want me?" She said, unsure if she was ready for the answer that awaited her.

"Many want you dead." The demon took a step closer.

Demitria instinctively stepped back. She became painfully aware of the others as those dancing shadows closed in around them. She'd been right about them. Her fingers itched to grab the sword she didn't have. The sword Evan had so expertly crafted. Demitria felt that emptiness hollow her. The blade had become like an extension of her own arm.

Her safety, and she'd give just about anything for the weapon right about now. Would pray to whatever gods she could to get it back.

"You've killed for both sides. Maybe you're here to exterminate both races?" Another step.

With each foot forward she took another one backward until the cool brush of taloned claws caressed along her back. She truly didn't know what this demon spoke of. Her only goal had been to survive the fucking onslaught of the planet.

She didn't want to be here. She needed to get out. She just didn't know how.

"I'm sure you're aware of the powers of a human soul."

Demitria wasn't. She had no idea what any of it meant. The demon circled in a taunting manner.

"He wants to break you, then take your soul. Eliminate you from this world."

Kill her. She'd figured that much.

"Who is he?"

"You'll find out in due time." The being waved her off with a toothy grin, each one ended in a pointed tip. "We have been prisoners for far too long. For over a millennia! It is time for a king to reign." At his words, the cavern exploded with sounds. Cheering, as the demons around her roared in agreement. The sound haunting.

Gods, there were so many of them. "He is coming for you. For all of you. Then this forsaken planet will be ours!" The being—demon lord, whatever the fuck he was, threw his hands in the air for effect. More cheering. Eerie voices chanted something she couldn't make out.

She shook her head. "I am worthless. I am nothing." The words weren't a lie. She'd felt them time and time again and knew them to be true. "There is nothing that I can give to help whoever your king is."

"On the contrary, Demitria. Your soul is powerful, and it is the key to setting us free."

"They'll stop you." She blurted out. Kellan and his siblings. They had to. It was their job. Balance. They needed balance.

"Who, my dear girl, is going to stop us?" He was in front of her again, dragging a sharp nail down her neck. The bile rose in her throat as he trailed it down her chest where it stopped, resting just below the collar of her shirt. "That little friend back at your home?" The demon gave her another wicked, toothy smile. Jace...they knew about Jace.

"Get your hands off me." She spat. That spark coming to life as a fire awakened. She'd been complacent long enough.

"And if I don't? Your Horseman isn't here to hear you scream." Demitria's eyes darted around the cavern at the shadowed beings surrounding her. Dozens of eyes in varying shades of crimson staring. Waiting. The one who'd captured her was smiling again, the amusement clear on its face. Even among more of his kind she'd been able to pick him out in an instant. His very being engrained in her mind, no matter how many times she'd tried to forget it.

Kellan wasn't coming, she knew that. Had accepted it when she'd been kicked awake.

"I said get off me." She made a grab for his throat, but he was faster. Much faster. Her back bit into the stone wall feet away as the breath caught in her throat. Darkness exploded around her, vision fading as what little light had been in the cavern slowly dimmed.

"Pathetic." His body hovered over her crumpled figure when she lunged. Willing whatever strength remained into her limbs. Unwilling to give up just yet. No matter what pain riddled her body.

She rolled the two of them to the ground. The demons watched but did not interfere as they grappled. But he was quick to gain the upper hand, pinning her to the rock floor by the weight of his body. She'd caught him off guard and nothing more. It was the only reason she was able to roll him. Demitria knew she wouldn't be able to do it again.

His hand enclosed around her throat, cutting off her air supply. She only had seconds. The demon smiled with a deadly grace, like the act itself had cost him no effort at all.

Ten seconds.

She struggled beneath him. Kicking out, scratching at his arms, but his grip never wavered.

Three seconds.

He smiled again, pulling them both to their feet.

Two.

She could feel her heart slowing with the lack of oxygen. The world around her fading into a thick mist. If this was how she'd go, Demitria would take it. Her arms fell limp to her sides and she closed her eyes, willing it to happen. Willed her body to just *let go*.

"Not today." The air returned in a rush as his grip loosened. Demitria had just enough time to open her eyes as he smashed her head into the rock before darkness overcame her.

Twenty-Three

KELLAN

For days Kellan had been behind, following the tracks of the girl's horse. They were easy enough to follow until they weren't. Having all but disappeared into nothingness the night before.

He shouldn't have even followed her, the logical part of his brain telling him to leave her to die, but the guilt over their conversation had been gnawing away at something he'd pushed into oblivion. Something he hadn't expected to resurface ever again, and that spiked even more curiosity within him. Too many questions, not enough answers.

Idiot.

He didn't know if it was him or her who was the idiot at this point.

They were close, though. He could feel their presence, like a beacon, and he knew they felt it too. His siblings were nearby, and it would only be a matter of time before they crossed paths and reunited. Convenient timing, he supposed.

Kellan continued on, pushing his mount further toward his siblings. He could feel them, their surge of power beating in a steady rhythm as he neared, as if they were calling out to him. His eyes scanned the land-scape. The waste of the expanse before him. So little green, and nothing but charred ash and dirt beneath him. The humans may have done unspeakable things to their planet, but he could say with absolute certainty that this devastation hadn't been from them. The demons had felled cities, destroyed continents...but the moments the angels rebelled against the council? That had been catastrophic. The council had never given full transparency on what exactly happened, but it was enough to know that the angels—Fallen, as his people call them—that did come down made their own play for the planet. Inciting a war not only with the humans, but the demons as well.

Another hour of riding and his siblings appeared on the horizon.

Their mounts thundered toward him. One as dark as the night sky, another as white as the moon. The third had been an agile, dappled gray. Each rider and mount fit together like they'd been carved from the same stone.

Gabriel, Death, atop the powerful black stallion thundering toward him at the front of the group, his golden blond hair a stark contrast against the dark clothing he wore. His scythe held high in the air. Their eldest brother, and the council's trusted contact. Gabriel could give and take life.

Eire, Famine, rode in on the dappled mare, her long dark braid flying wildly behind her. The second eldest of the group. Her power derived from those around her, siphoning their very life essence to fuel her body. She left nothing but husks in her wake.

Kane, Pestilence, sat atop the white stallion. The white blond of his hair matching the beast below him. As his given name suggested, his power brought forth an infectious plague to all who'd become prey to his deadly arrows.

"Brother!" Gabriel was the first to call out. Kellan rode out to meet them, urging his mount into a canter. When they were feet away, he reined the beast in, sliding to a stop before his siblings.

"Where have you been?" Eire eyed him up and down, her gray eyes wild, waiting for an answer. The dark gray of her cloak billowed around her and over the mare as she crossed her arms over her chest, letting the leather reins dangle loose around her mounts neck.

"I found the girl," he said. "I tracked her down to a nearby community a few days west and—" Kellan kept one hand tight around his reins as his mount pawed at the ground before finally settling among the group.

"So, we can return home?" Kane was quick to cut him off, pale blue eyes hopeful as he stared at Kellan. Most times, Kane hated going out more than he did, and could never wait to return home from a mission.

"Let me finish." Silencing him with a hand, Kellan continued. "I found the girl, and am tracking her now."

"So... you lost her is what you're saying." Ever sarcastic Eire. The only one who he loved to no end, despite actively wanting to drive his sword through her chest.

"A technicality." Kellan waved her off. "I'm confident that she is near."

"Gods above, you have no idea what you're doing." Her groan had been loud, exaggerated for effect as she rolled her eyes at him.

He ignored her. Knowing that if he gave in, his temper would only soar. "She is not who the council portrayed her to be. I do not understand the order to eliminate her." There was no skirting around the truth with them. They could not lie to one another.

"So, you're saying that you had her and didn't finish the job when you had the chance?" Eire's voice rose an octave higher, anger swirling through her gray eyes as she threw her hands in the air. "When did you find her?" Her gaze narrowed in on him. Kellan braced for a moment, readying for her reaction.

"The day we got here."

"You had one fucking job, Kellan. One job, and you fucked it up." Eire pointed at him, and he could feel the power within the gesture. "Multiple chances to end her life and send us home, and you couldn't even do that!" She raged; her brows knit together as her lips curled inward. "You'd forgone a different choice every gods damned time. I could care less that you felt the council was wrong. It is not our job to make these decisions. Our job is to obey!"

Kellan could feel his own features mirror hers, his eyes narrowed as the muscles in his jaw went taut. "A human simply cannot cause this much damage. We are sent to restore the balance. Killing her did not seem like the solution." He rebutted. "There are other things at play here." Reining in the anger swirling through him, he ran a hand down his face.

"Like what?" With a hand in the air, Gabriel silenced anything that Eire might have said.

"They sent an Archangel." Kellan sighed, tearing his eyes from his sister to meet the forest green of Gabriels. "Noel."

His siblings exchanged confused glances. "Why did they dispatch us, only to send out one of the Angels of Death?" Gabriel questioned, and Kellan could see the calculating look on his face.

"It just doesn't make sense." Kane was the first to break.

"We were ambushed shortly after the girl and I crossed paths." He explained what happened then. The words the angel had spoken. The threat. How he'd come after not just her, but him as well. He'd been willing to kill off one of the councils prized Horseman over a human. "It doesn't add up. Killing her would not bring balance."

Gabriel gave him a knowing look. At least he agreed with his decision, despite going against a direct order. The one task they had been sent there to complete. He may have completely fucked it up, but he'd had good reason to.

"The girl mentioned a run in with a demon before we crossed paths. It threatened her home, saying someone was after them. After her. It knew who she was, by name." One by one, each of his siblings faces hardened into stone. A look he knew all too well. "They aren't telling us something."

"Are we really supposed to believe the word of a human?" Eire asks, her eyes narrowing in on Kellan once more. She'd fight him with everything in her. It was how they'd always been. Especially since the council had gotten hold of each one of them, stripping away pieces of their soul in punishment.

"After the events I've been through these last few weeks, yes. Everything I've witnessed has led me to believe none of it has been a lie. I was there when a demon came for her. Knew her by name, and threatened her." He challenged. Waiting for her to fight him on it. She didn't, and the relief flooded him. "The council refused my summons, and I don't know why."

"They have never refused a summons before." Eire countered. "They don't ever refuse."

Kellan met her with a hard stare, eyes narrowing as his sister fought him again. "You seem to forget your place, sister." The growl rumbled through him deep within his chest. "You dare to call me a liar? They ignored every single one of my calls, and there were several. Now tell me, why the fuck would they do something like th—"

Thundering hooves pulled them from the conversation and they all turned in that direction. A dark blur on the horizon quickly came into view, each step pounding along the ground as dust kicked up behind its heels. The creature was spooked, Kellan realized, galloping as hard as it could, driven by fear. Kellan recognized the jagged silver scar along his body, knowing an identical one was on the other side hidden from view.

Kellan's body tensed. "Atlas." Demitria would have never left him alone. Not in a millennium. "Something isn't right."

"Is that a—" Eire went quiet as Kellan dismounted from his horse, stepping into the path of the terrified beast. Atlas let out a knowing snort at the sight of him before sliding to a stop meters away, his breathing heavy, like he'd been running for hours, and had nearly exhausted himself. He pranced, unable to keep himself still as if deciding whether or not he still needed to flee.

"Shh." Kellan soothed, hand outstretched toward him. Atlas skirted away from his touch, eyes ablaze in panic.

What in the world has him so spooked?

It was unlike him. From what Kellan had seen, he'd never balked at anything, which was expected of a beast with his blood. Prized for their unflappable demeanor on the battlefield. He tried again, slower this time.

The beast's chest heaved with each breath, but he stood on still legs. Shaking his head, Kellan was able to touch the soft velvety skin of his muzzle. "It's okay," he whispered, running a hand down the slick fur of his sweat coated neck. Atlas heaved another heavy sigh. Safe. He was safe. Grabbing hold of the reins that hung dangerously low to the ground, he led the horse back toward his siblings.

"Why is a pterippus grounded?" Gabriel asked. Kellan was almost certain of the beast's heritage, despite the many questions surrounding him, but Gabriel had confirmed his suspicions.

"He belongs to the girl." Kellan explained. "Something is wrong. She would never let him loose beyond the walls."

"Why does a human have a pterippus?" Eire roared, feeling the surge of power in her words as it all but begged to release. They shared a homeland. Or rather, they had before this one was grounded. Yet another question that he didn't have an answer to, and that frustrated him.

"That's beside the point." He growled back. "Him being out here means that she's in danger."

"Leave her be!" Eire challenged, pinning him with a stare. "Let whatever is out there finish the job for you." Her gray eyes as dark and cold as a swirling storm. "Balance, brother! It's why we're here!"

"I've already made my thoughts on the matter clear. I am leaving, whether you like it or not." Kellan didn't know what he was thinking as he swung his body into Atlas's saddle. Any other time, he would have been thrilled to be on the back of one of these beasts. He would never care to admit it, especially to his current company, but it had been a dream of his to soar through the sky on one of them. Even just once in his lifetime. But the beasts were usually reserved for the higher-ranking Archangels working for the council, and for obvious reasons, they did not get along due to the *impurity* running through his blood. He *hated* the Archangels.

"She's made you soft." Eire balked, the surprise on her face clear as she sat back in her saddle.

"Life debts are funny things." He muttered, nudging the horse away. He didn't owe anyone a life debt, or had he? When she had brought him home for help that should have been the end of it all, yet he couldn't shake the compulsion to move forward. *Answers*, he reminded himself. He was doing this to get his answers. The others may not have been on the same page as him regarding the council, but he didn't believe a word they said. Not after years of questionable assignments, that looking back now, didn't make sense to him. Of the doubt that had slowly festered with each order to kill. Demitria had been the catalyst to the spiraling questions that surrounded him.

"Help me find her." Whispering to the horse, Kellan loosened his reins.

As if in answer, Atlas let out a loud snort before exploding on powerful legs and leaving Kellan's siblings in their wake. He could have smiled as the horse soared over the ground. Atlas may not have wings, but he truly felt like he was flying.

Kellan stole a glance behind him as he buried his hands in the dark strands of the horse's mane, feeling the coarse hair beneath his fingers. Already nothing more than spots behind him, his siblings kicked up after him in pursuit.

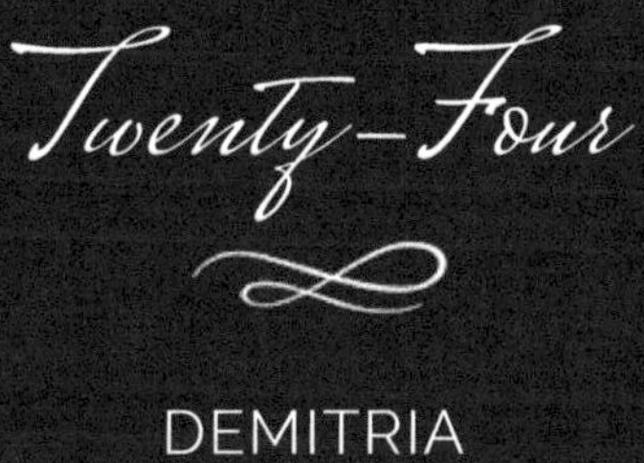

Twenty-Four

DEMITRIA

Pain.

So much pain. Searing through her entire body like she was burning from the inside out. Demitria awoke screaming. The blood pooled around the blade plunged into her abdomen, trickling down her sides and onto the smooth rock below her. Warm. Wet. Sticking her clothes to her body.

The demon lord stood over her, his depthless eyes meeting hers for a short moment. Grinning a wicked, toothy smile, he plunged it deeper. Feeling as the blade tore through muscle. Another scream ripped through her as tears welled in her eyes. Throat hoarse. Dry. Everything ached.

"You've been out for a day." He purred. "I told you we weren't finished yet." An entire day? She didn't want to think about what could have been done to her in that time. She tried to move her body, even an inch, on the stone beneath her, but everything burned.

"What do you want from me?" Demitria's body trembled, her voice shaky from the pain coursing through her as a wave of nausea took hold.

"I'm sure Reim has mentioned the need for the human soul," he said. The creature had a name. Reim. *Reim* had eaten her parents. She wished she could give Kellan his name in hopes he would kill the demon in a fit of rage. For revenge after the blow he'd been dealt, and evading them since. Demitria committed the name to memory, for whatever purpose it served. She didn't care who killed him at this point. She just wanted the creature dead.

"We're harvesting souls for the King. Yours in particular is said to hold great power." His inky eyes nearly gleamed as he walked around her, trailing a finger along her arms as he did. Giddy, she could see it in his face, hear it in the lilt of his voice. "And once I take yours, my subjects are free to take whatever they wish." The Demon Lord smiled again, and she shivered, that itch along her neck returning for a fleeting moment. "Reim likes the human heart. Especially when it's still beating."

Demitria couldn't help the gasp that escaped her at the mention of the creature. He was going to eat her, just as he had her parents. It took everything out of her to fight back the nausea rising in her throat. *It would have all been for nothing.*

"Tell me, girl," Taking a step back, he walked a slow circle around the rock slab she had been draped over once more. "Do you know the difference between a soul that is broken and one that is whole?"

No words left her mouth. She didn't have an answer to any of the questions he asked her. Demitria fought back the whimper threatening to spill from her lips. Focusing on the rise and fall of her chest, she kept her breathing slow. The pain coursed through her from her fingers to her toes. She pushed away the thought of the knife and the warmth of her own blood as it dripped from her body.

When she still didn't answer him, he continued, "The King feeds on souls. It is the base of his power. But a broken soul? They are near magical. The sheer power that radiates from them is like nothing you've ever seen before. Through you, he will conquer this world."

Demitria didn't understand any of it. Human souls, Demon Lords. Hell, fucking Horsemen of the Apocalypse. She didn't get any of this damned mess.

The Demon Lord took another step back, eyes zeroing on her face. He stood tall behind the rock slab, shoulders pitched back as he held his arms wide and shouted, "She's all yours, boys!" Cold fear rushed through her as the darkness around the room morphed into something else entirely.

From out of the shadows stepped eight creatures, scarily similar to Reim. Each one wore a look of hunger as they watched her, as if she was nothing more than a delicacy.

I am exactly that.

Reim was on her first, his claws digging into her skin as he looked her over, as if deciding which part he would eat first. The others waited for him to make his move. He must have outranked them all. Another scream tore through her as his serrated teeth sank in just below her collar bone, tearing through her flesh with ease. His clawed fingers dug into the wound, prying it apart as flesh separated from bone. Demitria's screams never stopped. She could feel those toxins coursing through her, the blood in her veins sluggish as it spread. In moments, the others joined in, biting into her flesh. Her wrists, legs, stomach. Everywhere.

She was being eaten alive.

"The heart is mine!" Reim roared. The absolute glee in his voice echoed off the walls around them.

There wasn't one inch of her skin that didn't feel like she had been doused in a sea of endless flames. Demitria didn't know how much more she could take.

KELLAN

It was the screams that alerted him first.

The sheer agony echoed, erupting from the dark cavern ahead. If it had been anyone else, they wouldn't have heard her. But with his heightened senses it felt as if he was standing right there. Even from far below the ground, he heard her. Atlas visibly tensed beneath him, like he could hear them too. Knowing exactly who they'd come from. Sensing her fear as she endured gods knew what.

The air stunk like them. Rotting. Burning. Demons had telltale signs if you knew what you were looking at. Smell was one of the biggest ones.

Kellan urged the horse faster, Atlas obeyed before he'd even touched him. Exploding toward the entrance where he slid to a stop. Kellan was running the moment his feet hit the ground, blade drawn. Poised. Ready for battle. Waiting for the bloodshed that he knew lay ahead.

"Where are you going?" Eire shouted angrily, but she was on his heels anyway. They all were at the scent. *The sounds.* Kellan didn't answer her. "Let them finish the job that you couldn't!"

He should have listened to her and should have let them have her nearly two weeks ago, but he couldn't bring himself to do it. Then she'd tried to save him, a being sent to kill her, and she'd still shown him kindness. Humanity. Then the rooftop. Hearing the story of her parents. The hardships she'd faced—

His questions that still needed answers.

Kellan couldn't let the girl die.

He didn't know how to feel about his decision. If he hated himself for letting things get so out of hand.

His feet propelled him forward. Faster as he raced into the darkness. Black all around him, the only sounds the pounding of their footsteps as they ran, one after the other. And her screaming. That was the loudest as they ran down the tunnel on agile steps.

They emerged into the fire-lit room as one. Shock. Disgust. Worry. A range of emotions took hold. Beside him, even Eire's breath hitched at the horrific sight before them. Her body, screaming and limp against the rock. The blood. *Fuck.*

His fingers clenched around the pommel of his blade, so tight he knew his knuckles were white as everything ignited within.

Eire's arrow hit her mark before he even managed another step. With his sword swinging, Kellan charged, the edge of his blade ricocheting from demon to demon as he made his way toward Demetria.

Twenty-Six

DEMITRIA

A rush of air whooshed past her cheek and suddenly, Reim was toppling over. Hands grasping at its throat as an arrow protruded from it. Scurrying into the shadows, he disappeared. Another flew, embedding itself into the forehead of another demon. She could just make out the small metal ring around each arrow, a crest carved into the center. Marking each one for who it belonged to.

A running horse.

Horsemen.

Her vision was starting to narrow, blurring more and more at the edges. Darkness seeped in. She willed it to come. Reveling in the feeling as it began to sweep over her.

A cloak. *Red*. Like a single flower blooming in the dead of night.

His cloak.

Demitria honed in on it, trying to keep her focus as the haze of color spun toward her. Blinking as if it'd help. Red. It was all she saw. Nothing more than a blur as it danced gracefully around the shadows, closer and closer before it was nearly in reach.

"Are you alright?" Kellan. The burning had stopped and she'd grown numb. His large body loomed over her as a gurgled scream echoed off the walls from somewhere in the cavern.

A new wave of tears swept over her. Kellan. She didn't care if he saw her cry. Not after this.

Demitria lifted heavy arms toward him, begging, reaching like a child needing to be coddled. She didn't care. Weak and shaking, her limbs looked pale white, inky veins snaking along her skin. His sword clattered to the ground in a heavy thud, and she slowly flinched at its intensity, the movement feeling dragged out. Shoving the hood of the cloak from his head, he picked up her bloodied body in his arms.

Kellan.

"I'm sorry we didn't get here sooner." Something woodsy and sweet wafted through her senses, triggering memories of a time long gone, but she grabbed onto it like a lifeline.

More tears. Like a gushing river. Instinctively fastening her fingers into the material at his chest, unwilling to let go

"You came." Demitria tightened her grip around him. She wanted to be held by him, something to anchor her. "There was nothing I could do." Weak. She was so weak, and her voice was no different.

"I found Atlas and knew something wasn't right." He said, "You should have never left without me." Atlas was safe? A new wave of relief rushed through her at the news. Atlas had been found safe... unharmed. Her lips tugged up in a pathetic excuse for a smile, and her body shuddered with the effort it took.

"Kellan!" A voice thundered from behind them, followed by a grunt. "You'll want to hear this."

Demitria didn't recognize the voice.

Kellan ignored them. "Why did you run? Why did you leave?" He was angry with her, and rightfully so. She had disobeyed his order and fled the community.

"I couldn't put them in danger." She strained against his hold as another wave of pain surged through her, squeezing her eyes shut as each breath burned. "I-I wanted answers, and I thought leaving was the only..."

"KELLAN!" That same voice shouted, louder, breaking her from the conversation. She couldn't see the beings over his large frame. Was too weak to try as her arms fell limp at her sides. Each breath throbbing, carving down her throat as if she swallowed a mouthful of glass.

"What the hell is the matter with him?" They scoffed. Female this time. "He took us in here, Gabriel. Now he's abandoned his post—again. The demon's fate falls in your hands."

Demon? Had Reim not gotten away? Gods, she hoped they were able to catch him. Hoped they would slaughter him where he stood, and get revenge for everything the creature had done. For every person he'd harmed and killed. Demitria was never one for needless violence, but she hoped he suffered endlessly. She tried to utter his name. To tell him the creature that had maimed her, but nothing moved past her lips save for another shallow breath that burned her throat. Sharp and excruciating as it moved.

"The Four Horsemen." The demon lord spat, laughing as he did so, despite the strain in his voice. Like he'd been talking through a hold. "To what do I owe the honor of your presence?"

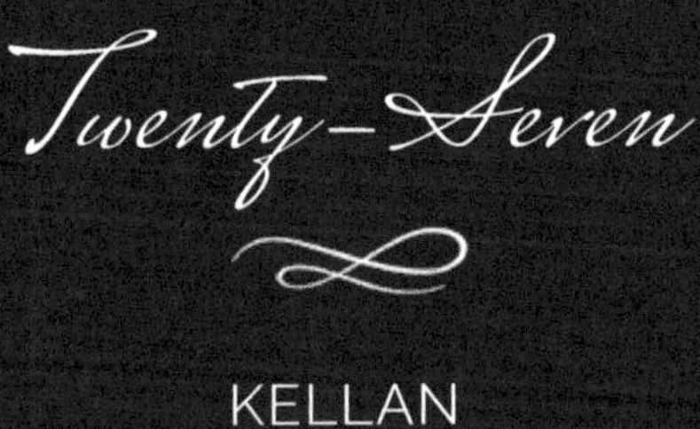

KELLAN

"The decision is mine." Kellan stepped away from the girl after gently setting her back down on the stone slab. "I will decide his fate. He will pay for what he's done." That familiar rage welled within. Burning a hole through him, igniting his blood. His body begged for the kill. To feel the flesh beneath the tips of his fingers as he ripped the demon to pieces. To hear the sound of his sword as it cleaved through the creature's bones, one by one.

His gaze lingered on the girl before him for a short moment, and he knew he had to tread carefully to keep himself in check. Before he could change his mind, Kellan turned, stalking toward the demon being restrained by his brother.

"We're supposed to be restoring the balance, not killing off more!" Gabriel's words were usually final, whether they liked it or not. "WAR!" The putrid being struggled beneath his brother's grasp, but Death didn't budge, his weapon held firm against the demon's throat.

From the corner of his eye, Kellan watched as the power behind his brother's voice made the girl flinch. He ignored him still. Eyes deadly calm as he honed in on his target, willing the room around him to disappear. He didn't recognize the Demon Lord, but loathed him all the same. Curling his lips inward, the male snarled at him, baring a set of deadly fangs.

"What did you have planned for her?" He asked, hand resting dangerously atop the pommel of his sword as he strode closer.

"Why do you care, Horseman? She on your side?" The demon shifted his weight uneasily, but the blade of Gabriel's scythe didn't get any further away from his flesh. Kellan watched as a thin line of dark blood dribbled from his unnaturally pale throat. Tracking it as it splattered against the rock at his feet.

"I am the one asking questions." The growl that erupted was near animalistic, and he felt it rumble through his chest. *Dial it down.*

"Are you abandoning your council? Are the Horsemen making a play for Earth?"

Kellan wanted to wipe that filthy smirk from his face. To cut him down limb from limb, but he refrained. Barely.

"Answer me, or your head will roll."

With a sigh that weighed heavily in annoyance, he spoke. "The King is returning to Earth." The demon stopped his struggles, accepting the deadly weapon before him.

Every bone in Kellan's body froze at the name. The rage he'd been trying to keep in check nearly ready to explode as it hit a new high. "And who are you to hold this knowledge?" He said through clenched teeth.

"Aaron, Lord of the shadow demons." The male stood taller, stepping further into Gabriel's scythe. "He's been looking for the girl, and I was to deliver her to him."

Kellan brought his gaze up to Gabriel, the knowing look mirroring his own before dragging his away, meeting the piercing eyes of Eire and Kane. Uneasy. Weary. If that was true, none of what to follow was good.

"We have hidden in the shadows for far too long. It is our time to reign." The demon laughed in a maniacal way, and it echoed throughout the cavern. "You're all in danger. He's already here."

Fuck.

Fuck. Fuck. FUCK.

There was something so much bigger going on. Bigger than they were told. The council had withheld vital information from them.

Demitria wasn't the enemy they had been led to believe, because there was no way the council didn't know about *him*.

"What does he want with her?" Kellan demanded, taking a step closer as his boots crunched something along the floor. He didn't care to look.

The demon glanced behind Kellan before looking back at him. "Her soul. I was to break it before delivering her soul." Gabriel tightened his grip on the scythe, pressing deeper into the demon lord's neck. More blood dripped from the wound, pooling along the floor beneath him.

"They were eating her alive! That is no way to break a human soul!" The anger. He was going to explode. Red. So much red. He couldn't see anything but red as his power surged within him, begging to break free. He could barely contain it, writhing through his veins, along his arms in dark tendrils.

"Do you *feel* something for this girl?" The demon lord laughed, spitting at his feet. "How disgusting. How... interesting."

He'd done it. Had pushed him so far over the edge Kellan had lost the ability to control his own body. Triggering the carnal disease that had taken over so many times before as that darkness within him broke free.

"Capturing her was the biggest fucking mistake you ever made." Calm, deadly cool.

The demon's head rolled feet away, blade heavy on the rock where it rested after his swing. It cut through flesh as easily as the wind tossed a leaf.

The sharp intake of air brought Kellan back. The cavern came into focus. His siblings, each and every one of them staring at him. No, at something behind him.

Demitria had slumped over, face pale. The blood pooling in her clothing, staining everything a dark crimson as it flowed. Inky veins marred her face. Every inch of her.

Shit.

Kellan was beside her in a heartbeat, his body moving on its own accord. So much blood. Too much blood for a human. He took everything in. The gaping wounds that littered her body. The darkening of her veins as the poison coursed through her system. "You need to help her!" He faced his kin, meeting each of their eyes. Pleading. "Please brother, I beg of you."

"It's one human girl, Kellan." Gabriel spoke quietly. "I can give life and I can take life, but I can only heal minor injuries."

"Gabriel, please! You are the eldest and strongest of us all. Heal her." He would get to his knees and beg if he had to. She would not die. Not on his watch. He picked the girl's slumped figure up from the rock, cradling her to his chest as he waited for his brother.

Gabriel fluttered toward them, graceful in his strides. Standing over Kellan as he cradled the girl in his arms. "I don't know if this will work." With a sigh Gabriel placed his hands above the most gruesome wound above her heart. His eyes closed as he concentrated, and Kellan knew what came next. He watched on as Gabriel commanded his power to leave his body and willed it into Demitria's.

Her eyes widened as she took in a sharp intake of breath. Kellan knew the pain she was in, feeling the power weaving its way through her body as her skin began to reattach, growing closed over the wounds. He'd felt the burn of Gabriel's power more times than he could count, and it never got easier. Demitria ground her teeth together, burying her head in his chest, fists clenched tight as she fought the scream he was sure threatened to emerge.

Gabriel opened his eyes and looked down at her, her breathing rapid as she lay there. "I never said it would be painless." He took a step back. When Kellan was sure she was stable, he set her back down.

"Thank you." She stared up at him with wide eyes. Her body was covered in blood, clothes torn, but she was... healed. "My name is Demitria Collins. I am indebted to you for saving my life. All of you." She met the eyes of each and every one of the Horsemen, driving the words home.

"You have obviously met my brother." Gabriel was the first to speak. "My name is Gabriel, but your people know me as Death. I am the eldest of the Horsemen. These two are my other siblings." He motioned toward them with a hand before grabbing the scythe he'd leaned against the wall, fitting it into the leather at his back.

Eire was leaning against the cavern wall, arms crossed tightly over her chest. "Eire." She mumbled, flipping a long black braid over her shoulder. "I am the second eldest, Famine." She stared at Demitria with questioning eyes. Kane walked straight over to them, extending out his hand as he smiled. "The name's Kane." He grinned. "I am the Horseman Pestilence. Now how in the world do you know our baby brother?" He said the word 'baby brother' in a near mocking tone, and Kellan could have killed him for it. He'd been dealing with his shit for over a millennium, and it never got easier. He knew they'd ask questions. His only problem? He wouldn't have the answers to any of them.

"He-He saved my life." She looked down at her hands, anxious at the attention as her fingers fumbled with the hem of her shirt.

"And she saved mine, a feat no other soul in existence has dared aside from you." Kellan didn't dare to meet the questioning eyes of his siblings. Refused to see the looks on each of their faces. "Why don't we settle for the night? The demons won't be back. We could all use a rest."

"Is no one going to talk about what just happened?" Eire questioned, her hands planting along her leather-clad hips as stormy gray eyes shot around the room between Gabriel and Kane.

"No, we're not." Kellan huffed, running a hand through his hair. He stared at them a moment later. At the blood that still coated them, and he'd seemingly streaked through his hair. Her blood. Any being would have been revulsed at the thought, but he'd seen so much bloodshed that even the thought of it didn't seem to faze him.

"What you asked of him goes against everything we were sent here to do." Eire took a step toward him, and he couldn't help the audible groan that left his lips.

"They were wrong." They'd all been through this. The claims made by the Demon Lord had proved it. The council kept tabs on the Dark King, and there was no way in hell they weren't aware of his presence here.

"You should have let them k—"

"Silence!" Gabriel shouted, cutting Eire off before she could finish as he stood between them. "I will not hear any more of this tonight." His nostrils flared, his jaw clenched tight.

Kellan turned from his siblings, eyeing the girl behind him. She hadn't moved from the rock slab, but watched the exchange between his siblings curiously, her full lips turned in a frown.

"Kellan is right. We'll rest for the night, convene in the morning." Finally, Gabriel sighed. "Someone should take first watch. I have some things to take care of." He watched as his brother disappeared through the mouth of the tunnel, and he knew exactly what Gabriel was doing. He already knew the council wouldn't answer Gabriel's summons.

"I'll do it." Flipping her braid over her shoulder, Eire followed behind their eldest sibling. "Don't bother changing me out."

Kellan watched her leave for a moment before turning away, the sigh heavy on his lips. He met Kane's icy stare and could see the questions in his pale blue eyes. He turned away from him, too.

Spotting the discarded dark cloak on the floor, Kellan swiped it up, setting it down on the cool stone along the wall, far away from the rock slab where she'd been brutalized. It was the one clothing item that hadn't been torn during the attack. He helped her off the slab, and she walked on shaking legs toward it before settling her back against the wall.

"I'm going to be okay." She whispered as he took a seat beside her.

She still looked weak, but the color had returned to her fair cheeks, now tinged with a hue of soft pink. Something akin to relief washed through him as the dark veins were slowly dissipating into nothing.

"No thanks to you... again." The chuckle left her lips as she rested a head on his shoulder, closing her eyes. Her body relaxed against his. Every bone in his body froze at the closeness, his body going ramrod straight. The willingness to lean against him. Kellan bit his tongue to suppress the shudder at the foreign feeling. "Why do you do it? Why do you keep helping me when everyone else wants me dead. I don't understand it."

Well shit...

"I don't know what it is about you." Kellan stared at the girl resting easily beside him as he felt the hint of a smile slowly creep its way across his face. "I can't explain it. What it is that you're doing to me." His words left him in a rushed whisper, the truths he so easily gave, sent a wave of shock throughout his body. "But I—" He didn't have a chance to continue as Demitria reached a tired hand toward him, soft on his face as she caressed his cheek. Those piercing green-gold eyes pinning him to the stone as she stared at him.

"Despite what others think, you're good, Kellan." She smiled up at him. Genuine. *Kind.*

He had no words. No words to describe the emotions within, like a bomb had ignited, exploding and tearing him open for the entire world to see.

Twenty-Eight

DEMITRIA

Demitria stretched her sore limbs out before her, the stone floor she'd slept on the night before doing little to ease the pain from her body. For the first time in gods knew how long, she'd slept the entirety of the night, dead to the world around her. Everywhere hurt, but it was the last thing on her mind. The searing pain, as if her skin had been ripped from her bones, had disappeared, only to be replaced with a relentless ache that wouldn't subside. Easier than the later, but annoying enough as it was. Demitria was grateful to be alive. Grateful to the beings that she'd hated with every fiber of her body. Because she'd hated every single one of them. Angel, demon, Horsemen... she didn't care that she'd yet to meet them. It made no difference to her, at least not then. Had it changed? Had she changed?

Then there was Kellan.

War, as he'd affectionately been dubbed by her own kind a lifetime ago. From another world entirely. Nephilim. Chaos incarnate, and she'd touched him in a way that should have sent her reeling. His skin had been warm against her palm when she'd held it there, like an inferno ready to consume her. And when he hadn't moved away from her touch? She didn't really know what had possessed her to let herself get that close. After the violence she'd endured, she needed something to ground her. A... gentle connection, of sorts, and Kellan had provided that and more. She couldn't even begin to comprehend the way he'd looked at her as she'd practically caressed his face. It just made things that much more complicated between them. Made everything more complicated than it needed to be. They were so different. Yet that night on the roof... that connection they'd somehow formed without either of their consent. She couldn't forget it.

Incessant yelling echoing throughout the cavern pulled her from her thoughts. Eire and Kellan were arguing. *About her.* About the entire gods damned war that they apparently now had to deal with.

"Have you lost your damn mind?" Eire shouted at him, anger dripping from her every word as she tossed her arms in the air in an animated gesture.

Kellan gazed at his sister, brows raised as his face contorted into what Demitria could only call confusion, absolutely dumbfounded at the words that had left the other Horseman's mouth.

"There is no place for a human with us!" Eire pointed at her for a moment, ignoring or quite possibly not even seeing the fact she was wide awake.

"You do not make the rules."

Demitria could see the struggle on his face as Kellan tightened his jaw, his fingers clenching and unclenching at his sides. The deadly calm he tried to paint on.

"And neither do you." Eire crossed her arms over her chest, face tight as she fixed her brother in a menacing glare. Kellan opened his mouth to say something but was quickly cut off as the eldest Horseman interjected.

"ENOUGH!" The immense power behind Gabriel's bellow ran a shudder through Demitria's body, unable to suppress the movement. "Both of you." Gabriel looked between the two warring siblings. "Childishness doesn't become either of you."

She should have no part in this conversation but she joined them anyway. "I can't go back." She'd fight tooth and nail to get her point across. She stood on shaking legs, her body still feeling weak from the night before, but she forced herself to walk toward them and stand beside Kellan. "Whoever this asshole is, he's after me. And if I go back, that's a death sentence not just for myself, but for my people too." Her tone rose as she met each of their eyes. Kellan's. Eire's. Gabriel's, then she roamed back to Kellan once more, giving him a sheepish smile before continuing. "I will not go back."

"This *asshole* is the entire damn reason you stupid little humans are in this mess." Eire sneered, as if Demitria should have known who the Dark King was.

Should she have? She didn't have a clue about their world, or the beings in it. Their hierarchy—she didn't know any of it. None of her kind did.

She didn't like Eire, and the feelings appeared to be mutual. The Horseman looked at her as if she'd kill her at any given moment and the condescending tone of Eire's voice each time she spoke couldn't be misinterpreted. If given the chance, Demitria really did think she would end her life.

"We have done nothing to you or your people." In a stupid fit of rage, she'd gone toe to toe with her as she ignored the burning in her limbs. Despite her brain screaming at her, telling her how much of a fucking idiot she was being, she did it anyway. Stood mere inches away from Eire. Gods, she must be close to a foot taller than her. *Idiot.* "And I will not be bullied by some insecure Horseman who acts as if I am beneath her."

The cool tip of a blade poked into the soft skin at her throat. Demitria felt a thin line of blood as it slowly trickled down her collar, disappearing into the fabric of her torn shirt. Eire's gray eyes were wild as she stared her down, like a rabid wolf ready for the killing blow.

"You little bitch." She snarled, but Demitria refused to back down as she stepped closer, into the dagger as the cold metal stung her flesh.

Before any more damage could be done, a strong, muscled arm ripped her body from its position, heaving her backward as her legs nearly gave out at the motion. Kellan's eyes were blazing. Dark as he stared between his sister and Demitria, his grip firm on her forearm. Gabriel now holding the latter by her shoulder in a firm grasp. Eire clawed at him, fighting to break free to no avail.

"You may match her in temper, but not in power. It would not end well." Kellan spoke, voice low in Demitria's ear. She shouldn't have shivered at the warmth of his breath, but she couldn't help the involuntary movement.

"I don't care. She needs to understand that I cannot go back." She turned hard eyes on him. Of everyone here, he needed to understand. He had to. "They are after me for a reason, Kellan. And if you send me back, it'll be the end of my home. You said that yourself. I can't let the entire community fall because of me. I want answers just as much as you do." Azure eyes softened at her words, but his grip on her arm never wavered.

"We need to look into the claims that were made." Gabriel intervened. "The Dark King is a bigger matter than what we were led to believe, and we need to investigate immediately." He spoke, finally letting go of a—somewhat—calmed Eire. She wasn't thrashing around anymore, and Demitria figured that was as calm as the Horseman would get. Yet the female still looked as if she'd kill her at any given moment.

"I want to help. He was after me."

"Do not make this about you, human." Eire spat at her feet, the saliva splashing on the top of her leather boots, and it took everything in her to not react. "Having you around would be nothing but a nuisance."

"Even I don't feel safe about that." Kellan sighed. "You don't know the things he's capable of. Even with us all there, I can't guarantee your safety." He gave her a knowing look as if there was more to the story. One that he wasn't willing to share. "But I understand your fear of going back. You have every right to feel that, but at least we know what we're up against, and can deal with it accordingly." Slowly, Kellan dropped his hand from around her arm.

Holding up a hand, Gabriel continued. "Which is precisely why we don't have the time for this. He is a bigger threat than we've deemed you to be. We don't have the luxury of waiting around for the orders to act on this. We will return you to your people, and we will ride out immediately."

"They didn't answer?" Kane finally broke. He'd been standing with them, quiet as they spoke, digesting the information just as she was, she was sure.

"I'm not going ba—"

"My word is final!" Gabriel roared, "I will not have you hindering any part of this investigation. Whether you are being targeted or not, that is not our concern." His dark cloak swished just above the ground as he strode toward where she and Kellan stood. Gabriel was terrifying in those moments, and looked every bit like the Death she had pictured. His dark, forest-green eyes narrowed into a hard stare as he reached them in mere steps. "You will not even have a world to call home if he succeeds, let alone your community." Gabriel pointed a finger at her, so close it nearly struck her chest.

Demitria willed herself not to cry. Begged every single muscle in her body to cooperate with her to keep the tears at bay. But she couldn't shake the inevitable feeling. Her people would die because of this. Because or.

Within an hour they were riding out. The rift between Kellan and his siblings now painfully obvious as they rode ahead of the both of them. She hadn't heard them utter a word since leaving the cavern, and had a growing suspicion that he'd been given the cold shoulder. It had been her fault, she realized. Broken, because of her. Something she seemed to be good at, it seemed. Her actions the other night had been damning enough when she'd reached for him, practically begging him to hold her. Him fighting for her today had all but sealed the deal.

Gods, what was she thinking.

She shouldn't have liked the way he'd looked at her last night. The thought foreign...forbidden, like it should never have crossed her mind. But the softness in his gaze had just—

"Thank you. For rescuing me, and taking Atlas in." Demitria looked down at her hands, focusing in on the detail of the leather reins in her fingers. She was so sure that she would never see him again. "I don't know what I would have done if something had happened to him."

"I know how much he means to you." Reaching over, Kellan rested a warm hand on her arm. She was quick to move away from his touch. Demitria didn't regret the softness that had fallen over her last night, not one bit. And she'd meant what she said to him. Kellan was *good,* and the thought of feeling that comfort scared her.

His face fell at her blatant rejection. He was probably so confused after last night. Hell, she'd all but fallen asleep in his lap! How quickly it had all changed. Gods, she hated it. Hated always letting people down. Demitria hadn't wanted to move away from any part of him last night, quite the opposite in fact, yet here she was, shying away from his touch like a fucking idiot. "Thank you." Voice no more than a whisper, but she knew he heard her clearly.

They rode in silence for another hour. Demitria focused on the sound of Atlas's relaxed breathing and the thud of his hooves along the hard, dirt ground. The rhythmic sound soothing in a way. Freeing, despite the dread pooling in her stomach as they journeyed back across the barren land toward her home.

Gabriel slowed his horse down beside her own. Kellan shot him a warning look, but his brother was quick to wave it off. "I meant to give you this earlier." Lightly tugging on her reins, Atlas came to a halt beside him. Atlas was tall, but Gabriel's horse seemed to tower over them as he pulled up beside her. Demitria marveled at the magnificent beast. The dark, ebony coat gleaming under the sun, almost as if he sparkled in the light. Muscles rippled under the faintest touch from his rider. Powerful, and she couldn't help but stare in awe at the creature. Gabriel unbuckled the sheath attached to the horn of his saddle, holding it out before her. The sword's familiar pommel glistened in the bright afternoon sun.

"You found it!" She had never been so happy at the sight of a weapon. Demitria pulled it free of its sheath, marveling at the blade, feeling it in her hands once more, like an extension of her own arm. She swung it with ease, unable to hide the growing smile on her lips.

"You have a skilled weapons master in your town. It is a beautiful blade." He nodded. She didn't know why, but his approval meant something. *It shouldn't have.*

She didn't even know why he'd given her the blade back. She had been their one assignment, and here they were, arming her once more. Much like she'd done for Kellan back in Solis. An offering, then. "Thank you." Demitria bowed her head. "All of you." With a tip of his own head, Gabriel nudged his horse on. Quickly falling into place beside Eire as they soundlessly moved on.

Right.

The landscape never changed. Everything around them looked the same. The rocky earth held nothing of desire, not anymore. She hoped the horsemen knew where they were headed. After the ambush she'd lost all her bearings. Couldn't decipher what direction the demon had even taken her in. It had been dark, her mind dazed. She couldn't help but shudder at the thought. Knowing he'd gotten away. *Again.*

Demitria found her eyes roaming to the Horseman beside her, his mount no more than an arms-length away. She studied him. The planes of his face, the broad shoulders and muscular chest. The azure eyes that had softened far too much in the short weeks he'd been around.

When Kellan caught her staring, she quickly dragged her gaze away. Focusing on *anything* but the male beside her. Her grip tightened around the supple reins in her hands. She needed to get ahold of herself, but her eyes drifted back anyway. Watching. Curious.

They continued on for hours on end, never stopping once. The sky turned dark as they pushed on, and she fought to keep her body awake, the pull of sleep an irresistible tug at the corners of her mind. It rippled with thoughts of the community. How would they even react? It hadn't gone well when she'd shown up with a dying—or so she thought anyway— Horseman. Now she was showing up with four, very much alive and at full power. They'd kill her. They'd try and kill all of them, actually. She probably wouldn't even make it to the gates. One well-placed arrow would have her dead before she'd even hit the cool earth below. The others would fare fine, but her people would pay dearly if they attacked. Kellan may have given his word, but she knew his siblings wouldn't just stand there if they were attacked. As much as she hated to admit it, she wouldn't expect them to, either.

Demitria looked at the faces that surrounded her. Eire. The lone female Horseman was stripped of all emotion. Or was that something else on her face? Anger? Hatred? She knew the female loathed her with her entire being. She'd made that point perfectly clear. Demitria couldn't help pondering the cause of it all. The incessant hate for humans. For the world. What had been done to her to cement those ridiculous notions in her head?

As if sensing her prying gaze, Eire hastily turned around in her saddle. She scowled down at her, her gray eyes radiating with such coldness, watching her as a lion would watch its prey before launching itself full force, unleashing that devastating blow. The scrutinizing look had her blood running thin, and Demitria tried her best not to stare, focusing on their never-ending surroundings instead.

"Don't pay her any mind." A soft voice came from behind. She turned to look at the second youngest Horseman that had ridden up beside her. He'd been virtually silent, or maybe she'd just been too lost in her own thoughts to realize. "She's brooding and cold, but wouldn't lay a hand on you." Somehow, Demitria doubted that. She couldn't shake the threat in Eire's eyes. Demitria could only nod. His reassurance had done absolutely nothing to ease her reeling mind. Telling Kellan was out of the question. They hadn't spoken a word to each other since she'd shied away from him. Starting another rift between the siblings wasn't something she wanted to be a part of either. It would be better if she took a step back. Better for the both of them. For *her*. She was trying so hard to deny him. Had fought whatever this connection was with all her will. She was failing. Could feel her mental blocks weakening with each passing glance. She hated it. Tried so hard to hate him.

Wanted to, but she couldn't.

"Are you tired?" Kane was still beside her. How easily she'd fallen prey to her mind once more that the entire world around her had ceased to exist.

"We can keep going." She refused to meet his gaze, despite her body still weak from the capture. An array of bruises painted her fingers in hues of purples and blues. The tear in her lip mostly mended, but still hurt. Gabriel had only mended the largest of her injuries. The life threatening, but the rest remained. A stark reminder on how truly fragile life was.

"Are you just saying that to not be a burden?" He'd seen through her.

Her presence felt like a burden among the Horsemen. She was slowing them down. They had a duty to perform, and returning her to the community—even though she didn't want to go—was keeping them from that. Demitria couldn't seem to keep herself out of trouble. How low they all must think of her.

"Let's call it a night." Kellan had been silent for hours now but he must have seen the tiredness in her face. She'd never admit it. Especially not to them. "The horses could use the rest." Her eyes made their way to his, seeing nothing but that gentle look. The gesture was enough. His boots hit the ground first, swiftly carrying himself to where she still sat atop Atlas. Demitria didn't reject his help to dismount as every muscle in her legs fought to hold her upright. And when his large hands wrapped around her, plucking her from the saddle with ease, she all but melted at their warmth.

Up ahead, the other two carried on a few more paces before finally coming to a stop. Eire mumbled something to her brother, but Demitria was too far to hear. Kellan's face didn't give any inclination on what had been said, either.

"How are you feeling?" He asked.

"Fine." She lied. Looking anywhere but his face, but he knew.

"No one else can hear you. They're all too busy arguing over who'll take the first watch." She let her gaze drift in their direction, toward Eire who seemed to be having an animated conversation with Gabriel before mounting once more and riding out of sight.

Kellan led her toward a small fire that Kane had promptly started upon dismounting. The warmth was a welcoming change for her body. Normally, she would have never entertained the idea of a fire out in the open like this, but with the Four Horsemen around it, she figured nothing would dare set foot within a ten-mile radius of them, unless they had some fucked-up death wish.

"Have I done something?" The plea in his voice had hit her far harder than it should have.

"I don't know how I feel anymore." She didn't. Toward him? His siblings? She just didn't know. "You've done nothing wrong." The sigh that left her lips was enough. "You've done everything right. That's the problem." Well... aside from trying to kill and or maim her in the beginning. They had moved past that. She'd moved past that. *Clearly.*

"Before all this," He motioned around them. "I was feared among my kind. Trained from a young age to fight. To kill. But my siblings were my life. They meant more to me than anything in the world, and I made it my mission to ensure nothing happened to them." Kellan leaned back, looking up at the darkening sky around them. "The scars that mar my body... I was punished, time and time again for what they called foolishness and insubordination. For protecting my kin the only way I knew how, through slaughter and bloodshed. For not completing my assignments in a *clean* manner, but I wouldn't have done anything different." Running a hand down his face, he returned those azure eyes to her as they darkened. "They stripped me of my very being, changed me, until I was this bloodthirsty monster that most coveted." A shudder ran through him, and she reached a steady hand toward him, resting it on his arm. Kellan stared at it for a long moment. "I—"

"I meant what I said." Demitria squeezed his arm for effect. "Whatever happened, you... you're still good. I can see it in your eyes."

"I'm anything but good." He laughed then, the sound full, hearty, as it rumbled through her.

"You went against a direct order to kill me."

"I had my reasons." He shrugged.

"Answers, right." Her own laugh bubbled through, and she stared off toward the horizon, looking for anything out of place. "Despite what I've said to you, you aren't that crazed monster." She'd watched him maim an Archangel, sure. He'd lived up to every thought in that moment. And maybe he still was that bloodthirsty being, but now? Deep down, Kellan was so much more than that.

"Will you look at me?"

She did. Kellan absently tucked a stray hair behind her ear. His fingers warm as they softly grazed across her cheek, the simple touch igniting a fire within her. Demitria felt her body moving closer. Toward the warmth that called to something in her blood. A pull, until she was no more than a hairs breadth from him. That sweet, woodsy smell wafting through her. *Consuming* her. And in that moment, she didn't care who was around them as she let that pull guide her.

Demitria grazed her lips across his. Soft at first. Tentative, and was just about to pull away when his large hand fisted in the back of her hair, his free arm wound around her, pulling her close until she was nearly in his lap. Kellan kissed her with a new found fervor. Rough. Hard, and a hunger filled her as that need welled up in her body. Could hear the rapid thump of her heart, so loud she thought it was about to explode.

When she pulled away a few moments later, breath heavy, she gazed up at him. "I'm sorry, I—" The words caught in her throat as she scooted away from him, turning herself away. What the hell had she been thinking? Begging for his touch had been one thing, but kissing him?

She'd crossed a line.

"Tonight was—"

Demitria cut him off. "It doesn't change anything." Or did it? Where did they even stand now? "It doesn't change how I feel about you. About your kind."

Her voice sounded hollow even to herself. It changed everything, and they both knew it.

Twenty-Nine

DEMITRIA

The morning sun broke through, casting a soft glow over their makeshift camp as Demitria stirred. She remembered curling her body along Kellan's side for warmth sometime in the middle of the night, despite her reservations. And from the warmth that still radiated around her, he hadn't moved a muscle since. She didn't remember being wrapped in the familiar red cloak, but smiled at the gesture anyway.

Hushed voices from the other three Horsemen were what roused her from a dreamless sleep.

"Wake her." Eire hissed. She'd been on patrol all night, refusing to change even when Gabriel had demanded it. Demitria had fallen asleep sometime after that, after hours of thrashing back and forth.

"No." Kellan refused. She could feel him tense beside her, but didn't move to get up, thinking it best they thought she was still asleep.

"Wake her, or I will." Eire grumbled, and she could faintly hear the sound of a knife freed of its sheath. "It will not be pleasant."

The growl rumbled through Kellan's chest, reverberating through her. "You lay so much as a hand on her—"

"Enough!" Gabriel shouted.

Demitria startled, sitting up at the intensity of his voice. Staring around at the four figures that surrounded her. She took them in. Kellan sat upright beside her, but his hand rested subtly atop the hilt of the sword at his left, that all too familiar animalistic look returning to his eyes. Nobody moved.

"Did I oversleep?" She broke. Kellan's features softened as he looked down at her. "I apologize."

"Everyone just woke." He smiled. "No need to apologize." She knew he'd lied. The look of his siblings told her enough. They were waiting on her. Again.

"We ride out now." With a hiss, Eire stalked away, seated atop her mount before Demitria could blink the lingering sleep from her eyes.

She rose to her feet. She felt better. Still tired, but not as weak. Her body stronger than the day before. "Thank you." She handed the cloak back to Kellan. Grateful for the warmth not only it but he had provided her that night. A repeating occurrence, it seemed. One she was slowly no longer beginning to mind.

Stretching her limbs out, the two of them walked toward the horses waiting patiently nearby. Atlas let out a soft whinny at her arrival, and she couldn't help the smile that tugged along her lips. She was alive, Atlas was safe, and that was all that mattered. Fuck Eire. Fuck her opinions. Fuck her attitude. *Fuck her.*

They rode out again through the seemingly endless, vast land. Through the dirt that crunched beneath the hooves of the horses as they pushed on, the blazing sun beating down on them.

Demitria silently wiped the sweat from her brow. It was hot. Too hot. She'd peeled her cloak off hours before, silently wishing for a cold shower. Water. Anything to help quench the heat that was taking hold of her body. Saving her water the other day had been her only smart move since she'd left Solis. Careless thinking would get you killed in an instant, as was evident with her most recent screw up.

She wondered how far from her home they were, her senses still feeling out of whack since the capture. They'd left the canyon behind the other day, so they must be getting close, at least.

Demitria tested her fingers. Bending and moving each one as she gripped the reins. The bruises along her body were lightening, but she was sure she still looked a mess. Her shirt was still torn in several places, dried blood crusted over making the material itch along her skin. She'd give anything for a shower. To cleanse away whatever the demons had done to her body, and rid herself of their touch.

"Can we talk?" Her head shot up at the voice of the Horseman. Kane had ridden up beside Kellan. They moved around her so easily she barely detected their presence each time. She stared at him, his face blank. Eyes staring into the distance. He wasn't talking to her, and she cursed herself for thinking otherwise. As if they would truly have any business with her. Demitria pushed Atlas into a trot, leaving the brothers behind a few paces as she rode ahead to give them whatever privacy they needed. Gabriel and Eire still rode strides ahead, taking up the front. She sure as hell wouldn't be joining them.

She and Atlas took up between the sets of siblings, and if she hadn't felt useless and out of place before, she did now. Demitria strained her ears, desperately trying to hear the conversation between the two behind her. She could make out pieces. Broken words here and there. Her name. Community. *Balance.* Always balance, and she was doing the exact opposite of that, it seemed. It was the same thing the others had been saying. She was sure of it. Kane must be trying to piece together the events leading them up to this morning. Trying to piece together his brother. Her.

Kellan had been absent from his siblings for a week before she'd run from Solis. Run from *him.* And since then? How can someone fuck up their life so badly in just over two weeks. The curse left her lips in a harsh whisper. She cursed them all. Every single one of them. Eire, the twins.

"A woman should never speak words as you do." She met the wise, forest-green eyes of the eldest Horsemen. The power radiated from him, and she nearly flinched at its intensity. He'd heard her curse. Damning his siblings. The residents of her community. *Shit.*

"I'm not a typical woman." She answered, gaze unchanging. The laugh rumbled through his chest, and it startled her. Her body begged her to shy away. Avert her gaze. She didn't. Wouldn't give them the satisfaction of the fear they so coveted.

"I've gathered that much." His smile never wavered. Never faltered as he stared at her. "Which begs the question. What exactly are you?"

Human. She was inexplicably human. He should know that. She

was nothing more. Nothing more than mortal flesh and blood. "I don't know what you mean?"

"You are different, Demitria Collins." He spoke, quiet enough that only she could hear. So quiet in fact, she could barely hear him. "Something about you has drawn him in." She followed the subtle nod of his head. Kellan. He was talking about Kellan. "Drawn him in so deep that he's lost himself in the process." Had he? She hadn't known him as his former self. Gotten glimpses, sure. The deadly warrior that those around had claimed him to be, but never the full extent. He was softer, maybe. But that could just as easily have been because of their mutual understanding of each other, or whatever the hell it was brewing between them. But lost himself? A Horseman couldn't lose himself in the few weeks that she'd known him.

"Brother." Kellan growled.

Gabriel knew to take his leave, and with a nod in her direction, he resumed his place at the front.

"What'd he say to you?" Kellan's eyes never left Gabriel's back. The challenge in his voice was clear, and Gabriel backed down. A movement that surprised him, she could tell, as it flickered in his eyes. Given their hierarchy, his brother giving in so quickly was nearly unheard of it seemed.

"It was nothing." She shrugged, glancing over at him. His face hardened, but he continued the fixation on his brothers back. He didn't believe her. "It's none of your concern." She added. Slowly, his eyes met hers. "Tell me, what did Kane have to say?"

"It's none of your concern." He mimicked. The amusement danced over his face. *Bastard*. She cursed him, too. Damning him. She heard the chuckle echo from the Horsemen ahead. Damn him *and* his siblings.

They bantered back and forth for hours, and she knew he enjoyed the frustration in her eyes as he grinned down at her. The anger in her face as he won, over and over again. Beating her at her own game. "You're an ass." She hissed. Kellan's smile only grew.

The sky around them paled, the air growing cooler. No one had mentioned the ever growing quiet as they neared their destination. Nothing scurried at their feet, fleeing at their mere presence. Demitria had experienced this once before. The night she'd met the deadly Horseman.

They smelled it before they could see it.

Smoke. The smell filled her lungs. Choked her senses. Clouded every thought as the panic, the pain, surged within. Consumed her.

Fire.

The community was on fire.

Thirty

DEMITRIA

Demitria broke free from the Horsemen as they surged forward. Atlas, sensing the urgency, like he could feel it in the way she clung to him, had never moved so fast. He sprinted, galloping at such a fast pace that she felt as if they could have been flying. The few hundred yards that separated them from the community flashed before her eyes in a blur of smoke.

Demitria jumped from the saddle before Atlas even came close to a stop. Her body surging through the air for a heartbeat before landing hard, the horse skidding in the dirt beside her. Atlas's normally docile brown eyes were blown wide, his nostrils flared at the scene before him.

Not the community. Not her home.

She stood in front of the large iron gate, panic surging through her. It hung loosely from its hinges, barely hanging on to the crumbling wall that surrounded the town. Nearly ripped clean off.

Solis was engulfed in an endless sea of bright orange flames. Kellan was screaming her name as she stumbled forward on shaky feet. Screaming, over and over again. She heard nothing. Blocked it out. Blocked everything out as the only thing she could focus on were the flames flicking up toward the sky.

What had happened? What had happened? WHAT HAD HAPPENED?

Her feet picked up pace and she was sprinting again. She was met with complete and utter silence. No screams. Nothing. Only the sound of the flames licking the wood. Engulfing buildings as it destroyed everything in its path, devastating the community, the red-orange glow taking over everything she saw.

Buildings were in shambles as they lay in heaps of rubble on the ground. Stone, metal and wood sticking up in every which way from their collapse. Bile rose in her throat when she spotted the first body. A limb, she realized. Gnarled and bloody, she couldn't truly discern where the body it belonged to was. Red everywhere she looked. So much blood, and she knew it was from her people. *Her friends.* But other splatters were dark, black, and she was proud that they'd at least made whatever pieces of shit had attacked, bleed.

Another body, intact, but Demitria couldn't bring herself to uncover their face from the rubble. She knew they were dead. There was no way anyone could survive this.

"I'm sorry." She choked back a sob, and ran.

She'd never run so fast. Couldn't think. Couldn't breathe.

"Jace!" The cry left her lips as she bounded toward the familiar building. She tried the handle, recoiling with a hiss as the metal burned into her palm. Her hand ached, but she didn't care. It didn't matter. *Get Inside.* With a swift kick, the door fell free from its hinges, collapsing to the ground before her. The smoke filled the foyer. Filled her lungs. Clouded her vision.

Jace. *Find Jace.* Her mind screamed. The only thought she clung to as she pushed through.

Find Jace.

Keep moving. Search.

Find Jace.

Her breaths were panicked. Labored as she frantically searched the burning building. Nothing moved. Not a cry for help.

"Jace!" She begged. Her eyes stung from a mixture of smoke and the tears that she couldn't stop. She had to find him. No matter what she did, she had to find Jace. That was the only thing that mattered to her now. Room after room, she searched. Coming up empty every time.

He wasn't there. Wasn't in the house. He had to be somewhere. Had to be. His brown, worn leather jacket sat draped over a chair in his kitchen where the flames hadn't yet reached. He never went anywhere without it. He'd been caught off guard, she knew it. Demitria didn't think twice before swiping it off the chair and flinging it over her shoulders. Like hell it was staying here. She grabbed stupid little keepsakes, stuffing them into his pack that she'd found sitting atop the counter.

The smoke was denser as she pushed through the house. Toward the back bedroom. His bedroom. Another kick sent the door flying open. Rifling through the drawers, she packed little clothing. A change of clothes from the bottom drawer of her things, but mostly his. A few shirts, a pair of pants. Anything that reminded her of him.

A picture. She'd seen it on his nightstand for years. Of the two of them, laughing as they embraced. Despite the current circumstances, she smiled at the memory. Touching her finger to the glass. Demitria had made a stupid trade for the polaroid camera. It hadn't even been worth it for her, but she'd wanted it. Wanted to feel some sort of normalcy in the world once more, so she did it. Another one. From eleven years ago. They were kids, four sets of smiling faces stared back at her. Her parents. *Their* parents. A new wave of pain took over, nearly engulfing her.

The crash from down the hall sent her skittering from her thoughts. Her throat ached, burning as she coughed. The building was coming down. She had to leave.

All the memories. All the laughter. Burning. Crumbling to pieces. She stood feet away outside, watching as the roof caved in. Sealing the rest of him inside.

Demitria made a run for her house, but it was too late. The flames had completely destroyed anything that was inside as it ripped through the windows, doors and roof. What little possessions she had was already lost to the burning inferno surrounding her. Demitria willed herself not to cry at the loss, but her tears broke free. For the memories she would never see again. The items she would never hold. She watched as everything from her previous life burnt into nothing.

A groan was the last thing she expected. Sent her reeling from her house toward the noise. She ran, blocking out even more lifeless bodies as she went. Tears blinding as she followed the sound.

Please be Jace.

The bag fell to the ground at her feet as she rushed to his side. Pieter lay propped against a stone building. Chest heaving as the blood leaked from his body. Pouring from his mouth as he coughed. *So much blood...* The dark, metal spear stuck clear through his chest, pinning him to the ground. The force behind that blow—she shuddered at the thought.

"Pieter!" Her legs felt like lead as she collapsed before him. "Oh Pieter." She cooed, "What happened?"

He coughed again, eyes opening at the familiar voice. "We were..." He grunted at the movement, pain lacing through his body. "Attacked." *What'd he mean attacked?* She pressed him for more information, even when she knew she shouldn't. "Ambushed."

"By whom? What happened?" She pushed. His wounds were horrific. Her heart tore, ached for him, but she didn't know what she could do. The wound was too gruesome. Too final for her to bring him back from it.

"Demon raid." He coughed again, flinching as the pain tore through him. "Never stood a chance." His body shuddered. "No time to react. They came looking for you."

Fuck.

She hated them. Hated every single one of those fucking creatures that continued to take and take every little thing away from her. People. A home. *Her life.* She fucking hated them all.

"Did anyone get out, Pieter?" He had to say yes. They had to have gotten out.

"Some." He nodded. "Not sure who."

"Jace. Where's Jace." She pushed, but his eyes grew distant. Breath slowing. He wouldn't meet her gaze. "Pieter, where's Jace?" *No. No.*

"He was on the front lines." Slowly, he looked up at her again. Even in all his pain, he sounded visibly upset. Distraught at the news he shared. "The demons killed everything in their path. Everyone perished so fast..." Demitria watched as the tears escaped, running down his face in soft lines as they mixed with the blood, dirt and gore that coated his skin. "There were no survivors."

NO.

She couldn't think. Couldn't think past the pounding in her ears. The aching that ripped through her chest. She wanted to curl up. To just lay there, unmoving as the world imploded around her. To let the flames engulf her. To slowly eat away at her flesh as she burned alive. She deserved to die like that.

But she couldn't. Pieter was still there.

The coughs shook his body in wild spasms. Even more blood pooled from his mouth. The spear made a sickening noise as she pulled it free from his body, and she threw it to the ground behind her. Tossing it like it had been a plague among her people. It had, in a way. How many lives that weapon had probably ended. She cursed it. Cursed them, before returning her attention to Pieter who didn't even flinch. Demitria took the man into her arms, his head resting in her lap.

"Shh," She whispered, hand softly wrapping around his own. Lightly stroking his cheek with the other. "It's okay." His hair. Anything to take his mind off the pain. "You're okay." Blood coated her fingertips, smearing across his skin, but she continued the movement. His breathing began to slow, and he gripped her hand tight. Squeezing it with the little energy he had left. Demitria wouldn't cry. Couldn't cry. She had to be strong for him. For Pieter. Finally, his grip loosened in her hand. She brought her lips to his forehead, placing a soft kiss as a sigh left his lips, and his chest fell still.

She was being pulled to her feet. Her body engulfed between warm, strong arms as he held her. That familiar sweet woodsy scent filled her senses. The scream erupted through her chest. Ripping through her. Tearing her apart as it echoed into the night.

Dead. Jace was *dead*.

He couldn't be dead. She didn't want to believe it. She hadn't even said goodbye. She hated herself. Hated herself for leaving, and walking away from him.

Another scream ripped through her as the sobs raked through her chest. "He's dead!" The tears ran down her cheeks in swift currents.

Pooling against Kellan's chest as he held her. Not daring to let her go for even a moment. "He's dead."

Kellan's grip tightened; his arms wound so tight as he anchored her. Keeping her from crumbling to the ground in a broken heap. Her fingers clenched so tight into the fabric of his clothing, not caring if it ripped.

"He's dead." She repeated the words, over and over again. It wasn't real. He wasn't dead. She couldn't believe it. Didn't want to. Her friends were gone. Her family. And she hadn't even been there to help them. To save them.

"We need to go." Finally, he spoke. She hadn't realized his hands had been doing circles along her back until they'd stopped moving. The fire around them had grown, closing in on what little remained of Solis. If they didn't leave soon, they'd be the next victims. "It's too dangerous to stay."

They came looking for you. The words echoed in her mind, threatening to drive her mad.

"I'm sorry," Demitria's eyes met the lifeless figure behind her, "I'm so sorry." Kellan ripped her away before she could say anything else. Jace was gone. They were all gone.

There was nothing left of her home. Nothing.

Kellan swiped the bag off the ground as he carried her toward the gate, cradled safely in his arms.

"Any survivors?" Gabriel's eyes met his brother's, and Kellan shook his head.

"No." Even Eire wouldn't meet his gaze. Did the Horsemen pity her? Pity the entire community?

"We need to leave." Kellan spoke, still not daring to set her on the ground. "She can't stay here."

"That was our plan! To bring her back, and leave!" Eire's eyes mimicked that of the fire. Harsh. Unforgiving.

"There is nothing left here!" He roared, eyes glazing over, darkening as the blood lust took over. Demitria watched as that familiar rage threatened to spill free from his incredibly thin restraint. "Nothing left for her to go back to."

"Leave her, let her find her own way." The snarl rumbled through Eire's chest, matching Kellan's own.

"She has lost her family, her home. Everything she ever cared about is gone, and you're telling me to leave her here?" Demitria let the whimper pass through her lips, her fingers tightening in his cloak as she turned her head into Kellan's shoulder.

Gone.

Everything was gone, and the only thing they could do was argue. She didn't know if she should scream. Flail. Anything to just...make it all stop.

"There's a town to the north." Gabriel's voice was calm, collected, which was more than what she could say for the others. "It's an eight-day ride, but that is where we'll go." Gabriel's eyes met Kellan's. "She'll be safe there."

She should be feeling grateful to them for not leaving her. Should be feeling *anything,* but she felt nothing. Paralyzed to the world around her. The heart wrenching pain that was consuming her.

Demitria couldn't bring herself to thank Gabriel.

"Unbelievable." Eire barked, cursing under her breath before turning away.

The darkness that swelled within was an endless pool of despair. Numb. Every limb. Every part of her felt numb. Couldn't feel. She didn't want to. Her own thoughts haunted her. Condemned her.

Everything she ever loved, gone. Her home. Her family.

Jace

Gone.

It was her fault. Everything was her fault. She'd been too late. *She'd been too late.* Had taken too long to return. She should have never left. She would have stayed behind had she known they'd come regardless. Running off had been the biggest mistake she'd ever made, and now she was paying the price. Would be for the rest of her life.

This pain wouldn't go away. It never would. His face ingrained in her mind until even that no longer served her.

His death had broken her. Torn her in two. Demitria couldn't live without him. Didn't even want to begin to think of a life without him.

It wasn't supposed to happen like this. She was never supposed to leave the community. It wasn't what they had planned for their lives.

He wasn't supposed to be dead.

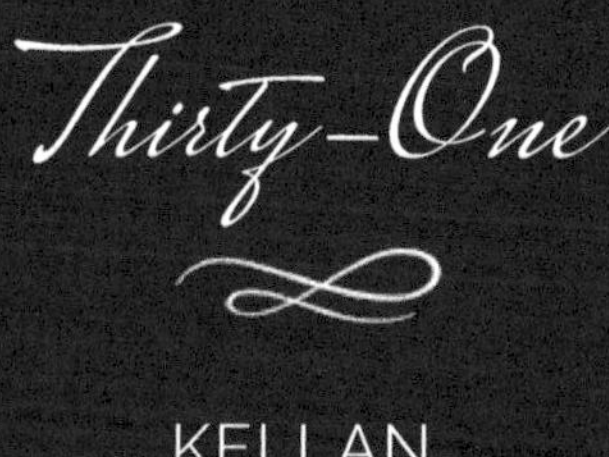

KELLAN

Kellan let the sigh pass through his lips as he ran a hand through his hair. Hours upon hours of silence haunted him, much like her screams had the night before. The sound tore through him, and then Eire? He'd barely been able to keep himself from tipping over that edge. Had never felt so disgusted by his own family before that moment.

"How is she?" Kane rode up beside him.

Demitria had been riding alone for hours, and Kellan thought it best to give her space to process, but he hadn't been able to help the lingering stares as he watched her.

Kellan didn't need to answer to tell his brother how Demitria felt. It radiated off her like a beacon. Lost. Broken. She wouldn't speak. Wouldn't look at either of them. Didn't even flinch as his sister launched into a string of insults. She didn't even look up. Her eyes glazed over. Demitria hadn't even reacted to his touch. "Bad."

He hadn't had time to process anything that happened leading up to this. The rift with his siblings, Eire specifically. Or how she'd changed her mind on him and his siblings? Not to mention how she'd *kissed* him!

Kellan couldn't get that part out of his brain. Had tried to, on numerous occasions, but his mind kept coming back to the warmth of her mouth on his. The way she'd tasted. He couldn't remember the last time he'd felt this way. *If* he had ever felt this way. There were so many years he couldn't remember. Too many to count, down in the trenches of the Underworld where he'd served *him* as a puppet. That was why he had his own reservations about bringing Demitria with them. He feared the Dark King, probably more than the lot of them combined. And fear was something out of his repertoire. Had been beaten out of him time and time again until he no longer felt it, but after those years, even he couldn't shake the fear of the male.

Kellan shook his head, running his hand down his face once more. He was fucked. So, so fucked. What he had done, what he was *continuing* to do, was forbidden. A Horseman and a human girl. He shouldn't even be thinking about it. It wasn't right, and Kellan knew that. He was no better than the bastard of a father that had sired him, but he couldn't help himself. He wanted her, no matter how impermissible the situation was. He was a Horseman of the Apocalypse, his job was to restore the balance, then return to his world with his siblings when it was all said and done. But now? He didn't know what he was to do anymore.

The wildly feared Horsemen, War, had changed into something that his siblings didn't recognize.

Something he himself didn't even recognize.

"Were they close?" His brother's words pulled him from his thoughts. Kane knew about Jace. He'd explained it briefly to the lot of them, but hadn't gone into detail out of respect.

"Unbelievably so." He remembered the way she spoke of him at the community. The day she'd broken down in front of him. Jace had meant the world to her. Even more than that. He'd felt something that day, too. Something he had no business feeling toward the male. Especially in that moment, but he wouldn't touch on that now.

"Have you spoken with Gabriel at all? About the council?"

"No," Kellan shook his head. "It's useless at this point." He reined the fiery red mount in beneath him, slowing the stallion's gait further before patting his sleek, muscled neck. "I know what I saw, and they refused my summons. Something more is going on here, and I will get to the bottom of it."

"Because of Lucifer?" Kellan had been avoiding the name, and he eyed his brother wearily.

"Especially because of him." His gaze traveled toward the girl before him. Waiting for her to turn around. When she didn't, he continued. "If what the demon lord said is true, he needs to be dealt with. Eliminated."

"I agree." Kane nodded, pulling the pale cloak over his head as those icy-blue eyes seemed to look through him. "We need to talk."

Kellan had been dreading those words. Had hoped that the others wouldn't pry, but if it had to be any of them, he supposed Kane was the best-case scenario. "About?"

"You already know."

"Unfortunately." He sighed. "Please, tell me how much of a fuck up I am." He shouldn't have laughed at the thought, but he couldn't help it. Kellan had truly, royally, fucked this assignment up so bad, he didn't think there was any coming back from it.

Kane fixed his gaze on Demitria. "I saw you the other night." Gods help him. "Are you mad?" Yes. Yes, he was indefinitely mad. Crazed. An absolute idiot. He could name off many things, and he was every single one of them.

"I think I'd rather talk to Gabriel about the council and Lucifer."

"Human, Kellan. The girl is human." He knew that, too. As if it hadn't been painfully obvious.

Gripping the bridge of his nose, he tore his gaze away from her. "Look...the concern is touching. Truly, but I think we have bigger things at hand, here." Like an entire fucking war about to befall this planet?

The council wanted balance, not an annihilation. And if they didn't stop Lucifer? That was exactly what would happen.

Defeated, knowing Kellan had been right, Kane sighed. "I know, brother. I just hope you know what you're doing."

He didn't.

Thirty-Two

DEMITRIA

Her fault. She blamed herself.

Jace was dead because of her. It repeated over and over again in her mind.

Her fault.

Beneath her, Atlas mimicked her every mood. The horse was sullen. Quiet. His feet almost dragging along the ground as they rode. Understanding the loss she had suffered. Jace's blood was on her hands. All of theirs. Stella, Cory, Evan... they'd all died because the demons had come for her.

She'd wished the Horsemen hadn't rescued her in that cave. They should have let her die. Let her soul break, and fed it to the Dark King, whoever the fuck that was supposed to be. It would have prevented all this. Could have saved the lives of those she'd lost.

The jacket hung heavy on her shoulders. Weighed her down. She didn't care. It still smelled like him. He'd always had that soft scent of mint around him, and the jacket was no different. Like it had been pressed into the leather. Worked its way through every fiber until it was wafting through her. Taking over every sense she possessed.

Jace.

It was all she could think about. His face. His smile. His laugh. Oh gods, his laugh. She loved it. Loved every damn part of him. No matter how mad she was, how far down she'd fallen, he'd always been there. Waiting. Waiting to pull her back up again.

But he wouldn't be there. Not this time. There was no coming back from this one. Never again would she hear him speak. Never hear the melodious sound of his voice as he softly hummed to himself when he thought no one was listening. Always some old rock song from before the Ascension. One their fathers would always have blaring through a speaker in a backyard filled with green grass as they played. As they laughed without a care in the world. *Never again.*

It had been ten days since she'd run from the community. Ten days since she'd seen his face. Four since she'd learned of his death. She took back every word she'd said about him. Every curse. Every damning thought she'd ever had about him, she took it back. She took it all back, like somehow, it would change things. Change everything.

She never got to say goodbye. Didn't get to see him one last time. His body could be anywhere. Eaten by those fucking creatures, or burned within the flames. Lost to the world. Lost to *her*. Lifting her eyes toward the bright afternoon sun, she blinked. Once. Twice. The tears welled in her eyes once more. Never ending. They never stopped. The pain never stopped.

Her fingers trembled along the reins. Focusing on their detail as she'd done so many times before when she'd been mad. Mad at him. But this time was different. The anger was placed solely on herself. She wouldn't even be here if she hadn't insisted on doing patrol some weeks back. Maybe if she'd just been there, she could have made a difference. Plead for their lives. His life. But they'd never been known to show mercy, either. At least if she'd been there, they could have died fighting side by side, and no longer would she feel this agony inside her chest.

The demons could all go to hell. Or was that what the Horsemen were trying to do anyway? Send them back there? She didn't know. Didn't care. They were the ones who had invaded her home first. Before the angels who had undoubtedly followed not soon after, but none of that mattered anymore. The humans hadn't attacked first. *She* hadn't attacked them first.

The High Council had played her out to be this murderous

monster. Had sent not only The Horseman, but an Archangel after her to eliminate the 'threat' that they claimed her to be. All she'd ever done was tried to survive in this fucked up world. Tried to live.

A deadly calm took over her. Body stiffening as the thoughts swarmed throughout. The burning community. Her parents' eyes. The blood pooled on the floor. All of it had led her here, to this moment.

She would be what they claimed her to be. Would become the murderous creature they swore she was. Demitria was out for blood. For revenge.

"What's wrong?" Kellan watched as her demeanor changed. The hardening of her features. The emotionless stare. It had been a carbon copy of the one she'd seen him don so many times before.

Demitria didn't answer him, just stared out at the horizon. The horse beneath her mimicked her calm. Alert. At the ready. His movements thunderous and deadly as he walked along. Like a shadow cutting through the night.

"I'm going to kill him with my bare hands," She growled. "And all those that follow him."

She only had one want now. One need, and she didn't care how she got there.

Demitria would cut each and every one of the fucking creatures down, starting with their gods damned king.

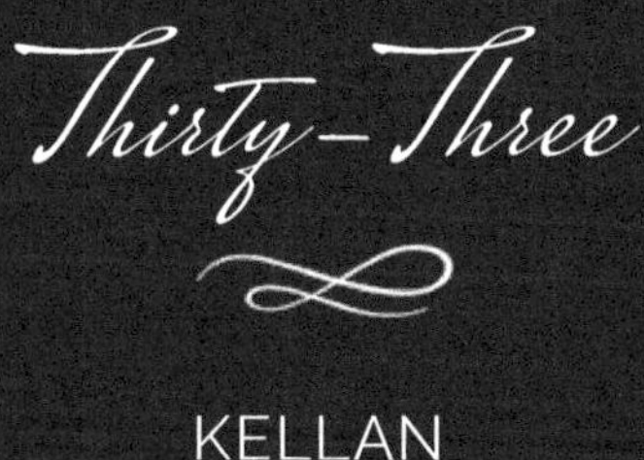

Thirty-Three

KELLAN

Kellan sat in front of the fire across from his siblings, his body barely fitting atop the large boulder he'd perched on. He glanced to his left, toward the mounts sleeping soundlessly a few feet away in the darkness that surrounded them before turning back to the others. He was used to the darkness, his senses sharp. Eyes that could see far more than the human fast asleep near his feet. He'd discarded his cloak the moment they'd sat down, offering it to Demitria as she rested her weary eyes. He found himself staring at her, too. At the way the curves on her chest rose and fell with each breath she took. He needed to stop staring. To get ahold of himself, and stop acting like an absolute fool.

It took him far too much effort to drag his gaze back.

"Have they answered?" Kane spoke, his voice barely above a whisper. Kellan already knew the answer. He knew Gabriel had summoned them every time they'd stopped riding to no avail. Heard the string of curses when they didn't answer. The council was refusing their summons, and that unnerved him more than it should have.

"No." Gabriel stared into the red-orange glow, the dancing of the flames reflecting in his dark, forest green eyes. His voice was gruff, stern, as if the very thought tasted foul in his mouth. His hands were balled into fists in his lap as he sat there, unmoving. So still, almost as if he was nothing more than stone.

"Why?" Eire chimed in. "Because of the girl?" She chided, shooting her sleeping figure a quick glance before meeting his own gaze. Eire rolled her eyes at him, her features contorted to one of disgust. "We're only in this mess because of her."

"I don't know." Gabriel didn't even stop them from the argument that was moments away from happening.

"Something more is going on. I've said it before, and I'll say it again." Kellan spoke, stretching out the kink in his arms. Massaging the muscles with deft fingers from being in one position for too long.

"You believe the claims, then? About *him*?" To his surprise, Eire's voice softened, her features doing the same as she mimicked their eldest staring into the flames. If there was one thing they could agree on, it was the gravity of those claims. What they meant to each and every one of them.

He didn't want to, but everything since he'd got here seemed to point directly to the male ruling The Underworld. And he hated that. Loathed it with every fiber of his being. The Dark King—Lucifer, was not a being he wanted any part of.

"I do." He sighed, his head falling back as he stared off into the sky above, watching the stars peek through the clouds.

"Then what? What does it even mean?" Kane asked. His features were such a stark contrast against the world around them. The white blond of his hair, the piercing blue eyes. Striking, as he watched on.

"It means we kill him." There was no other answer. Nothing that he could come up with, other than ending the male's life.

"You think we can do that?" Eire laughed, then. Her gray eyes practically glowing as if he'd just said the most humorous thing. "We barely got you out of his clutches, and you think *you* can kill him?"

"We don't have a choice!" His voice rose, deepening, as his brows knit together.

"We can't just go off and kill him, Kellan. We need to wait for the council's orders, that has always been law." Kane reasoned, and Kellan rounded on him. He was supposed to be the one that agreed with him. The easygoing one out of all of them.

"They don't give a shit about us!" He almost yelled, the anger dripping from him. What didn't they understand? Even after everything that's happened, why didn't they believe him? "In case you haven't noticed."

"Gabriel?" Silence fell over them as Kane spoke, waiting for the final orders.

It seemed like eons before he finally answered. "We continue this path." Gabriel answered, voice low. He still hadn't broken from that stare, and Kellan wondered what was coursing through his mind. "Wherever he is, we find him, and we apprehend him." It was Kellan's turn to laugh. *Apprehend him?* There would be none of that. They wouldn't survive it if they tried.

"And what then, brother?" Kellan narrowed his eyes at him. Killing Lucifer was the only option they had. Gabriel knew that.

"We apprehend him, and take him to the council. To hold a proper trial, and they will punish him as they see fit."

Fucking delusional.

He loved his siblings, but gods...sometimes they made it so damn difficult.

"And the girl?" That look returned to Eire's face, and he was nearly ready to smack it off her. His temper flaring from the conversation.

"We indulge her." Gabriel looked at him, then. "Accompany her until she reaches the town safely, then we forget this assignment ever happened."

They broke from the fire minutes later, but Kellan stayed in his seat. He didn't care where the others went right now. Not after that conversation. Lucifer was a risk that none of them could take, and they all knew it. He couldn't fathom the thought of trying to capture the bastard, let alone bring him in front of the council. He of all people knew that would never happen.

He was angry. Too many *emotions* swirling around inside him. Rage. Always so much fucking rage. Confusion...even shame at the way his brother had looked at him. Spoken his final orders as if they were directed at him. And that made him even angrier.

So, when Eire left in the middle of the night, he didn't try to stop her.

"We're being tracked." She'd been harsh. Absolutely sure of herself.

"There is nothing out here." Kellan sighed, exasperated. He felt like a void. There was nothing, and had been nothing for miles. The smoke had driven away any individual. Nothing wanted to be near the blaze. That was why they had yet to encounter a single demon, angel, or creature of earth. "The air here is making you hallucinate. Nothing is following us." He'd let himself slip to the ground some hours before, settling his back against the cool stone as he sat beside Demitria.

"I'm telling you, something is out there." She glared at him from across the fire, already several feet away from their makeshift camp.

"You're mad." He rolled his eyes, losing interest in her claims as quickly as she'd brought them up. He hadn't sensed anything, and the others hadn't spoken up about it either. Eire had always been the tracker of the group, but someone else should have picked up on it too. "There's nothing out there, Eire." He sighed, slinging his arm protectively over the sleeping figure nestled into his side.

Eire swung her body up atop the gray mare and her heels dug into the horse's sides in a harsh jab that sent her reeling off into the dark night air, grumbling about proving her point as she left.

Kellan knew the others were awake. Listening to his interaction with Eire. Their eyes were closed, but he could tell. Kane and Gabriel had come back to the warmth of the flames sometime within the last hour, sitting much the same as he had, their backs propped against a stone. He knew they were absolutely sick of breaking up the two of them, it was their usual dynamic, even before things seemingly went to shit. Violence almost always was involved, especially as of late, it seemed.

Morning crept up on them all too soon, and they all stirred as the first rays broke over the horizon. There were no signs of Eire, or the being she had claimed to be tracking them since the burning community. Kellan was sure it had all been for show. Whether it be to scare Demitria, or something entirely different, he didn't know. Maybe even to get away from him. Some days, he felt as if he hardly knew his siblings anymore.

"Thirsty?" Kellan held the canteen out, motioning for her to take it. Demitria didn't flinch. Didn't even blink as she watched his movements. She hadn't changed since the other day. The deadly calm still radiating through her. The claim about killing the Dark King still hung fresh in his mind. She'd die doing it, he knew that. Hell, he might die doing it. But none had questioned her on the proclamation. He wasn't sure if it was because the council still wanted her dead, and they'd seen it as a way to have her eliminated without setting a finger on her, but it would make sense. Kellan didn't want to know, so he didn't ask.

"Where do we even start?" Kane asked.

"I know a place." Demitria said, catching him off guard. "We got word of a group of angels that took up residence not too far from here. J—" She caught herself, only faltering slightly at the near mention of his name, before continuing. "Sent a few scouting missions to keep an eye on them, watch what they were up to." She finally took a large swig from the canteen, screwing the lid back on before passing it back to him. "They've been here for a few years. Never caused any trouble, so we never bothered them. It was...where I was headed before—" *Everything*? She didn't need to say the words for each one of them to know what she meant.

He and his siblings stared at the girl. They'd defected? Being on Earth meant those angels had abandoned the council and its orders. They were Fallen.

They had known about some angels going rogue every once in a while, abandoning Eden for Earth, leaving behind the responsibilities of the High Council with them. Kellan had thought about it once. Maybe twice, albeit briefly. Being shackled to the council, having to obey their every order when sometimes they just didn't make sense. *Like now.*

He stared at Demitria again. He still had so many questions. Too many to count. Now this? The Fallen were always found, and always eliminated. It was only a matter of time before the council would send out an Angel of Death. Usually weeks, sometimes months. Their freedom never lasted long. But years?

"They will know where the Dark King resides. Where he hides, I'm sure of it." Demitria met the eyes of each Horsemen present as if in challenge. She stared the longest at Gabriel.

"Lead the way." He motioned toward their horses, waiting patiently for them to mount up and ride out. She stared, one last long look before swinging her body atop Atlas. The rest followed, only moments behind as she took off northbound.

Eire had yet to return, but she'd track them down without a problem. It was what she was best at, after all.

~

"How do you do it?" Demitria asked hours later. They'd been riding at a fast pace all day, following closely behind as she led them toward the Fallen. She'd slowed her mount down now until they were in line to speak. "How do you kill with no remorse?"

Gabriel was the first to answer. "We do not kill without reason." He watched the human as Kellan had the day before. Recognizing the dark depths of where she now lay, the rage that leeched its way through her, eating away every ounce of humanity. One he'd seen on Kellan far too many times. "Our purpose is balance, and nothing more."

"That's nothing but a lie, and you know that." Face hard, she glared at the eldest.

"I do not thrive on killing. It is my job, and nothing more." Harsh. Final. Kellan stayed silent, unsure on what to say. He did not have a clean past, and the blood on his hands was far too great. He could drown a thousand times over in it. His hands had never been clean from the moment the council trapped him in their clutches. Not like his siblings.

"We are required to keep the balance. Our job is to eliminate anything that threatens that, and nothing more."

"So why me? Why was I deemed a threat?" She asked.

"I do not know." He answered.

"Does my existence threaten the balance so much that I had to be killed? Where is the logic in that? Why did they want me dead?" Demitria was irritated, they all could see it.

"I do not know that either." Gabriel sighed, pulling his gaze from her.

"Do you know anything?" She quipped.

"Only what they wish us to know." His answer silenced her. Kellan knew his brother had just as many questions as he did, if not more. As their leader, he was granted most of his knowledge directly from the council themselves. And yet they'd held back, even from him.

Why?

"Follow your orders. Do whatever you wish with me, but I will kill him first." Those green-gold eyes had gone dark. "Regardless of what you have to say, I will follow you on your quest to eliminate him. The attack on my family made things personal." He didn't have it in him to tell her Gabriel hadn't wanted the male dead. That they were to attempt to capture the being, to leave this world and bring him before the council to stand trial. She wouldn't even get the chance.

If the Horsemen hadn't known better, they could have sworn she had been one of them. Nephilim. The power she exuded. The command in her voice as she challenged them, it was like one of their own. Like Gabriel.

"I don't care what you do with me afterward, but I will kill him for everything he has done."

Gabriel was silent, now his turn to watch her. Kellan waited with bated breath, unsure on the road his brother would take. His breath left him in a whoosh as the faint hint of a smile graced Gabriel's features before promptly disappearing. "I look forward to seeing how the council's most wanted killer works."

Thirty-Four

KELLAN

Kellan hadn't brought up the events that had led them here. Wouldn't dare, in fear of the girl shutting herself off again. She still harbored that deadly calm on her face, at least she reacted to his touch, but he was worried regardless. Knowing full well how it felt to shut that part of yourself off. Emotions...Humanity. He was amazed his siblings had tolerated it for so long, even after they'd pried him from the hands of his captor. From the being that had encouraged such hatred, such bloodshed, that he'd essentially turned off any ounce of compassion he'd possessed.

Kellan was exactly what Demitria had thought of him, a monster, killing for the hell of it. Feeling the power of somethings life in his hands. The sea of red as he rampaged through the vast worlds. The crimson blood that inevitably always fell. He once reveled in those feelings. Now he was just ashamed. Seeing the destruction. The pain it had caused the inhabitants of Earth, and Earth wasn't even his fault. He saw the carnage from the demons on her community. On the entire fucking world when he'd showed up weeks ago.

Kellan remembered what it had been like before the demons rose. So much like Eden. Beautiful and green. He didn't care for the steel buildings and machines they'd built, but that was another story. This was the one planet where his hands were clean. In terms of mass destruction, at least. Because even here he'd spilled blood. The only difference was that it had been warranted. For survival, his and the girl beside him.

They pushed on, the never-ending terrain of nearly identical barren land until they entered the large canyon that would bring them to the angels' camp. The wall of rock extended high overhead, hundreds of feet. No life bloomed within, but that was rare in itself anywhere these days it seemed.

An eerie feeling settled over him. Like a thousand different eyes were now watching. Like all at once, something had awoken, waiting for them to get there. He could handle demons, hell, even more Archangels. He just hoped it wasn't the latter, knowing it would end in even more bloodshed. And in this moment, he wasn't so sure what side his siblings would stand on.

He scanned over the canyon walls. Up to the highest peaks, willing himself to focus. Listening for the smallest sound. A creature scurrying, anything. Those eyes, whatever they were, burned into him. The world beyond blurred, like he couldn't hone in on anything. Kellan blinked furiously, trying to rid himself of that fogginess that seemed to grip into the corners of his mind.

He couldn't discern if it was the residual smoke from the community clouding each of his senses, or if there truly was something fucking with him from within the canyon walls. He couldn't tell. Couldn't fucking tell anything, it seemed. Gripping the pommel of his saddle tighter, he glanced at each of his siblings. Gabriel and Kane shared similar looks. Their jaws taut, fingers clenched around their weapons.

Kellan urged his mount up beside Demitria for the first time in days. Unwilling to yield to whatever it was that lay hiding in the canyon. He'd promised to keep her safe, and he'd do just that. Granting her the space she needed to grieve, he wouldn't let up when danger was on the horizon.

"Are you alright?" He asked, his mount so close their legs brushed. "With...everything?"

"I don't have a choice." She replied, eyes focused on the slowly winding path ahead. Kellan reached behind him, fetching the canteen from his saddlebag before extending it toward her. She watched it for a moment, finally taking it from him with a nod.

"Everyone has a choice." He whispered.

"I've never had a choice. Not in any of this." Demitria unscrewed the cap, pressing her lips over the rim as she took several swigs before closing it again. "The Ascension, this price on my head, being taken against my will." Technically, she'd agreed to go with him. But it had been through brute force. Ever the monster, he was. He lived up to that name every day, even if he hated it.

"I'm sorry." And he was, truly. Kellan had his own choices stripped from him so many times, and now he was no better than those who'd hurt him. Following blindly to the authority of the council. Even the Dark King when he'd been his pawn.

"I don't claim to know about your past beyond what has been said," She started, slowly meeting his piercing gaze. "But from what I gather, you and I have shared similar fates. Bound to those we love to a fault, and doomed to a life we can't live."

Words had never resonated with him more.

Kellan felt his features softening as he lifted a tentative hand toward her. He needed to stop himself. Needed to pull so far away from this... this *human* before he caused himself anymore grief.

He dropped his hand.

They rode in that uncomfortable silence that had her squirming in the saddle, and he watched from the corner of his eyes as she repositioned herself over and over, a heavy sigh passing through her full lips. Kellan felt her staring at him, but he didn't return the look. Focus. He had to focus on the task at hand. Find the Fallen. Figure out where Lucifer was scheming—*what* he was scheming—and subdue him for long enough to bring him before the council. Those were his brother's orders. He could do that.

"Do you feel that?" Gabriel rode up beside him, his beast of a horse falling into step with his own. Kellan's mount shook his head at the closeness, letting out a loud snort of annoyance. He ran a hand down the creature's muscled neck to soothe him.

"No." He didn't feel anything, that was the problem.

"Exactly." Gabriel narrowed his eyes as if the movement would help him hone in. When he frowned, Kellan knew his struggles were the same.

"Are you worried?" Kellan asked. His hand inched toward the sword strapped to his back. Readying himself to wield the blade that seemed to almost call out his name as his fingers neared. One glance at Kane, and he already had his bow drawn.

"I don't know yet." Gabriel answered. "Hold." He raised a hand, signaling for Kane and him to stand down, but Kellan freed his blade anyway. He'd been on edge since the cave.

He dared a glance at the girl who'd yet to draw a weapon of any sort. He'd been about to bark an order at her when her mount planted his hooves and came to an abrupt halt. Atlas's ears perked, his nicker echoing around them through the canyon.

A whinny in answer from somewhere around the bend, and to Kellan's relief, Eire rounded the bend one hundred feet ahead of them with a body strapped to the back of her mare, its legs and arms bound tightly. At neck breaking speed she galloped toward them, only sliding to a stop feet away before colliding. Effortlessly, she sliced the bonds on the wrists and legs before tossing the body to the ground at their feet. Kellan watched as the man landed with a grunt.

Thirty-Five

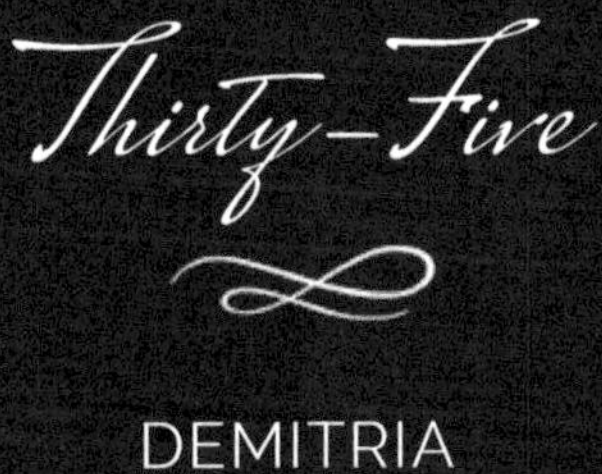

DEMITRIA

Demitria's heart stopped, catching in her chest. Feet flying from the saddle, she was running before the others could even blink.

Warmth. Strong arms.

Through all the blood, dirt and sweat, *mint*. It overtook her. Overwhelmed her. He was alive.

Alive

Her brain screamed, over and over again. Alive. Alive. Alive.

Jace was *alive*.

"Jace." Voice hoarse, her throat burned from lack of proper use. His hands tangled in her long, brown hair. "Oh God, Jace." The sobs overtook her body. She couldn't see, blinded by the tears that were once again falling as she clung to him. Afraid that if she let go, he'd disappear forever. This had to be real. She couldn't survive it if it wasn't. Jace was alive. He was here.

"I thought I'd never see you again." Jace was crying as he grabbed her, touching her arms, her face, as if in disbelief.

And she was laughing. Gods, she was laughing, because he felt *real*.

"I thought you were dead." Demitria buried her face into Jace's chest. Pressing her body to him. Suffocating herself at their closeness. "I didn't know what to do. Couldn't breathe." She was hyperventilating.

Her entire body trembling. Alive. He was alive. "I'm so sorry for leaving. I'm sorry. I'm so sorry." She apologized over and over again as another wave of guilt crashed through her. She pictured the bodies lying on the ground. Limbs torn free or buried under rubble, and in her mind, suddenly it was Jace. Staring at her, eyes glazed over and lifeless. She held on to him tighter. "I thought you were dead, and I... I'm so sorry."

"It's okay," He whispered. "I'm right here." Jace ran a hand through her hair in a soothing motion. "I'm right here."

"You were dead." Her brain was in overdrive. Couldn't tell up from down. Everything stopped. Jace. The only thing that mattered was Jace.

"I'm here." He soothed. "I'm not going anywhere. Never again. We're together." His hands roamed over her face. Her sides. He couldn't stop touching her, like he couldn't believe *she* was real.

"I thought I lost you." Her knees buckled beneath her, and the two were sent crashing to the ground. Pulling her body into his lap, Jace embraced her tighter, unrelenting in his grip. Refusing to let her go. "I thought I lost you." She repeated, voice no more than a whisper. Demitria closed her eyes, and all she could see were the flames that burned their homes. The bodies in the streets...

"I'm here." He rocked the both of them gently and her body melted into him. Her fingers aching from the grip she had on him, but she couldn't let go in fear that he'd disappear once more.

"How did you get out?" Kellan's strained voice broke through her thoughts, and she pulled away from Jace to look at him. At all of them seated atop their mounts. Gabriel's face hardened, jaw clenched as he looked at his sibling.

"Everything happened so fast." Jace looked up, eyes meeting each of the Horsemen towering above him. "We didn't even have a chance to react before they hit the gate." He didn't move from his spot on the ground. Content with Demitria safely back in his arms as she listened to the steady beat of his heart. "They slaughtered everything in their path. Set the city ablaze." Shaking his head, the shudder worked through his body as he recalled the events.

"We knew you were on the front lines. How were you spared?" Kellan pried.

"I shouldn't have survived." Jace hung his head, almost as if he was ashamed. "I tried to get everyone out. Tried to hold off as many of those damned monsters as I could while the others escaped." Demitria's hand entwined with his own, willing her strength into him. He smiled down at her, and it didn't go unnoticed by Kellan. The Horseman turned from them. "Stella took a death blow for me. She shouldn't have been fighting. I *watched* her leave with the first group that left." Bringing his gaze back up to Kellan, he continued. "I didn't even know what happened until it was too late. I didn't know she came back. She shoved me out of the way with a strength I didn't even know she possessed, and she took the blow that was supposed to be for me." More tears ran down his fair cheeks

Something in her cracked at the news as she choked back a sob. Stella... Demitria had even dared to hope that she'd see the woman again. Her sweet, smiling face as she greeted her. As she taught her about plants and medicinal herbs in the greenhouse. How to grow food. So much of her knowledge was from the woman, like the mother she'd lost, and Demitria never got to say goodbye. She was grateful to the woman for saving Jace's life, but at what cost?

Another body. Just another body added to her list of people she couldn't save. Of loved ones lost.

"She sacrificed her life for yours." Kellan's voice was quiet. Knowing. Demitria watched his features soften as his eyes met hers, and he bowed his head at her, as if in condolences.

"She told me I had unfinished business. That I wasn't done yet." Jace shook his head, a new wave of tears taking over. "I didn't even get to thank her before Evan was dragging me away." His fists clenched around the cloak at Demitria's back. "Like a coward, I ran. I followed him out. I abandoned everything."

"There was nothing more you could have done. You did what you could, Jace. Running doesn't make you a coward. You would be dead and the community would still be burnt to the ground had you stayed." Demitria squeezed his hand.

She'd run from them all, too, and felt exactly like the coward she'd claimed him not to be. Was she any different? Did that make her a coward?

"They came looking for you, and I panicked. It scared me to no end, but knowing you weren't there—I should have saved them. Should have gotten them all out. I was their leader..." His voice trailed off into nothing, and she felt the tremble of his fingers as he spoke.

Her. They'd come looking for her. She wanted to scream. Wanted to let those emotions welling up inside consume her until she was nothing but unyielding rage.

"You got out as many people as you could. The attack wasn't your fault." It was hers. None of this was on Jace. She was the one responsible for it. And as a guardian, she should have been there. On the front lines with him, holding those creatures back until her arms couldn't wield a weapon anymore or she was dead.

"How many people escaped?" Gabriel had been silently watching when he dismounted, striding over with an unearthly grace before holding a hand out toward them.

Jace watched it tentatively, unsure, but finally took it and Gabriel pulled them both to their feet. "Five others made it out with me. We lost contact with Pieter and Braun in the beginning of the raid."

"Pieter didn't make it." The thought of him stirred something in her chest. Him lying in her arms, whispering to him softly as he took his last breath. Jace's gaze met hers at the sound of another friend's passing. She watched that guilt pass through him as silver lined his eyes, pooling down his cheeks as he cast his eyes downward. "I held him in my arms until he took his last breath. He wasn't alone."

"Thank you. For being there for him when no one else could." He smiled softly. "What of Braun?"

"We never saw him." Demitria wondered if he was one of the many bodies that littered the ground in Solis. She hadn't been strong enough to check. Despite their quarrels, she wished she would have.

Jace nodded, his face sullen. "Cory, Tyler, Evan, and the twins made it out with me. I just...I can't wrap my head around everyone else being gone." Demitria felt a flutter in her chest at the names. Cory and Evan, Tyler. Hell, even the twins, she was happy about. She didn't wish death upon anyone, not like that, no matter how much they hated one another.

"Great, now we have two fucking humans." Eire spoke up from behind. One by one, everyone turned, all eyes focused on her. "I brought him back thinking we could ditch this one. She was already bad enough." Eire motioned toward her, and she couldn't help the roll of her eyes.

"Sounds like we're about to have seven, actually." Kane chuckled from behind, clapping his sibling on the back as his mount moved toward hers.

"Who is this lovely piece of work?" Jace whispered, his voice laced with a hint of amusement as he shrugged the comment off, stretching out his arms, rubbing the aches from the bind on his wrists. "I had a feeling she was one of them." He motioned toward Kellan.

"Don't even get me started." She grumbled, the chuckle leaving her lips effortlessly. It amazed her how easily he pulled her from the depths of that darkness.

Demitria moved to look at Kellan, following that inexplicable pull seemingly dragging her gaze toward him. Kellan had been unexpectedly quiet, and she wondered what was going through his head as azure eyes anchored her to the spot. She felt that look deep within her, pooling in her, and had to force herself to look away.

"What happened after you left?" Gabriel prodded for more information; his arms crossed over his chest. The dark cloak billowed around him, caught in the breeze that swept through the canyon.

"We've been holed up in a nearby shallow cavern. We traveled on foot for days. Everything is gone..." Jace stared at the eldest horsemen. "Every community we've come across has been destroyed. Burned to the ground. There is nothing left but ash."

Demitria looked up at Kellan again, his expression visibly hardening at the news they'd just received. He was aware of the being that was threatening the entire existence of this planet, but there was no way any of them anticipated just how quickly things were going downhill.

"They were taking me to Augustus." Demitria nodded at the Horsemen. "For refuge while they investigated further."

"It's gone."

Demitria's breath caught in her throat.

"Valencia was burned to the ground shortly after you left." Jace said.

Another community gone. Burned by the fucking monsters that were a plague on this planet. Demitria refused to cry.

"Just fucking great." Eire threw her hands in the air.

"This cavern, will you take us?" Gabriel asked. "I said I would return you to your people." Forest-green eyes turned on her. Hard. Final, as if she had no say in the matter.

"I told you I'm not—" He cut her off midsentence, hand raised to silence her.

"You will do as I say." Gabriel took a step toward her. Demitria's fists clenched at her sides. The Horseman held no sway over her, but his tone had been so stern. So...matter of fact. Law. "I mean you no disrespect, but things have been rather...difficult with your presence." Her features dropped, hands falling limp at her sides as she shot quick glances at the siblings. Did they all think the same? Eire, she already knew. But the others?

She was an idiot.

"I-I apologize." She turned away from those piercing eyes, her head hung in shame.

"Brother." Kellan interjected, dismounting from his horse and moving toward her.

"I don't want to hear it." Gabriel barked, stopping him in his tracks. Demitria knew a rift had been created between the siblings over whatever it was going on between them. She hadn't meant for that to happen, either. "Where are your people?"

Jace schooled his features as he glanced in her direction. She knew he would never give up the whereabouts of their people, especially after everything.

"We can trust him." Gripping Jace's arm in a reassuring gesture, she nodded toward Kellan. Deep down, she knew she could trust him. The others? She still wasn't so sure.

"Mount up." Was all Gabriel muttered before he turned away from them.

Kellan watched her move toward Atlas, as if waiting to speak with her. She wanted to say something, anything, to try and change their minds, but with Jace on her heels, all she could do was smile.

"What happened out there? How did she get ahold of you?" Demitria asked, climbing into the saddle. Jace scrambled up behind her, and she scooted as far into the pommel as she could to make room. His body seemed to mold around her as he anchored his arms around her waist for balance. They'd doubled on Atlas many times before, but never with the saddle. It made her seat awkward. Sloppy.

"I was out looking for survivors when I came across hoofprints." He started, his breath ghosting across her ear. "I'd hoped it'd be you and Kellan, but it turns out I wasn't so lucky." He laughed, the sound rumbling through her.

"I'm glad you're safe." She whispered, the sigh heavy on her lips.

Demitria nudged Atlas in front of the group to let Jace lead the way. They passed Kellan, that tug forcing her gaze up, over the planes of his face. The softening of his features as he looked at her, smiled at her.

Shit.

She needed to get herself together. Had to stop thinking about the way those eyes seemingly roved across her body. The warmth of his lips against hers when she'd kissed him just days ago...

Forbidden. Every single one of her thoughts was forbidden. Demitria knew she shouldn't—couldn't feel it. Her fingers tightened around the pommel of the saddle, moving that tortuous look to the land ahead.

They all rode in silence in a slow procession, one after the other. Kellan rode directly behind her, followed by Eire, Kane, and then Gabriel took up the rear. She heard nothing but hoofbeats and the steady rhythm of her heart beating in her chest.

She should be happy more than anything. She was returning to her people. Keeping her *life*. Yet... why did she feel upset? She'd made a vow to end the Dark King, and had told the Horsemen just that. But the thought of not fulfilling what she'd now set out to do? That irked her.

Demitria wanted her own answers, now. And if she returned with Jace and the others? She wouldn't get them. She wanted to know why a price had been put on her head. For what reason? Had she been destined to do something so wrong? What if she still was? She wanted to know how to change that, because what if their council just sent someone else for her in a year's time?

"We're wasting time." Eire groaned, and Demitria could all but picture her head leaned back, eyes to the sky in sheer agony at the sound.

"Don't listen to a word she says." She muttered, turning her head so Jace could hear her better. "She feels like she has some sort of entitlement to the world. Better than everyone." With a roll of her eyes, she chuckled.

"I can hear you!" Eire shouted, a vulgar gesture on full display for her siblings to see. "Humans..." She growled.

She heard Kellan's own laugh rumble through him, like a song to her ears. He'd told her how much his family meant to him, and yet, he seemed to enjoy the way Demitria all but taunted Eire, and that only made her smile grow. She was happy for the small distraction.

Jace lead them through the canyon, pointing around winding turns for what felt like hours before the large, rock walls opened up to the barren land.

"To the left, it's just around this bend." He motioned, and she steered Atlas in the direction he'd pointed. The horse moved on steady feet beneath them, despite the added weight. Demitria let her fingers trail down his soft neck, feeling the muscles beneath her hand, smoothing out the long, black mane. He deserved a long break.

Demitria spotted the opening some twenty feet away, large stalagmites jutting from the ground like an open maw, ready to devour them. As they approached the cavern, the others emerged, weapons drawn and ready in case of an incoming attack. She counted four bodies. The twins, Tyler, Cory, and Evan stood outside, like they'd all been waiting for Jace to return. Unaware that he'd been captured and held hostage by a Horseman. Aside from the twins, Demitria was happy to see the others. With a smile, she reigned Atlas to a halt before pulling her body free from the saddle and dismounting as she rushed to greet the other three.

Upon spotting her, Sam rushed them, grabbing Demitria in a choke hold before she could react. His hands enclosed around her throat, squeezing the air from her before she could muster the energy to evade his grasp.

"It was your fault!" Sam screamed, tears streaming down his face as his hands held her in an unrelenting grip. Demitria had never seen him cry. It all happened so fast, he had her pinned against the stone before she could blink. Her nails dug into his arms as she tried to break free of his hold, but the guilt consumed her once more, and she was unable to contain her sob as it broke. She knew. She already knew it was her fault.

"I left to prevent it, but they came anyway." She cried, barely able to get the words out. The image of the fire burned her vision. Their home. The bodies. "I didn't mean for any of this to happen."

"You're the reason everyone is dead!" Flecks of black began to dot her vision. She couldn't breathe, the panic setting in as new images replaced the burning inferno in her eyes. Reim and the Demon Lord exploded from her mind and she grew frantic. A wave of panic surged through her as the memory of the demon's hands flooded her thoughts. The unrelenting grip of his hold as he'd brought her closer and closer to death. She clawed at his arms. Face. Anything she could reach.

"They came looking for you. You! You killed every single one of them. I'll kill you for what you did!" The air came rushing back as Sam lay splayed across the ground, the tip of a sword ever so slightly piercing through the flesh of his throat.

"Remove your hands if you wish to keep them." Kellan snarled, his lips pulled back over his teeth. Murderous. "If you touch her again, I won't hesitate to end your life where you stand. Your head will roll, you understand?" *Rage.* So much rage filled his entire body. He left Sam in a heap as a thin line trickled down his neck as a reminder.

She sat there, panting on the ground as Kellan made his way toward her, helping her sit up.

"Are you alright?" He steadied her as she caught her breath. His hand warm on her back as she leaned into his firm grip.

"Yes, thank you." She coughed, finally able to find her voice once more.

"So help me God, Sam!" Jace had the man by his shirt as he shook him. "Are you insane? What is wrong with you!" He dropped the twin to the ground.

Demitria looked up at Kellan as the tip of a blade grazed his neck. She felt her breath hitch at the movement, but his face remained neutral. Unbothered as he didn't dare break his gaze from her. It took every ounce of strength to pull her eyes away.

Will's fingers curled around the knife's handle.

"Back off, human." Gabriel said, his voice calm. Smooth, as he stalked behind Will before coming to a stop behind him. Kane and Eire had arrows notched in their bows, the glint of Gabriel's scythe shone in the sun as the Horsemen pulled their weapons on the brothers.

"One more step and it's the last thing you will ever do."

Will hesitantly took a step back, helping his brother to his feet after sheathing his own blade.

"Remind me again why I should be saving your people." Amusement danced across Kellan's face as he extended his hand, pulling her back to her feet. She shouldn't have found it funny, but the laughter came easily, slipping free from her lips.

His hand lingered in hers for a moment longer than it should have, neither one quite willing to part first. With a sigh, Demitria finally dropped his, taking a step away from the warmth of the Horseman.

As quickly as it started, the fight was over. Satisfied, the other Horsemen sheathed their own weapons, moving away as the twins scrambled back to the mouth of the cavern.

"You're alive?" Cory was the first to step forward, eyes wide. Demitria wrapped her arms around him in a friendly embrace. "I'm glad he found you." He whispered, nodding toward Kellan still standing in close proximity.

"I sure hope so." The playful tone returned to her voice. It came easy with him. Cory came to the community shortly after Jace had taken over, and had been a constant, brotherly figure in her life since. One she had surely missed. "And so am I." Her voice lowered, feeling that pull between her and Kellan standing behind her. Demitria took a step back, moving to greet Evan. He gave her a sharp nod.

"Good to see you."

"Glad to see you made it out." It was a stretch of the truth. A half-truth, really. But she extended it all the same. "We should get inside. We need to talk." Demitria moved past him and entered the cavern, Kellan on her heels.

Jace motioned the others inside. The other Horsemen hesitated for a moment, before entering between the gap of the stalagmites.

Demitria took in the darkness of the cavern. The musty smell that wafted through her senses. Little belongings littered the floor, but she could tell they'd been here for a few days at least. Toward the entrance, the soft glow of a fire illuminated the front of the room as flames danced along the walls. She shuddered at the sight as she drifted toward the cavern with Reim, and she pushed further away from the flames that haunted her. She could hear the footsteps as the others followed behind, but her mind was reeling.

She should be happy that some of them had made it out. Should be absolutely rejoicing that Jace and Cory and Evan were alive, but couldn't shake the fact that this was it. That the Horsemen would leave her here, and stop whatever—whoever this Dark King was.

Demitria wanted her answers. She needed to find out why they all wanted her. She was afraid that when they left out of that cave for good, she would never know.

And she *wanted* to know why these beings sought her out. Why they wanted her dead. Why she felt this...pull between the male she had no business knowing, let alone having these thoughts about. He was a Horseman of the fucking Apocalypse, and she was supposed to hate everything about him. Like the way he carried himself. So confident and sure of himself. Or the soft, velvety laugh that rumbled through her. Or—

Demitria ran a hand across her face and through her hair, turning on her people she looked from Jace to the others around her.

"There's...something going on that I think you should know." She didn't know if she was ready to tell them *why* Solis had fallen, but they deserved to know. Sam had tried to kill her for it minutes ago, and he didn't even know why. "Everything that happened, has been because of me." Her gaze drifted toward Kellan. He was at the back of the group now, but his eyes never left hers. Behind him, his siblings hadn't moved past the mouth of the cave. Whether they were listening or talking amongst themselves, she didn't know.

"We know they came looking for you." Sam glared, rubbing the side of his neck. The puncture in his throat had stopped bleeding but the faint outline of a bruise now graced his throat.

She didn't bother answering him. "There's a price on my head, and those creatures came looking for me. I don't know why. I don't know what they want with me, and I'm sorry for everything it caused." Demitria swore she wouldn't cry again, but she could feel the tears lining her eyes, desperately trying to break free.

"Whatever it is, we'll fix it. We'll do what it takes." Jace took a step forward, reaching a hand toward her.

"You saying you're special or something?" Will scoffed. "Like they want you or something? Please, whatever it is can't be that bad." It took every effort not to shout back a retort. Not that bad? People had *died* because of it. They'd lost their homes. Everything. She settled on rolling her eyes, instead, unwilling to cause a rift with her own people.

"This is a bigger threat than you can even fathom, boy. I suggest you shut your mouth and let the adults speak." Kellan glowered. "The destruction that you have witnessed is not something any of us should take lightly. The fact that it is happening this fast is... alarming." He added.

"What do you mean? Is something coming?" Cory asked, turning from the conversation at hand, and back toward the other Horsemen, as if drawn to whatever it was they were saying. Demitria could see them talking quietly, but couldn't make out what it was.

"This could mean the end of life as we know it." Demitria's voice hardened. "Something big is coming. Probably already here, and he wants nothing more than the destruction of every civilization here, and won't stop until we're all enslaved."

Jace went silent. She knew she should have tried to explain it on the way here, but she hadn't been able to bring herself to do it.

"What is coming?" Like his brother, Sam glared at the Horsemen. At Demitria.

Kane spoke, moving from the entrance to join them. "A being that you don't want to be anywhere near here if he succeeds. We could have used you over there." He turned to Kellan.

"While you were wasting your time with the humans, Gabriel tried summoning the council again." Eire stated, her arms crossing over her chest. Every part of the female looked deadly.

"And?" Kellan raised a brow.

"They didn't answer." Kane sighed, his pale blue eyes turning to the floor. Demitria watched the siblings, that curiosity spiking through her.

"We can't let him succeed." Gabriel said. Through his clenched hand, she could see the faint hint of red as it leaked past his fingers. "I will not allow it."

"Who is he?" Tyler asked. Demitria turned toward the boy. The family she had vowed to never let another member fall, and she hated having him out here. One more body to protect with her life. One more she couldn't let die.

"The Dark King is a power none of you will survive if we don't stop him before he reaches his potential. Before he comes into the power he seeks." Kellan's eyes fell to Demitria. She knew he must have felt the same as her. The Dark King wanted her very soul, and they needed to know *why*

"They mentioned west." Cory's voice echoed off the walls. Loud, to ensure he was heard the first time. "I heard one of them tell the others to bring the bodies west." He shook his head. "Wish I knew more. For all of our sakes."

Bodies? Had they taken people from Solis? Did more survive?

"No one faults you. Any bit of information helps." Kellan smiled at him. Surprise widened Jace and Tyler's eyes.

"I was headed to the angel encampment when they found me. I wanted answers, and they were the only beings I could think of." Demitria told them. She wouldn't tell them about her capture, none of them needing to know the horrors she'd endured. Jace especially. "We were nearly there when Eire came across Jace." When she'd *captured* him, really.

"The last report I received they were through the canyon. That was why you were there?" Jace asked her.

Demitria nodded, turning to face the Horsemen once more.

"I will still take you there. I meant what I said earlier."

Eire opened her mouth to cut her off but Kellan silenced his sister. "Let her speak." He barked.

"I want answers, just as much as you do." She focused on Gabriel as she spoke. Willing her words to hit true. "This is my life at stake, and I deserve to have a say in what happens."

"You're just as stubborn as he is." Gabriel groaned, rolling his eyes. He sighed. "You will show us the way, and I will make my decision then. For now, I will give you the opportunity to rest. We ride in a few hours." Gabriel didn't wait for any further comment before turning away from them and exiting the cave.

She was grateful for the reprieve, however short it may be. Despite the rest, she needed to figure out a way to make herself useful if she were to stick around.

Demitria had vowed to kill this Dark King. To find her answers and end the creatures that hunted her people for nothing more than sport.

She would find a way to accompany them on the rest of their journey.

Thirty-Six

KELLAN

The night had grown cold in the cave around them. The orange glow of the flames softly illuminated the smooth rock exterior within. The heat was a welcomed necessity as nearly all the humans had fallen asleep an hour before, aside from the twins whispering before the flames. Three of the siblings had initially fought the idea, but Kellan had won out on giving them extra time to rest until dawn. He needed more time. Anything to help delay the inevitable. The battle that he knew they were racing toward. The slaughter that they were now leading them to. The humans wouldn't survive a fight against *him*. After talks had dwindled down hours before, Demitria and her group had decided they'd all journey to The Fallen with them. Despite their protests, he found himself glad for the extra company.

Kellan's eyes traveled to Demitria's sleeping figure on the other side of the blaze. *More time.* Her head was tucked softly into Jace's chest. His fingers balled into fists on his lap, jaw clenched as that familiar sensation of boiling blood took hold. The anger swelled within him, despite every bone in his body telling him to behave.

He'd known for a while now that things had changed between them, and was sure she had too. Yet despite knowing better, he was angry. At himself. At Jace. He didn't even know anymore.

Kellan looked up to find the twins staring at him.

Maybe it was the laughter that echoed off the walls as the twins both sported that familiar shit-eating grin. "What does she mean to you, Horseman?" Sam nodded toward Demitria.

Kellan didn't answer, and it spoke volumes.

"Does it make you angry? Seeing her with him?" Will added, his smile wicked through the flames. Kellan had to avert his gaze before he did something stupid.

"Jace is the only man she's ever let in." Sam taunted.

"In more ways than one." Their laughter erupted again.

He needed to get out. So close. He was so close to stepping over that edge. One more comment and he'd—

"She doesn't want you. She chose him." Will motioned toward the two sleeping figures in their tangled embrace.

Kellan was on his feet, exiting the cave before he'd make any rash decisions. If he'd waited one more minute. One more second, the brothers wouldn't be breathing, and the cavern would be painted in blood. He could imagine their flesh in his hands, their throats constricting beneath his fingertips as they gasped for air. He wouldn't lie, it would have brought him immense pleasure to have them die by his bare hands. Strangling them wouldn't have been his preferred method, but in the moment, it would have sufficed. Anything to silence their mouths.

It shouldn't have bothered him, seeing them like that. Wrapped around each other as they slept. It shouldn't have mattered. She'd said they were friends from a young age, and that was all it was. *Why did that even matter?* Kellan ran a hand down his face as he groaned. Maybe Eire was right. Maybe he was growing soft. Losing touch with himself and the world around him.

Toeing a rock with his boot he kicked it, watching it fly, disappearing into the darkness beyond them. He listened, waiting for it to land as it crashed into the dirt. His senses still felt out of sorts, but beyond the canyon things felt that bit clearer. Like he could finally breathe again. He'd find out what was blocking his abilities later. Before they left in the morning. Kane could have been doing just that, judging by the lack of a lookout.

"I can punch them out if it'd make you feel better?"

Kellan was so lost in his thoughts he startled, turning as he looked down at her. She was standing right outside the entrance, arms crossed over the swell of her chest as she watched him with bright eyes. Something like amusement, maybe even more. She'd left the familiar dark cloak inside, and Kellan let himself take her in. The fitted clothing that seemingly hugged her every curve. He fought against the smile threatening to break at the sight of her as that incessant pull flared to life. He was so fucked. "It's nothing."

"Not what it looked like." She shifted her position, now leaning casually against the stalagmite. Her eyes didn't leave his. "They're annoying, I know, but don't let it get to you. They want to make you angry."

"I don't like it." He grumbled. Dislike would have been a complete underselling of his feelings, but he wouldn't get into it with her. Not wanting to cause even more of a rift between her and her people.

"Whatever they said, don't believe it." He was sure she was fast asleep when he'd practically run outside, and although he hadn't wanted to believe them, that jealousy reared its ugly head. "They're nothing but a bunch of assholes."

"Kind of hard not to when it's right in front of me, staring me in the face." Kellan pulled his gaze from her, looking the other way. It took more effort than he cared to admit. He didn't dare meet her eyes. Hated how vulnerable she'd made him feel. Despised it, yet he couldn't get her out of his head. Longed to feel the softness of her skin on his. To race his fingers up and down her arms. Kellan shook his head, frustrated all over again.

"Kellan." She stood in front of him, grabbing his arm. His name like a song on her lips. One he wanted to hear again and again. "Kellan." She repeated, more stern the second time around. Slowly, he returned his gaze, eyes meeting once more. "Ignore every single word they said." Kellan managed to hold back the shiver that threatened to course through his body as she ran her hand slowly up his arm and up to his chest where it rested. *Barely.*

"I don't know what to think anymore." Before he could stop himself, Kellan's palm was resting against the warmth of her cheek, so soft beneath his fingertips. "The way I was. Everything I knew…" He trailed off. Kellan moved to turn away again, but stopped himself. "It's you. I don't… I shouldn't." Shaking his head, he forced his eyes closed. By the fucking gods, he knew anything between them was out of the question. Anything between him and a human girl was utterly forbidden, but he was losing the battle and couldn't stop himself.

"Kellan." Demitria's voice was no more than a whisper, breath wavering at their closeness. He couldn't hold back any longer. Kellan's eyes shot open, lips meeting hers in a fiery kiss. She stumbled back into the rock at its intensity, but didn't make a move to break away. He near collapsed into her, pushing himself closer. He'd lost all control. All ability to think rationally the moment she'd touched him.

In a dizzying haze, Demitria was untying his armor, shoving it to the ground until he'd been stripped down to nothing more than the pants he wore. Her fingers trailed up his abdomen from the waistline, up toward his chest. Feeling the warmth of his skin beneath her fingertips, and the sheer muscle as she passed over them. To the thin silvery white line of the new scar that graced his chest from the hit he'd taken for her.

Kellan let his own hands explore every inch of her he could. Softly up her sides, slowly working their way underneath the hem of her shirt. The shiver worked its way through her body, eliciting a grin as he nipped at her bottom lip. Couldn't get enough. He couldn't get enough of her.

"Whatever they said, it isn't true." She whispered, hot against the sun-kissed skin of his chest as ever so slowly, she let her mouth trail down, down, down. Kellan groaned at the sight of her kneeling before him as wicked thoughts filled him to the brim. Imagining what it would feel like to have that mouth wrapped around him. When delicate fingers traced along the waist of his pants, his only thoughts were to throw his head back against the rock behind him. He was fucked. So, so fucked as those green-gold eyes met his. As they stared into his *soul*.

Grabbing her wrists in his large hands, Kellan pulled her to her feet before spinning them, pinning her figure to the smooth rock. So small, as he held her arms above her head with just one hand, the other pressed firm beside her head as his hulking figure towered over her. He watched her chest heave, up and down with each breath she took.

Kellan stepped further into her, feeling her up against the planes of his body, and let his free hand roam along every inch of her, relishing in the sound as her breath hitched. Claiming her mouth with his once more, tasting her, he let that hand wander further until a small sound slipped through her lips.

He was so ready to lose himself in her. To toss all caution to the wind, and absolutely devour her. Kellan imagined taking her right then and there on the ground. Imagined running his hands over every speck of skin as he mapped her with his fingers, trailing them along the smooth skin of her stomach, her thighs, before delving them inside until she was writhing beneath him, making that noise that drove him absolutely *feral*.

But when he imagined his hands again, they were tainted red. Dripping that scarlet liquid between his fingers as she lay on the ground motionless, blood pouring from the gruesome slash across her throat.

Something snapped in him at the thought, so much like the brutal death his mother had suffered. Like the crack of a whip, pulling him from the frenzy he'd been in, breaking him from the spell of the human girl before him. Not regret. Definitely not that, but something akin to it. Guilty. He'd felt guilty over what had transpired, because it made him no better than his father. For taking a human when it was utterly forbidden. The council had *beaten* it into them so many times that he couldn't even enjoy what had just transpired. Because fuck, he wanted to. Wanted to explore the sounds that had come out of her mouth as he touched her, igniting some long-smothered fire within him.

Kellan took a step back, pulling away from her touch as he regained some form of restraint within himself.

Demitria was the first to break the silence. "I'm sorry—I shouldn't have."

He wasn't, not even for a moment. Neither one had been willing to break their gaze, but her cheeks blossomed into warm shades of pinks. She reached a tentative hand toward him, but dropped it just as quickly. For a moment, he'd thought she'd felt regret, but it was something similar to what he'd been warring with himself. Everything they'd ever known. Been told—

"I know." He replied. It took every fiber in his body to convince himself to take another step back. For his hands to remain at his sides.

Demitria was stronger than he could even fathom. She straightened out her clothing, the breath shuddering through her shoulders as she willed her body to calm before turning away from him on shaky legs. He watched as she evened out her breathing before hesitantly returning to the cave. She stopped short, nearly out of eyesight before turning around to face him once more. Opening her mouth to say something, the heavy sigh left her lips instead, and she disappeared back into the awaiting darkness.

Kellan ran his own shaking hand down his face, his breath leaving in a rush. He waited a few more minutes outside before he dared follow. Needing to calm his own breathing. Despite his body screaming at him, he had to let her walk away. He shouldn't do whatever the hell it was they were doing, but at least he knew where she stood.

Thirty-Seven

DEMITRIA

Demitria watched the entrance with bated breath, listening as the argument raged on beyond the entrance as she leaned against Jace. She could hear Eire shouting as the siblings fought and had a growing suspicion it was over what happened last night between her and Kellan. Her people had been none the wiser, the Horsemen were different.

Demitria didn't know how to go about the morning. The sun had broken over the horizon nearly an hour ago, yet they stood waiting in the cavern as the embers of the nights fire died into nothing, sucking the remaining warmth with it.

When Kellan rounded the corner, her heartbeat quickened at the sight of him. She could see his narrowed gaze from where she stood. The scowl on his face as he all but stormed through the entrance. He didn't look happy. She felt her body take a step in his direction. His eyes met hers. She should say something. Anything. Neither of them had said a word to each other after last night.

"Morning." Not exactly what she'd had in mind, but it was something. Absently, she took a step away from Jace. Putting distance between them.

"Good morning." His gaze didn't break. Staring at her. Into her.

Like he was reading every thought. Like he knew exactly what she was thinking. It took every ounce of strength she had in her to not take those few steps forward. To throw her arms around him and press her body flush against him like she wanted.

Stop.

Her mind screamed at her. Scolded her for even thinking it. They'd agreed it wasn't right. That they couldn't pursue anything between them, despite that tether pulling them together. But the way he'd felt last night. The warmth of his skin beneath her fingers. The feel of his hands on her as she—

Enough!

"I take it we're leaving?" She had to look away. Her body would betray her if she didn't. Any moment, she'd lose.

"Your little tiff with your sister over?" Will laughed. She was thankful, for once. His outburst had drawn Kellan from her. Pulled those azure eyes away, and she could feel her breathing even. Her heart slowing.

"Get your things together." He huffed. She could hear the hardness in it. He was angry. He wanted to say something, but he wouldn't. Demitria imagined fighting with his siblings drained him. "We're leaving." All she could hear was the thud of his boots along the rock as he left once more. She should go after him. Talk to him. Figure out what exactly had been bothering him.

She didn't.

Jace looked at her, his brow raised in question. She couldn't tell him what had happened with Kellan while he slept. Didn't think he'd understand any of it. Hell, even she didn't, really.

She must be sick. Twisted, somehow. Kellan had tried to kill her merely weeks ago, but she'd let him touch her last night. Hadn't wanted him to stop when he'd pulled away as quickly as he had. She'd contemplated begging him to come back as that feeling pooled within her.

Demitria just shrugged. "We should probably head out. Gabriel said we leave at dawn, and we're already late." She took another step away from Jace, placing one foot in front of the other until she was passing between the stalagmites at the entrance, and out into the early morning air.

The siblings sat atop their mounts, waiting for her and her people with hard expressions on their faces. Gabriel's lips held in a firm line, while Eire scowled toward the entrance. At her, it almost seemed like. Kane was the only one looking away, his piercing blue eyes fixated on the canyon before them.

Kellan stood beside his mount, holding his reins in one hand while the other held Atlas. He whispered something to the horse. Atlas nudged him softly, blowing a soft breath from his nose as if in understanding. Curiosity spiked within her, and Demitria found herself wishing to know what he'd said, and if Atlas had truly understood.

The silence was unnatural. For hours, the air had been tense. The Horsemen had split themselves among the group. Gabriel took up the front, Eire at the rear. Kane rode silently in the middle. Evan, Cory, and Jace walked together, but neither of them spoke. The twins conversed quietly behind. Laughing over something that she didn't care to know about. Demitria rode alone on Atlas, but Kellan wasn't ever too far off. She stole a glance toward him, only to find him already watching her. She couldn't help the smile, and his features softened. Eyes gentle.

"Is everything okay?" She asked, voice barely above a whisper, but he heard her. Kellan only nodded. "Would you tell me if it wasn't?" Nothing. Didn't shake his head, just continued watching. Her sigh was loud as she glanced away.

"I would tell you." His leg brushed hers as Kellan pushed his mount up beside her. So close their shoulders nearly touching. "Always."

"What's going on?" She wouldn't meet his gaze. Could feel the eyes of the others as they burned into her back. Watching. Straining to hear the conversation being had between them.

"Nothing I can't handle."

She could hear the amusement in his voice. Demitria stole another glance at him. He was looking straight ahead, but the smile was there.

"Kellan." She sighed again.

"She knows."

She knew who he was talking about. It shouldn't have come as a surprise after last night. "That's what it was about. She knows, and she lost it." Demitria stayed silent. Waiting for him to continue. "Threatened to turn me into the council."

"She can't!" She didn't think as her hand reached for his. Enclosing around it as her heart near stopped. She remembered what he'd told her about his parents. How the council slaughtered his mother because of the choices his father made. Would the council kill him, too? "She wouldn't do that!" Pulling Atlas to a halt, body whirling around in the saddle so she was facing him. Not daring to let go, or caring who was watching.

"You don't know her." He shook his head, eyes roaming over her. "There are things you don't know. Things about her past—our past, that shaped us into who we are today." There was more to the story, but she wouldn't push him. He would share it if he wanted to.

"You really think she'd do that?" Demitria couldn't fathom the thought of his own sibling turning him in. Couldn't even grasp the fact. It was his sister. How could you do that to your own family?

"You have no idea the things we've seen." His grip on her hand tightened, and she reveled in the feeling. The warmth of it against her skin. The sheer size of it engulfed around her own. She knew she should let go. Move Atlas away. Avert her gaze. Something. Anything to get herself away, but she couldn't. Or refused to. She didn't know anymore. Found it harder and harder to tell the difference as the days went on. The more time she spent around the Horsemen, the more confused she felt.

Demitria wouldn't push him for answers. Knew well enough when to leave it alone. The look in his eyes said it all. Whether it was his story or not to tell, she wouldn't question it. Question him.

"Okay." It took a moment, but she finally let herself sit back. If Eire was really going to turn him into the council, it wasn't going to be on her account. She didn't know much about them. Actually, she knew nothing. But by the way he acted, and the brutality caused to his family. she knew it wouldn't be pleasant. Having him turned in was the last thing she ever wanted.

"We should continue on."

Kellan didn't drop her hand at first, but after several heartbeats, he finally let it go. With a curt nod, he nudged his horse forward and walked off. She easily fell into step beside him. "It'll be fine," he said. "They can't hurt me anymore than they already have." Something in her hardened at his last words. The whisper of them as he wouldn't look at her when he'd said them. The council had... hurt him? And Eire had still threatened it anyway?

They rode together in silence for another few minutes before Demitria finally broke it once more. "Has the plan changed?"

Kellan shook his head, "No. Everything is still as before. Finding the angels is our next target. Then we move from there."

Demitria nodded. Once they found the angels, she didn't know what they were to do. She had her own goal, that still remained. Jace was alive, thank whatever gods had made that happen, but she wouldn't let the Dark King live. Not after everything. Her community. The surrounding ones. She would find a way to continue on with them, then she would end the being if it was the last damn thing she did.

For several hours they pushed on, until the sun was high in the sky. Regrouping briefly to decide on their route, with the consensus being to get above the never-ending rock walls surrounding them for a better view. Finding a spot for their mounts to climb up had been tedious and downright frustrating, but they'd managed. Somehow, without anyone getting injured. Demitria felt for the others making the tedious climb on foot.

As they crested the ridge, they came upon a densely wooded area of charred trees. They'd never climbed the canyon during their scouting missions, and neither of them had known what to expect. It called to her, whatever was up here. Pulling her toward it.

"Well, this is just great." Sam grunted, crossing his arms over his chest as he stared out at the forest of ash.

"They're leading us into a trap, and they're going to kill us all." Will added, glaring at each of the Horsemen before him.

Demitria rolled her eyes. She hated that the twins had come along, and wished they would have come across a community that hadn't been ravaged, and left them there. Forever.

"Shut your mouths before I do it for you." She snapped. Demitria had grown increasingly tired of their quips and had very nearly reached her limit on what she could take. The constant bickering. The talking down. She was ready to explode. One job. One goal. It was all she had, and so help her if they stood in the way of that...

"We need to decide our next course of action." Gabriel met the eyes of each of them. "Something feels... off about it." He turned, staring intently at the charred forest.

Despite being only human, she couldn't agree more. Something about the woods. The eerie mist that seemed to hang unnaturally around it. Nothing about it seemed normal. Well, as normal as things got these days, at least.

But it beckoned her. Called out to something in her blood that she couldn't quite explain.

"I vote we go through it." Eire stated. "I can't sense anything of the Fallen anymore. Not since we were down below. I don't know if it's the stench of these trees or what, but going through will be faster than going around."

"That's exactly why I'm voting to go around. It isn't safe for them." Kellan countered, toeing with his sister once again. A regular occurrence, it seemed.

"Why should we listen to you? You have been nothing more than a human-loving piece of shit as of late, Kellan. Have you forgotten your place so quickly?" She snarled.

"Have you forgotten yours?" Kellan matched her tone for tone.

Demitria dismounted, leaving Atlas as she took a step forward. Not toward Kellan. Toward the woods. Toward the siren song that called out to her from within. Tapping along the edges of her mind. She moved further. Away from her friends. From Kellan. She could almost touch it. Could feel the cool sensation of the mist along her body. Tingling— itching against her skin as it crawled around her. Pulling her into the thick of it. Before any of the others had noticed her, too engrossed in the conversation among the Horsemen.

"What are you doing?" Kellan shouted, tearing himself from Eire. Too far. He was too far away, and she couldn't make her body stop. She kept moving, one foot in front of the other until she couldn't hear them anymore, and the trees seemed to swallow her whole.

Thirty-Eight

DEMITRIA

Demitria had given in to whatever pull had summoned her. She couldn't explain what it was that drew her in, but knew that it was something she needed to do. If she was to continue walking this path she was on, she needed to follow.

All around her was dark as if the mist had swallowed any life that lay within. Not even the sun's piercing rays could break through. The air was hazy, and she could only see a few feet in each direction. Still, she pushed on. Slipping her hand to the hilt of the sword, she slid it free of its sheath. Readying the blade as she pushed further in.

Don't run. Don't be afraid.

Like a mantra, she repeated the words. *Don't run. Don't be afraid.*

She had to push forward. To face whatever it was that was inside. Whatever it was that she needed to see.

All around her the air smelled stale. Musty, yet burned. The trees, despite the raging inferno that must have swept through the area, stood solid. It was shocking to see them still so tall. Strong. Even though a fire had very clearly torn through the woods, they'd refused to fall. Refused to bow down to the forces that sought to end them.

She could feel herself drawing strength from them. From the

thought of it. They were broken and charred, their habitat utterly decimated, yet they stood.

I am strong, and I will get through this.

Demitria took in a breath, peering around the darkness. She may be flawed, but she was not broken. Being here was proof of that. After all that she'd endured, she was still standing. She pushed forward. As she did, the mist around her lightened, the darkness lifting enough that she could see her surroundings.

Demitria was in the thick of the trees, but had wandered into an open clearing within. Whatever had been beckoning her inside had vanished. That tug pulling her deeper was gone. Or had she just gotten where she needed to go? Raising her sword higher, readying it, she let her eyes scan the area. Searching for something. Anything that could have called to her.

"We meet again." She couldn't move as the wave of fear tried to root itself within her and take hold of her body.

I am strong, and I will get through this.

She repeated again.

I am not afraid.

Before her stood the creature who had murdered her parents. The creature who had taken her hostage and brought her to the Demon Lord. The creature who had tried to eat her alive. Reim smirked at her, a terrifyingly toothy grin as those crimson eyes shone bright. Wicked. That familiar numbness tried to take over once again. A dark prodding at the wall she'd resurrected.

"While you were following the darkness so blindly, your friends entered after you." The demon circled her, its smile never wavering. "They shouldn't have come here."

"It was you." Demitria took a tentative step forward. "What did you do to them?" She demanded, holding back the tremble in her voice. *I am strong, and I will get through this.*

"You've been told the human soul holds great power." Reim circled her. "Your people proved to be quite...delectable." The demon licked his lips, his forked, snake-like tongue a deep shade of purple. Her people? Had he eaten her people? Stolen their souls to get to her? "What if I were to give you a choice? Their life for yours?" Reim ran a clawed finger down her arm as he circled her once more, like she was his prey. Light enough that he hadn't broken her skin, yet hard enough that her body remembered the toxins that had nearly killed her as that familiar revulsion filled her. Demitria suppressed the shudder that threatened to overcome her.

"What did you do?" She asked, the lithe, inky, humanesque body stopping before her. Watching with those terrifying eyes.

Reim held up a familiar gold object, and her blood ran cold. "Stupid, stupid human." The demon twirled the pocket watch in his taloned fingers. "It's a shame he and your Horseman followed after."

It had captured Kellan and Jace. Maybe even the others, too. Were they being held by demons, somewhere in here? How the hell had she not heard them come in? Surely, she would have heard them shouting after her.

"If I give myself up, will it end the war?" She'd do it. If it meant stopping the Dark King, she'd give herself up. Wanting him to die had been her goal, but stopping the war? She could save humanity. Kellan or Jace wouldn't be happy, but she knew they'd find a way to kill him when the time came.

"Stupid girl." It laughed. "We are beyond that point. He's here, raising his army as we speak." *Shit*. Were they too late? Had this entire search been for nothing after all? Had Eire been right that they were just wasting their time? The demon stepped into her, so close she could feel the cold press of his body, her hair standing on edge as every nerve ending seemed to misfire. Wrong. The demon felt so wrong to her.

"You're lying." Gods, she hoped he was.

"Enough about the inevitable." Reim growled. "I want to play a game." Another clawed finger trailed across her neck, and every inch of skin itched where he'd touched her. "Let's make this interesting. One lives, one dies. The choice is yours." With another terrifying grin, Reim stepped back. The mist receded again. In a tangle of shadow and charred branches, Kellan and Jace lay pinned. Heads lulled to the side, unconscious, as blood seemed to pool around them. Her heart raced at the sight of them. Near ready to explode from her chest as a panic began to set in. Was this the power of a human soul? Of several? Had it given him so much power that he'd captured a Horsemen?

"Don't make me choose." She wouldn't choose between them. Couldn't, for that matter. Jace, the permanent figure in her life. Her best friend. The one who had been by her side for as long as she could remember. Kellan. Whatever they had brewing between them was something she couldn't explain. And despite the rules saying otherwise, she wanted to explore what it was. To know all there was to know about him. To explore *him*.

Like hell she would choose.

I am strong and I will not be afraid.

Her stance widened, blade poised.

I am strong and I will not be afraid.

And for the first time, Demitria pushed on. Launching herself at the demon. "I will not be afraid!" She roared. The deadly edge of her blade skirted across the demon's shoulder. Not enough to render him incapacitated, but she'd drawn blood as that black substance oozed from the wound. She swung again, and he dodged backward. His steps never faltered.

Back and forth they went, trading blows. She hadn't landed another since the first, but she'd been lucky to avoid the poisonous claws. Demitria knew what it could do to her if it broke skin. She wouldn't let that happen. Not here, not now. Not ever again.

"I can smell your fear." Reim taunted, resuming his circling of her. Like a hungry shark readying his strike. She wouldn't fall for it. Wouldn't let him touch her again.

"The fear you smell is nothing but your own." She growled. Turning with him, meeting his gaze every step of the way. She wouldn't be afraid, not anymore. She was strong, and she was still standing.

Demitria dared a glance toward the unconscious figures. They hadn't moved, but nothing had changed either. That was all that mattered. A brief glimpse of the rise and fall of their chests was all she needed to know to keep going. To keep pushing.

"This is all over if you choose." He lunged, claws pointed for her chest. Demitria rolled out of the way with less than an inch to spare. Narrowly escaping the deadly blow he'd tried for. He was fast, but she'd been quicker. Her blade swung again, this time it pierced flesh. A deafening roar of pain erupted from his body as he twisted, striking for her.

She rolled again. He was slowing, but she wouldn't let her guard down. "I'll take my time killing you." He seethed, "Taste your flesh like I did your parents. I still remember how your mother tasted. Her blood sickly sweet." Another toothy grin, an effort to get under her skin.

It worked, just not how he'd hoped.

Demitria let the rage consume her as the guilt she'd been forever carrying disappeared. Let the fire she'd barely contained overcome her, and launched at him with such fierceness, the demon couldn't move. She moved so fast he hadn't had the chance to.

She was screaming, roaring, as she exploded. Embedding the blade through the demon's chest with an ethereal force she didn't know she possessed. Ripping any ounce of life from the creature's body.

"My name is Demitria Collins," She panted, standing over the demon that had ruined her life. Those crimson eyes bore into her own. *Fear.* She could see the fear in them as she towered over him. Could taste it in her mouth as a familiar itch radiated down her spine. "I am not afraid." She plunged her sword deeper. Deeper until it pierced the dirt beneath him, and the demon ceased to exist.

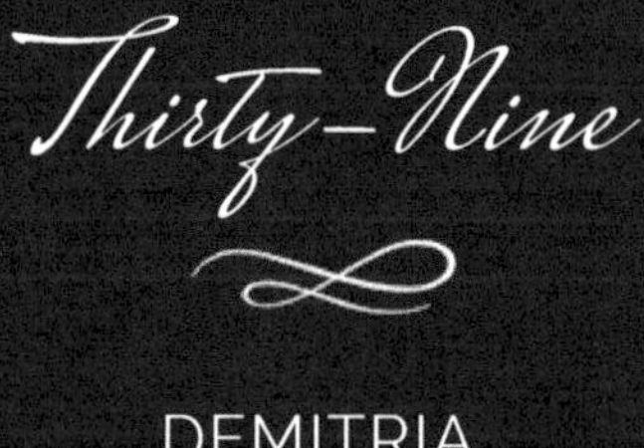

Thirty-Nine

DEMITRIA

She couldn't move. The adrenaline that was pumping through her body had left her feeling numb. Legs nearly useless. Despite it all, she'd made it. The body beneath her was proof of that.

On shaky legs, she crawled off the demon, snatching the golden pocket watch from his talons as she did. A lightness had enveloped her body. A warmth, like a soft caress that eased every worry she'd had. It was the guilt, she realized, that no longer plagued her. That utter feeling of despair and worthlessness that had been dragging her for so many years, torturing her at every waking moment, was gone. Killing Reim had lightened her. Healed her soul in a way that no one else had ever been able to since the death of her parents.

Using her sword as a crutch, Demitria stood, taller than she had in years. The mist began to dissipate, and with it, the bodies of her friends vanished into nothingness.

"Demitria!" Kellan reached her first. Her name rolling off his tongue like a prayer, for the first time, she realized. And she—she'd *loved* the way it sounded coming from his mouth. He'd come from the opposite direction from where his body had been minutes before. Had it... not been real? Had he not been caught? "By the gods, we couldn't reach you." Kellan held her face in his hands, and she realized her entire body was shaking. Reim's corpse still lay unmoving feet away. That had been real. She'd felt it in her entire body when he'd died. "I'm so sorry you had to face him alone." Kellan crushed her in an embrace she didn't dare break away from. Hugging her body so close to his they'd felt like one.

"I killed him." She whispered. "All that pain... the guilt. It's just... gone."

"They'd be so proud of you." His breath ghosted over her ear, and the shiver wreaked havoc on her insides at its warmth. At the things it did to her. "I'm so proud of you." Kellan had known the strife the demon had caused her. The pain that had engraved itself under her skin at what Reim had done. He knew, more than any of the others aside from Jace, just how hard that had to have been on her. The trauma it would have caused.

"You were taken, and I just... Jace was there, and I couldn't let him kill you. Either of you." She held them in for as long as she could. The tears fell freely from her eyes, soaking his cloak as they trickled down her cheeks.

"He consumed human souls." Kellan spoke. "I'd recognize that power anywhere. That's why we couldn't reach you. To tell you it wasn't real. We couldn't touch anything in the clearing without succumbing to that power ourselves. But you won. You overcame it all, and you beat it." Pulling away from her, Kellan cupped her face in his hands softly so all she could see was him. Staring into those azure eyes that'd she'd grown so fond of these weeks since he'd captured her. His thumb gently caressed her bottom lip, her body igniting underneath the touch. Begging him to close the distance, despite the others that surrounded them. In that moment, it was only her and Kellan.

"You're beautiful." He whispered, as if seeing her for the first time. In a different light than before, like watching her had ignited something within him.

"What...was that?" Demitria pulled away from Kellan at Jace's voice. *He didn't know.*

"That is what killed our parents." She wiped the back of her sleeve across the tears lining her eyes. "It's what I couldn't tell you back in Solis."

Jace stumbled backward, hand clenched to his chest as the words left her lips. Pain. Grief. She watched it change his features, hollowing his face until his own tears fell.

"Wh-What do you mean?"

"When I didn't come back from patrol, he found us. He remembered that night, and taunted me with it." She couldn't hold back the new wave of tears that fell. She wasn't consumed with her own grief, but Jace. The heartache she watched him relive again. "He was after me, and Kellan took the blow. That was why I brought him back."

"The life debt you said you owed." Jace's jaw went slack, his green eyes blown wide.

Demitria nodded. "Now you understand, the things I've done up until now. The things I've seen out here..." She let her voice trail off. She wouldn't tell him about the capture. How Reim had nearly killed her. She'd save him from that horror. His grief today was enough.

Jace wound his arms around her, pulling her into his embrace. "I'm sorry you had to face him alone. That I wasn't there. That we didn't face him *together*."

"That demon means nothing to us." She whispered, hugging him for a moment before stepping away. "He has no hold on me, not anymore." Demitria wiped her eyes once more for good measure.

"We have company." Gabriel broke. "Draw your weapons." His voice carried far, as if he'd been standing directly beside them, not on the other end of the clearing. Demitria's eyes wandered the land. Surveying. Searching for an oncoming attack, but through the mist, she couldn't see a damn thing. It had lightened some, but not enough. She cursed her human eyes.

Kellan immediately moved to the defensive, pulling his sword free from its sheath as he wrapped a protective arm around her. Pressing his body into hers as a shield, eyes solely focused to the west of them. "Stay behind me." Eire had her bow drawn, arrow notched in place. As much as she hated protecting the other humans, she couldn't disobey a direct order. Not from Gabriel, so she and Kane fanned out between the remaining humans.

"Multiple." Kellan called. "Be ready." Demitria didn't know what was coming, and Kellan was too preoccupied to answer any questions she may have about it, so she did the only thing she could think of. With tired arms, she lifted the sword up that had been dragging along the ground and readied it as best she could. Her arms felt weak. Heavy, as she readied herself the best she could.

"If anything happens, you run. I will not let you fight. Not anymore."

Opening her mouth to protest, five bodies broke through the mist, filling the sky above them. Wings so dark they were like shadows themselves. The angels were nearly upon them by the time Demitria could make the figures out clearly. She recognized the leader immediately from the only scouting mission she'd gone on years ago. Liquid golden eyes that she could never forget, and much like the last time, they seemingly sought her out. She could feel herself inching closer to Kellan. Seeking the warmth of his body as a chill ran through her, nearly freezing her in place.

"Arakiel." Kellan's sword never wavered as he watched the angels' leader with a cold stare. "I thought you were dead."

"The Four Horsemen." Arakiel inclined his head in a bow, his feet gently touching to the ground before them. His long, golden curls swaying with the slow breeze. Wings ruffling, restless against his back. The other four followed suit, landing down behind him. "We've been waiting for you."

Before Kellan could snap back a retort, Gabriel stepped forward. "To what do we owe the pleasure." He was the voice of reason. As the leader, he had to be.

"We heard of your mission given by the council." Another stepped up, taking position beside what Demitria knew to be her leader. "We have eyes everywhere." The angel's amber eyes falling to her own. Demitria could feel her body tense, and she took another step into Kellan. Closing what little space she'd gained, the angel moved toward her, keeping the remaining distance the same.

"One more step and your wings will be gone." The growl rumbled through Kellan, and she couldn't help but shiver at its intensity. Again, the angel took another step. "I mean it, Laylah."

"I won't hurt her." She smiled sweetly, muttering something to another with strikingly similar features. "I'm... curious." Laylah was the essence of perfection. Everything you'd think an angel would be. Her long blond hair fell in soft waves down her back. The unearthly grace had been absolutely mesmerizing to watch. She was beautiful, and Demitria couldn't help but stare. Stunned by her mere presence.

Kellan's eyes darkened at the mention of her, pulling her body closer until she was flush with his own.

Behind the angel, another waited. Silent. Watching with warm chestnut eyes as they conversed. Her fiery auburn hair fell to her waist, framing a beautiful, feminine face. Something about the angel drew her gaze, but at her smile, Demitria found herself pulling away.

"Stand down." Gabriel warned, and the Horseman hesitated. "Everyone." Eire and Kane were quick to drop their weapons. Returning their arrows and bows to their backs once more. "Kellan."

"We're on your side, Horseman." Arakiel walked toward him, toward the sword pointed for his chest. "We want balance."

"You deserted?" He held the angel's gaze. Daring him to speak. "We were told you'd died."

"We don't believe in extermination. That is why we are Fallen."

Demitria didn't know if she could trust them. She'd been hunted by angels before. What made them different? "There are other things at work here. Things that you need to be made aware of."

"I'm listening." He lowered his sword slightly, but didn't put it down. Not yet. The other Horsemen seemed convinced, but not Kellan.

"There are bigger things at work than you realize. There is no extermination of both sides. You all know there must be balance to go on." He nodded. "The Dark King. Lucifer."

Lucifer. Fear ran through her at the name. A being known only in myth by her kind. The personification of evil, ruler of the Underworld, and he was who the Dark King truly was. Some part of her must have felt it, the significance in the name. Why it had stoked such a reaction from her body upon first hearing it.

Lucifer was the Dark King, and he was here.

"We already know that he's here." Kellan shifted his weight, but his blade stayed still.

"Lower your weapon so we can continue. There is more you must know."

Kellan slowly looked toward his eldest brother. Gabriel nodded, urging him to comply. With a sigh, he sheathed the sword. "Leave the humans back and come with me." His golden armor, while beaten and scuffed, still glistened in the light that pierced the mist. "I won't go far." Kellan whispered, another breath ghosting over Demitria's ear. "If anything happens, I will come for you." She wouldn't protest. She wanted to fight, but doubted her body would let her again. She'd wanted to stay by his side, but Kellan was so on edge over the Fallen that surrounded them that she listened. His fingers bit into her arm, holding her to him.

"Okay." Turning, she held his stare for a moment longer before pulling away from his ironclad grip. Kane shot her a knowing glance before following behind his sister.

"She comes." Arakiel turned, finger pointed to her retreating figure. Everyone stopped at the angel's voice. "Demitria Collins."

Slowly, she faced him. Hands clenched. His smile didn't falter as he beckoned her over. Eire glowered down at her. As if she didn't feel out of place enough. Demitria nodded at Jace once before she took a step forward, head high as her eyes never left the angel. She would never again show weakness.

They walked in silence to the other edge of the clearing where the angels finally came to a halt. Kellan had fallen into step beside her almost immediately. His presence brought a wave of calm.

"It is a pleasure to finally meet you." Arakiel bowed his head, and it took a moment for her to realize that it had been directed at her. Surprise filled her, and Demitria stood in silence. Watching him with curious eyes,

"You know of me?" She asked, finally finding her voice. The angel nodded. She couldn't discern if it was a good or bad thing that another being seemed to know exactly who she was. "How?"

"That doesn't matter." Something in his gaze, Demitria couldn't place it. He knew something that she didn't, and he wasn't going to tell her a thing. "I know everything about you. About your parents, your life before the war..." His voice trailed off, and finally, he settled his eyes on Kellan before bringing them back to her once more. "Known about you for a very long time."

Demitria shuddered at the intensity of that look. So many questions overcame her. How had he known about her parents? Her entire life?

"Tell me what you know about Lucifer." Kellan demanded as his full lips pulled back into a scowl, eyes narrowing on the angel. "Tell me what you know."

"Very well, Horseman." With a nod of his head, Arakiel turned golden eyes away from her, focusing on the Horseman. "We've been hearing things for months. Rumors. Rumblings about Lucifer's involvement in the war." His eyes roved over the bodies around him. "Tracking him and his army, here. He's been planning this. Waiting. Harvesting souls." With a sigh, he continued. "In just over a few weeks' time, when the moon turns red, he'll make his move."

"The blood moon." It left her mouth before she could hold it back. How she even remembered was beyond her. Growing up, her mother had always referenced the red moon, but it didn't make any sense. Not then, and not now. "When the sun falls to darkness, and the moon fills with blood, the seal will crack and he will come." Demitria recited the words her mother had spoken time and time again. She could still hear her voice whispering the words as she held her in the rocking chair, smoothing the long, wavy hair down Demitria's back.

"From the heavens they will fall, and the beasts reign free, Tartarus will soon be free." Kellan turned to her, his face pale, azure eyes blown wide. "Where did you learn that?"

"I—" She stuttered. "It was this silly little rhyme my mother used to say." Stumbling backward, she took a step away from him. From all the siblings as each one turned in her direction, their expressions mirroring one another.

"That was something our mothers used to tell us." Eire took a step toward her, regaining the distance Demitria had put between them. "Why would your mother know that?"

"I don't...I don't know. It never meant anything back then, I just—" *Why* had she known it?

"What secrets have you been keeping." Gabriel's tone was hard. "That has been around since before our time."

She didn't know. Didn't know anything, it seemed. For so many years, these stories about monsters, winged beings, and creatures from the under-world where nothing more than that. Stories that her parents told at night around the fire. Myths. Legends. How was she to know they were very real?

"The girl knows nothing of our world." Arakiel waved a hand at the Horsemen. His large wings furled, folding neatly against his back. "Shall we resume?" Those liquid gold eyes roved across them all before settling them back on her. Always back to her. "The blood moon is in two weeks." He nods. "Lucifer needs to be stopped before that happens."

"We know of the prophecy." Despite their reactions, Kellan took a step toward her. "What is he planning?" Kellan asked.

His siblings watched her with unease. "We were always told he would come for Eden, not here."

Arakiel shook his head. "Lucifer will see you fall. He wants Earth and its resources for his creatures, and the blood moon is when he's strongest. He's been collecting souls to gain power, and if he isn't stopped—If he succeeds, there won't be anything left." The angel's words stung, and all she could think about was protecting those she loved. "He'll use that power to bring forth a new empire. To bring Tartarus to Earth."

Everyone broke out in a frenzy. Lucifer was raising Tartarus. Earth would be doomed. They didn't stand a chance. Aaron, Lord of the shadow demons had mentioned harvesting souls. Now she knew why. It all made sense.

"We've had eyes on him for weeks. He was spotted in those moun-tains." The angel on Laylah's right pointed beyond the canyon, off in the distance. He bore an uncanny resemblance to her. The same high cheekbones, the structured face. It was almost like looking at a mirror image of the two. They had to be related.

Laylah nodded. "Oriel and I have been tracking him."

Demitria's brain was in overdrive. Planning. Working something out to get every soul as far away from those monsters as she could. No one was safe in the vicinity. Not with Lucifer so close. "We need to move. Now." Her boots swiveled in the dirt as she stalked toward the others. Waiting, watching the exchange with curious eyes.

. . .

"The humans stay out of this!" Eire was before her, yanking Demitria's body back before she even managed to walk ten feet away. The force was so hard, it was like running into a wall.

Demitria could feel her anger rising. Blood boiling as the Horseman grabbed her, the grip so tight she could feel her skin burning. Bruising under Eire's harsh hand.

"They will only get in the way." Steel gray eyes met hers. Eyes that spoke a thousand words. Hatred. Anger. Even sadness, but the fire in them was what broke through. "Leave them. They deserve their fate."

The maneuver shocked Eire, and Demitria hadn't even realized she'd done it until the female lay flat on her back, Demitria's boot pressed firmly to her chest.

"They are my people." Eire had pushed her one too many times. "I refuse to leave them in the dark. To let them go on blindly, when such a threat looms overhead. Even bigger than I was led to believe." Her boot pushed harder, inching slowly toward the Horseman's throat. "You call yourself a warrior? A Horseman? You're nothing." She spat, venom lacing every word. "You don't want balance. You only do what benefits you, most. You see those mountains? There is an entire community below them. They never asked for this. None of us did. Your kind came down, invaded *my* home. Waged a war against us, when all we wanted was to survive." She'd never felt like this. The rage. The power behind her voice, it nearly froze her in her tracks, shocking those around her. She continued on. "Those are my people, and we refuse to back down without a fight." Because they deserved to fight, now more than anything. When it had just been her life in question, she was fine with leaving. But raising an empire? Another war against humankind? Before doing something that she'd immediately regret—like pulling a weapon —Demitria stormed off. Gait faster, chin high as she left the Horseman on the ground.

Eire was too perplexed to move, stormy eyes blown wide. Dumbfounded at the strength Demitria had possessed. "You'll regret that." She spoke in no more than a whisper, but her voice held the ferociousness of a predator, gaze trained on the girl's receding figure.

"What happened?" Jace rushed her, sprinting away from the others as he met her halfway, hand held firmly on her forearm. Demitria looked him over. He wouldn't be happy. This mess so much bigger than they'd ever imagined. Bigger than the both of them, and now he'd gotten caught in the middle of everything. And it was her fault. Again.

He'd made the choice, hadn't he? Jace had chosen to follow her and the Horsemen since they'd been found. He could have stayed in the cavern, and looked for a community still standing, yet... she hadn't actually given him much of a choice to begin with. Demitria had just assumed he would come along because she was there.

"Lucifer." She told him, coming to a stop before the others. Her green-gold eyes met each one as she pulled away from Jace's iron hold. The twins wouldn't care. They already looked bored and uninterested in whatever it was that she'd had to say. It didn't bother her. Not anymore. "He's been planning this all along. For years, this was his plan." A warm hand rested on her shoulder. She didn't need to turn around to know it was Kellan. Could feel his presence cascading around her. That sweet woodsy scent enveloping her. "He's been collecting souls. Harvesting them to harness their power. He's been feeding off us!" Her eyes burned, but she wasn't willing to let the tears fall. "He's going to raise an empire." Jace stared at her in shock, face paling at the news. Slowly looking from one Horseman to the next before settling on the Fallen.

"How do you know they're telling the truth?" Cory stepped forward, taking a stance beside Jace. "How can we trust them?" The question had thrown her off. He was right. How did she know the whole thing wasn't an ambush? Some sort of trap? They were Fallen, just like Lucifer. Demitria had been so engrossed with the news, so mad, that it hadn't even crossed her mind that the angels could be lying. But the stupid little rhyme her mother had told her. The fact that the others seemed to know it, too. She knew they weren't lying, something in her blood resonating with it. With them.

"I know Lucifer." Kellan's voice was meek. Whatever he was about to say burdened him. "Worked alongside him for a long time." He shook his head before dropping his gaze to the ground below. Plagued by a guilt that Demitria couldn't place. "I know the way his mind works. He wants power. Craves it. It's the truth." She wanted to ask him about his time with the fallen angel. Talk to him about what it was that bothered him so much. Talk to him, and find a way to get him through it.

"And just like that, we're supposed to believe you?" Tyler had been quiet for so long. He'd barely done so much as glance up at either of them since they'd returned. She noticed he'd been spending an alarming amount of time with the twins, and it unnerved her. "How do we know you haven't been working for them all along?" He questioned Kellan. Questioned all the Horsemen, accusing them.

"Yes, you are." She stepped up, planting herself in front of someone she once thought a friend. Someone she had vowed to keep safe so many years ago. Before the twins had corrupted his mind. "He's on our side." Demitria dared him to challenge her. Waited for him to make a move, and she'd strike. The hatred had gone on long enough. Determined now to put an end to it. "Anyone else have a problem, you come through me." There was no more questioning where his loyalties lay. He'd proved himself time and time again. Even against his own siblings, he'd always picked *her*. "I'm sick of your accusations. Your opinions." She scowled at the twins. "This ends now." Her words final. She wished one of them would step forward. Willing it with every fiber in her body. She should feel ashamed, but she didn't. Every part of her wanted to end the brothers, but she wouldn't stoop to their level. Wouldn't give in to the craving that called out to her blood.

"When did you decide to take over?" Sam finally questioned. The uneasiness on his face was clear. Unsure if he should be interrogating her or not.

"I don't remember voting you in." Will snapped, not as easily convinced as his brother. His eyes narrowed, brows furrowed.

"By all means, feel free to step up." She smirked. There was a time when she'd let their words run her life. Feeding off them. Letting them affect her to no end. Those days were gone. Something in her had snapped the night she'd found the community in flames. Neither one stepped up. "That's what I thought." She glanced around at the others. Waiting.

"I stand behind you." Jace shot her a smile. "Always." She could see the relief in his eyes. His position had burdened him for so long, and she knew it all too well. Jace hated being in charge of the community, and had voiced it many times before. He didn't need to think twice before stepping down. Wouldn't fight it.

"I'm with you." Cory nodded, his expression mirroring the man beside him. It meant everything to her, having the both of them back her up. Their opinions meant the world. To see them stand behind her, no questions asked, was all she could have asked for.

"Me too." Evan inclined his head toward her.

She looked again at the twins. At Tyler, who seemed to be standing even closer to them, but neither met her piercing gaze, their eyes trained to the dirt at their feet.

"So, it's decided then?" Arakiel and his angels had been quiet. Watching the exchange in silence. His face held the thin lines of a knowing grin as he looked at her. Demitria wanted to know the thoughts swarming through his mind. He'd been staring at her with an expression she couldn't quite figure out. Hope? She nearly scoffed at the thought. He held some form of knowledge. Both he and his group knew something that the others did not, and she was determined to figure it out.

Forty

DEMITRIA

For days they traveled toward the looming mountain beyond the canyon. Haunting each and every one of them with what could very well come to pass. Would they even be able to stop Lucifer? The way Kellan had spoken about his time with the Dark King scared Demitria more than anything. Her being nervous was one thing, but him? The Horseman, War? That was something else entirely.

They passed nothing during their journey. No life along the way. Lucifer's army seeming to have decimated every community in their wake, beating them to every ounce of life that had been in their path. Demitria could tell that it bothered the others, Jace especially. Having lived through demon destruction once, seeing place after place burned to the ground was igniting a rage in him that she'd never seen until then. His once fluid movements now harsh, his stature hardened. Every time he spoke his answers were short. Never once had she seen him so tense. So filled with a rage, akin to the one she'd harbored. Gone were his carefree ways, and the simple smile he'd been known for around Solis.

For so many years they had hated all of their kind. Angels and demons alike. But things had changed since the Horsemen had come around—for her anyway.

Jace hadn't bore witness to the gentle side of Kellan. The side that, despite every bone in her body telling her otherwise, she'd been drawn to inexplicably. Ensnared in a web that she couldn't get out of. She wasn't so sure she even wanted to anymore.

She still hadn't been able to bring herself to tell Jace everything about Reim. About how she'd been captured and tortured to the brink of death by him, and other demons like him. By a Demon Lord. She couldn't suppress the shudder that took hold. A wound still too fresh. *She wouldn't tell him.*

"Are you alright?" Kellan rode beside her, close enough to rest a warm hand on her thigh. "You've been quiet all morning." She honed in on that hand. The muscle beneath that touch. It nearly sent a shudder through her. After the way he'd held her in the mist she couldn't get the thought of him out of her mind. The way he'd soothed her. Caressed her.

Fuck.

Demitria hadn't been able to get the thoughts out of her head. Not since that early morning at the cavern, in fact. Filthy thoughts that she'd had no place to be thinking. Not now. Not when what loomed ahead. Maybe when they had a promise of another day. When a battle wasn't days away.

If they made it out alive, she'd do more than just thinking those thoughts.

"Just thinking." She replied, begging the heat in her body to simmer. It cooled considerably as she thought about the Dark King. "About everything. Reim... Lucifer."

"That demon filth has paid for what he's done. Don't give him any more satisfaction by paying heed to what he's done." Kellan's eyes were dark as he spoke, the topic striking a chord in him.

"It's Lucifer." She sighed. "I'm scared." It was hard for her to admit it, and he respected her that much more for it.

"You have nothing to fear." His smile was genuine. Kellan squeezed the leg his hand had still been resting on, driving his words true. "I will not let anything harm you."

She believed him. Gods, did she ever.

They'd nearly reached the expanse of the mountain, now. The canyon days behind them as they rode for hours on end. Some of the angels went ahead to scout, only coming back the night before with word of a large homestead. They'd decided, as a group, to travel there. To take up residence before they made the trek to Lucifer.

She saw the large chain-link fence surrounding the land, first. Then the massive expanse of the house, with several outbuildings further back. An estate of some sorts it seemed, from many years ago. A winding, overgrown gravel road led toward the home. And from what they could see, it was mostly intact. From a time when wealth was power, and people collected more than they needed. Living in luxury, and owning lands the size of a small town. It could have been that, a community to many people. And yet... the estate lay barren. Overrun. As the mountain range drew closer with each passing hour, it was time to plan. To strategize how they'd kill Lucifer, and end the war that threatened their entire world.

A large stone and iron gate loomed overhead, nearly eight feet tall. She and Kellan spent nearly twenty minutes inspecting it, and found it to be in surprisingly good shape. A welcoming barrier from the demons she knew would be prowling the area. The yard was overgrown with weeds and bare trees. Not burnt. Possibly even *alive*. She couldn't let herself get excited at the possibility. Dry grass as high as her waist sprouted in places while muddy vines climbed their way over the brick and wood siding of the massive house, eating its way through it like a disease.

Eire and Kane peeled off from the group to scout. Arakiel and his angels took to the skies for an overhead view while Kellan and Gabriel waited with the others. Watching should anything come after them.

"The house is empty." Gabriel spoke. "Has been for some time." Demitria knew he had abilities far greater than anyone here. It was why he'd been the unspoken leader of the Horsemen.

"We go inside." Kellan nodded, motioning for Demitria to follow behind him. She did, the others followed suit in a tight line.

Kellan nearly kicked down the front door, only managing to stop himself inches before his boot hit the hard wood. Forgoing for a different approach. Less openings, the easier it would be to defend. Having your enemy waltz in the front door would be frowned upon. Laughed at even.

Realizing he knew no other way than to break his way through, Will stepped in. "Allow me." He smirked, pulling a long, needle-like blade free from a hidden sheath. Demitria hated that he was the one who stepped up. She sneered at him.

Will knelt before the door and inserted the blade into the delicate lock. Listening, then twisting. Shaking it ever so slightly. The audible click came a second later. He'd gotten them inside. It still didn't change her feelings about him.

Giving the two of them a grin, Will flung the front door open and motioned them inside. "After you, your highnesses."

She could hit him. Hit him so hard she'd render him useless. Gods, she hated him with every bone in her body. His attitude, his personality... everything. Everything about the man just made her mad, and his twin was no different.

"Not worth it." Kellan muttered, as if reading her thoughts, and guided her inside before she could do anything stupid.

Inside the massive house was drab. Frames and vases broken to pieces lay along the floor. Carpets stained with gods knew what, curtains torn and shredded, and tile flooring cracked and broken in more than one spot throughout. It had been lived in, probably by multiple people on numerous occasions. It was a miracle it was empty now. But it was a place to stay nonetheless, and Demitria was grateful to just have a roof over her head and to not be sleeping in a cave again.

She walked with Kellan, inspecting room after room. Each one trashed beyond repair. Hardly any furniture remained intact. There was no food in the kitchens, but she hadn't expected there to be any really. Jace and Cory had offered to go hunt for it, claiming to have spotted signs of rabbits on the property. She nodded, letting them leave with the promise of their return. Between the angels and the Horsemen, she was confident they'd be protected on all fronts. At least for tonight.

It took an hour for the others to settle in and pick rooms for the night. The Horsemen staggered themselves around the house. For protection, they'd claimed. The angels did the same. Demitria lost track of just how many rooms the house contained. Too many, really. More than anyone should have ever coveted.

Demitria took up residence toward the back of the building.

Surprisingly cared for, as far as cleanliness went. She still didn't trust the blankets that were on the bed, and a piece of her ached at the one she'd lost to the flames back in Solis. But the mattress? Gods, she'd take the gamble to sleep on a mattress again. The back of the room opened up to a tall, glass door that led outdoors. She promised herself to explore outside once she was more settled. See what the estate really had to offer. In another life, she could have been happy there. Content, to spend her days on a property like this. There was more than enough room to farm whatever she wanted, and she swore a greenhouse lay at the back of the property. There seemed to be plenty of edible grass for Atlas, and she'd never have to worry about him ever again. She'd repair the iron fence somehow, make it safe for those that chose to join her. Jace. Cory. Kellan.

In another life.

She didn't get that luxury. Didn't get to live her days, happy and carefree. Not with him. Not when they were so different. Worlds away.

A knock on the door pulled her from thoughts of what would never be.

"Nice place." Jace let himself inside, letting his weary body flop down onto the soft mattress. "Managed to catch a few rabbits. One of the angels said they'd prepare them for everybody." He patted beside himself, beckoning her over. With a smile, she obliged. Jace shuffled over the remaining foot, and she curled into him. The familiar smell of mint wafting through her nose as her eyes closed.

"I miss this." She sighed, not moving away as he threw an arm around her. "When everything was easy. Before everything happened."

"I don't miss the responsibility," He started, laughing for the first time in days. "But I agree. I miss spending time like this. I know we haven't been traveling long, but I feel like I hardly get to spend time with you anymore." Jace couldn't be more right. She'd been so caught up with this gods damned war, and most importantly, Kellan. So caught up in her own emotions that it felt as if their friendship had been tossed aside. They'd always fallen back into that seamless rhythm again. It came easy, but the distance was different this time. Both of them knew it.

"It was like that before we got here." *Before he got here,* she thought. Demitria didn't have the heart to say it aloud. Knowing very well how her feelings with the Horsemen had affected their relationship. How she'd found herself instinctively stepping away from her best friend's touch, when before she'd reveled in their closeness. Sought it out for years to ground her. Jace only nodded, agreeing. He wouldn't voice the issue, or rather *his* issue with Kellan.

"Want to know what else I miss?" He asked, voice barely above a whisper.

"What?" His fingers softly trail down the smooth skin of her arm, and she moved it away.

"That damned roof." Leaning back so she could look at him, her face straight for only a moment before she erupted with laughter.

"Even waking up in the rain?"

"Even waking up in the rain." He grinned. They said nothing for a moment, but he sat up. Moving away from the bed. "Do you ever wonder if this is worth it?" Refusing to meet her gaze, his eyes fixated on a chair in the corner. Looking for something, anything of interest in the grain of the wood.

"Jace? What do you—" The bed groaned softly under her weight as she sat up. "What are you saying?"

"Exactly what it sounds like. Is everything with *them* worth it? All of it." Jace's words were heavy, filled with a hatred she hadn't been able to place.

Demitria hadn't realized he held such a resentment toward the Horsemen. She hated how the conversation had turned so quickly. One minute, they were reminiscing about old times, now it was the Horsemen. Not openly admitting to it, but she knew he'd directed every word about Kellan. She hadn't noticed the change in Jace. Always knew that he was weary of him, but the sudden hostility was something foreign to her. Something she was just beginning to see. The mistrust of the siblings was widely known, but this? When they—when *he* had done nothing wrong? Had never even laid a hand on him, or hurt him in any way. Protecting her was the only thing Kellan had done since the moment the two had met, even when he'd been following orders. And if that was a crime? Jace would be guilty a thousand times over.

"Where is this coming from?" Closing the distance between them, she put herself between Jace and the chair he'd been so intently staring at. Forcing him to look at her. "How did all of this just come out of nowhere?" Her eyes narrowed, one hand resting on her hip as the other clenched into a tight fist. "Why does everything have to be so different with you?"

"You think I'm the one that's different? That I'm the one who's changed?" Taking a step toward her, the friends were barely more than a foot apart. "You might want to look in a mirror before you go around saying I'm the one that's different." Words laced with venom, he'd never before spoken to her like this. "It's beings like them that killed our parents, Demitria." The blow was low, and he knew it. Knew it had wounded her as she gaped at him in horror. "Yet you're so keen to spend all your time, running around this damn world with them."

"*He* didn't kill our parents, Jace. The fucking demon rotting in that clearing, did. Kellan never raised a hand to any of us. If it wasn't for him, I would not be standing here." Side stepping away from him, she made for the door. Getting away was the one thing she had to do. To leave the damned room before anything else could break her heart. He was her family, the closest thing each other had left of it, but his words had stung. Like a poison working its way through her, numbing her to the bone.

The bedroom door slowly opened before her. She could hear Jace turn from the creak of the floorboards. Could practically hear the cringe as his face contorted into a look of pure disgust. "Impeccable fucking timing!" He spat the words, hands thrown skyward as he brushed past, shoulder connecting with her body as he stormed out the door. Shoving the Horseman in the process.

Kellan met her stare. It was strange, seeing the emotion his face held. Gentle, yet guilty. So soft as he looked on. Demitria knew he had heard the conversation with his innate sense of the world around him. Maybe not all, but the parts about his siblings and himself, she was sure. Whether he'd been standing at the door when it happened, or caught it as he'd neared, she didn't know. Maybe he pitied her? Felt sorry for the series of unfortunate events that had seemingly turned into her life. But the bright light from the oil lamp seemed to magnify the expression in his azure eyes, portraying the sadness and guilt he felt. He was blaming himself for everything. For the falling out with her people, and her fight with Jace.

"I'm—"

"This is not your fault." She whispered, nervously toying with the sleeve of her shirt.

"I can't help but feel somewhat responsible for all this." The sigh that left his lips tore at her. More than when Jace had spoken to her.

Her body ached, begging her to reach out. To touch his hand, arm, anything. She yearned for the contact. Every part of her craving the feel of him pressed up against her once more. "Don't apologize for something you played no part in." With a sigh that could rival his own, she took a step toward him. "He's being a pig-headed idiot. None of this is on you, Kellan."

"I came to tell you we were all meeting in the dining hall. To go over our plan. The others are all waiting."

"What about Jace?" Despite what had happened, she knew he'd be at it. As mad as he might be, abandoning her was something he wouldn't do.

"Gabriel met him at the front door. He's there." Kellan tapped a finger to his head, as if she needed a reminder of the many abilities he possessed. Another thing that set them worlds apart. With a nod of her head, Kellan led her out the door, hand resting comfortably on her back as he guided her down the halls. She didn't pull from his touch. In fact, she delighted in the way his hand pressed into her. The finger that lazily stroked soft circles against her lower back.

She shouldn't have been thinking about this. Her mind needed to be elsewhere. Away from the hand that was igniting everything within her. They had a battle, a war that they needed to plan for. Something that required her undivided attention. But that was quickly swaying, and had been for some time now. Finding it harder and harder to keep her focus around him.

Kellan didn't drop his hand until they entered the room.

Somewhere, they'd found a large white oak table and placed it in the center of the room. Around it, the three remaining Horsemen stood, along with the angels as they mulled over what looked to be a map. Jace and Cory stood amongst themselves, toward the back of the room. It didn't surprise her that the twins and Tyler were nowhere to be found. Evan not being there did, though. It took everything in her not to meet Jace's piercing look. To smile softly at Cory before tearing herself from them both as she strode to the table.

"So glad you two could join us." Eire met her gaze, and all Demitria could do was shrug as she looked away. She wasn't in the mood to fight with the female. It was exhausting, and she just didn't have the energy for it. Not after the fight with Jace.

"This is the mountain range." Motioning her over, Gabriel pointed. "The angels tell me he's somewhere in here." With a calloused finger, he traced along a section midway up the largest peak. "I can sense the tunnels throughout, but as to their extent, I do not know."

"If what my mother said is truly important, he'll be somewhere in the open, right? Somewhere you can easily see the sky?" Demitria spoke softly. "If the blood moon is when he'll be strongest, it'll be essential for him to have that." Her eyes wandered over the paper, committing as much to memory as she could. It bothered her, knowing this...prophecy. A knowledge that felt so foreign to her. The others. Snippets. Secrets that she should not know from memories long since faded.

"There are several paths leading up to where we believe he is. Some easier than others." The angel shrugged, tucking a strand of golden hair behind his ear as he leaned forward.

"What's the catch?" Gabriel asked.

"They're in plain sight." Arakiel answered. "I sent my scouts weeks ago." His hand grazed over the map, pointing with a steady finger as he spoke. "You're right about him needing an area in the open. There is an outcropping here, which will give him a perfect view of the moon at night. Several entrances around, but all in the open. Except for one." His eyes meet her own. "It isn't safe for humans. We could fly in, but the climb is dangerous to... others."

"So, we have no choice but to waltz right in?" Kane slammed a fist down on the table, and she swore it splintered under his blow. "We'd be walking into a trap!"

"We can go this route, but it will have its consequences." Theliel had been quiet for almost the entire time she'd known him, which hadn't really been all that long, only learning his name once they were riding out from the canyon, and she'd rarely heard him speak more than a few words. And only when the need arose. "Lives will be lost before the battle even begins. The humans will not survive."

"So we have some casualties. This is war!" Eire droned. "Lives will be lost no matter what. It is one of the many consequences. We have the element of surprise, here. It shouldn't even be a question which path we take."

"Eire is right." Kane refused to meet his brother's piercing eyes, keeping them fixed to the map on the surface before him. "It's secluded. Lucifer wouldn't know we were coming. We have no idea how many we're even dealing with. Surprise is something we need." He knew better than to look up. Demitria was sure he could feel the burn of Kellan's stare as he sided with their sister.

"Surprise is everything! There is no debating that. We take the secluded path!" Eire bellowed. The angels watched the exchange silently. Neither of them choosing a side.

"I will not subject my people to that journey when it could put their lives even more at risk." Demitria broke, daring a look toward her friends leaning against the wall at the back. Jace may have said some things to hurt her, but she was bigger than that. She couldn't even entertain the thought of asking him to make that climb. "They have given me more than I deserve. Following me blindly into this war. I refuse to ask this of them. We won't be taking that path. I will proudly march into the open, alone, knowing that I could keep my own safer."

"You are nothing to me. You hold no leadership, no command over my siblings, nor I." Eire's gray eyes grew cold as she looked down at her. "You have no say in this matter."

"You're stepping out of line." Kellan stood before his sister, his large frame towering over her. "Watch your tongue." An all too familiar growl rumbled through his chest. One Demitria had grown accustomed to after he'd fought on her behalf time and time again. One that may have incited something within her that sure as hell should not have, especially right now.

"I've heard just about enough out of both of you." Gabriel gripped the bridge of his nose in frustration. "We must listen to both sides before coming to a decision." The exasperated sigh left his lips as he sat himself down in the wooden chair, elbow resting against the table's surface as his other hand clenched into a tight fist at his side.

"The world has seen many losses since the start of this war." She knew her words meant nothing to some, but for her friends, her people, they were everything. Their very lives hung in the balance. "Species have gone extinct. I know a few human lives don't seem like much in the bigger picture, but to us—to me, they are everything. These people are my family. My home, and I will not ask them to make that trek. They risk enough fighting with us. If this is the path you choose, you walk it alone. We will find our own way in. With or without you." Demitria knew all eyes were on her. Could feel them burning into her skin. "I won't back down from this challenge. I will fight until my last breath to save this planet, but I will not follow you if it means putting them in more danger than necessary. I will walk alone."

"It's decided then." The ever-knowing grin returned to Arakiel's face as he looked on with those liquid gold eyes. "We will take the safest route, meeting them head on."

"You've got to be kidding me!" The chair toppled over as Kane jumped to his feet, fists slamming the table again in his rage. This time, she visibly watched it splinter beneath his fingers as the audible crack echoed throughout the room.

"You are at your strongest when you work together." Arakiel looked around the room. She couldn't explain how, but every time the angel spoke it brought a sense of calm over her entire body. "Alone, you will falter. *Together, you are everything.*" Golden eyes met Demitria's. A gaze that held so much knowledge, so much power that she nearly shied away. But she didn't break from the stare, hypnotized by its intensity.

"She's going to get us all killed!" Eire shouted her displeasure, but no one gave in.

"What do you suggest as a strategy?" Gabriel asked, analyzing the room as he did so.

"The blood moon approaches in one week. Lucifer must be stopped before then. We have little time to prepare. We will provide air support and cover to those on the ground. I suggest you four lead the charge with *her*." He turned his gaze back to her, and all she could do is nod. "We will not have the element of surprise, but we have sheer force.

Lucifer will be waiting in the open. Do not take him on alone. We ride out in the morning." Heart already hammering in her chest, it nearly stopped at the angel's proclamation. Having known they would be leaving soon shouldn't have surprised her. But morning? She thought they'd have at least a bit more time than that.

"And what of your plan for us once we reach the summit?" Jace casually asked from the back of the room. He'd been silent, leaning against a wooden bookcase as he and Cory listened. "We don't have the...abilities that the others do. What is our plan?"

There had been no set plan that Demitria was aware of. Neither of them knew what to expect up there, or what they'd be walking into. There was no enemy count. No assessing the situation before storming in. They were going in blind. The only thing any of them knew was Lucifer had to die at whatever cost. *That was the plan.*

"We kill Lucifer however we can." Gabriel's voice had quieted, and Demitria could feel the apprehension in it. He was nervous. Something she hadn't ever seen on him. The Horseman of Death was scared, and that terrified her. She didn't know about the fallen angel. About the history between he and Kellan. She'd ask if either of them made it out alive.

At the table, Arakiel went into conversation about the path they would take. Which direction to follow, and which turns to avoid. He mapped out the safest route, reciting each landmark until it had been drilled into their minds. By the end of it, Demitria knew the way like the back of her hand. She could close her eyes and almost picture it. The winding, rocky path up the mountain. The sheer cliff surface she'd have to climb in order to reach the next landmark. It scared her to no end that this was the safest route possible. Voicing her concern now, after gaining the support of those in the room, would be stupid and unwanted, so she kept it to herself.

"So, everything has been decided then?" Kane asked. His face had permanently hardened. Unhappy with the outcome. He was on his feet as he addressed the group. "This meeting is over." He walked out of the room, and didn't stop until he reached the front door, slamming it shut behind him.

The chairs scraped along the floor as the others followed suit, filing out of the space after him. Each going their respective ways to live out what could very well be their final night.

Demitria was nearly the last to leave. She'd hoped to have a word with Jace and Cory before the morning, but the two had fled the instant Kane ended the meeting. Hunting them down was always an option, but giving Jace the night to cool down would maybe be for the best. Besides, no one had really come up with a concrete plan for tomorrow. There wasn't anything to talk about.

"Would you care to take a walk?" Kellan called to her halfway down the hall. His hand light on her arm. Stopping, her eyes met his, the tug of a smile edging along her lips as that familiar pull ignited within her. "Unless you have other plans..."

"None at all." She couldn't hide the smile any longer, the toothy grin taking over. "Come on."

The house was silenced by the oncoming battle. The stakes were high. Not a soul wanted to lose this war. It wasn't an option, but failure was something that floated through even the strongest of minds. Gnawing its way through any tendril of hope that remained.

More silence filled the night air as they emerged from the house, aside from the low coo of an animal hiding in the distance. Someone had placed a few lanterns around the massive house, the soft glow illuminating the overgrown path as the embers burned. It was peaceful, in a way. Fitting for what could potentially be their last night. One last moment to enjoy the small beauty of their world, and the warm breeze that blew through the yard.

They wandered the property for an hour. She should have been nervous being so out in the open, but with him she felt nearly invincible. Like nothing could touch her out here. They walked, following along the fence line until they reached the large building at the back of the property. The one Demitria had spotted from her room. It must have been a greenhouse before the war, she realized. Glass walls from floor to ceiling. She couldn't see inside. Whatever they had been growing had taken off. Grown out of control. The glass cracked and broken in spots where trees had blown through the roof. So much life her heart hammered in her chest at the sight of it. Ten years, and she hadn't seen even close to this much *green*. She motioned for him to follow before breaking her way inside.

They shoved through the foliage. Ducking under branches as they climbed through the broken doorway, and emerged into a treed oasis. The building inside was even warmer, despite the broken glass that let in the outside air. With a grin, she took his hand, pulling him further to explore. Kellan didn't hesitate.

Pushing through another set of heavy greenery, they emerged into an area with a floor made of river stone, and her breath caught in her throat. She never thought she'd see anything like it again in her lifetime. Slipping her hand from his, she sat along the edge of the water.

Hidden oasis indeed.

Whoever had owned this estate before the war had turned their greenhouse into a hidden, now overgrown, pool. The water, to her surprise, was nearly clear. And if she remembered correctly, it was partly due to the water lilies floating around among the other plants thriving. It was breathtaking. Mesmerizing, and it called to her. A familiar feeling of a past memory. A past life.

She shook her long hair free from its braid as Kellan took a seat beside her. Happy for the other's company. Neither one of them wanted to be alone tonight.

"So, tell me. What is it like? You must have seen so many places. Witnessed so many battles, and just..." Demitria's voice carried off. She wanted to know so much. Whatever Kellan was willing to tell her, she was interested in it all. He'd been to other worlds, and met so many kinds of beings. The sheer thought of what else could potentially be out there intrigued her to no end. His home. Eden. She wanted to know it all.

Kellan shook his head and smiled as he leaned back, softly laying back along the cool stones as he turned to focus on the night sky through the broken panes above, stars shining as they illuminated the greenhouse. "It's different from here, but not as interesting. I've seen bloodshed. Done so many things I'm not proud of..." Kellan let his own voice trail off into nothing as a haunted looked took hold of his features.

"With *him*?" She didn't dare say his name. Not when Kellan looked so vulnerable. So wounded at the things he'd done. He just nodded. "I don't want to push you if you can't talk about it. About what happened—"

Kellan stayed silent, as if reluctant to speak his truth. Rolling over to his side, he faced her. She was still sitting straight up, watching him with the softest expression.

"For thousands of years I was under his control. Unable to make my own decisions. I was a monster. A murderer." He sighed, but continued. "I was his prized warrior. The general of his army. His right hand. I killed for sport. Killed because I liked the way it felt to hold someone's life in my hands, and be the one to end it. Seeing the panic and pain in their eyes as they slowly died." Kellan stared at his hands like he could still see them coated in the blood of the beings he'd slain. "He stole from me what little humanity I had left. Took every choice I had, and turned me into the monster that he wanted."

"That wasn't you." She whispered, reaching over and resting a soft hand atop his own. "The things you did. The beings he made you hurt. It wasn't you."

"How can you say that when you weren't even there." Kellan moved to pull from her hand, but stopped himself. Yet still, that look haunted him. Haunted her, as the Horseman before her seemed so vulnerable. So wounded, like he might break. "Every life lost at my own hands was my fault."

Demitria moved before he could register it, the weight of her body shifted down on him as she sat in his lap. With soft hands, she cupped his face, holding him as she stared into his eyes like no one else in the world existed. "I don't blame you. For any of it. For the things you did when you had no control over yourself. Right here and now, showing me this side, I know that it wasn't you."

Finally, Kellan let the smile creep along his face, azure eyes brightening as she leaned in closer, her breath ghosting across his face.

She smiled at him, and then she was gone, leaving him blinking up in the spot she'd just been.

Demitria stood at the edge of the water. "Would it be bad if I wanted to just jump in?" Her gaze slowly fell to his. To the puzzled expression that adorned his features. She couldn't help but chuckle.

How easily her mind had wandered. But she was shaking. Trembling. Her body begging her to go back to him. To that touch.

"... what?"

"Swimming. I haven't since I was a kid. I know we technically shouldn't, but I—" She couldn't help her voice trailing off as her gaze returned to the shimmering water once more. She wanted him. Wanted him so badly she couldn't think straight.

"If it would make you happy, then I won't stop you." Kellan righted himself, a soft smile tugging along the corners of his mouth.

"Really?"

"Really." He nodded.

"Come with me." She met his stare. Eyes pleading.

"You didn't even need to ask." Motioning for him to turn around, he obliged. She was quick to strip down to nothing more than her bra and underwear before sprinting the remaining distance to the water. It was cold. Freezing. The icy water tingled her entire body. Voicing her displeasure as a string of curses left her mouth, she turned on her heels to flee before colliding with Kellan.

"Oh." She squeaked, letting her hand slowly drop into the water from where she'd caught herself on his chest. Neither of them moved.

Demitria was frozen in her tracks. Unable to move even a finger as he stared down at her for what seemed like hours. The slow shiver that ran through her body was the first indication that she'd regained movement. Beneath the surface, his fingers lightly brushed against her own before latching together, and he took another step into her.

He kissed her. Soft. Gentle at first, before it turned hurried. Frantic as the hunger for the other became almost unbearable.

Demitria didn't dare pull apart as he lifted her from the water, setting her body down along the edge so only her feet dangled within. Kellan stepped between her, hands unable to leave even an inch of her untouched. His thumb roved in tantalizing circles along her inner thigh, coaxing a soft moan from her lips. She'd beg for it. Beg for *him* if she had to. At the noise, Kellan dipped his head to her. Into her neck where his teeth grazed ever so softly down. Down until he reached the area before her collarbone and nipped. The whimper left her before she could hold it back, and could feel the smirk on his lips as they traveled across her exposed skin. Kellan's hands continued to trail up, teasing as he went. Resuming those lazy circles as he neared the hem of what little clothing remained.

This should have been the last thing on her mind. They were getting ready for war, and she needed to prepare herself. But there was something about the Horseman that had drawn her in from the moment they'd met that she couldn't even fathom the thought of breaking from his grip. Like her body had been waiting solely on him. Waiting for this exact moment, and maybe, this was precisely what she needed.

A stroke of his hand had her forgetting every thought of what was waiting for them tomorrow. Pulling her back into the present, into him, as large calloused hands pulled her forward. Leaving her on the cusp of plunging into the chilling water, but he held her there. Held her steady as his lips found hers once more. She didn't know where to touch him. Couldn't decide where to for that matter, so she slid her arms around his neck

His hand ran down the length of her spine and she arched into his touch. Kellan took it as an open invitation and tore his mouth away from hers as he unclasped her bra before discarding it beside them. Demitria had almost been ready to pull him back when he trailed down her neck. Agonizingly slow with his tongue. Further down still. Across her chest before hovering over her breast. The warmth from his ragged breathing sent her entire body trembling beneath him as that heat pooled within her.

"Tell me to stop."

"Gods no." She begged. Pleaded. And he was kissing her. Taking her into his mouth as his teeth grazed across her nipple. Another moan left her lips, and she didn't care who heard. Because nothing had ever felt this damned good. She slid her free hand down his front. Down the hard length of him that strained against the minimal clothing between them. Ready to burst free. She wanted him. Wanted him so bad it hurt. Kellan let out a guttural moan against her touch, and she was pulling his face back up to hers once more. Needing to feel him. To taste him.

She lost all control as his fingers bit into her hip. Dipping down before settling over the sensitive bud between her thighs. He pressed into her, his thumb working deep circles through the fabric as another breathy moan escaped her. She was falling apart in his hands. Coming completely undone, and she loved it. Loved every torturous sweep of those fingers as he stroked her.

"Kellan." She was begging, and she didn't care. Could feel him smiling against her neck as he stopped his movement. Near laughing at the growl it elicited from her to continue. Demitria ground herself into his hand as he toyed with the waistline of the fabric. He didn't need to be told twice, and his fingers found her core. Teasing at first. Toying with her. She drove her hips into him again, and he obliged, sliding a finger deep into her awaiting warmth. Curling inside her. She nearly screamed. Her body rocking against his hand as he inserted another finger. Slow at first, sliding in and out of her at an excruciating pace. And when he quickened, pumping into her, she saw stars.

She was close. So close to that sweet release that would leave her breathless against him. She whimpered. Moaned again and again as his fingers drove into her over and over and over. He kissed her neck. Bit again into that sensitive spot before her collarbone and she exploded around him. Body trembling at the wild release that consumed her, and he rode her through it. Held her as she slowly came down from the peak of her high. And then he was kissing her again. Soft. Sweet. But she still ached for him. Wanted nothing more than to feel the solid length of him embedded deep within her.

To hell with the rules and the fucking high council. She wanted to feel every gods damned inch of him, and didn't care who she pissed off in the process, not when she'd endured so much. Fought so hard to be here, in this moment, with him. When denying that pull had been unbearable. She'd given in, and so had he. Holy gods, did they ever, and she wouldn't change a single moment of it. Wouldn't trade this feeling for the world. Because she deserved it more than anything. She saw that now. Because through all the bloodshed. Through all the pain, she was allowed to be happy. *She was allowed to hope.*

Demitria didn't know when they'd left the greenhouse. When their clothes had been picked up only to be strewn about the floor of the room she had been staying in for the night. The euphoric high had been so great that it had all passed in a blur of motion. A messy movement of rushed kisses and dancing fingers along warmed skin that gleamed under the moonlight in a sheen of sweat.

It wasn't until she'd been backed into the wall of the room that she'd been able to come to. As Kellan claimed her mouth with his own. She ran her hands up his bare chest, feeling the rough scars beneath her fingertips. A story lay behind each one, she was sure. Stories she'd hope to hear at some point, if he was willing to share. After the battle, she'd ask. Demitria wanted to be fully present for whatever awaited her tonight. No lingering thoughts but the feel of him moving inside her. His hands everywhere on her. That was all she wanted.

Kellan lifted her with ease, holding her slim body in his arms, and she felt every glorious inch of him pressing up against her. Her hand tangled itself within his dark hair as she fervently kissed up his throat. His chin, and then to his lips. Nipping at them with enough pressure to sting, but not hurt. To portray the need she felt so deep within her. He answered by leveling her on the bed. Hovering over her like he was a predator ready to devour her whole. She'd let him. Gods, she'd let him do whatever the hell he wanted to her.

Demitria could feel the pressure of him at her core, yet he moved at an intolerably slow pace. Waiting. Questioning if she'd back out now. She could see it in his eyes as he restrained himself before her. She needed him. Needed to feel every inch of him, stretching her as he pounded into her over and over again. Wanted him to fuck her so hard she'd forget her own name. Digging her nails into his back, she pulled him into her. Pulled him in until he was fully seated in her, and she kissed him. Held his face, her forehead pressed to his own as he pulled out slowly. Out until only the tip remained and he plunged into her again. Faster this time, in one smooth movement. Stretching her to the brim. Filling her with every inch of him, deeper than the last, and she pulled his mouth back down to hers. Craving the taste of him. The only thing she could do as the pleasure soared through her.

He thrust into her with a new fervor, and she lifted her hips to meet his. Arching against him as that unyielding need built within her again. She clenched around him with each stroke, every time he buried himself deep within her. Kellan growled at the sensation of her tightening around him. Groaning at the wicked grin that laced her lips.

"You should have tried harder to kill me in that cave." His body shuddered, voice husky as he sheathed himself inside her again. Harder. Faster than before. Each thrust grinding her into the bed. "Left me for dead."

"Not a chance." Breathless, she barely managed the words. Could hardly think straight as the feel of him took over her senses, and nothing existed except the way he was moving inside her. She was on the verge of that threshold again. That wild power building up, up, up until it was ready to explode. Kellan kissed her, muffling her cries as she came undone around him, more intense than the last. Her entire body unraveling as he kept his pace, never breaking rhythm until his own release found him moments later.

Panting, their eyes never broke. It wasn't until Demitria had moved to cup his face that he lowered himself, still housed within her. She kissed him again, nuzzling into his neck as his arms wrapped around her. Like he could shield her from the world.

Nothing mattered but the feel of his body against hers. The war going on around them, the battle they'd meet tomorrow, nothing. She'd stay in this room with him until her last dying breath if she had the chance.

Her only regret was fighting the pull between them for so long.

.

Forty-One

DEMITRIA

The warmth emanating around her body was enough to keep her in bed until the end of time. There wasn't a thing in the world that could make her get up at that moment. Resting firmly in his grasp, the smooth skin of his chest warming her to her core was all the more reason to stay in bed. Lying here beside him, after everything that had happened leading up to this point, this was the moment she had been waiting for. What the both of them had been waiting for. Like they'd been attached together on a string, their very beings pulled toward one another as it slowly wound and wound around them.

"Are you awake?" Her voice soft, cutting through the silence as she whispered. His arms wrapped tighter around her and she couldn't help the smile that crept its way across her lips.

"I'm awake." Kellan's voice was just as gentle, and Demitria could feel him nod his head as he nestled it into her neck. His lips caressing along her throat as he trailed gentle kisses across it. That burning igniting within her, body craving the feel of him once more. After last night she wasn't sure if she'd ever be able to have anyone else again.

"I don't know if I'm ready... to go today." It had been on her mind for hours that morning as she lay there, unmoving while Kellan slept soundlessly beside her. Listening to the soft breaths pass through his lips as his chest rose and fell. The reality of their situation sunk in. It could very well be the only chance she ever got with him. The only moment she was able to truly wake in his arms. She needed more time with the Horseman, and was cursing herself all morning for pushing her feelings aside for so long. Because the thought of losing him made the bile in her stomach rise, and she nearly fell ill.

It wasn't fair. But nothing in this life had been fair, either. She knew that, better than most. The argument in her mind had fallen silent just as quickly as it had arisen.

"Don't go," Kellan whispered. "Stay here, where you'll be safe. Stay in this room, and don't leave until I return." He pulled away to gaze at her, and the look in his eyes had her weak, her body coming apart at the seams. "Stay in this house, and away from this battle. This war isn't yours to get caught up in, and I can't—I can't lose you." She felt it, deep within her chest. That incessant ache as he pleaded with her.

"This is my people... I have to protect my people. My world. I may not feel ready, but I can't abandon them." Demitria closed her eyes, shutting out the thought of something happening to them. To all of them.

"I admire you. For everything you've done, and continue to do." His lips grazed lightly across her, ghosting over her collarbone as the shiver coursed through her. "You're stronger than any being I've ever known, but your bravery scares me." Kellan closed his eyes, letting out a trembled breath at the thought. "I can't lose you. Not when I've only just had you." He trailed his fingers slowly up her arms and down her sides where he finally rested them on her hip. The caress sent sparks shooting throughout her body, skin on fire everywhere he touched.

"I don't want to talk about today." Voice still quiet, Demitria tangled a hand in his hair, pulling him closer to her. "I want to live in this moment. With you." She kissed him. All those heated exchanges, the frantic moments when either of them would cave into the other, it was nothing compared to this. Didn't even come close to what she'd had last night. Now that she'd experienced what it had been like to really have him, to hold him in her arms. To kiss him without having to hide it from the world, she didn't want to let that go. Not now, not ever.

"We could both just stay here." He inquired, teeth nipping softly at her bottom lip. "Hide away and find our own little community where no one knew who we were. Abandon all responsibility."

Demitria couldn't help the laugh that escaped her mouth. She wanted to tell him that she wanted nothing more in this world than to run away with him. To live a life without fear or death.

To be free.

"Kellan..."

"I know... wishful thinking." He grinned, propping his large frame up on his elbows as he looked down at her beneath him.

Demitria lay there, bare, for only his eyes to see. His azure eyes intoxicating as he stared at her, drinking her in. Like he was looking into her soul, his own exposed wide open for her in mutual understanding. As if they were two halves of a whole, and like called to like.

"The sun has already risen; we should be moving soon." Leaving was inevitable. No matter how badly either of them wanted to stay behind, they'd be found soon enough. There wasn't a place on this earth where they could hide away from it all. From Kellan's siblings... the council. They'd all find them eventually.

"I know." Her long sigh could rival his own. With an embrace that neither of them wanted to back away from, they slowly removed themselves from the bed. Demitria hesitated before pulling the thick, form fitted black pants up her body, fastening the button at her waist. Glancing behind her, she stared at Kellan who hadn't moved a single muscle to get himself dressed. "They might wonder why you're fighting naked." She winked. Snapping him from his daze, he grinned sheepishly at her, closing the distance between them in two long strides.

"Who said anything about fighting?" Laughing, his arm snagged around her body, nearly pulling her off her feet at his quick movements. "I'm stalling, and it's painfully obvious, isn't it?"

"Very much so." He kissed her softly before settling her feet back firm on the ground and reluctantly pulling his own pants up. Demitria let her fingers graze gently along his chest before pulling the dark, long-sleeved shirt over his head. She fastened the leather armor across it, slowly buckling the worn straps together. Kellan helped her fasten the sturdy leather bracers to her wrist. One of the only pieces of armor she had, and he whispered a curse at the realization. He took it upon himself to strap the sword around her curved figure, letting his fingers softly run along the waistband over her hips. The sigh was heavy on his lips as his azure eyes slowly made their way up toward her as he reluctantly took a step back.

The two stood at the door, unable to move. Outside their small group was waiting for them, and in less than an hour they'd be marching up the mountain to face gods knows what. No one really knew what they'd find, and even Kellan had told her he couldn't discern if it was a trap or not.

"Once we go out this door…" His hand wavered as he gripped the doorknob.

"We will fight and we will win." Demitria's fingers dug into his arm as she gripped him tight. "We will return together." She could feel it brimming in her eyes, the tears that threatened to pour. Feeling so vulnerable in that moment, but she didn't care. Not anymore. "We will come back here. I don't care what they think. You and I—" Kellan didn't let her finish the sentence. He engulfed her entire body in his arms, pressing himself firmly against her as he kissed her like his life depended on it. It felt like time itself had stood still, and when he pulled away, she thought her heart might explode from her chest. He'd made her feel so many things. So many different emotions…

"They're waiting." With a sigh, Kellan stepped back. Hand slowly turning the knob and opening the door to the hallway beyond.

The house was quiet. The others who wouldn't be joining them most likely still sound asleep in whatever bed they had chosen. Blissfully unaware of the turmoil her and the Horseman endured as they took what could be their last steps through the hallway. Awaiting their return with news of their victory.

The cool air nipped at Demitria's face as they slowly made their way to the large stoned area that had once been a driveway. Their arms brushed as they continued. Neither one hiding the newfound closeness between them. Kellan lightly grazed his fingers across her own. They'd been balled into fists, but at his touch she relaxed them.

They had been the last to arrive, and all eyes turned toward the Horseman, and the human girl that arrived together. Kellan made a point to stand as close as he could get to her.

"You disgust me." The venom dripped from the female's mouth. The disbelief was wild in her eyes. Eire had her bow drawn and aimed straight at Demitria. The tip of the arrow resting on her chin as the rage consumed her.

Demitria didn't flinch. She knew his siblings would be more than aware of the difference between her and their brother, and had accepted it last night. They both had accepted their fate when they had finally given in to the pull that continuously drew them together time and time again.

"You do not have any say in this." Kellan spoke, eyes never leaving his siblings. The challenge clear.

"She's *human*!" Eire spat. "What has she done to you." Eire's lip quivered for a moment, and then it was gone. Any emotion drained from her face. The arrow was replaced in her quiver before Demitria could even blink, and the female was stalking away. Down the stone covered road and headed toward the gate where her dappled gray mare waited.

Demitria knew he was staring at her but she couldn't bear to meet his eyes. She could feel his gaze burning into her, eating away at her very being, but she wouldn't look. Jace had never liked the Horseman. He had made that perfectly clear to her when they'd fought. He'd tolerated them, but deep down she knew his true feelings. Now everything was different. *They* were different. There was no coming back from last night, and she knew that. She was okay with it, in fact. But Jace would never let that go. Not after everything they'd been through together.

"I don't regret anything." The whisper left her lips, hand softly grazing across his forearm in reassurance.

"Neither do I." She knew his gesture would not be received lightly by those around them, but he didn't seem to care as he brushed his thumb across her lips. She watched the war on his face as he forced himself to back away before the exchange turned intimate. Eire had been his only sibling to cause a scene, thank the gods.

"Is everyone ready?" The eldest Horseman left his post beside Arakiel and slowly walked toward them. The look in his eyes said everything. Disappointment. Both of them knew what they'd done was against every rule the council had ever set, but neither of them cared about the repercussions. But while there was disappointment, she also saw understanding.

Arakiel made his way toward them. "We must complete the last of our preparations before we are to continue." The soft waves of the early morning sun glittered like starlight along those perfect dark wings that he held so proudly. Not a single feather out of place. It was hard to imagine that they'd soon be tainted and covered in blood. "Your Smith has been working through the night on some things." He motioned for the remaining Horsemen to follow him as he disappeared behind the large house. Kellan shot her a longing glance before he finally followed behind.

Demitria knew she had to talk to him. They were about to start the grueling journey up the mountain together, but she couldn't leave things the way they were between them. Her breath came out in a huff as she finally turned toward them. Sad, green eyes were watching her, gaze never faltering as she closed the distance between them.

"I'm glad you both are here." She started, slowly finding her voice. "I don't think I could do it without you by my side." Not once did she pull her stare from him. She needed him to know that despite everything, she still *needed* him by her side.

"I'm going to give you guys a minute." Cory broke, patting Jace along the back. "I know you have things you both need to talk about." Without a second thought, the copper haired man made his way toward the remaining angels down the driveway.

She was thankful for him, always. Cory could read the room effortlessly, and knew exactly when someone needed space.

"I'm scared." The words had been hard, and Demitria couldn't look at Jace as she said it. Having worked so tirelessly to always keep her emotions in check, admitting when she was afraid wasn't something that came naturally or easy. "I'm terrified to fight, Jace." He didn't say anything to her, but wrapped her in his arms instead.

"I'm sorry." He whispered softly, squeezing his arms around her even tighter. "I have no right to judge you on the things you do, or the people you choose to have in your life." She knew the tears were flowing down her face. Could feel them soaking through Jace's shirt as she clung to him. "I know nothing I say will change your mind, but please stay back. Lock yourself away somewhere and let us fight."

"You know I can't do that." Finally, she released her hold. "I need to fight alongside them. I need to fight with you and Cory. This is my fight, more than it is yours." Because in truth, the fight had nothing to do with them. They all seemed to want *her*. The council, Lucifer—they'd only gone after Solis to get to *her*. Jace nodded his head, understanding everything she had said. She could see it in his eyes, that heaviness. The fear, in having her fight. But above all else, she knew he understood her reasons for pushing forward.

"The time is now." Arakiel raised his arm, waving the others over toward the group that had assembled around him after returning. With a curt nod, the two made their way to him.

"I suppose everyone is ready?" Gabriel asked, walking toward them. Demitria watched as Kellan tucked what looked to be daggers into his armor. He couldn't help but smile as he caught her gaze.

"Your Smith has been working on these for you." She took the cloth bound item from him and unraveled it quickly, revealing two shining new daggers similar in size and shape to her previous blades. "It looks like someone had attempted their own little haven here, and he found an abandoned forge in the back shed."

Demitria had been so caught up in *him* last night, that she hadn't even cared to find out what her own people were up to. And Evan had worked tirelessly through the night to arm them?

She wouldn't let herself feel guilty for last night. Everyone had chosen to spend what could be their final evening doing whatever they liked, and that was fine. She'd wanted—needed to spend it with Kellan. Exploring him, like her body had been begging her to for days on end.

"I'll have to thank him when we return." The daggers effortlessly tucked into her attire. One in the top of her left boot, the second in her right bracer, and the third strapped onto her back between her shoulder blades. Demitria's eyes made their way around the others before her. Watching as some fiddled with weapons or armor, others, like Eire, stood waiting at the gate. She hadn't moved from her position, but her mount was gone.

The wind blew softly as they left the confines of the estate. Demitria tucked a few strands of hair that had flown out of her braid behind her ears as she turned, giving one last look back before moving on. She had so many thoughts. So many emotions swirling through her mind as they began the ascent. What if this really was a trap? Could they survive? They had such low numbers to begin with, would they be able to make it out alive?

In answer, a sharp whinny echoed throughout the land before them. A promise. A call from the creature that had been her rock time and time again. An oath that they would see each other again. That she would return, and they would reunite once more. She smiled, nodding at the bond shared between them.

"We will return." His soft voice pulled her from her thoughts, sending a new wave of calm over her body. She regretted fighting against the pull for so long as that nagging feeling bubbled to the surface once more, wishing they'd just had *more time*.

So she made a promise to herself. To fight and to win, against whatever odds were against them. To reunite with Atlas. To return to this estate, and return *home* with Kellan.

Forty-Two

DEMITRIA

The path ahead grew smaller and smaller as they climbed until they were walking single file. The wind had all but disappeared, and the air grew hot as they pushed on. Demitria watched as Kellan scanned their surroundings, listening for anything out of place. She watched his features harden, unnerved at whatever he did—or didn't—hear.

Kellan had insisted that Demitria climb in front of him. Should anything go wrong, he would be there if she so much as faltered. She was glad for it. Her nerves had always made her clumsy, and the rugged path onward was growing steeper by the minute. Sharp rocks jutted out on either side as they advanced. Sharp enough that she knew they would maim should she fall. The ground beneath her was loose. Stones the size of her palm littered their path. Nothing about it was solid, and they broke free with each step, waiting to take one of them down. It would only be her people, that much she knew. If anyone should misstep, it would be one of them. Jace. Cory. Her. She at least had the protection of the Horsemen. The other two would be utterly helpless, unless someone else stepped up. Despite this trek, she doubted any of them would have. Eire especially. Demitria was glad she led the charge, far away from her own people. She wouldn't have to watch the female stand there, grinning as one of them fell to their deaths, and Demitria wouldn't have to try and kill her, despite being on the same side.

Because she would do it, she realized. She would kill Eire if the female pushed her hand. Wouldn't even think twice before drawing her blade.

"Relax your body. You're expending too much energy before the climb." Kellan's hand was soft on her arm, pulling her back from the blood thirsty thoughts that had taken over and plagued her. She hadn't even realized how rigid she'd gone, or the fists that had been clenched tight. Demitria relaxed her hands, fingers already aching. "I will not let anything happen. To you or them." He reassured her, and gods did she believe him.

With a smile, they pushed on. Over the rocky terrain as they climbed to the biggest obstacle of the trek, aside from whatever lay at the top. Whatever was waiting for them. The only sound she could hear was the drag of her boots across the path. The slipping as rock after rock broke free and she stumbled, only to be steadied with a solid hand at her back.

Much to her surprise, the angels had stayed on foot. Demitria had been sure they would have flown alongside as they hiked. To keep their bodies honed. Primed to fight whatever came at them. To save whatever strength they could, but they walked along with the rest of them. Like a team. Arakiel had said that together, they were the strongest. She just hadn't realized that had included them as well.

Laylah kept pace with Eire. Meeting her step for step as the Horseman ascended at a godly pace. Her body effortlessly traversed along the rocks. Nimble. Graceful. Demitria hated it. Despised the way she carried herself, as if better than the rest of them. Like she deserved the world, and they were nothing but a smear among it.

Further down the line, Cory and Jace climbed close together. Leaning on the other for support. She was grateful for Cory. Once upon a time, that would have been her up there. Beside Jace. Fighting along-side him. They'd been glued 'o each other's hips for years. How different things had played out. The path she had chosen.

His foot slipped, and she felt herself lurching forward. Knowing that no matter how fast she moved, it still wouldn't be fast enough. She wouldn't get there in time. Demitria nearly screamed as Jace tumbled. It was Arakiel who reached him first. Wings carrying him swiftly toward her friend, grabbing hold of his arm before he could plunge down to his death.

Demitria nearly vomited, and was all too grateful for the lack of breakfast that morning. She was trembling as she watched the silent conversation. Jace's face pale as the angel spoke, then nodded at whatever he'd said. Then he was looking at her. Seeking out her gaze, wanting to make sure she knew he was okay. Wanting nothing more than to embrace him, her body shook slightly.

Family.

Jace was her family, and she'd nearly just lost him. Again.

It reminded her why she was doing this. Why she was choosing to fight and not stay back like he and Kellan had begged her to do. Having lost nearly everyone she cared about, she had vowed to never let that happen again. They'd both made that promise, so many years ago, that they would never feel that pain again. Never know that feeling of truly being alone. Because they always had each other, and nothing would ever change that.

She would kill everything that threatened to break that. Every being that sought out her family. Every creature that so much as looked maliciously at anyone she cared for, she would slaughter them where they stood. Lucifer had played his cards. Had sent his army to eradicate the world.

It was her turn to play hers.

"I'm going ahead." Eire had turned around, closing in on the rest of them that she'd wandered away from. "Can you feel it?"

"I feel nothing." Kellan eyed her.

"That's exactly it. Nothing." She met the stares of her siblings. The angels. Eire didn't bother to look at Demitria or her people. "There have been no demons. None of their creatures."

"Something isn't right." Kane agreed.

"It's a trap." Kellan had suspected it. From the moment they'd stepped foot on the mountain, he'd known something wasn't quite right, and told her as such. He'd hoped that his instincts were wrong, but that wasn't proving to be the case. It had been why he'd been so quiet. So focused. Demitria let the shudder course through her as any hope she'd let herself feel dwindled.

"We don't break." Gabriel's voice was stern. Law. "We stay together. Especially now."

"I respect you brother, I really do. But don't force me to go against your will." Eire's voice nearly cracked at the thought of it. "If we are to end this here today, we need eyes up ahead. You know that."

No one spoke as Gabriel debated what to say. What Eire's next course of action was. They all knew she was right, but was he willing to split them? To send her off into the unknown, when they knew it was a trap?

"We have come too far to turn back now. Failure isn't an option." Demitria stepped forward. "At all costs, Lucifer cannot succeed. And if letting her go scout ahead makes the difference in us defeating him, trap or not, we take that chance. No questions asked."

"Why don't you send one of your own, before sending mine off to what could be her end." Gabriel's voice rumbled through the group, but she didn't back down from his challenge. It was reassuring when Kellan took up beside her. Agreeing with her.

"I'd go myself if I knew it would help us, but we all know where those skills lie. Who would be an asset, and who would falter."

"I'll go." Kellan stepped forward past her.

"No." Demitria and Gabriel shouted in unison, but it was her arm that reached him first, hand gripped tight to his muscled forearm.

"Eire is the tracker. The scout. She will go." Gabriel finished when she'd gone quiet. He faced his sister. "You make it up the cliff, and you wait. No farther. Scout the path. Only return if you find something."

With a nod, she was gone. Disappearing up the path in a near sprint. Energy that she was shocked the female still possessed after the climb they'd already done today. Demitria hated to admit it, but she was jealous at the stamina the female possessed. The skills that made her such an asset to them. But she herself was human. The only thing she'd brought to the group so far had been her stubborn refusal to back down, and her innate pull for finding trouble.

"We should keep moving." Gabriel spoke, his eyes never leaving the spot where his sibling had been. Watching. Waiting for anything out of the ordinary. Demitria knew what he was feeling right now. The worry. The fear as his family left into the unknown. Because it was exactly how she felt watching Jace make that trek.

He waited only a few moments before resuming his swift pace toward the cliff, the rest of their group keeping pace with him.

It felt like hours had passed before they reached the cliff side. Only then had they decided to take a moment to catch their breath and refuel. The angels handed out small amounts of dried fruits and meat before passing around a few canteens of water. She was grateful for it. That first climb had been brutal, her body was already running on near empty, and that hadn't even been the worst of the climb. That part was next. She ate anyway. The exertion on her body was enough to chance the sickness that could follow the grueling climb.

The cliff was steep. More so than any of them had realized. Especially to her own people. They didn't have inhuman strength or wings should they fall. The angels had agreed that flying was a last resort. It would give away whatever position they had, if that even mattered. Regardless, flying them up had been out of the question.

The smooth surface of the rock had little for foot and hand holds. They'd have to go slowly and carefully. But with the sun nearly peaking in the sky, she knew they couldn't afford to dawdle. Didn't have the luxury to take things slow. There would be no camping out on the mountain and fighting tomorrow. Once they emerged on the flat outcrop, they would engage. Regardless of how tired any of them were.

Craning her neck, she looked up. Up the sheer face of the cliff that taunted them. A few hundred feet to the top, then another small hike before they reached the outcrop. If they were to make it before nightfall they would have to leave any minute. The short reprieve not nearly enough for her aching body. Muscles near spasming as they strained.

She could do this.

Because if she didn't, it meant the end of life as they knew it. If they didn't make that climb before the sun fell, she knew it would be over. Regardless of the blood moon still days away. Lucifer and his army would find them, and eviscerate everything she knew. It had to end today, at all costs.

Eire had yet to return, and Demitria hoped that had been a good sign. That she hadn't encountered anything, and was waiting for them at the top.

Or she was already dead.

"We need to move." It was her turn to lead. Not because of Eire, but the fear that they had already downed a Horsemen. The fear of what losing one of them could mean for this entire fight. Could they even win? They had Arakiel and his angels. Kellan. Gabriel. Kane. Jace, and Cory... would it be enough? "If the sun falls before we get there, we're done. We've lost."

Demitria strapped the sword to her back before checking to make sure her remaining blades were tucked away in her clothing. Losing any weapons on the way up would be bad. Another thing they couldn't afford.

Tightening her boots, she stepped up to the cliff. Heaving a breath before pulling her body up. No one made a sound as they followed behind her, and she could feel his presence directly beneath her. Like a shadow lying in wait. When she moved, he moved. When she faltered, he was the hand to steady her. To keep her from tumbling.

The muscles in her arms roared in protest as she pushed higher. Fingers bleeding at the tips, nails cracked and bloody as she grabbed for anything she could manage along the rocks surface. When even the smallest ledge could mean life or death for her. For any of them.

Gabriel and Kane had surpassed her within minutes. The angels, too. She knew Kellan would have easily, but he stayed behind with her. Warming something within her chest. He wouldn't let her fall.

The next foothold had been higher than she'd anticipated, and she stretched. Reaching with outstretched fingers as she dove for the small alcove. It had been nearly in her grasp when the stone beneath her crumbled. It took every ounce of control to hold back the scream that would give whatever advantage they might have away. She was silent as the world slipped out from under her.

"No!" It was Kellan who roared, making the leap for the foothold she'd missed, his hand digging into the sword strapped to her back as he slammed her body into the wall with him. Holding the both of them steady as the silent tears fell down her face in streams. "I will not let you fall." He whispered. She couldn't see his face, but knew he was staring at her. The warmth of his breath ghosted along her neck. The stone bit into her face, hard enough she knew it had drawn blood, but she didn't care. She was alive. "I'm going to push you up to the next hold. Take a deep breath and calm your mind. Don't rush this." Demitria could only nod. The words had left her.

Kellan did as he said and gently pushed her up to the next divot on the surface. Grasping it with an iron grip, she pulled with everything she had. Ignoring the screaming fear in the back of her mind.

I'm not afraid.

Daring a glance upward she nearly sighed in relief. Gabriel and Kane were just cresting over the edge. She was close. She could make it. Jace was there too. He'd caught up to the angels and was staring down at her. Willing her to make it. Had he seen her nearly fall to her death? She'd never have been able to live with herself if this was where she met her end. Before the battle even began. Before she could even do anything to help her people. The world.

A slim hand reached for her at the top, and the offer shocked her. Eire stood, stone faced with her arm outstretched for her to hold on to. Demitria waited. Contemplated it. Would she let her go?

"Grab my hand you stupid girl." Eire's voice was harsh, demanding as she dangled out that tether toward her. Finally, she grasped it, the Horsemen hoisting her up the remaining feet of the cliff. "Don't say I never had your back." She huffed, spinning on her heel as her long, dark braid flipped over her shoulder, leaving Demitria wide eyed and mouth agape.

She didn't dare look down at how far they'd climbed. Couldn't stomach the thought, so she stood there, bent over with her hands on her knees as she panted to catch her breath. Kellan brought over a canteen filled with cool water and she drank it greedily. Lips dry from her labored breathing.

Eire gave the others a few moments to catch their breaths before reporting.

"It's a trap," She stated. "I found nothing. Literally nothing on my way up. Not a single demon. They know we're here."

"Fuck." Kellan cursed. Each one of them had hoped for a different outcome, but it hadn't surprised them one bit.

"What do we do now?" It was Cory that broke. Asking the question that neither she nor Jace couldn't bring themselves to do. Fearing the answer that deep down, they all already knew.

"Our plans don't change." Kane glared at him. "We end him here. Trap or no trap. No matter what lives it costs." He hadn't said it, but she knew. Their lives. Her friends' lives would be a sacrifice that he was willing to make. That all of his kind would be willing to make if it meant they'd succeed.

"They don't have to continue, but I will." She stepped up. "Jace and Cory can stay back. I will fight for them. I refuse to have them forfeit their lives." She was responsible for them. They were all in this mess because of her. They could have all lived their lives, blissfully unaware of the mass destruction that threatened their world if she hadn't gone back to Solis. And if they died, the blood would be on her hands. Demitria would never forgive herself.

"That isn't your choice to make." Jace grabbed hold of her shoulder. Hard enough to hurt, but she didn't flinch. "Where you go, I go." He whispered. "We do this as a team. Together." It took everything in her to hold back a new set of tears. The sacrifice he was so willing to make to stay by her side.

She didn't deserve him. Didn't deserve the undying love and loyalty that he showed her, time and time again. She knew it would be the reason he died one day. It would be because of her.

Finally, she looked at him. Hoping. Praying to whatever gods were listening to keep him safe. Begging him to see the words in her eyes that she couldn't say. The love she felt for him.

They didn't have long to wait before needing to push on. They were so close to the top. So close to the end that would either break them or save the world. Demitria righted her blade, settling that familiar weight alongside her hip once more before she drew it.

The air around them was wrong. Eerie, and it set her on edge. Senses screaming at her to turn around. To come back the way she came, knowing that the climb down was the lesser of the two evils before her. But she pushed it down. Down, down, down until she felt nothing. Until that fear was replaced with an unyielding need for revenge.

They pushed on, weapons drawn, with a new wave of energy. Up the remaining rocky terrain that would lead them to Lucifer. To the battle that waited for them, and they emerged onto the outcrop together.

She wouldn't say a goodbye to either of her friends. Because they would get through this together if she had her way. Each and every one of them would return from this fight. They'd trek back down that fucking mountain and go back to the estate. They'd reunite with Atlas, and cultivate the land around them. Build a community anew. Better than the last. Better than that she'd ever known, and she'd live.

Demitria would live. She'd love.

She'd be free.

"We've been expecting you."

Forty-Three

DEMITRIA

Demitria wasn't prepared for the horrors that awaited them, and her entire body itched at the sight of them. For the beasts that snarled their ugly pointed teeth as saliva dripped from their gaping maws. The long, slender arms that dipped into sharpened talons. Each one deadlier than the last. This was why they hadn't seen a single demon on the mountain their entire climb. They were all here, waiting for them to walk right into the trap.

Legs like lead, Demitria felt as if she couldn't move. The creatures of nightmares stared her down with those same crimson eyes that Reim had possessed, and it unnerved her. She may have conquered those fears, but it had never prepared her for this. For the sheer numbers Lucifer's army had on their own. She didn't even know if they stood a chance.

The rock beneath their feet had been worn smooth. Weathered from years and years of heavy rains. The clawed gouges were new, had been used to sharpen talons into even deadlier points than they already were.

"The Four Horsemen." The Dark King looked just as his name suggested. His armor, forged of the darkest materials, glared under the sun as ivory skin peeked out from beneath it. He wore no helm, but a spiked obsidian crown sat poised atop his head. Regal, yet deadly. Demitria fought the shiver that threatened to course through her entire body at his presence. Long, thick inky hair fell over his shoulder in soft waves as dark eyes, like twin pools of the deepest ocean, took them all in. He was beautiful, in an ethereal way, and she hated to even think it. "War. My dear old friend." Lucifer smirked, taking a step toward them. They didn't concede any space, and Kellan only growled in answer. "You look well... changed, perhaps?"

From beside her, Kellan clenched the hilt of his sword tighter. The only indication of the rage that was swelling within him. She fought the urge to touch him. His arm. His hand. Anything that she could do to reassure him, but she knew better. Knew any sign of whatever they were could be used against them, so her hand stayed rigid at her side.

"Cut the bullshit," Eire's voice erupted. "You knew we were coming."

"Of course I did." He grinned. "I have eyes and ears everywhere, or did your brother forget that?" Lucifer took another step forward, and it was Kellan that stepped up. Slowly closing the gap. "How many years has it been? Hundreds? I wouldn't particularly blame you for it if you did." A beast of a creature writhing in darkness crept up beside him. Eyes trained solely on the humans in the group. Its body was dark, sleek with elongated legs that ended in five sharp claws. Curved horns sat atop its lupine skull.

"Call your hounds off," Gabriel snarled. "We can end this quietly, without the bloodshed."

"Now where's the fun in that?" Lucifer patted the beast along its muscled neck. "Especially when you foolish beings brought humans."

She supposed it wouldn't have taken much to notice the differences in her kind, but the call out had sent a ripple of nausea roiling through her stomach. Not for her sake, but for Jace. For Cory. Would this be where they died?

"What's the point in a war when you know there will be nothing left of the planet you are trying so desperately to rule?" Kane spoke, his bow loaded and ready, aimed for the creature at Lucifer's side.

"You know my conditions." Lucifer grinned again. "My price to back down is the same as it always has been. One that none of you are ever willing to pay."

"I will not subject my brother to your bloodthirsty clutches." Demitria hadn't seen Gabriel this angry before, and it scared her. He scared her. Death. He was the Horseman of Death, and it radiated off him like a beacon. The air cooled around him as he called forth that blinding power within as shadows writhed beneath his skin. "Stopping a war or not, he will not be sacrificed. We find balance another way."

"The girl. Give me the girl and I shall think about it."

"Out of the fucking question." Kellan growled, and in that one short moment, he revealed her importance to him. Lucifer's eyes narrowed as he gazed on at them. Studying. Putting the pieces together.

"Oh?" His smile widened. "A Horseman and a human girl. I heard you were tasked with elimination. And yet you've let her crawl into your bed." He laughed then. "A pity... but an outcome I expected none-theless." Lucifer shrugged, a look of disinterest on his face.

Demitria wanted to be the one to kill Lucifer, but as that rage set across Kellan's face, she wasn't so sure she'd be the one to plunge her sword into the male's heart, but she yearned for that sweet revenge all the same. For the communities he'd decimated. The planet he'd lain waste to. For all the people he had killed. *For Kellan*, and the suffering he'd endured.

"You never did like to do things the easy way, did you?" He sighed, and Kellan lunged. Lucifer was faster, and he disappeared into the dark-ness that was his army. Gnashing teeth met Kellan's blade as he swung. Flesh tore and fell to the ground in bloodied heaps as he advanced after the fallen angel.

"Coward!" He bellowed, his sword moving so fast Demitria could barely track its movements. His scream was all they needed. The war cry that sent them all into the fray, weapons swinging in precise movements as the darkness unleashed around them.

I will not be afraid. Those familiar words repeated themselves as she charged after him. Into the hoard of nightmares that clawed and snapped at her every which way she turned, but still she followed. Ducking under the slash of talons, dagger poised above her as Demitria sliced the limb from palm to elbow, her body sliding along the smooth stone. The creature roared in frustration and swiped again. She'd barely evaded this one, narrowly missing her thigh as her body rolled out of the way. Inky blood from its wounded arm dripped down her legs. So cold she felt it through her pants. Demitria sliced upwards with her sword as the guttural cry left the beast's body before it crumbled to the stone beside her. She was running before it even made an impact.

Darkness wreathed around them as shadows danced in moving tendrils along the ground. Grabbing, reaching for anything that moved.

"Kellan!" Demitria screamed after the Horseman. Her only visual on him was the red cloak that whipped and swayed with his body as he attacked. He hadn't been on the defensive once, the bodies in his wake were proof of that. Still, he kept moving as if he hadn't heard her calls.

She couldn't waste time watching over the others. A quick glance was all she could spare as she fought her way after him. Gabriel, Kane, and Eire had amassed bodies of their own, and she was confident that they'd be okay. The angels had fanned out to her left as they attacked from the air. Unleashing their silver and golden weapons upon the darkness that threatened to consume them. But those shadows were faster, deadly, as they wound around Laylah's leg and pulled her to the ground. Her piercing scream echoed across the battlefield, and it struck her in the chest. Heaving the breath from her lungs as the shadows consumed the female's body.

A wicked laugh filled her, almost numbing her, as another cry pierced the air. "You think you can beat me? I wrote the fucking book on your maneuvers. You are nothing!" Lucifer bellowed over the screams as his power erupted.

Demitria pulled herself away from the screams. Away from the wails of Oriel as his sister fell to the darkness, and she kept running. Pushing the tears away that threatened to fall with each step further.

I will not be afraid.

She told herself, again and again as she pushed on. Willing the words into her very being.

"You're not going alone." Jace panted, reaching out for her arm to stop her from running further. He'd fought like literal hell to get to her side. His temple coated in blood. Red, which meant it was either his or Cory's. "I'm okay." He added, dropping his hands to his knees as he sucked in breath after breath. "Cory is with Arakiel." Demitria nodded once.

"I'm going after Kellan. Stay with the others where it's safe." She pleaded. Going after Kellan was foolish enough. Having Jace follow her into it was outright suicide.

"We agreed that we do this together. Don't push me away." Jace grabbed hold of her arm again as if it would stop her from whatever stupid decision she was planning on making. "I'm going with you."

Demitria knew she couldn't fight him. All she could do was nod, and the two burst into a sprint after the red warrior. Her and Jace fought side by side. If one would block, the other would slash. They moved in tandem, swords hissing through the air as blades met flesh. She was covered in blood. Some of it inky, some of it red. Her own, Jace's too. He didn't look any different, but they pushed on. She could already feel her body tiring and knew that Jace must be close to empty. The hike had taken a lot out of them. More than they both would care to admit, but to fall now could mean defeat.

She watched as Kellan advanced further, swinging his blade at the darkness that threatened to incapacitate him as Lucifer let out wave after wave of power. Farther toward the open mouth of the mountain. What the hell was he doing? She'd lost sight of Lucifer. Hadn't seen him since he'd disappeared into the darkness, but she'd heard his laugh. Seen the devastation of his power as shadows whipped about the battlefield.

Another scream ripped through the air, but Demitria didn't have the heart to turn around and see who had fallen next. Angel? Horseman? Even Cory? She didn't know.

Another body. Another mark on her soul of people she'd lost.

When Kellan darted into the opening, Demitria almost screamed. "It's another trap." She gasped. Lucifer was baiting him into the mountain. Away from his siblings. Away from the angels. "Jace, he's running right into a trap."

"I know." He huffed, sword piercing through the neck of another creature. He'd realized shortly after she had.

"Fuck." With a speed she didn't know she could muster, Demitria took off, dodging around the remaining creatures that stood in her way. Jace quickly trailed her as blade met beast.

Kellan was running right into a trap that Lucifer had set, baiting him into whatever area would give him the best advantage. Demitria didn't know if there were other more powerful demons lying in wait for him. Waiting for their chance to strike the Horseman down. She couldn't let that happen.

Not when they'd made a promise to each other. To return home *together*.

Forty-Four

KELLAN

As he ran through the hoard of creatures, Kellan couldn't believe the cowardice of Lucifer as he retreated into his army. The sharp metal of his blade pierced through beast after beast, the sound creating a rhythm as he moved fluidly through them, following Lucifer to the back of the mountain. This was the one being Kellan cared about most. The only one he cared to truly drive his sword through. That familiar urge beckoned him to let it free. To completely take over his body and just give in to the blood lust that called to him. With a shake of his head, he ran. Ran faster and harder through the demons that came at him. He was gaining ground, catching up to the fallen angel of death and destruction as he chased him through a narrow path between the emerging peaks. Kellan didn't know where it led, but he followed anyway.

Lucifer banked left down another small passageway, tossing out a wave of his dark power before disappearing from his sight. Kellan sensed it moments before it was upon him, no more than a heartbeat between the time it took to throw his large frame to the ground as those piercing shadows slashed out overhead. He felt it graze across his forearm, tearing the fabric and breaking skin, but he didn't stop. The moment they receded, he was on his feet and running.

Kellan was angry. At himself for giving whatever he and Demitria were away before they'd even fought, but mostly at Lucifer. For using any weakness against them that he possibly could in order to get whatever he wanted, even if that thing was him. But he had killed far too many souls for Lucifer. Kellan had done so many things he wasn't proud of during that time with the dark angel, and it had taken him hundreds of years to forgive himself. It had taken a human girl to truly set him free.

So he'd fight, he'd decided. For a brief moment, before he'd sprung free, he'd entertained Lucifer's demand for himself. He would fight until he no longer could. Until his legs had been rendered useless, and his arms had been torn to ribbons. Kellan would fight until his sword lay bloodied on the ground, his enemies strewn around him as his battered body stilled on the cool stone if it meant he had a chance. A chance to walk away. To be happy.

With her.

The closer he got to the fallen angel, the more his brain screamed at him. To go back. To wait for help. Kellan knew it was a trap, yet he didn't care.

"My offer still stands." With just enough time to dodge the attack, Kellan stumbled into the rocky mountain side as a golden-silver blade missed his throat by only a few inches. In all his time with the Dark King, the male had never shown an angel blade, and he couldn't let the thought sink its ugly, taloned claws into his mind, despite the fact that there was a very real chance he wouldn't make it off the mountain.

They'd just emerged into another smaller, flat outcropping that overlooked the war raging on below when Lucifer jumped him. Kellan didn't even have the chance to check on the others down below before the male was upon him.

"I want nothing to do with your cause." He swung, and the angel easily evaded his efforts.

"Don't you miss it?" Lucifer grinned, swatting away Kellan's maneuvers as if he'd been wielding nothing more than a stick. "The killing? The bloodshed? I can see it in your eyes, Horseman." Kellan could feel it too. "We conquered so much together, you and I. Waged wars on so many cultures." Like flames, those shadows danced down his arms, twining with the golden-silver blade in his hands. He'd be so, so fucked if Lucifer got ahold of him. The edge of his blade grazed across Kellan's forearm and he flinched, feeling the burn as it sunk into his skin, as the shadows tried to fillet the flesh from his bones, but held his ground.

"That was a long time ago. I'm not the same as I once was." He hadn't even had control over his own body during most of those years with the Dark King, but he'd changed, regardless.

"No, you've grown soft." Lucifers eyes trailed toward the emerging humans, grinning as a pair of green-gold eyes caught his own. "She'll be your downfall, you know. Your complete undoing." Another swing, and Kellan managed a strike. The thin line of blood trickled down the fallen angel's dark armor where the Horseman had pierced through. "Join me, Kellan. Horseman of War. Join me again." His power surged again, and for a moment, Kellan was in total darkness. Like he was freefalling between worlds, and his surroundings came back to him in a flash. Every inch of his body burned from the darkness and the shadows Lucifer possessed. As they found their way into him through even the smallest wound, scorching him from the inside out, and he felt it throughout his entire body as it fought to incapacitate him.

"I refuse to join you again. Refuse to allow myself to fall into that once more. To kill innocents. The bloodshed ends here!" Kellan moved to strike, but he was a fraction of a second too slow, his blade tied up with his enemies as that familiar silver-gold of an angel blade nearly struck him stupid. More of those shadows surrounded him. Prodding, slashing him as it tore into him again and again. Kellan could feel the warmth of his blood as it welled within his clothing. Soaking the fabric above the wounds. The Dark King had always been a force to be reckoned with, even against himself, and he struggled to gain the upper hand.

The blow to his knee had been unexpected, and his body tumbled to the ground, rolling out of the way a heartbeat before the blade had come near inches from his face. Lucifer was stronger than he remembered, and Kellan was struggling. He hadn't been prepared for this power. It was nothing compared to what it had been like so many years ago. Back then, his siblings had barely managed to claw him away from

Lucifer's grasp. Now? Kellan felt like he'd be lucky to survive another five minutes.

At the echoing footsteps around the bend, he glanced behind him, watching as Demitria rushed toward him, her own sword poised in attack as she lunged toward the fallen angel.

He was on his feet, slashing at those shadowed tendrils that shot their way toward the second human in his entire existence he'd ever found himself caring for in a millennium. "This is not your fight." Kellan growled, his arm pinning her against the mountain's rocky surface while the other held firm on his sword. "Get back." He tossed her aside with such carelessness that she was nearly tumbling to the ground. "Stay out of my way." He snapped, his attention wholly focused on the dark angel before him, not even sparing a glance in her direction to insure she'd been okay.

She screamed something at him, but he couldn't hear it through the ringing in his ears. As his blood boiled, and he fought to control the rage threatening to take hold of him.

"Get her out of here." He muttered through clenched teeth. Jace's grip was firm around her, but she fought him with everything she had. Struggled against his arms that held firm around her. Clawing at him to let her go. Yet the human held strong, and something akin to pride washed over him.

"Let me help you! You're hurt!" Demitria cried out. Kellan knew he was. Could feel the fatigue that was threatening to overwhelm his body with each new wound the fallen angel opened up across him, but he wouldn't let it stop him. He'd fight until he was dead. Protecting her until he couldn't anymore.

"I don't want your help." Lucifer stumbled as Kellan feigned left and swung, the tip of his blade connecting as it submerged into the Dark Kings left thigh. He growled, a deep guttural and animalistic sound as he recoiled from the blow. Kellan couldn't help but grin as his opponent's face was laced with pain.

"I'm getting tired of these games, Horseman." Lucifer thrust himself forward, throwing his weight into his next swing and Kellan barely managed to evade the sword as more of those shadows fought against him, winding around his wrists. Kellan clawed at them, ripping them free as they seared into his skin, marring the exposed flesh where the fabric of his shirt had all but shredded. He hadn't accounted for the dagger that embedded itself into his side, piercing through his armis-suento the tissue below his ribs. He hadn't meant to let the sound free, but a slight yelp escaped his lips as he stumbled to his knee. Panting, as that agonizing pain took over him. Lucifer had been too fast. Spinning on his foot, his sword barreled toward his exposed chest, and Kellan knew this was where he'd die.

Then everything was in slow motion. The screams that ripped through the air. The heavy footfalls across the stone beneath them.

The sickening sound of piercing flesh echoed through Kellan's ears as a roar erupted through the battlefield.

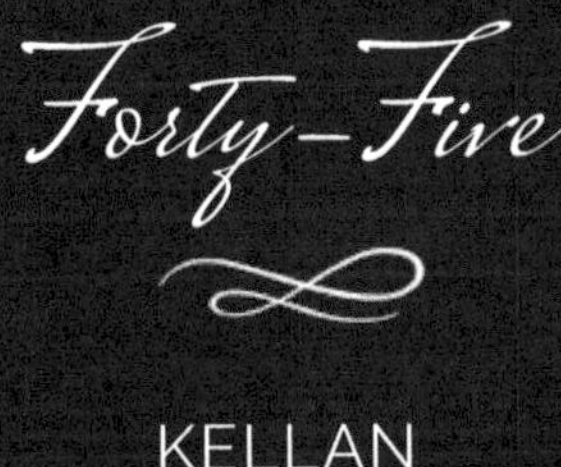

Forty-Five

KELLAN

In his rage, Kellan's sword severed through a limb. Blood spurted across his face, his clothing, and along the edge of his blade. He'd taken Lucifer's hand from the wrist down, and it tumbled to the ground beneath his feet, muscle and bone protruding from where the chunk of flesh once sat. With a blood curdling scream, Kellan was consumed in a wall of darkness for a mere moment before stepping out of it completely as the Dark King disappeared, his wounded figure retreating further up the mountain.

Kellan turned, fighting back that welling sea of rage that threatened to become him.

Demitria's eyes were unnaturally wide as she gripped her abdomen with trembling fingers. Lucifer's sword pierced clean through her body, staining the golden fuller of the blade.

"Kellan..." Her voice wavered, and he'd never heard that melodious voice so panicked. The terror in her eyes as she looked up at him, her body swaying as she crumpled to the ground beneath his feet. Kellan was beside her in a heartbeat, catching her frail body in his arms before she made impact. Holding her to him as he knelt there. Willing. *Begging* that growing inferno within him to subside. To just give him time to think. To figure something—anything, out.

"No... no." His own fingers trembled as he reached for the blade marring the beautiful ivory of her soft skin. He was horrified at the events that had played out. It couldn't be happening. It was supposed to be—should have been him. *Him*, that died on this battlefield. Not her. Never her.

Kellan's hand curled around the blade, feeling it cut into his palm as his own blood mixed with hers. Panic set in, and he was ripping the sword from her body, hurling it away as if it had burned a permanent scar into his hand. Kellan could feel the blood on his fingertips. Her blood. They were both coated in her blood. It pooled around her, into his lap and across the stone, and he couldn't make it stop as she began to bleed out.

He could feel it writhing beneath his skin, like a serpent, winding and slithering just below the surface as his power begged to be freed. To consume. To lay waste to anything and everything in his path.

"I'm... sorry." She coughed, spitting up more of the crimson liquid that began to fill her lungs, and that tether went taut.

"Don't say that. Don't say you're sorry." He cried out, shaking his head. He couldn't hear the words. Couldn't let her say them. "You stay with me." Kellan's hand brushed across her face. Over the trembling bottom lip as he caressed her. Feeling as the warmth, her lifeforce, began to leave her body. Demitria coughed again, and it coated his armor. His shirt. "I mean it, Demitria. You aren't going anywhere."

He'd been a fucking idiot. Had led her into the trap that would take her life. A life that he wanted—needed more time to explore. To learn and map out every inch of her skin. Every freckle and scar. To commit every *noise* to memory. But there was always blood. More blood on his hands. Blood he had never wanted to spill over a war he had never wanted to happen.

"Kellan... I-I need you to know something." She swallowed, wincing from the pain that coursed through her body from the gaping wound in her chest.

"Anything. Just stay here. Stay with me." He pleaded, his fingers digging into her that little bit harder, as if she'd do just that.

Her eyes closed briefly, the movement slow and dragged out, and she laughed softly before the sound died out as she winced once more. "I was falling for you. Hard." Kellan knew the sharp intake of breath sent another wave of searing pain through her, but she pushed on. Knowing the words needed to leave her lips before it was too late. "Harder than I ever thought was possible." A hint of a smile graced her full lips, and he rubbed his thumb across them once more. "I think I love you."

Something in him shattered. Like every single bone in his entire body broke at those three *beautiful* words. He was completely torn wide open, shattered into a million little pieces by that damning phrase, but he smiled at her anyway. Willing it to meet his eyes. "There was a reason I couldn't kill you when we met. A pull I still can't explain." He whispered, not letting the panic that threatened to take hold, the tremble his body fought, find its way to his voice. "I needed you, more than I've ever needed anyone before. Now I need you to stay here." Kellan's forehead rested on her own as he closed his eyes. Something rumbling through him. A feeling he hadn't felt before, almost as if he'd been the one who had been pierced through the chest. "I love you, Demitria."

"I was sure I wouldn't get to hear you say it, but I'm glad I could, even just once." She smiled again, and Kellan could tell she was growing weaker with each breath she took. "I've wanted to hear it for a while." Her breathing was shaky now, and a ragged sigh left her lips. "I hope we can meet again... someday." She stared into his silver lined azure eyes as she drew her last breath, and her chest fell still.

For the first time in as long as he could remember, Kellan, one of the Four Horsemen, War. Warrior and bringer of destruction, hung his head and cried.

JACE

Loss. Grief.

Guilt.

Jace had yet to move from the ground where he'd fallen when Demitria broke free from his grip. Staring at his hands as if he'd been the one to stab her with the sword. He'd been an immovable fortress, and she'd still tossed him away as if he'd been lighter than a feather.

"Let me take her." Jace whispered. His hands shook. Trembling with his own grief coursing through him. His only family. The only person remaining that he truly *loved*, and she was gone. Had slipped through his fingers before he could get a better hold of her. Before he could anchor himself around her frame, and never let her go. Now she was dead. Her body unmoving as the Horseman cried. "Let me take her." He repeated, voice wavering. Weak. Pathetic. He didn't care.

Kellan didn't move. Whether unwilling to answer him, or had been so lost in his own emotions, Jace didn't know.

"Please." He broke, choking back the sob that tore from his throat. He couldn't make himself move. To get up and take her body from Kellan's hands, so he sat on the ground. The bite of the stone in his knees, the blood from his own wounds swelling to the surface, and he couldn't even feel it. Everything was numb, yet he was broken. "Kellan let me take her." Jace couldn't help the tears as they flowed freely from his eyes. They'd promised to return. To end this together.

They'd promised each other they would never be alone. To never leave the other, and stay together. And even with the deaths of their families. His parents. Their entire world, he'd never felt alone, because she'd always been at his side. But now, that was all he'd ever be.

Alone.

On steady legs, Kellan moved toward him. Passing Demitria's limp body to his awaiting arms. The grief that had overtaken him had vanished, replaced with a killing calm.

Jace cradled her to his own body, pressing his forehead to hers. Still warm. Still smelled like she had, after all those years, it had never changed. Like a field of lavender on a crisp morning. Never again would he smell it. Never would he breathe it in, wishing that it would just overcome him.

"You weren't supposed to leave me. This wasn't supposed to happen." Jace rocked their bodies back and forth. Pulling his head away only to brush the tousled hair off her face. The tips had been stained with her own blood, and it smeared on his fingers, cold, and no longer warm. He didn't care, but wished it was his own. What he wouldn't give to see her smiling again. To stare into those green-gold eyes he'd grown so accustomed to—so fond of, over the years. To take her place. He'd give anything to trade places with her, right here and now.

His own scream echoed over the mountain.

Anger.

Grief.

Regret.

It hit him with a slamming force that could have cleaved the mountain in two. As if his very being was shattered the moment her body fell.

A piece of Jace died with her.

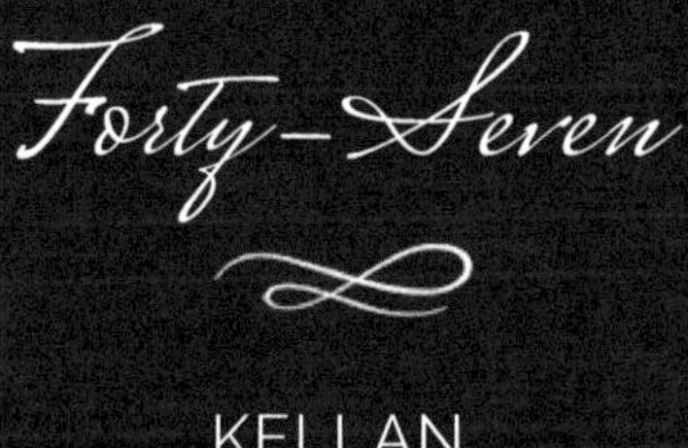

KELLAN

Kellan watched the human wailing as he rocked Demitria back and forth as he brushed her face with gentle fingers as if she'd come back to life under his touch. Kellan felt it deep within his chest, that nagging feeling again. The loss he knew Jace must be feeling. He'd had years with her, and Kellan knew what it looked like when a human was broken. When they'd given up on everything. Jace was the spitting image. His face was hollow, pale, his eyes dull. Lifeless, like something in himself had died. As if any light that had been within had gone out the moment Demitria had taken her last breath.

Kellan could feel himself slipping into that rage, willing every ounce of it to come pouring into him. Feeling the surge as it thrummed in his veins, pumping through his blood as it *rejoiced*. He was murderous. Craving nothing more than destruction and death. What he had been groomed to be. A being of mass destruction, and he welcomed every fucking ounce of it.

Kellan crossed the threshold and let the darkness take over.

With his sword in his hand, he stalked in the direction Lucifer fled. A fiery darkness emanated from him, nearly identical to the one Lucifer wielded, winding itself around him as it clung to everything that he was. Like a power of the gods, it pulsed through him. Igniting. Burning.

Kellan was hell incarnate. This was why the Dark King had held him in his clutches for so long. Why he had led that army through countless wars. He was fire, he was rage, he was darkness. And it mirrored everything that Lucifer was.

The remaining Horsemen were quick on his heels, readying themselves for the fight that was coming. A battle that he knew had been on each of their minds for so long now, but Kellan whirled around, turning his sword on his own siblings.

"I go alone." The growl rumbled through him. His eyes dark. Murderous, as he stared at each of them. "Back off."

"You can't do this alone. Not like this." Gabriel stood his ground and toed toward his brother. Kellan swung his blade, and Gabriel jumped back a foot to miss the deadly point. Friend or foe, he could hardly discern the difference. Not when he could *feel* his eyes turn into that depthless pool of black.

"Follow me and I will turn on you. Back the fuck up." He had such little restraint as something told him to swing. To pierce his sword through flesh, and let the bodies build before him so he could bathe in their blood. Drink it in.

"Kellan you'll be killed!" Eire cried out, silver lining her stormy eyes as she reached a hand toward him. He contemplated cutting off her limb, too. Kellan was so much more than the last time his darkness had taken over. The incessant rage. The bloodlust. He very nearly killed them all the last time. Now? He didn't know if he could hold himself back. Not as that voice whispered for blood.

"Then so be it." Kellan left them standing there before he disappeared into the mouth of the mountain.

Following the Dark King was easy. Blood trail aside, he could *feel* the fear wafting from the male's body. The metallic, iron tinge to the air, and Lucifer hadn't gone far. Kellan ducked into a narrow passage, and the blood trail thickened. Fallen angel or not, Lucifer would not come back from that wound without a healer. He'd lost too much blood. It smeared across the rocky ground and the walls around him. Dripping and pooling along the ground as it slushed beneath his boots. Another fifteen feet of the passage and he emerged into a shallowed cavern.

Kellan could sense him. Could smell Lucifer's fear as he cowered.

Alone, without another demon in sight. As he waited to die by his hands.

"You can still join me, Horseman. We can put the past behind us. Create a force that even the council couldn't reckon with." Lucifer stumbled back as Kellan advanced. His dark hair was plastered to the pallid skin of his forehead with blood and sweat. Lucifer's lips trembled, cracked and dry as the irregular breaths fluttered through Kellan's ears. Gone was the cocky, confident, fallen angel he'd served so many years under.

"You're pathetic." He laughed, the sound reverberating off the walls around them. Wicked, as it filled every inch of the cavern. "It's over for you." He stopped, waiting. Watching to see Lucifer's next move.

"We can still beat them. Help me take what should be mine. Help me take this planet, and I will free you from their grasp." Something in the fallen angel's voice had his body begging for more blood, stoking that fire burning within him.

"I'd rather die than work for you again." Kellan spat. He advanced a step, and the fallen angel flinched. Loose stones crunched beneath his boots, but his legs were steady. Nothing phased him when he was like this. Like the world around him no longer existed once he set his sights on his target. It was how not only the council, but Lucifer himself had groomed him. Had embedded it in his brain to tune every sound and movement out of his mind until it was nothing but him and his prey.

"Kellan you don't want to kill me."

"You're delusional if that's what you believe. I want nothing more than to absolutely obliterate you." He laughed again, almost in a near manic state.

"She needed to die. What's the life of one human girl? Surely my life means more than that slimy rat."

Kellan lunged, his steps faster than Lucifer could comprehend. He swung, but held back just enough for it not to be a killing blow. He had vowed to take his time with Lucifer. To make him suffer like he had. Like so many before, and still continued to, suffer. He would have made it last weeks. Months. Even years if he didn't have one last mission after he was done with Lucifer. He'd be brutal, but it would be faster than the angel deserved.

With the deadly point of his blade, Kellan severed the tendons at the back of Lucifer's heel, and the male crumbled to the ground. Howling in pain as he tried—and failed—to get back to his feet.

"Kellan don't do this." Lucifer's eyes grew wide as the reality set in. He knew he wasn't walking away from this. Not this time. "Kellan, I have so much left to do. I'm not ready."

Kellan reveled in that look as the being pleaded for his life. That sick, twisted part of it calling to him, and he enjoyed every fucking moment.

"How dare you plead for your pathetic excuse of a life." With a flick of his wrist, another appendage fell free from his body. The scream that erupted from him was like so many Kellan had heard before. The wounded cry of a dying animal, and he grinned.

"Kellan!" The pool of blood thickened and expanded beneath him as he continued to bleed out. There was nothing left of the fallen angel's left arm. In sheer moments, Kellan had reduced it to nothing more than a hunk of flesh.

He palmed the dagger, striding toward the trembling being. "Begging will get you nowhere." Down Lucifer's chest he dragged the blade, plunging it into his abdomen before tearing into Lucifer's flesh with his bare hands, enclosing them around whatever he could grasp, and yanking them from his stomach. Lucifer's blood sprayed, and Kellan could feel it dripping down his skin. Tasted it in his mouth, but he continued on. Severing the tendons in his right arm, *ripping* them from his body, and rendering him completely immobile.

Lucifer's pained wails echoed throughout the cavern. Over the mountain where an entire army had fallen still at the ear-piercing sound. Kellan should have been disgusted, but he felt nothing. No remorse. Held no mercy for the being beneath him, despite him begging over and over again for his life.

Suffering. It was the only thing Kellan wanted Lucifer to feel. He wanted him to suffer. To beg for his death.

"Balance, Horseman. Killing me throws the balance."

"Fuck the balance."

Lucifer's severed head hit the floor, rolling a few feet away from his still body. Eyes glazed and unseeing. His mouth still hung open in a pained, silent scream.

Only then did Kellan let the weight of his actions fall heavy on his shoulders. Not with remorse. He didn't feel anything for the dead angel. But relief. This world had been rid of the monster that had plagued them since the dawn of time.

KELLAN

His heavy footsteps were the only indication that he was returning. The three remaining Horsemen didn't move, already aware it was him. Kellan saw the track Eire had worn into the ground with her pacing, but the sigh of relief hung heavy in the air. Gabriel and Kane didn't speak, unsure of the state he was truly in. He had been enveloped in such darkness it was a wonder he even knew who they were.

Behind them, Jace had refused to set Demitria's body down, Kellan had been gone long enough to know her warmth had begun to slowly seep back into the world as her skin grew colder and colder.

Kellan was covered in blood. So much that his siblings didn't even know where his enemies ended and his began. Could see it in their eyes as each one looked him over. He was wounded, but none of the injuries were new. Not since her death. He was a force to be reckoned with before the rage, but once the darkness took hold? Kellan was untouchable. His siblings circled him in a rush of motion, weapons drawn as he prowled closer.

He was strong enough to keep himself in check.

With a thud, Lucifer's severed head rolled to Gabriel's feet. The Horseman stopped it with a dirtied boot. Kellan tossed the dark angel's blade down beside it, sickened at its sight. For what it had done. To her and to him, and he spat on it for good measure.

He shrugged off the others. Kellan didn't want to talk about any of it. Not about what happened or the brutal way Lucifer had met his end. And he sure as hell didn't want to talk about how *he* was feeling. Not to them. Not when he'd had one thing on his mind this entire time. His one remaining mission. He knew they would protest it to no end, but he didn't care. Not after this.

He couldn't bring himself to truly look at her. He glimpsed Jace still cradling her lifeless form from the distance and it was like he was broken all over again. That piece inside him swelling and screaming as it shattered into tiny pieces over and over and over. Kellan couldn't bear to look down on her and see those bright, vibrant eyes dulled to nothing. That infectious smile forever stilled.

Instead, he turned away. Walking toward the path leading down the mountain.

"Where are you going?" Eire reached to grab his shoulder, but he moved too fast away from her. Like he couldn't handle her touch on his body.

"To plead for her life." He didn't turn around. Unable to stomach the looks he knew were on their faces at his confession.

"Are you out of your damn mind?" Gabriel shouted. Like a switch had been flipped, the Horseman's anger soared to new heights at the stupidity he had just admitted. "You know as well as any of us we can't beg for a life, Kellan."

Eire opened her mouth to say something, but closed it in a thin line. Unable to bring herself to do it.

"That's grounds to kill you! The council will never stand for that." Kane shouted at his retreating figure. Kellan hadn't stopped moving. Slowed some, but he never deviated from his path. "Even if they did decide to listen to you, they'd strip you of everything you have. You'll have nothing left!" He added.

He'd be okay with that, he'd decided. To lose everything he was. To be stripped bare, if it meant bringing her back.

Finally, Kellan stopped. "I am prepared for whatever the consequence." They wouldn't understand, no matter what he said. They'd beg him to stay. Would do anything in their power to prevent him from seemingly forfeiting his life, but he wouldn't stop. This was his last mission, he'd decided. The last thing he would do, then he was done. If they granted his wish, he'd rid himself of the council for good.

"Kellan!" Eire roared. "Where are you going?" She couldn't hide the pained look on her face as she asked him again. As if hoping for a different answer than the last. But she already knew. Already knew as her hands clenched into tightly bound fists at her side.

"I told you. To plead for her life." He resumed walking. Slowly, his feet carried him away from the piercing stares.

"To whom?" They asked in unison. Pleading for a life was forbidden. Against every rule they had ever been taught. Especially a human life, and he'd do it anyway.

"To anybody who will listen."

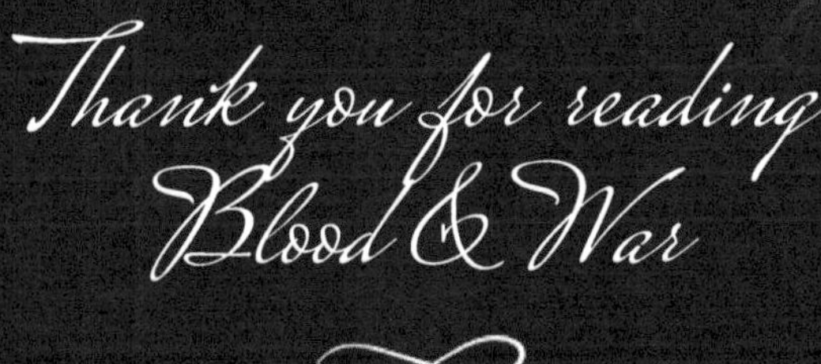

We hope you enjoyed it as much as we enjoyed bringing it to you. We just wanted to take a moment to encourage you to review the book. Follow this link: Blood & War to be directed to the book's Amazon product page to leave your review.

Every review helps further the author's reach and, ultimately, helps them continue writing fantastic books for us all to enjoy.

Also in series:
Blood & War

Want to discuss our books with other readers and even the authors? Join our Discord server today and be a part of the Aethon community.

Facebook | Instagram | Twitter | Website

Join our non-spam mailing list by visiting www.subscribepage.com/aethonreadersgroup_romantasy and never miss future releases.

Looking for more great Romantasy?

To be a Keeper is to dedicate one's life – and heart – to protecting another. *Jasmine wasn't ready for it. Less than a year into her training at Sanctuary, a college for Keepers and mages alike, and with a fresh start from a brutal life of thievery in the slums, all she wanted to do was continue mastering the sword arts and avoid her other responsibilities. Those plans are ruined when she's assigned to be the protector of a young nobleman whose family was murdered. Her new charge is cocky, smug, and drives her up a wall at every opportunity. Forced to protect a man she can't stand with her life, Jasmine needs to find time that isn't there to continue her training and keep assassins from killing both of them, all the while learning magic and discovering that there's more to life than survival. And yet, Jasmine starts to find herself inexplicably drawn to him. In the slums, Jasmine never had room to care about anything other than putting food on the table. But she's not in the slums anymore, and she can't keep her feelings tied down forever. Unfortunately, burgeoning love is the least of Jasmine's problems. As pieces of a malevolent plot start to unfold around them, she and her charge realize that there might be only one thing left that they can rely on. Each other.* **Keeper of Scarlet Petals *is the first book in a new romantasy series with a strong female lead, heartwarming romance, and cursed magic. It's perfect for fans of* Scholomance *and* Fourth Wing*!***

Get Keeper of Scarlet Petals Now!

MYTHIC
SPARK
CC HARTLY

A shattered life. A dormant power. An arms race between realms—for her. *When twenty-one-year-old Nyleeria met King Thaddeus for the first time outside her family's rickety cabin, she had no idea how irrevocably her life would change. The Spark. Magic. Spellcraft. Fae. The Great War. All elements wiped from human memory and written histories—an ignorance Nyleeria would have gladly maintained. But fate had other plans when it shattered her world with the disappearance of her siblings and the brutal murder of her parents all because of a latent power she unwittingly possessed. The primordial Spark lying dormant within her was coveted by two opposing realms who would unquestionably use its force to extinguish the other. In a war she never knew existed, where the veil between human and fae realms is becoming dangerously thin, Nyleeria finds herself in possession of the very magic that can alter the fabric of her world.* ***Don't miss this captivating adult Fantasy Romance by debut author CC Hartly. With its intricate magic systems, believable characters, and richly developed world-building, it's sure to delight romantasy and epic fantasy readers everywhere!***

Get Mythic Spark Now!

For all our Romantasy books, visit our website.

Acknowledgments

To my husband, Ben. I would not have finished *Blood & War* if it weren't for you. Thank you for your patience throughout this entire journey—for every day you kept our boy busy while I was writing, and giving me the time I needed to pour my blood, sweat and tears into this, and troubleshooting my damn laptop when it failed at every turn. For being my rock and my biggest supporter. You believed in me when I didn't even believe in myself. I love you.

To Rowan—Follow your dreams. If I can do it, so can you.

To my parents, Carmen and Henri—You fostered my love of reading, and gave me the space to explore this passion of mine. For taking me to the library to check out a literal stack of books each week, then to the bookstore for more as I filled up my dream library (sorry you're still stuck storing all those books). I would have never mustered the courage to pursue this if it wasn't for you both. I can't thank you enough for your unconditional love and support.

To my siblings, Renee and Jamie—Thank you for your enthusiasm during this entire journey, and thank you for believing in me. I did the thing. *insert Tina joke here*

To my forever friend Liz—My smut researcher (I told you I'd do it). But for real, thank you for reading this book before it was *this*. For your insurmountable feedback and critique, and helping me untangle the mess it was. LOVE YOU.

To my writing friends Heather and Julia—Thank you for being so supportive, and pushing me to get this story out into the world. I'm so grateful to have stumbled upon both of you. I can't wait for the world to hold your magic.

To the team at Aethon—Thank you for making my dream come true. For believing in this story and helping bring it to life. There's always that fear of handing your story into someone else's hands, but it wouldn't be what it is without you all. Thank you, thank you, thank you.